A CONTRACT, A WEDDING, A WIFE?

CHRISTY McKELLEN

HER MAN ON THREE RIVERS RANCH

STELLA BAGWELL

MIX
FSC
FSC C007454

This book is produced from independently certified FSC™ paper to ensure responsible forest management.

For more information visit: www.harpercollins.co.uk/green

Printed and bound in Spain
by CPI, Barcelona

MILLS & BOON

First Published in Great Britain 2018
by Mills & Boon, an imprint of HarperCollinsPublishers,
1 London Bridge Street, London, SE1 9GF

A Contract, a Wedding, a Wife? © 2018 Christy McKellen
Her Man on Three Rivers Ranch © 2018 Stella Bagwell

ISBN: 978-0-263-26485-2

38-0418

Formerly a video and radio producer, **Christy McKellen** now spends her time writing fun, impassioned and emotive romance with an undercurrent of sensual tension. When she's not writing she can be found enjoying life with her husband and three children, walking for pleasure, and researching other people's deepest secrets and desires. Christy loves to hear from readers. You can get hold of her at www.christymckellen.com.

After writing more than eighty books for Mills & Boon, **Stella Bagwell** still finds it exciting to create new stories and bring her characters to life. She loves all things Western and has been married to her own real cowboy for forty-four years. Living on the south Texas coast, she also enjoys being outdoors and helping her husband care for the horses, cats and dog that call their small ranch home. The couple has one son, who teaches high school mathematics and is also an athletic director. Stella loves hearing from readers. They can contact her at www.stellabagwell@gmail.com.

Also by Christy McKellen

Unlocking Her Boss's Heart
One Week with the French Tycoon
A Countess for Christmas
The Unforgettable Spanish Tycoon
His Mistletoe Proposal

Also by Stella Bagwell

The Arizona Lawman
Her Kind of Doctor
The Cowboy's Christmas Lullaby
His Badge, Her Baby...Their Family?
Her Rugged Rancher
Christmas on the Silver Horn Ranch
Daddy Wore Spurs
The Lawman's Noelle
Wearing the Rancher's Ring
One Tall, Dusty Cowboy

Discover more at millsandboon.co.uk

A CONTRACT,
A WEDDING,
A WIFE?

CHRISTY McKELLEN

CHAPTER ONE

Risk—a game of strategy, conflict and diplomacy.

HE WAS NEVER going to find someone suitable to marry at this rate.

Xavier McQueen let out an exasperated sigh as the woman who had seemed like his best hope—on paper at least—gave a firm and very final no to his admittedly completely barmy-sounding proposal before putting the phone down on him.

Apparently only being married for a year before divorcing wouldn't look good on her dating CV. She was under the impression it could put off real prospects in the future because they'd be worried about her coming with baggage from such a short previous marriage.

Closing his eyes, he slumped back in his chair.

Three *months* he'd been wasting his time with this ridiculous endeavour and now he only had six weeks left before the Hampstead mansion where he'd lived for the last four years—the home that had been in his family for the last hundred and fifty years—would pass to his money-grubbing clown of a cousin.

Damn his great-aunt and her jeopardous eccentricity.

He thought she'd loved him—certainly more than his parents ever had—but this bizarre stunt she'd pulled with her will had made him wonder about that.

Shoving a hand through his hair and trying not to pull it out in his frustration, he stared out of the floor-to-ceiling window of his office, barely registering his view of the majestic Tower Bridge stretching out across the fast-moving River Thames.

He'd not wanted to widely advertise exactly what he was looking for in case it brought out the crooks and the crazies but that meant he'd quickly run out of people to ask to help him out. The problem was, the chosen candidate needed to be someone he could trust, as well as someone he'd be able to get along with, but all his good female friends were already married and he didn't fancy taking his chances with any of his exes. A year was a long time to live with someone who detested the very sight of you.

The other two women, who had also been put forward as possible candidates by his friend Russell—the only friend he'd trusted with his problem—hadn't worked out either. Not being able to have sex for a year hadn't appealed to either of them. They'd both been looking for the real deal. Soul mates. An ideal he had no faith in whatsoever any more, not after being left humiliated at the altar five years ago by the woman he'd thought he'd spend the rest of his life with. His disaster of a non-wedding, which he now liked to think of as a near miss, had put paid to that ridiculous notion.

Nope, it was short-term, uncomplicated relationships

for him from here on in. Or a purely business one like this needed to be, thanks to the bizarre demands stipulated in Great-Aunt Faith's will.

Just as he was reaching for the glass of water on his desk to relieve his parched throat, there was a loud knock on the door and a petite woman with bright blue eyes and a riot of blonde curls walked purposefully into his office and placed a small basket of assorted cakes on his desk with a flourish.

He frowned down at them, then up at her. 'I didn't order any cakes.'

'I know. They're an excuse to get some face-to-face time with you,' she said, folding her arms and looking down at him with a determined expression that made his stomach sink.

'I've been trying to get a meeting with you for weeks but your PA keeps fobbing me off,' she went on before he had a chance to say anything. 'So I've been forced to take drastic action. On the other hand, I've brought you some really fantastic cakes. I made them myself. So it's actually a win for you.' She flashed him a half-smile that didn't entirely convince him she was as self-assured as her spirited speech had made her seem.

He leant back in his chair again and studied her in bemusement.

She looked young, maybe early-to-mid-twenties, with a sweetly pretty face. Her abundance of curly blonde hair, which she'd tried to tame with an Alice band, stuck out around her head, probably due to the windy day. She surveyed him back with intelligent eyes, her button nose, which was scattered with freckles, wrinkling a little under his gaze. She seemed to him to have the air of someone who could cause a great deal of mischief if she put her mind to it.

As he scrutinised her she shifted on the spot and visibly swallowed as if rapidly losing her nerve in the face of his silence. It seemed her blustery, confident entrance had all been an act to get past the temporary PA sitting outside his office. Soon to be his ex-temporary PA.

'And you are?' he said with a sigh. He really didn't need this extra hassle today; his nerves were already strung as tightly as they'd go and he had an important meeting in ten minutes which he needed to have his head in the game for.

'Solitaire Saunders. Soli for short. That's what everyone ends up calling me, anyway. It's a bit of a mouthful otherwise.'

His eyebrow twitched involuntarily upwards.

'Solitaire? Like the diamond?'

She gave a self-conscious grin. 'No, like the card game. My dad was a huge fan of games. He set up our board game café on Hampstead High Street—in the unit we rent from your company.'

Board game café?

He was surprised anyone could make a living from a business like that, though, judging by the increasingly irate letters he now remembered receiving from the woman running the place—presumably this woman—after they'd notified her of the upcoming rent raise, perhaps she didn't.

Despite his reluctance to get into this with her right now, he knew he ought to nip the issue in the bud while she was here in front of him. His executive assistant was fed up with having to field her constant phone calls asking to speak to him directly and he'd never been one to shy away from a legitimate business conflict when it reared its head. Its pretty, curly blonde head in this instance.

'The trouble is, Soli,' he said, splaying his hands on the desktop, 'the market's moved on a lot since you last signed the rental agreement a couple of years ago—'

'Four years ago,' she butted in. 'And it was my father who signed it. I've been running it without him for the last three of them.'

'Okay, I don't have the exact details to hand right now,' he said, trying to remain patient, 'but I do know that the market's moved even more since then.' He lifted his hands, palms towards her. 'We're not monsters here, we've actually held back on increasing the rent on a lot of our property because we know how hard it can be for small independent businesses to survive in London, but we have to move with the times.'

'You know how hard it is to run a struggling business, do you?' she shot back. 'How utterly heartbreaking it is when a once thriving business starts to fail? How demoralising that can be?' Her voice rose on each question. She glanced pointedly around his plush office with its high-end furniture and enviable London view then fixed him with a challenging look, her cheeks flushed a deep shade of pink but the expression in her eyes unwavering.

He experienced a shiver of guilt, but knew he couldn't let it get to him. Everyone he came across these days seemed to have a sob story to tell him so that he'd agree to charge them less money for the property they rented from his company. He couldn't let his personal feelings get in the way. This was business.

'We live above the café,' she said before he could form his careful reply. 'If we can't afford to keep the business going we'll lose our home as well, but then I don't expect you'd know how a threat like that feels either!'

If only that were the case.

He began to shake his head, but she took a step closer to his desk and put her hands over her heart, her cute little nose wrinkling again in a way that made something twist uncomfortably in his chest.

'Is there any way I can persuade you to hold off for a little while longer?' she asked in a voice wobbly with emotion. 'Please. Just give me a chance to get a bit more business in.'

'How do you intend to do that?' he asked, genuinely interested. 'Aren't there a lot of other café options on Hampstead High Street?'

Her bold stance deflated a little. 'Yes. Unfortunately there are. But they're all chains owned by big corporations.' She waved a dismissive hand. 'We offer a more local, family-run atmosphere. And board games! Who doesn't love playing board games?'

He shuffled a little in his chair. 'Can't say I'm a huge fan of them.'

'You just haven't played the right ones yet,' she persisted. 'If you come in you'll see how much fun they can be. We have four hundred games to choose from. Something for everyone. We'll even teach you how to play them.'

He shook his head, holding back the smile that was pushing at the corners of his mouth. Learning to play board games was the last thing he could imagine wanting to do with his precious time off. 'As appealing as that sounds,' he said, trying to keep the irony out of his voice, 'that doesn't tell me how you're going to start making enough profit to pay your rent.'

'I'm working on it,' she stated, but her gaze wasn't meeting his now; instead she was staring out towards the river, her hands clenched at her sides as if she was fighting to keep her composure. 'I just need to find some time to do a bit of local advertising, update the website and post to the social media sites we're on,' she said, almost to herself. 'Trouble is, I work long hours. I have a cleaning job at a gastro pub from seven-thirty till ten, then I have to make the cakes and prepare the sandwiches we sell at the café, then we're open from eleven till three. When we close I have to go shopping for supplies for both the café and the family and take care of anything my mum needs and then the café's open again from five till ten pm. So there's not been a lot of time for developing a high-concept business strategy.'

More guilt tried to shoulder its way in as she looked back at him with tired eyes.

He shook it off. This wasn't his problem. He couldn't allow it to become his problem either. He had enough of his own troubles to deal with right now.

'Look, Soli, things are complicated for me at the moment and I'm afraid I don't have time to deal with this today. I have an important meeting in a few minutes, so if you leave your contact details with my PA—'

She flinched at the hard edge he'd given his voice now, but didn't move from where she stood.

'Complicated? You think your life's complicated? Beat this, buster.' She pointed her finger at him. 'I'm desperately trying to save the business my late father built from scratch, our family's legacy, so I can afford to get my mother, who's suffering with Parkinson's disease, the care she needs whilst also trying to scrape together enough money to support my younger sister, who's a brilliant mathematician with an offer from Oxford University, but who can't afford to take the place there. And you're making it even harder for me to do all that by raising our already extortionate rent. *That's* complicated!'

The ensuing silence rang out loudly in the still air of his office.

'Okay. Fine,' he said resignedly when he saw a glint of tears in her eyes. 'You win the "complicated" competition.' He made a placating gesture. 'But only just— *believe* me. My life isn't exactly easy right now either.'

'Look, is there some sort of arrangement we could come to here?' she asked desperately, blinking back her tears and looking a little embarrassed about losing her cool. 'Any sort of deal we could make which would give me a bit more time to try and turn the fortunes of the café around and make the money we need to afford the rent hike? I can't lose the place. Not after all the love and hard graft my father put into it. It's all we have left of him now.' Despite her efforts, a single tear ran down her cheek.

He looked hurriedly away, frowning down at his desk. 'I've already held back on rolling out the new rent and if I do it for you I'll have to—'

'Please. Have a heart,' she broke in hoarsely, clearly aware she was losing the battle but seemingly not prepared to accept it. 'I'll do anything. I'll come and work here for you when I'm not working at the café. I can type and make coffee, file things. Documents. Tidy up! I'll do whatever it takes to keep our café running.'

The ring of hope in her voice clawed at his chest. He had to give her credit, she was certainly determined.

Or maybe just desperate.

His heart gave a hard thump. He knew what desperate felt like and he wouldn't wish it on anyone.

'Whatever it takes?' he asked slowly, meeting her eyes again now. He wasn't sure where he was going with this, but he had the strangest feeling there could be a solution here that he hadn't quite hit upon yet.

'Anything. Just name it,' she said, her eyes wide with anticipation.

He sighed and shook his head. 'The thing is, I have a PA already. There wouldn't be anything for you to do here at the office.'

'At your house, then? I'm a great cleaner. Fast and totally reliable.'

'Got a whole team of those.'

'Then what *do* you need? There has to be something.'

And there it was.

The idea.

But he couldn't suggest that.

Could he?

No.

He shouldn't.

'Please,' she whispered in a broken voice, tears brimming in her eyes again.

'What I need most right now is a wife,' he said roughly, losing the grip on his restraint as the idea pushed harder at his brain and compassion loosened his tongue. 'At least, I need to find a woman that's prepared to get married in the next few weeks and stay married to me for a year.' Catching the expression of shock on her face, he silently cursed himself for letting that slip out.

She must think he was a total loony.

'Are you serious?' she asked in a faltering voice.

He sighed, feeling tiredness wash through him. 'Unfortunately, I am.'

'Why do you need a wife so fast?'

'Like I said, it's complicated.'

She surprised him by perching on the edge of his desk and fixing him with an intent stare. 'Well, you listened to my problems; let me hear yours.'

His pulse stuttered. 'I don't think it's appropriate—'

She held up her hands in a halting motion. 'Just tell me. Perhaps I can help.'

He frowned at her, taken aback by her unexpected forcefulness. 'I very much doubt it.'

'Look, I won't say anything to anyone if that's what you're worried about. I'm good with secrets. Maybe it would help to say it all out loud. That's what my dad used to do. He used me as a sounding board and often I didn't need to say a word: he already had the answer; he was just having trouble accessing it.'

He took a moment to study her, trying to judge whether he could trust her not to blab to all and sundry once she'd left his office. The last thing he needed right now was for this to be circulated around social media or the Press. He was already taking enough risks talking to the women he'd approached so far and it could only be a matter of time before his luck ran out.

'Go on. What harm can it do?' she murmured, giving him a reassuring smile. There was something about her that encouraged confidences, he realised, and for some reason he felt, deep down, that he could trust her.

He sighed, deciding that he may as well tell her the whole sorry tale since she knew most of it already anyway. Plus, he didn't really have anything more to lose at this point. And who knew, perhaps she could help in some way?

Stranger things had happened.

Getting up from his chair, he paced over to the window and stared out at the pleasure boats transporting tourists up and down the wide river. 'My late great-aunt owned the house I live in at the moment.' He swallowed past the dryness in his throat. 'It's the place I've considered to be my home for my entire life. It was meant to go to my father next, but he passed away a few years ago, so I'm next in line to inherit it,' he said, glancing back to check she was listening.

She was. She gazed back at him with an open, interested expression, her hands folded neatly in her lap.

'It's been in my family since 1875, ever since it was built for my great-great-grandfather,' he continued, turning back to look at the river again. 'It's the house where I spent all my holidays from boarding school and the home I intend to live in until I die.' He paused for a moment, feeling his throat tighten as he remembered how he used to say it was the place where he and Harriet would always live, before—well, before his whole life was turned upside down.

Shaking off the tension this memory produced, he moved away from the window and sat back down on his chair.

'In order to inherit the place, though, a covenant in the will states I have to be married within the next month.' He tried not to grimace as he said it.

She nodded slowly. 'Okay.' Frowning now as if a little puzzled, she said, 'Could I just ask—why the rush? Haven't you known about this for a while?'

'No. Apparently my great-aunt wrote it into her will a couple of years ago, but she was in a coma for eighteen months after suffering a massive stroke. I only found out about it three months ago when she passed away.'

He paused and swallowed, shaking his head as a wave of sadness at losing the woman he thought of as more of a mother figure than a great-aunt flooded through him. 'I only inherit it if I'm married by my thirtieth birthday and remain married for at least a year, otherwise it gets passed on to my cousin, who is already married,' he grimaced, 'and the most immoral, wasteful, tasteless man I've ever met. He'd sell the place to the highest bidder in the blink of an eye.'

There was a heavy pause where he watched her eyes widen and her mouth twitch at the corner.

'And before you ask, no, he wouldn't sell it to me. We don't exactly get on.'

'I kind of gathered that from your description of him,' she said with a smile.

He tried to smile back but he couldn't quite muster the energy needed. Mirth was a hard response to summon when you were about to lose the only place in the world that really meant something to you. The place that held all your childhood memories and felt like an integral part of your history.

Your home.

He'd feel baseless without it, adrift, disenfranchised.

'Well,' she said, her eyes alive with what looked suspiciously like amusement, 'that's quite a conundrum you have there. It's like something from a soap opera.' Her mouth twitched. 'And not a very good one.'

Rubbing his hand over his brow, he felt the tension this predicament had caused under his fingertips. 'I'd have to agree with you.'

'Your great-aunt sounds like a real character.' Her eyes still sparkled with amusement but her smile was warm.

'She was a little eccentric, yes.'

Crossing her arms, she peered down at him. 'And I'm guessing no one you've asked so far has said yes to this rather unusual proposal?'

'Correct. Not that there have been many suitable candidates.' He leant back in his chair and mirrored her by crossing his own arms. 'The fact we'd have to live together to make it look like we're a real couple—apparently a solicitor will be deployed at random times to check on this,' he added by way of explanation, 'but not have a real relationship hasn't exactly caught the attention of the women I've approached so far. I'm really only interested in getting married as a business arrangement; I'm not looking for true love.'

Her brow furrowed at this. 'You don't want to fall in love?'

'No.'

There was a small pause before she asked, 'Why not?'

He shrugged. 'It's just not for me, that's all. Despite my great-aunt's insistence that it was the best thing that ever happened to her, I don't believe falling in love with someone can really make you happy.' He sat up in his chair. 'In fact, I think it does the opposite. It didn't work out for my parents, or for a large population of the country, and I intend to learn from their mistakes.'

Not to mention his own near miss—though he wasn't about to tell her about that humiliating experience.

'Just out of interest, what does your temporary bride get out of this arrangement?' she asked in a faltering voice, jerking him out of his scrambled thoughts.

There was a tense pause where they looked at each other and he weighed up what he'd be prepared to offer her if she meant what he thought she meant by that.

'The candidate would be able to keep the rental cost on their property the same for the next five years,' he replied slowly.

'And would there be some sort of pay-out as soon as she'd signed the marriage register?' she asked, her gaze intent on his now.

'There could be, if it was a reasonable request.'

'But she'd have to live with you,' she appeared to swallow, 'in your house?'

Noting the renewed flush of her skin, he could guess what she actually meant by that.

'It would be a purely business arrangement,' he re-assured her, 'which would mean she'd sleep in her own bedroom. There wouldn't be any conjugal expectations. In fact, it would be a totally platonic relationship, to avoid any complications.'

'I see,' she said, her shoulders seeming to relax a little.

Despite his wish to keep sex out of the deal, he couldn't help but feel a little miffed by her apparent horror at the idea of sleeping with him. Was it really that off-putting an idea? He shook off his irritation, tell-ing himself not to be an idiot. The woman didn't know him from the next man, so of course she'd be nervous about the idea of any expected intimacy between them.

'We'd also both have to agree not to have any sex-ual relationships outside the marriage, again, to avoid complications.'

'Okay,' she said without expression, not giving him any clues about her feelings on that one. Would that be a deal-breaker for her? She was an attractive, sparky woman and he guessed she must get plenty of male at-tention. There was something really appealing about her, especially when she smiled.

'One of the other stipulations would be that she'd need to take my surname for the duration of the marriage,' he said, pulling his attention back to the matter at hand. 'It would just be for appearances and she could change it back again afterwards, of course.'

'Afterwards?'

'After the divorce. There'll be a pre-nuptial agreement to sign so she won't be able to petition for money or property during the legal severance of the marriage.'

There was a pause in which the air seemed to vibrate between them.

'Oka-a-ay,' she said slowly, her voice sounding a little breathy now.

He frowned, panicking for moment that she might be stringing him along for a laugh.

Before he could start to backpedal, though, she fixed him with a steady gaze, her lips quirking into a wide smile—triggering a warm, lifting sensation of hope in his chest—then took an audible breath and said, 'I'll do it. I'll be your wife.'

CHAPTER TWO

Monopoly—move around the board for the chance to collect money and new property.

SOLITAIRE SAUNDERS HEARD her father's voice in her head as she gazed anxiously back at the man who had the power to turn the course of her and her family's lives around with a mere nod.

'Your tendency to run headlong into things without thinking is going to get you in serious trouble some day, Soli,' her father's voice warned her.

He wasn't wrong.

She knew that.

But you're not here any more, Dad, and I'm doing the best I can.

There was a chance, of course, that she was actually dreaming all this and would wake up at any moment in bed with her heart racing and her palms as sweaty as they felt right now.

But she really hoped that wasn't the case.

In fact, she knew it wasn't possible because when she'd actually rolled out of bed this morning, and been unable to eat her breakfast because her stomach was jumping around so badly with nerves and worry, she'd never felt so awake—and afraid. The pressure of her mum and sister relying on her to stop both their home and livelihoods from being swept out from under them weighed heavily on her.

So she was hyper-aware, sitting there now in her smartest clothes with her wild hair as neat as she'd been able to get it, that how well she performed in this meeting could change all their lives for ever, one way or another. What she hadn't expected when she turned up here was to be confronted with such an unusual and nerve-racking way to do it.

This—this incredible stroke of luck—could be the answer to all her problems.

If she could handle it, that was.

As far as she could see, the most challenging thing about it would be having to see Xavier McQueen, property baron and high-society mover and shaker every day for the next year.

And be his *wife*.

The thought of living with this powerful, domineering stranger made her heart thump harder in her chest.

The guy was seriously attractive, with a lean but muscular physique which she imagined he kept looking that fit with regular trips to the gym. His face was angular, with high cheekbones and a strong jaw, and he had light green, almond-shaped eyes, framed with dark lashes, which gave him a nerve-jangling look of stark intensity. And he had really good hair. Thick and shiny and the colour of melted chocolate. It sat neatly against his scalp as if it had been styled deliberately to do that by a master hairdresser at a top salon. Which, she mused, it probably had. Her fingers twitched at her sides as she fought a powerful urge to reach out and touch the soft waves, to see if it was as soft and smooth as it looked.

'I have some non-negotiable demands if I'm going to do this,' she said, a little more loudly than she'd meant to out of nerves.

'I thought you might have,' Xavier replied, with an ironic tinge to his voice. He had to be the most sardonic person she'd ever met. Throughout all their exchanges it had seemed as though he'd been having trouble taking anything she'd said seriously.

Still, he wasn't exactly laughing now. In fact, despite his sarcasm, he was actually looking at her as if she might be the answer to all his problems.

'Okay. If I'm going to be your wife for a year I need to know that my mother is being taken care of properly, so I'll need to have a live-in carer provided for her while I'm away. She'll be mostly okay during the day, but she'll definitely need someone there overnight to help her get ready for bed and to get up when my sister's not there. Which leads me on to the next stipulation. I also want you to pay for my sister's tuition fees at university. She'll get a job to cover her living expenses, but it won't go any way towards the fees.' Her heart was racing as she laid all this out, wondering whether he'd just tell her to get up and get out because she was being too greedy.

But he needs you, a voice in the back of her head told her, *so front it out.*

There was a long pause while he looked at her with such an intense gaze she felt it right down to her toes.

'Okay, so let me get this straight,' he said eventually; 'you want a full-time carer for your mother, tuition fees paid for your sister, a stay on the rent on the café for the next five years *and* an as yet undisclosed sum of money as soon as we're married?'

She swallowed hard, but held her nerve. 'Yes.'

'And how much were you thinking of for your lump sum?'

Shakily, she said an amount that she thought would cover the wages at the café for the next year as well as giving her some spending money which she could use for marketing or renovations to the café once they were divorced.

He surveyed her for a moment, his right eyebrow twitching upwards by a couple of degrees.

Soli held her breath, aware of her pulse throbbing in her head.

Had she blown it by asking for too much?

'Okay. It's a deal,' he said finally. 'But, considering you'll be losing your wage from the cleaning job and you'll have to employ someone to cover your position in the café, I'm prepared to give you an additional twenty per cent on top of that.'

Soli swallowed hard, his unexpected generosity bringing tears to her eyes.

'As long as you agree to marry to me within the next month and spend the majority of your time in my home,' he added quickly. 'I don't mind you visiting your mother and working part-time at the café, perhaps one or two days a week so you can keep an eye on it, but it needs to look as though the majority of your time is spent living there with me. Particularly in the evenings.'

'So I can only work during the day?'

'Yes. I'd like it if you were able to attend any work or social events at the drop of a hat. For that, I need you focused on your life with me as much as possible.'

She suspected that what he wasn't saying out loud was that he wasn't the sort of man to have the owner of a board game café for a wife and he didn't want to have to explain himself to anyone.

'So what will I do for the rest of the time?' she asked as indignation rippled through her. What was wrong with working in a board game café? She really enjoyed it. It was sociable and kept her fit because she was on her feet all day.

He frowned, momentarily stumped by her question. 'Perhaps you could work on that "high-concept business strategy" you haven't had time for?' He waved a hand. 'I'm sure you'll find plenty of things to do with your day.'

'And what do you want me to tell people when they ask what I do for a living?' she asked, still riled by her suspicion that he didn't value her choice of livelihood. 'What do the kind of women you normally date do for a job?' she added, perhaps a little tetchily.

He rubbed a hand over his forehead, looking taken aback by the directness of her question. 'Most of the women I've dated have either had a media job or been a doctor or solicitor.'

'Well, I don't think I'm going to convince anyone I'm

a doctor or lawyer,' Soli said, raising a wry eyebrow. 'My sister got all the brains in the family.'

He frowned, apparently a little bemused by her now. 'Okay, well, if you want to choose a different career for yourself, go right ahead. What would you have done if you hadn't taken over the café? Do you have any burning ambitions?'

His question stumped her for a second. It had been a long time since she'd thought about doing anything but running the café. 'I don't know. I wasn't exactly focused at school so I never expected to have a high-flying career. I liked designing clothes, but I did that in my spare time. My dad pressganged me into taking academic subjects to "give me a better chance in life".' She put this in air quotes, remembering with a sting of shame how she'd rallied against this notion, thinking it would bore her to tears to have a professional job in the future. All she'd wanted when she was in her mid-teens was to have a family of her own and perhaps make a living in some sort of arty career.

How naïve she'd been.

'Well, why don't you have a think about what you'd feel comfortable telling people you do? You're a business owner; why don't you go with that?'

She nodded slowly, her earlier irritation at his imagined snobbery subsiding. 'Okay. Business owner it is.'

He nodded. 'And what do you intend to tell your family about our arrangement?' he asked in a careful tone.

'I'm going to say I've taken a job as your live-in housekeeper, for which you're going to pay me an exorbitant wage.'

He nodded, then pulled out his phone and began to type onto the touch screen, presumably making a note of her demands, and his, so they'd have something to refer back to should there be any issues in the future.

'They'd buy that much more readily than the truth—that I'm marrying a total stranger,' she added with a strange tingling feeling in her throat.

It felt so odd to say those words. Whenever she'd imagined getting married, which hadn't been very often recently, owing to her life being too complicated for her to think that far into the future, she'd imagined herself meeting a guy, their mutual love of board games bringing them together, and dating him for a couple of years before moving in together, then him proposing to her out of the blue in some far-flung romantic destination, like Hawaii or Morocco, or maybe on a Mediterranean island whilst sailing through the clear blue water in a yacht.

They'd get married in a quaint little church with all their friends and family watching and throw a huge party afterwards, where they'd dance the night away together. Then, a year or two later, after they'd had some time together as a couple, they'd have kids, maybe three or four of them.

She'd always wanted a big family.

When she was younger, sitting bored and frustrated at school during subjects she couldn't get a handle on no matter how hard she tried, she'd fantasised about what it would be like to be a mother. How she'd make her kids big bowls of hearty food, which they'd gobble down gratefully before going off to play happily with their toys, or do finger-painting with her at the kitchen table, laughing about the mess they were making together. Or she'd imagine ruffling their hair at the school gates and receiving rib-crushing hugs in return before they ran in, with her shouting that she loved them, which they'd pretend to find embarrassing but would secretly adore. Then later in the evening she'd tuck her sleepy, happy kids up into bed before spending the rest of the evening with her gorgeous husband, chatting about the day they'd had before retiring to bed together hand in hand.

That all seemed a million miles away now though.

It had been ages since she'd been on a proper date with anyone and even then they'd barely got to the kissing stage before her lifestyle and responsibilities had got in the way of things developing any further. She'd made it clear that her family came first and that had destroyed the chances of a relationship.

Not that she blamed her mother and sister. Not a bit. In fact, despite their difficult circumstances, she quite liked being the head of the family. The one that everyone relied on. It gave her a sense of purpose that had previously been lacking in her life.

Yes, anyway, it was a good thing that Xavier had insisted on a purely platonic relationship. It wasn't like she had any time for romance.

'How old are you, Soli?' Xavier asked brusquely, jolting her back to the present.

A shiver of disquiet tickled down her spine. Was he worried she wasn't mature enough to deal with this?

'I'm twenty-one,' she said, setting back her shoulders and fixing him with a determined stare. 'Old enough to know my own mind,' she added firmly.

His eyes assessed her for a couple of beats more before he nodded. 'Okay, then. I guess that's everything we need to discuss today.' He put his phone down on his desk, arranging it so it sat parallel with his keyboard, before looking up and giving her his full attention again. 'Look, I appreciate this is a lot to take in right now, so why don't you go away and have a think about it, to make sure you're comfortable with everything we've discussed? It's a big decision to make and I don't expect you to sign up for it until you've had a chance to check me out first.'

She nodded jerkily. Despite her bravado, she was actually glad of the chance to go and think about this away from his discombobulating presence, just to make sure she hadn't overlooked something important. 'Okay. I'll do that. It really wouldn't do to marry an axe murderer by mistake,' she said, flashing him a jokey grin.

Ignoring her attempt at levity, he opened a drawer in his desk and took out a business card which he handed to her. 'This has my personal mobile number and address on it. Give me a call when you're ready to talk again.' He paused and frowned. 'But don't leave it too long or I might find someone else to marry in the meantime.'

For a second she wasn't sure whether he was joking or not. He didn't seem to *do* smiling, at least not the kind that made him look as though he was genuinely happy. Cynical. That was what he came across as. And reserved.

She wondered fleetingly what had happened to him to make him like that, but pushed the thought away. It wasn't important right now and she really shouldn't allow herself to get emotionally attached to him any-way, not if this was going to work as a purely business arrangement.

'Okay, thanks. I'll get in touch very soon,' she replied, taking the card from his fingers.

She shot him a tense smile, then got up from the desk on shaky legs and turned to go.

'And Solitaire.'

She turned back.

'If I find out the details of this proposition have been leaked to the Press I'll know where to find you.' There was a heavy pause before he added, 'And you'll find your business and your family swiftly evicted from my property.'

'Understood,' she said, then left the office of her po-tential future *husband*, wondering what in the heck she'd just got herself into.

Back at the café, she relieved Callie, who waitressed for them a lot and had kindly agreed to work an extra shift that morning so Soli could go to the McQueen Property office. Once she'd caught up with the daily tasks and served a sudden rush of customers, she sat behind the serving counter with her laptop and typed Xavier's name into the search engine with trembling fingers.

She'd already looked him up before the meeting, of course, scouring the web pages for something she could use in her defence against him, but to her frustration had found him to be squeaky clean. At least at first glance. She needed to put in more thorough due diligence here though if she was going to commit to live with the man for a year. The last thing she needed was to find herself sucked into something she'd not anticipated and then couldn't escape from without causing more harm to her situation.

But as hard as she looked, she couldn't find anything that threw even the meanest of shadows over his reputation.

The only things that came up about him were on gossip sites, where they mentioned him in relation to the high-society women he'd had flings with over the last few years. The man appeared to be some kind of international playboy, always showing up at high-profile fundraisers and gallery openings with a different, instantly recognisable woman on his arm. He was like a character from one of the romantic novels she liked to gobble up like sweets for escapism from her busy, stressful existence. She'd never really believed such a person could exist in real life, but here he was, a living, breathing, alpha male business tycoon.

So he checked out okay online.

Picking up her phone, she called a friend who was a police officer in the Met and asked him if there was any way he could have a check around about Xavier, pretending she was doing it for business reasons concerning the café. Mercifully, her friend seemed to buy that and asked her to leave it with him.

She spent the rest of the day in a jumpy, nerve-filled state and was mightily relieved when her friend called her back in the early evening to let her know that nothing negative at all had come back to him with regard to

Xavier, either personally or with his business. It seemed he was an upstanding citizen of the realm.

The only thing left to do now was to check out exactly where his house was using an online map app—just to make sure he wasn't expecting her to live in some kind of broken-down hovel. Not that she expected to encounter that. Judging by the high-end furniture and breathtaking elegance of his office, she couldn't imagine his house being a place she wouldn't like to spend time in. She could have happily lived right there in his office if he'd asked her to, with that wonderful view over the water. It certainly beat the one she had from their living room window over the busy, vehicle-choked high street, or the one of the bins in their small back yard from the bedroom she shared with her sister.

Not that she was complaining about her lot. Home was where her family was and she'd been happy living here above the café with them. Staying in this flat had made her feel closer to her father somehow. She could still picture him sitting in the battered old leather armchair by the window after long shifts in the café, with a paperback resting on his knee and his requisite tripleshot black coffee on the small table beside him. He'd hated working at the bank and after twenty years he'd finally given up corporate life and they'd all downsized so he could run the board game café, a dream he'd had for years.

Sadly, he'd only worked there for five years before he died. Still, Soli was glad he'd had the opportunity to realise his dream. Ever since she'd lost him the café had become a symbol of hope for her, as well as a reminder that hard work and dedication paid off—something she'd been slow to learn in her younger years, to her everlasting shame.

Shaking off the guilt that always gave her a painful jab when she remembered how selfishly she'd acted in her teens, she got up from behind the counter to close up after the last stragglers made their way out onto the street, waving cheerily to her and calling their thanks. If only they had more regulars like them, the type that bought food and drink every hour as they played, the café would have some hope of survival.

She just needed to find a way to entice those types of people to walk through the door.

After locking up behind them and giving the floor a sweep and the tables one last wipe, Soli walked into the middle of the room and tried to survey it with objective eyes. Why weren't people coming in as much as they'd used to? Sure, it was a bit shabby-looking now after years of wear and tear and it could probably do with a bit of sprucing up, but it had a friendly, comfortable aura to it, and didn't people love shabby chic these days?

She hated the idea of messing with what her father had done to the café. He'd sanded and varnished the wooden tables himself, painted the walls, chosen the now slightly chipped crockery, and she couldn't imagine any of it changing. It would be like wiping her father's soul from the place.

She shuddered, hating the very thought of that.

No, she'd try advertising first, then think about any alterations they might have to make once the money was flowing in again.

Assuming they didn't lose the tenancy in the meantime.

Taking a breath, she focused on calming her suddenly raging pulse. All she needed to do was marry Xavier McQueen and everything would be okay.

The utter bizarreness of that thought made her laugh out loud.

Shaking her head at the surreal turn her life had taken, she went to the till to make sure it had been cashed up properly, grimacing at the sight of the meagre takings for the day. Yes, something definitely needed to change.

Picking up her phone, she tapped in the number he'd given her. He picked up after two rings.

'Xavier McQueen.'

'It's Soli.'

'Hi,' was all he said in reply.

There was a pause in which the weight of expectation hung heavily in the air.

'So I checked up on you and it turns out you're not an axe murderer,' she quipped nervously.

There was a uncomfortable pause when he didn't respond.

Okay, then. Jokes weren't deemed appropriate right now. Wow, this guy was so businesslike.

Probably best just to get down to business, then.

'So I've thought about it and I still want to go ahead with our deal.'

'Great, that's great.' She could hear the relief in his voice. 'I'll arrange for a solicitor to draw up a pre-nuptial contract and another one that states the terms of our deal, which we'll both need to sign.' His tone was professional again now.

'I'll give notice at the register office that we want to get married but we'll have to wait twenty-eight days before we can legally perform the ceremony. The closest one is near St Pancras Station, but I'm assuming you won't have an issue with where the formality of it takes place.' It wasn't a question, she realised. 'It's not like we'll be having a big celebration with friends and family,' he added when she didn't reply right away.

'Er, no, that's fine.' The words came out sounding confident, but something deep in her chest did a strange, sickening sort of flip. This really wasn't the way she'd imagined it happening. Getting married. But, as he'd rightly pointed out, this wasn't meant to be a romantic event, it was a business transaction and should be treated as such. There was no room for any kind of emotional attachment. She'd make sure her real wedding, to the guy who loved and cherished her, was a big, exciting affair, with all her friends and family present. That one would be a cause for a true celebration. She just needed to keep that in mind when she signed the register. True love would come later in her life, when she finally had the time and energy to consider it a possibility.

'Okay, good. I'll let you know the details as soon as I've set it up. I'll need some personal documents from you which I'll swing by and pick up tomorrow, if that works for you?'

'N-no problem,' she stuttered, feeling suddenly as though her life was running away from her a little.

It's not surprising; you're getting married in a month.

A shiver of nerves tickled down her spine.

There was a lot to sort out before then, not least accepting the university place for Domino and finding a full-time carer for her mum, as well as giving notice at the gastro pub and hiring someone to cover her shifts at the café.

The mere thought of all the work and organisation ahead of her was exhausting.

This is for the family, she reminded herself as panic threatened to engulf her. *And it's only temporary.*

In a year's time her life would have taken on a whole new shape. She was doing this for all the right reasons and once she and Xavier were divorced she'd be free to fall in love and get married for real.

With that thought in mind, she told Xavier goodbye and hung up.

Trying to ignore the now almost overwhelming wave of nerves, she turned off all the lights in the café, hid a yawn behind her hand and trudged up the narrow staircase to the flat, first to check that her mother didn't need anything, then to spend the next hour or so planning how best to kick-start the beginning of her brand-new life.

CHAPTER THREE

Scrabble—choose your words carefully.

THEIR WEDDING DAY was glorious. At least the weather was, with the sun pouring in on them through the large picture widows of the register office as they stood at the desk reciting the lines they were asked to say.

The huge room, with its rows of chairs facing the desk, was eerily empty except for Xavier and Soli, the registrar, Xavier's friend, Russell—the only friend he'd confided in and who had drawn up the contracts in his other role as a solicitor—and one other witness, who was a complete stranger to them all. Xavier had approached him outside on the street, pretending that their second witness had been delayed in traffic, and offered him a wad of cash for half an hour of his time.

Glancing around the room, he remembered all too well the last time he'd been in a place like this as echoes of a clawing sense of shame and dread pricked at his skin. He'd promised himself he'd never set foot in a register office again and hadn't attended a wedding since his own disastrous debacle. He'd actually intended to avoid them for the rest of his life, if at all possible.

But he hadn't counted on his Aunt Faith's iron-like will.

So here he was again.

At least this time the bride had turned up and actually married him.

Well, you got what you wanted, Aunty. I hope you're happy now.

Soli, to her credit, didn't say a thing about the lack of guests or the stranger signing the marriage register beneath her name. In fact, she'd seemed more than happy to let him deal with all the arrangements and go along with whatever he'd asked her to do. She'd told him it had meant she'd been able to focus fully on making the necessary arrangements for her family and the café before she came to live with him. Apparently her sister was off to live in Oxford over the summer to earn rent money at a job she'd found there before her first year began and her mother now had a full-time carer living in the flat with her. All thanks to his money.

Not that he resented it. It meant he was able to achieve exactly what he wanted after all.

In his experience, money always smoothed the way. It was the only thing he could ever really rely on.

'Congratulations,' the registrar said to the two of them once the ceremony had come to a close. She didn't seem at all fazed by the lack of guests or the sombreness of the occasion, but Xavier guessed she must have seen it all in the course of her duties.

'Thank you,' he said, giving her a nod of gratitude.

'Yes, it was a lovely service,' Soli added with a barely discernible quaver in her voice.

He glanced at her, wondering whether she was having a moment of regret, but she just smiled back at him as if nothing in the world was wrong. He appreciated her professionalism.

He'd not really looked at what she was wearing when they'd met in the lobby only minutes before their slot because the registrar had come straight over to introduce herself then whisked them straight in, but as he surveyed Soli now he realised she'd made a real effort with her appearance today.

Her wild curls had been tamed into an elegant up do and she'd put on more make-up than he'd previously seen her wear, which accentuated her big bright eyes and full, rosebud mouth.

The simple cream-coloured sheath dress she wore exposed her slim, toned arms and flowed over her curves, drawing his gaze to the tantalising swell of her breasts under the thin fabric.

Hoping she'd assume he was looking at the small posy of flowers she clutched in front of her, he cleared his throat and raised his eyes to give her a tight smile.

Yes, she definitely looked the part. She was a very attractive woman and no one would find it strange that he'd chosen to marry her. At least on the surface. As long as she kept her mouth shut about the terms of the deal they'd worked out, his secret would be safe.

Hopefully there wouldn't be many opportunities for their charade to be discovered anyway. He'd asked her to be ready to attend functions with him but he wasn't actually intending to take her along to many. Just one or two, so it didn't look odd if anyone checked up on them.

He'd already alerted his great-aunt's solicitor to the fact he was getting married and had been told to expect spot checks in the next few months, just to satisfy her conditions. After a year the title deeds to the house would pass into his name.

Then he'd be free to live his life as he chose again.

One year wasn't too long a time to maintain this farce. He could manage it.

'Well, Mrs McQueen, now that's over, shall we get out of here?' he suggested once the registrar had departed, more than ready to leave the place now.

To his surprise Soli pressed her lips together and pulled a mock horrified face. 'You know, I thought Solitaire Saunders was bad, but Solitaire McQueen?' She raised both eyebrows. 'My father will be dancing with glee in his grave.'

The sad edge to her voice gave him pause. 'How did your father die? If you don't mind me asking?'

She shrugged. 'I don't mind. I guess you should know now that we're husband and wife.' Taking a breath, she pushed her shoulders back a little, as if using the action to give her courage. 'He was knocked off his bike by a guy who was texting whilst driving. He died instantly.'

A prickle of horror rushed up Xavier's spine. 'Ah, hell, that's awful. I'm so sorry.'

There was an awkward pause while she blinked back the tears that had pooled in her eyes.

'Thank you,' she whispered, smiling bravely. 'I still miss him every day, but he'd want to know we were all getting on with our lives without him.' She glanced down at the slim white gold ring he'd placed on her finger only minutes ago with an expression of incredulity on her face, then flashed him a wry smile. 'I'm not sure what he'd think about me marrying a stranger though.'

'I'm sure he'd approve if he knew you were doing it for the right reasons,' Xavier pointed out.

Nodding, she let out a small chuckle. 'Yeah, I'd like to think so. He always said I'd get myself in a knotty situation one day with my impulsiveness, but I don't think this was quite the scenario he had in mind.'

Her cheeks had flushed an attractive shade of pink and he had the strangest urge to stroke his fingers across her skin and feel the heat he knew must be there.

Don't be a fool, McQueen.

Instead he nodded jerkily in response to her joke, then gestured towards the exit. 'Well, anyway, we should leave the room before the next wedding party arrives,' he said stiffly, wishing he didn't sound like such an uptight prig.

Giving her body a small jiggle, as if shaking off her melancholy, Soli nodded in agreement.

He marched ahead of her, trying to blank his mind of the way her voluptuous body had shimmied in his vision as he held the door open for her.

A hubbub of noise surrounded them as they entered the lobby and walked through a large group of people that had gathered there, presumably to attend the next marriage that was taking place in the room they'd just vacated.

Russell and the other witness appeared beside them

as they made their way towards the exit. Xavier hadn't noticed them slipping out while they were talking to the registrar, but he suspected Russell had suggested they made themselves scarce so he wouldn't find himself having to answer any awkward questions.

'Let's go out to the front of the building and I'll take a couple of photos of you both in your wedding gear, then we'll see if we can grab a passer-by to take one with the four of us in it,' Russell murmured into his ear.

'Good idea,' Xavier agreed, heading towards the large doors at the other side of the vestibule.

Once outside, they posed next to the register office sign while Russell fiddled with his XLR camera, which he stood on a tripod. Once it was set up, he directed them to stand closer together, with Xavier's arm around Soli's waist and her body pressed close to his. They shuffled awkwardly into the pose and Russell had just taken the first photo when a loud and uncomfortably familiar voice boomed out behind them.

'McQueen? Is that you, old boy?'

Turning reluctantly, with his heart in his mouth, Xavier came face to face with the one person he really could have done without bumping into today.

'Hugo. Good to see you. What brings you here today?' he said, letting go of Soli and taking a deliberate step in front of her so she was obscured from Hugo's line of sight as he shook the man's hand.

'A colleague's getting married and I promised to attend.' He leaned towards Xavier conspiratorially and cocked an eyebrow. 'He's on track to become my boss one day soon so I thought I'd do the smart thing and turn up today. Show willing, you know?'

'Sure. I hear you,' Xavier said. He knew exactly how these old boy networks worked. It wasn't wise to snub someone who had the potential to either help your career or ruin it for you in the future.

'Is Veronica with you?' Xavier asked, a little panicked at the thought of having to save face in front of Hugo's scarily perceptive wife as well.

'No, she's off on some girls' retreat, lucky mare!' he said loudly, adding in a jovial guffaw for good measure. It seemed Xavier's attempt to hide Soli hadn't been successful, though, because Hugo leaned to one side to peer past him. 'And who is this, may I ask?'

Xavier swallowed down his exasperation. 'This is Soli.'

She took a step forwards and held out her hand, giving Hugo a warm smile. 'Solitaire McQueen,' she said, as if happy to have the opportunity to test out her new name for the first time.

Bad timing, Soli. Very bad.

Not that she could have known that.

'McQueen, you say?' Hugo boomed, giving Xavier a confused glance, then looking towards where Russell stood with the camera. 'Have the two of you—' he waggled a finger between them '—just got married?'

'Yes, just a few minutes ago,' Soli confirmed, to Xavier's chagrin.

'Well. You are a dark horse, McQueen. We had no idea marriage was on the cards for you.' Hugo's confused frown deepened as he looked between the two of them.

'No, well, it all happened very quickly,' Xavier said, his heart sinking through his chest. 'We've dated on and off for years but only recently decided we should make a proper go of it,' he lied, silently begging his friend to take him at his word.

'Really?' Hugo said with a tinge of disbelief in his voice. 'It happened so quickly you couldn't even wait to invite your friends to the wedding?'

Damn. He was well and truly busted. He'd never hear the end of it from his old friends now.

'Neither of us wanted a big do,' Xavier said gruffly, feeling heat rise up his throat. The last thing he needed was Hugo and his old social group to find out he'd had to pay Soli to marry him in order to keep his family home. He hated the idea of that getting back to Harriet. His humiliation really would be complete then.

'We thought we'd have a party for close friends and family some time in the near future,' he said, deciding the only thing to do was to bluster his way through this.

Hugo flashed him a knowing smile. 'Fair enough, old chap. I suppose I can understand why you'd choose not to shout about it to all and sundry.' Turning away before Xavier could comment on that, he asked, 'And what do you do, Soli?'

He noticed her shoulders stiffen at the question and silently prayed she'd be able to handle this unexpected confrontation without making Hugo suspicious about the real state of their relationship. 'I'm a small-business owner in the catering industry and one of Xavier's clients,' she said, somewhat mechanically.

Xavier cringed at how that must have sounded to

Hugo, but mercifully he didn't seem to find anything odd about it.

'Well, I must congratulate you, Soli; I never thought I'd see a woman manage to make an honest man of Xavier McQueen,' he said, aiming a cheerful grin in her direction. 'Any particular reason for getting married right now though? Do we have the patter of tiny McQueen feet to look forward to?' Hugo asked with a sly wink.

'No,' Xavier stated coldly, feeling the atmosphere thicken between them. 'It just felt like the right time for us both,' he added, trying to smooth over the extremity of his reaction.

Hugo didn't take offence though and slapped him hard on the arm. 'Sorry, old chap, didn't mean to put my foot in it. The wife's always telling me off for that! Very happy for you both, obviously. I'll have to tell Veronica I saw you; she'll be delighted.'

He felt Soli look round at him but didn't turn his head.

'In fact,' his friend went on, completely oblivious to the discomfort he was inflicting, 'if you're not going on honeymoon right away—' He paused and looked at them expectantly.

The only thing they could do was shake their heads dumbly, caught out by the question.

'Well, in that case, why don't the two of you come over to our place next weekend? We're having a bit of a do to celebrate our fifth wedding anniversary—all Veronica's idea, you know,' he added with a pseudo grimace towards Soli. 'I know she'd be delighted to see you, McQueen, and to meet you too, Soli.'

'I'm not sure—' Xavier began to argue.

'Don't be a bore, McQueen!' Hugo broke in before Xavier had chance to air an excuse. 'You can't hide from us for ever. And Veronica will never forgive you if you don't accept at least one of our social invitations. We've not seen hide nor hair of you for years! Now you're married you've no excuse not to come along to see the old crowd. You don't want folks thinking you're shunning them, now, do you?' he said this with a laugh in his voice, but Xavier knew it covered a real sense of hurt. Clearly Hugo was nursing a sense of resentment about being ignored and avoided for so long.

He was trapped. Damned if he did and damned if he didn't.

They'd have a week to prepare for it though. That ought to be enough time for him and Soli to get to know each other well enough to convince Hugo and Veronica, and anyone else they'd invited, that they were a real, loving couple.

'I'm pretty sure we're free then,' he conceded. 'We'll check our diaries and let you know.'

'Great! I'll get Veronica to send you an official invite,' Hugo said with affable gumption. 'You still in your aunt's Hampstead pad?'

'Yes. I'm still there,' Xavier said, feeling a desperate urge to get away from his friend now so he could regain his shaky composure. 'I look forward to receiving the invite, Hugo. Anyway, we'd better get on. We need to take a couple more photos, then we have some celebrating to do,' he added in an upbeat voice that didn't sound like his own, forcing himself to give Hugo a happy-looking smile.

'You've picked a real charmer there, Soli,' Hugo said with another wink in her direction. 'I hope he's intending to treat you like a princess today.'

'Oh, I fully expect him to,' Soli replied, smiling back. 'He's the most generous man I've ever met.'

Xavier experienced a rush of gratitude towards her for that.

'I tell you what, Hugo,' Xavier said, as a flash of inspiration struck him. 'Since you're here, let's have you in the photo too. It'll only take two seconds. We just need to grab someone to press the button for us— it's all set up.'

'Sure! Be happy to!' Hugo boomed, clearly pleased to be included. 'This lovely lady will do it for us, won't you?' he said, making a large beckoning motion to a woman in a big red hat who was just about to enter the doors of the register office.

'Er...yes, of course,' she said, looking over at first Xavier, then Soli, and giving them a warm, indulgent smile.

So they all bunched together and the lady took a couple of pictures of the five of them.

'Thanks so much,' Xavier said, pleased with his quick thinking. It would look much better to have at least two of his friends in the wedding photos.

'We should do one more of just you and Soli, for safety,' Russell said to Xavier, before they all dispersed.

'Ooh, yes. You make such a gorgeous couple,' the woman said, beaming at the two of them. 'You should do one with the two of you kissing. I always think they're the nicest ones to have displayed.'

There was a small pause where neither of them reacted.

'Er…yes, good idea,' Soli said a little too loudly beside him and he felt her slip her arm around his back and lean in towards him, giving him a slightly awkward cuddle.

For a moment he stiffened under her touch before realising how odd that would seem to the small group that were looking at them intently now.

Without allowing himself to think about it, he slid his hand against her jaw, tipped her head towards him and kissed her fully on the mouth.

She drew in a small, breathy gasp, but didn't pull away, instead sinking into the kiss and wrapping her arms tightly around his waist as he instinctively opened his mouth against hers. The soft, flowery scent of her enveloped his senses and he breathed her in deeply, struck by the distinctiveness of her taste and smell.

Delicious.

Her lips were so soft and perfectly pliant he experienced the strangest sensation that they were somehow made to perfectly fit with his. His stomach swooped at the thought and he became aware of something deep inside him—long buried—beginning to stir.

Sensation fizzed along his veins, causing his breath to shorten and his heart to pound against his chest.

Oh, Lord, that's not good.

Pulling abruptly away, he didn't dare look her in the eye again in case she saw even a hint of the heavy need that now pulsed through him. 'Was that okay? Did you get it?' he asked Russell, who was standing behind the camera looking at the two of them with an odd expression on his face.

'Yes, perfect. I got it,' his friend replied, quickly rearranging his features into a smile.

Xavier's stomach twisted as he realised that the spark he'd felt between them had outwardly showed. Not that that was necessarily a bad thing. At least to Hugo it would have looked as though they were genuinely attracted to each other.

When he glanced back at Soli he noticed she looked as bewildered as he felt and his stomach knotted even tighter.

'Well, I'd better get inside before I miss the beginning of this thing,' Hugo said loudly, strolling over to give Xavier a slap on the back and jolting him out of his tangled thoughts. 'Looking forward to seeing the two of you next weekend.' And with that he gave them both a farewell salute and strode quickly away.

Xavier swallowed, his mouth suddenly dry and his head tight around the temples.

'I'd better go too!' the lady in the red hat said, glancing at her watch and moving towards the door of the register office. 'Congratulations, you two, and good luck for the future!'

Luck? Yes, they might need a bit of that if this fake marriage was going to go without a hitch.

'I guess we'd better get on, then,' he said, pulling himself together and turning to look at Soli.

'Okay. Sure. Great,' she replied, her expression still a

little shell-shocked. Something tugged hard inside him as a strangely protective instinct appeared from nowhere.

He shook it off.

He needed to get on top of this weird, edgy feeling that was messing with his head. It was this place, it had to be; it was bringing back too many long-suppressed emotions. He couldn't allow himself to develop any kind of feelings for Soli, or encourage her to have any for him. It could cause all sorts of problems.

And extra problems were something neither of them needed right now.

CHAPTER FOUR

Snakes & Ladders—a frustrating game of ups and downs.

SOLI STOOD IN front of the register office, having just kissed her new husband for the very first time, trying to deal with a strange sort of unease at finding she'd enjoyed it much more than was probably healthy for a woman who was now expected to live a life of celibacy for the next twelve months.

How had it been possible to feel so much in so few seconds?

She'd thought it would be fine, kissing Xavier for the camera with everyone looking on, but she'd been shocked by how her body had responded to him. Her skin had flushed all over as if the sun had concentrated all its power on her in those moments and her heart had done a triple flip before sinking to somewhere in the region of her stomach.

It had been wonderful and terrible all at the same time.

She wished she hadn't liked it quite so much because

she now had a year to think about how wonderful Xavier's mouth felt on hers without being allowed to experience it again. He'd made it very clear this relationship wasn't ever going to be anything more than as friends.

Friends. But were they really? *Could* they be?

'I'll go and get your bags from the cloakroom,' Xavier said brusquely.

All she could do was nod in agreement, then watch him stride back into the building where she'd stashed the two cases she'd packed so carefully the day before. They represented the sum total of her worldly goods, apart from a few items of clothing she'd given to Domino and a small box of mementoes from her childhood which she'd left back at the flat because she'd not wanted to lug them over to his house.

Taking a moment to compose herself while Xavier wasn't around, she took a breath and pushed back her shoulders, uncomfortably aware that her legs were still wobbling like mad after she'd put herself through the most nerve-racking half-hour of her life—first the actual marriage ceremony, during which she'd felt as though she were looking down on herself from above, then the whole surreal exchange when Xavier's friend Hugo had appeared out of nowhere and she'd had to scrabble for the correct way to act in front of him.

In the heat of the moment she'd just gone for it and introduced herself as Solitaire McQueen without considering that this might not be something Xavier would approve of, but she'd realised from the way he'd stiffened, then scowled at her, that it had been a mistake. But then, how was she supposed to have known how he wanted her to act in front of his acquaintances? They'd been so busy sorting out the legal side of things they hadn't got round to discussing the day-to-day business of being married yet. It had all been such a whirl.

She'd tried hard not to take offence at his obvious reluctance to introduce her to his friend, but it still rankled. Obviously Xavier wouldn't want the marriage of convenience part to be public knowledge, she understood that—he was clearly a private and proud man and if people found out the amounts of money he'd promised to pay her to go through with it neither of them would come out looking particularly good—but surely he wasn't planning on not telling his friends that he was married to her.

Judging by Hugo's reaction it sounded as though Xavier had kept the marriage a secret from *all* of his friends too, apart from Russell, of course, who had written up the legal documents for them to sign and so was clearly a necessary confidant.

She turned to look at Russell now, who was standing quietly beside her, and wondered what he thought about the whole strange undertaking.

He must have felt her gaze on him because he turned to look at her and asked, 'How well do you know Xavier?' as if he'd been wondering the same things that she had. From his expression she suspected he was actually a bit concerned about what his friend had just done.

'Uh, hardly at all,' she said with a pained grimace. 'We've not spent a lot of time together because we've been too busy sorting out our personal situations before the ceremony. It's all been a bit of a whirlwind to be honest.'

Russell nodded thoughtfully, then gave her an encouraging smile. 'Listen, I know he comes across as a bit distant sometimes, but he's a good guy. He's just been through a lot during his life, that's all, and it's made him a bit hard to reach. Emotionally, I mean.'

'Really? What happened?' Soli asked, intrigued by what Russell might have to tell her. If Xavier was going to keep her at a distance, talking to his friends would probably be the only way to really get to know more about him.

Russell looked uncomfortable. 'I should probably let him tell you all that himself. It's not really my place.' He rocked back onto his heels and crossed his arms. 'You've got a year to get him to lower his barriers, after all,' he said, his smile a little strained now. 'I'll just say this—' he paused, as if searching for the right words to use '—you should keep in mind that he's unlikely to want to commit to the marriage fully. What I mean is, don't get your hopes up that he'll let it become a real relationship. I don't think he's really cut out for that sort of commitment. Not any more.'

Soli nodded, but couldn't help but frown, feeling a bit overwhelmed by it all now. 'Don't worry, I'm not looking for it to turn into a real marriage either,' she said assertively, though something in the back of her mind let out a small squeak of protest.

No. She'd be a fool to even consider that happening. She was only doing this for the year, then she'd be in a much better position to commit her heart for real. With someone who truly cared about her.

The momentousness of what she'd just done suddenly hit her full force, sucking her breath away.

She was *married* and about to move in with a man she barely knew.

Adrenaline surged through her body, making her hands shake.

'A year suddenly feels like an awfully long time to live with a stranger,' she blurted.

Russell gave her a reassuring smile. 'Don't worry, he'll look after you. He's nothing if not a gentleman.'

Xavier reappeared through the doors with her bags then and came over to thank Russell for his help, giving him a friendly slap on the back, before turning to face her.

'Are you ready to go home?'

Home.

His home though, not hers.

'Yes, I'm ready when you are,' she said, summoning a smile, which she hoped wouldn't give away how nervous she was.

Xavier nodded, not seeming to notice her jitters, and set off at a brisk pace with her bags to where he'd left his car. He loaded her cases into the boot while she slipped into the passenger seat.

The car smelt wonderful: of new leather and Xavier's distinctive scent, a mixture of the aftershave he wore and a musky, masculine fragrance all of his own. She'd been hyper-aware of it in his office when she'd first met him and it had haunted her ever since, the olfactory memory appearing in the air at random moments, though she'd known she was only imagining it. Her mind was good at playing tricks on her like that. It had done the same thing after her father died, conjuring his scent at odd moments, bringing with it a surge of such painful grief she'd often been immobilised by it.

But this definitely wasn't a time for immobility. She needed to make good on this opportunity and she was determined to do everything in her power to make this deal work out well—for both of them.

Sensing Xavier needed a few minutes to process what had just happened too, Soli stayed quiet as they pulled away from the kerb and stared out of the window, watching the busy London streets slip by.

When he still hadn't said a word to her as they began to drive through Hampstead Village towards the road where he lived—where *they* lived—she found she couldn't stand the silence any longer. Turning to look at him, she experienced a wave of concern when she caught sight of his rigid profile.

'Is everything okay?' she asked quietly. 'I'm sorry if I did something wrong back there. I thought Hugo was a friend of yours so it'd be okay to introduce myself. Surely you weren't hoping to keep me a secret for the next year.' Pausing, she took a shaky breath. 'Were you?' She laughed nervously, concern creeping over her skin as she considered the possibility that she'd hit upon the correct answer.

'No, no, of course not, it's fine,' he said, but his tone wasn't exactly convincing. 'I hadn't really thought about how I'd handle telling people about us, so it caught me off guard, that's all. But I think he bought the whirlwind marriage thing.' He turned to look at her now and his set expression softened a little. 'No point dwelling on it though. It's done.'

'No. Okay.' His answer hadn't done much to calm her nerves but she decided to push her concern to the back of her mind. He was right—there was no point worrying about it. She'd figure him out eventually.

They'd need to spend some quality time together this week if they were going to look like a convincing couple at Hugo's party next weekend though. The last thing she wanted was to put her foot in it again with his friends. She hated the idea of making a fool of herself in front of them. If she and Xavier weren't careful something like that could potentially cause resentment and tension between them, which would make for a really uncomfortable home life. She *really* didn't want that. Not if they were going to have to live with each other for the next year.

After driving along the long, wide road locally referred to as 'Millionaire's Row' she'd expected Xavier's house to be impressive, but as they swung in through the automatic gates at the end of the driveway, which magically opened for his car, the true magnificence of the place struck her like a blow to the stomach. Built in the arts and crafts style, it loomed above her like an enormous geometric citadel, its two wings standing like sentries either side of the grand entrance.

'Home, sweet home,' he said, turning momentarily to raise both eyebrows at her as he pulled the car up to the front of the house, then turned off the engine. 'I'll grab your cases, then I'll show you around.'

Taking a moment to get another swell of nerves under control, she watched him get out of the car and take her bags out of the boot, then dragged in a deep, steadying breath and got out too, following him to the front door, which he was opening with a swipe card.

It was like walking into another world as Soli took her first step into the house and she let out a gasp of wonder.

'You weren't expecting me to carry you over the threshold, were you?' Xavier asked gruffly, possibly mistaking her stunned awe for upset as she stood there, gazing around the cavernous, marble-floored entrance hall with wide eyes.

'No, of course not,' she said, giving him a reassuring smile before returning her gaze to the dark wooden-banister staircase, which drew the eye upwards towards an ornate mullioned window, its many panes of glass winking in the late-afternoon sunshine. Looking at it, she wouldn't be surprised to find this one room had the same square footage as her entire café.

'Wow. I can see why you wouldn't want to lose this place. It's spectacular!' she said, turning to flash him an impressed expression.

He glanced around him as if checking out what she meant, then gave her a taut smile back.

'It's been in my family for nearly a hundred and fifty years, but I've only had the privilege of living here for the last four—since my great-aunt was taken into hospital after her first stroke.'

'That must have been hard. Coming to live here on your own when she was so ill.'

He shrugged but didn't say anything. There was a glimmer of sadness in his eyes though, she was sure of it.

'Have you done much to it?' she asked, sensing his intention to keep the subject on a non-emotional level.

'Hardly a thing, which was great for me because I could just move straight in.' He gesticulated around the large, elegant entrance hall with its neat marble-topped table and large vase of fresh flowers sitting invitingly in the middle of the space. The subtly coloured walls were hung with striking pieces of modern art, and there was a huge gilt-framed mirror on the far one which reflected their images back to them.

'She had really good taste and a love of interior design, so kept up with all the trends. She was always poring over those house and garden magazines,' he said with a faraway look in his eyes, as if remembering her fondly. 'I'm sure she would have been an interior designer if she'd had the chance but my great-uncle didn't want her to work. He was pretty traditional like that.'

'Right. Wow.' She couldn't imagine a world in which she wouldn't be allowed to work. She'd be bored to tears.

'Let me give you the tour,' he said, already moving towards one of the large mahogany doors that stood open to the right of them.

He guided her around the frankly massive ground floor: through the sitting room with its classy antique furniture, the library with its shelves stuffed with old books, the snug with a huge widescreen TV on the wall and a squashy-looking sofa facing it, and then on to what he called the morning room, which looked as though no one ever used it. She guessed the William Morris wallpaper in there was original, due to its slightly faded look.

She couldn't help but watch Xavier closely as he walked through the rooms ahead of her, his broad back straight and his long-legged gait a little tense. He intrigued her. Why was such an attractive, successful man living here alone? Maybe it had something to do with the not-believing-in-love thing.

Best not to think about that, though. She didn't want to get herself in any kind of emotional tangle. She had enough to deal with right now.

He then led her towards the back of the house, where there was a fully equipped gym, and on through another frosted glass door leading to an indoor swimming pool, which was surrounded by green-leafed plants in pots standing against the beautiful mosaic-tiled walls.

'You can use this any time you like,' he said, waving his hand at it as if everyone had one and it wasn't anything special.

A little bubble of nervous excitement, that had begun to form in the pit of her stomach as soon as she'd entered the house, rose up to her throat and tickled her tongue.

This incredible place was going to be her *home* for the next year.

They ended the tour of the main house in a huge kitchen diner, which was the most well-worn looking place in the house. Even so, she guessed the oak kitchen cabinets and marble-topped work surfaces would have cost a pretty penny.

This room was clearly the heart of the home and Soli

immediately felt much more relaxed in here. The rest of the house was beautiful, but it had been a bit like being shown around a stately home where you weren't allowed to touch anything.

She could imagine spending lots of time in this room though, making meals for them both and perhaps baking her locally famous cakes and biscuits for Xavier to sample. She'd welcome the chance to impress him with her cooking skills. It would make her feel less insignificant in the face of his overwhelming prowess.

He'd leant back against a scrubbed oak table in the middle of the tiled floor as she looked around, and she glanced over at him, wondering how many times he'd sat there to eat in his lifetime. She could imagine him as a bright-eyed, but serious, little boy with a wicked grin, when he chose to deploy it. Not that she'd seen any evidence of it so far. Any smiles he'd given her had seemed perfunctory and lacking in any real emotion.

What must he have gone through to not have any warmth in his smile? The thought of it made her inordinately sad, especially when it occurred to her that he might well have lost his spirit when he was a little boy.

But perhaps that wasn't the case. He seemed to have genuine love and affection for his great-aunt and clearly adored living here judging by the reverent tone he'd used when showing the rooms to her.

'Did your great-aunt have any children?' she asked, thinking what a wonderful house this would be for games of hide and seek. You could probably go for hours without being discovered with all the nooks and crannies available.

'No. I think she wanted them but it never happened. My great-uncle died before I was born so I never met him, but I used to spend a lot of time with Aunt Faith and I think she considered me the child she never had. She always invited me here during my holidays from boarding school.'

'And your parents were okay with that? Didn't they want you at home with them?'

He let out a low snort. 'They didn't mind at all. They're not exactly "kid people".'

'Oh.' The sharp edge of tension in his voice disturbed her. Was he telling her that his parents didn't want anything to do with him? How heartbreaking.

'Anyway,' Xavier said loudly, making her jump, 'let me show you the room you'll be staying in. Part of the ground floor was converted into a bedroom for my great-aunt to live in, but wasn't used because she had the second stroke before she could move into it.'

She followed him out of the kitchen and back to the entrance hall, suspecting there would probably be a lot of Xavier suddenly changing the subject when things started to get too personal for his liking—which would be frustrating, considering she needed to get to know this enigmatic man a lot better in a very short space of time if they were going to come across as a convincing couple.

'It's down here,' he said, guiding her along a hallway towards the back of the house, then through a door with its own mortice lock and into a large, airy bedroom.

So her bedroom was to be downstairs? As far away from Xavier's as possible, perhaps. Not that she had any right to question this. It was his home after all and she was, to all intents and purposes, his guest.

Like the kitchen in the main house, the bedroom was decorated in a warm, homey style, which immediately made her feel comfortable. There was a queen-sized bed against the wall on the far side and the rest of the room was kitted out in tasteful modern furniture, which, she suspected from its pristine gleam, had never been used before. Her heart fluttered as she realised there was a walk-in wardrobe. She'd only ever had half a small wardrobe at home, where she'd shared a room with Domino.

'You'll need to put some of your things, like toiletries and clothes, in my room too, just in case one of the solicitor's people drops round without giving us any notice and goes snooping. We don't want to give ourselves away by overlooking details like that,' Xavier said, crossing his arms, making him seem even more intimidating than usual.

The thought of being caught out like that only increased Soli's anxiety about them not knowing each other well enough yet. What if she had to answer questions about him that she didn't know the answers to? He could potentially lose his inheritance if the solicitor didn't believe they were a real couple, which would mean their deal would fall through and that could signal the end of the café.

'I can't lose this place, Soli, and I'm definitely not going to let it go to my money-grubbing cousin because we messed up the small stuff,' Xavier said, echoing her thoughts.

'Okay. No problem,' she said, trying to sound reassuring. She'd do everything in her power not to let that happen.

'Good. Well, now you've had a look around I'll bring your cases in here and you can get settled in.'

Following him out of the bedroom and back to the grand entrance hall, she tried not to let a feeling of being on the very edge of control overwhelm her.

She needed to focus on the positives, such as this amazing place being her home for the next year.

It would be so exciting to be here.

Or terrifying—depending on which way you chose to look at it.

Xavier seemed like a good guy though, if a little cold and reserved. Everything she'd found out about him had been positive, she reminded herself. Especially the things she'd read about his business practices. And her father wouldn't have rented a property from a shyster after all; he'd always been a very cautious and thorough businessman himself.

'Why did your great-aunt want you to be married in order to inherit this place?' she blurted as they reached the front door. It had been playing on her mind as he'd shown her around. 'It seems a little extreme in this day and age.'

He turned back to face her with a grimace. 'Yes, well, my great-aunt had very traditional values. Her marriage was arranged by her family and she stayed married to my great-uncle for forty-three years, until he died of a heart attack. I think she had some romantic notion that if she forced me into getting married I'd end up the same way she did. Blissfully happy.' He pulled a face.

'Not convinced, huh?'

'Not one bit.'

'Shame.'

He frowned. 'What do you mean?' From his tone she suspected he was unnerved to hear her talking about marriage in such a positive way. Perhaps because he was worried she might become more attached to the idea of being his wife than he was comfortable with.

'Don't worry,' she reassured him quickly. 'You're really not my type. When I get married for real it'll be because I'm in love with my partner and I want to spend the rest of my life with him. That won't happen with us.'

He continued to look at her in that unnervingly intense way he had, as if he was trying to read her innermost thoughts and catch sight of any lies she might be telling him. She stared boldly back, trying not to think about how devastatingly attractive he was.

'I promise you, I will not want to stay married to you after the year is up,' she reiterated firmly. 'I've got too much going on in my life to be a wife and mother right now.'

She was sure she saw him flinch when she said that, but before she could say anything more he nodded curtly and said, 'Anyway, you'll need these for the doors.' He pulled a plastic key card and a key for her apartment out of his pocket and handed them to her.

'So you're not planning on keeping me locked up inside all day, then?' she asked in as jovial a tone as she could muster.

'Of course not,' he said, waving away her words as if they were completely ridiculous.

Her skin prickled as she remembered how reluctant he'd been to introduce her to Hugo as his wife earlier, but she bit her tongue. She really didn't want to have a row with him on their wedding day. Not that it seemed they were actually going to celebrate it in any way.

This was confirmed when Xavier said, 'Well, I've a lot of work to do today so I'll let you get settled in. There's food in the fridge or takeaway menus by the phone in the kitchen if you want to eat in tonight.'

Disappointment trickled through her. 'We won't be eating together?'

'Not tonight. I need to deal with something that's just cropped up at work right away.' He gestured towards his phone. 'I'll put your bags in your apartment and catch up with you tomorrow.'

'No, don't worry, I can take them.'

He paused, then nodded distractedly, and she watched him walk away and mount the stairs, heading up the wide staircase to the top landing.

She suddenly felt very small and alone in the huge, dark house.

Looking down at the sheath dress she'd made especially for the ceremony out of one of her mother's old dresses, she felt a heavy sense of trepidation sink through her.

No, Soli, don't let it get to you.

Why she'd thought she needed to look good for this farce of a wedding today, she had no idea now. But it had been important to her to make an effort, even if Xavier hadn't appreciated it. He'd not said a word about how she looked.

She hadn't sewed her own clothes for a very long time, but being strapped for cash and not wanting to waste money on buying a proper wedding dress, even a second-hand one, she'd decided to make her own. She'd worked for three nights straight on it and was really pleased with the results. Whilst working on it she'd remembered how much she'd enjoyed designing and making her own clothes before her mother had become too ill to look after herself and her father had died, requiring her to step into his role as carer, parent and bread-winner. Experiencing that had made her appreciate just how hard he'd worked to keep them all in the lifestyle she'd taken for granted. She wished fervently now that she'd had the opportunity to tell him how grateful she was to him for providing that for her.

She hoped he would have been proud of her for what she was doing here—making sure that her sister and mother were well looked after.

The way she needed to look at it was that Xavier was providing her with a unique opportunity to set them all up for the rest of their lives.

All she had to do was make sure she didn't do anything to jeopardise it.

CHAPTER FIVE

Frustration (UK)/Trouble (US)—roll a six before you can make a move.

THE NEXT MORNING Xavier came down to the kitchen at seven a.m. to find to his relief that it was empty of his new wife. He'd been hoping that Soli wasn't an early riser and wouldn't expect to have breakfast with him so he could continue with his usual morning routine of sitting at the kitchen table and reading the news on his tablet whilst sipping his first cup of coffee of the day in peace.

It looked as if he was in luck.

As he set up the coffee machine, he noticed some cake tins and spatulas and a few bags of ingredients on the worktop. The sight of them sitting in what he thought of as his personal space sent a tingle of annoyance through him.

Telling himself to relax, he tamped down on his irritation, knowing he was going to have to get used to sharing his house with Soli for the next year and getting uptight about a few pieces of kitchen equipment lying around wasn't a good way to start. Anyway, it needed to look as if she lived in this house, he reminded himself, so having a few of her things scattered around would actually be a good thing.

He was just pouring the coffee into a mug when there was the sound of footsteps behind him and he spun around to see Soli standing in the doorway wearing a slouchy pair of pyjamas with a cartoon character on the front and her hair wild and sticking up around her head.

'Morning,' she said, hiding a yawn behind her hand. 'You're up bright and early.'

'I always leave at this time,' he said, averting his gaze as the idea of seeing her as she'd just rolled out of bed suddenly felt way too intimate.

'So you don't have time to have breakfast with me?' she asked, moving towards the kettle, which she flicked on to boil.

'No, sorry. I need to leave in a minute.'

'Oh, okay.'

She looked disappointed, but he pushed aside the sting of guilt this brought about. He couldn't just change his routine to fit in with her. She'd need to work around him.

As if she'd sensed this, she leant back against the work surface, smiled at him and said, 'Perhaps we could spend some time together this evening instead? It'd be nice to get to know you a bit better since we'll be sleeping under the same roof for the next year. We could spend a bit of time drawing up a list of dos and don'ts for the relationship.'

He frowned as the uncomfortable reality of having

someone at home waiting for him every night struck him. 'Yes, of course, but perhaps not tonight. I have a really heavy day at work and I'll want to relax this evening. Once my workload's calmed down a bit we'll have plenty of time to do that.'

'Perhaps we could just play a board game or two, then. It'll be a fun, unpressurised way to learn more about each other,' she suggested. 'They're great ice-breakers and it'll give us something else to concentrate on so we can chat freely. Our café is a popular destination for first dates precisely because of that. At least it used to be.' A frown flickered across her face. 'I'll cook us a light meal and we can play afterwards?' she suggested brightly.

His phone had beeped for the third time in as many minutes and he plucked it out of his pocket distractedly and glanced at the screen, seeing with a wave of concern that it was a message from his financial director. There must be an urgent issue for him to get in contact before the working day had begun. He glanced up from the screen to see Soli was looking at him with a questioning expression. 'Er, yes, okay. I should be back by about eight o'clock,' he said, wondering what could have happened for Rob to try him three times already.

'It'll be useful for us to know what makes each other tick,' she added.

'Yes. Quite right. We'll need to put up a good front at Hugo and Veronica's party and it'll be good to be prepared for that,' he said with a sigh, running his hand over his jaw as the idea of it sent a twinge of frustration up his back.

Would they really believe he'd married someone like Soli of his own free will? She really didn't dress, or act, like the type of woman he usually dated.

'I've been thinking about your question about what you're going to do during the day when you're not working at the café.'

'Oh, yes?'

'I'm going to arrange for a monthly stipend to be put into your bank account which you can use to go shopping for new clothes and book hair and beauty appointments and the like. Those sorts of things ought to keep your free days busy enough and they'll be practically expected of a woman who's married to me and not working full-time, so it'll fit our story.'

She lifted a hand to smooth down her wild curls, then adjusted her pyjama top, her brow creasing into a bewildered sort of frown. 'Okay. Well, thanks.'

Feeling satisfied with this act of generosity, he cleared away his empty mug and gave her one last nod before striding out of the house and setting off for the office, feeling a strange sense of relief at having something to focus on outside of Soli and his brand-new marriage.

Soli let out the sigh of frustration she'd been holding in when she finally heard the front door slam closed behind Xavier.

Well, that had been an incredibly frustrating meet-up.

Awkward didn't even cover it.

It was clear he wanted them to look like a convincing couple at the party, but he seemed reluctant to actually spend any time with her.

Work, apparently, was going to take precedence.

Her heart sank at the anticipation of the fight she might have on her hands to get his full attention.

She shook off her worry. She'd find a way to make it work. Her family was relying on her and there was no way she was going to let them down now.

Pouring herself a reviving cup of coffee, she mulled over what he'd said to her just before he'd left. She really hadn't expected him to give her even more money—not that it wasn't welcome. She'd been acutely aware as she'd hung up her clothes in the wardrobe in her room that the sort of things she wore—mostly high street store outfits or things she'd picked up from a great little vintage clothes stall in Camden Market—probably wouldn't look quite right for someone married to Xavier McQueen, but his insinuation that she wasn't the sleek, sophisticated-looking woman he'd hoped for in a partner had still stung a little.

Not that she couldn't fix that if she splashed the cash around a bit.

It was going to feel pretty strange spending his money on frivolous things like that though, and she was going to have to get over that. If he was happy to give it to her, she should just be grateful for it.

She took a breath and straightened her spine, imagining herself into the role of the lady of the house.

The first thing she needed to do today was plan what she was going to make for their 'getting to know each other' meal. She wanted it to be something that looked as if she'd made a bit of effort, which of course actually meant making a lot of effort. Despite the fact they were only pretending, for the sake of her pride she wanted to be as good a partner as she could be.

Perhaps she could do steak with a peppercorn sauce and some lovely fresh seasonal vegetables. And Dauphinoise potatoes. Her sister loved it when she made that dish—which wasn't often because it was pretty labour intensive.

Yes, something like that perhaps. And she'd make a dessert from scratch too. Something with lots of fresh fruit, like a summer pudding.

Her spirits rose again.

While she was out shopping for all the ingredients she could pick up a couple of board games for them to play this evening too. Games that might lead them to interesting discussions and help them to get to know each other a bit better.

With a sense of positivity and purpose surging through her now, she sat down at the table and began to make a list, planning a wonderful evening of food and entertainment for her and her new husband.

It would be great to finally feel as if she was on top of things and acting like the kind of daughter her father always wanted to have.

Yup, she was a grown-up now and determined to prove to Xavier that he'd made a good choice in her and that it would be money well-spent.

He was going to be so pleased he'd married her.

It was ten-thirty before Xavier made it home that evening, after having to deal with the crisis at work that had kept him, his PA and his financial director in the office, scrambling to close a property deal that they'd been working on for the last three months.

It had been a taxing day, but Xavier was pleased with the way it had gone in the end. He felt buzzed with success as he let himself in through his front door and made his way across the entrance hall towards the back of the house.

Striding into his kitchen, he experienced a shiver of disquiet as something niggled at the back of his brain.

He'd not even had a chance to let Soli know he'd be back late; in fact, he'd been so engrossed in what he was doing he'd not noticed how late it was until his PA had jokily pointed out they should eat before all the takeaway outlets shut for the night, but he'd figured it wouldn't matter. Soli had plenty of things to entertain her here in the house and she seemed like the resourceful type.

After flicking on the kettle, he leant back against the kitchen counter and took a moment to look around the kitchen. There was something different in here, he was sure of it. It *smelt* different. A bit like the French restaurant he loved to go to on the bank of the Thames in Southwark. Garlicky and delicious.

The kettle boiled and he made himself a cup of tea, lifting the teabag out with the spoon after swishing it around in the boiling water for a few seconds. He never had the patience to let tea brew properly. When he lifted up the lid of the food-waste bin to dispose of the teabag, the garlicky smell grew even stronger and he paused, staring down inside the bin's depths. It looked as though there was a whole meal in there—what looked like Dauphinoise potatoes and cooked vegetables. What was Soli doing throwing so much food away? How wasteful.

And then it struck him and his stomach turned over with unease. She'd made dinner for him and he'd not turned up for it. He hadn't even phoned her to let her know he'd be too late to eat with her.

He snapped the bin lid shut and stepped away from it, feeling a strange mixture of self-righteousness and guilt. It wasn't as though he'd deliberately not turned up for the 'getting to know each other' dinner, he'd just forgotten about it. Work had had to take precedence today; it had been imperative to get on top of the problem before it had snowballed.

He'd explain all that to her tomorrow and apologise for missing dinner. There was no point in feeling guilty about it though. They had plenty of time to get to know each other and she'd have to get used to him having to work late without giving her any notice. That was how his life worked and he wasn't about to change it for someone who was fundamentally in his employ.

She'd understand that.

Frankly, he was paying her a hefty chunk of money to understand and accept that.

With that assuring thought in mind he added a splash of milk to his tea then took it through to the sitting room to drink it, determined to enjoy a few minutes of his evening before he had to retire to bed.

When Soli turned up in the kitchen at seven o'clock the next morning, hoping to catch Xavier before he went to work, she was frustrated to find he'd already been and gone.

Had he done it on purpose so he didn't have to see her?

She'd been disappointed and a bit hurt when he hadn't come home in time to eat the food she'd spent so much time and energy on, but she'd tried not to take it to heart. She'd decided to give him the benefit of the doubt and assume he'd just forgotten about it.

And her.

The uncomfortable twisting sensation that she'd experienced when she'd finally accepted he wasn't coming home last night reappeared.

She needed to get a grip. There were bound to be a few misunderstandings until they got to know each other better. He was a very busy man who ran his own company, so of course he was going to be working long hours and would be prone to forgetting she was at home, waiting for him.

But the dissenting voice in her head whispering that he was deliberately avoiding her wouldn't shut up.

She felt wired and restless now as if there was something portentous in the air.

Perhaps it was the ghost of Xavier's great-aunt who had come to check up on the state of the marriage and was most displeased with what she saw.

Not that I blame you, Aunt Faith—I'd be pretty annoyed too if I found out he was playing the system to get round my wily attempt to force him to emotionally connect with life.

By eight o'clock that evening she'd just about given up

hope of him appearing for dinner again and was about to start making enough food for one when she heard the front door open, then slam closed.

Heart thumping hard, she waited with bated breath to see whether he'd come to try and find her in the kitchen.

When he appeared in the doorway he seemed almost shocked to see her, as if he'd completely forgotten he had a wife.

'Soli, hi,' he said, frowning at her.

Steeling herself against a wave of disquiet, she said, 'Hi. How was your day?'

Oh, man, why did she feel so awkward talking to him? Perhaps because he was still frowning at her as if wondering what she was still doing here.

'It was fine,' he said distractedly, glancing around the kitchen.

'You're back late again.' She forced herself to smile graciously then waited to see whether this would trigger an apology for missing the dinner she'd made him the night before.

He ran a hand over his eyes and let out a sigh. 'Yes. It's not an uncommon occurrence.'

'I see.' So she wasn't getting an apology, then.

'How was *your* day?' he asked instead.

He still wasn't looking at her though; instead his gaze ran over the kitchen surfaces where she'd left some of her cake-making equipment.

'Pretty good, thanks,' she replied, pleased that he'd at least asked about her even if he wasn't entirely engaged in the conversation.

'Are you planning on making stock for the café here?'

he asked abruptly, the terseness in his tone shooting a shiver of discomfort down her spine.

'No, this is just some of my baking stuff from home. You don't mind if I keep it in here, do you?'

He seemed to seriously consider this request for a second or two as if deciding whether he'd be prepared to share the space with her. 'Sure. Why not?' he said eventually.

'Thanks,' she said, slightly discomforted, hoping he wasn't going to be this possessive about the rest of the house. Clearly he wasn't used to having someone invading his territory.

Perhaps a goodwill gesture would make him more tolerant of her presence here.

'You know, I make a mean chocolate fudge cake. It's a particular favourite in the café. I can make one for you, if you like. It's yummy.'

She looked at him expectantly, hoping for some spark of interest.

'No. Thanks. I'm not a big fan of desserts.'

The pleasure she'd initially felt at the thought of spending time with him tonight was rapidly draining out of her.

'Oh. Okay.' She forced an undaunted smile, despite the sting of rejection she felt. 'No problem.' She swallowed. 'Have you eaten supper? I can make us some chilli. I've got all the ingredients right here.'

'No. Thanks,' he said again. 'I had a late lunch and I've got a few calls to make to the US so it'll be a while before I'm done. You go ahead and eat without me.' He gave her a curt nod, then turned to leave the room.

The last dregs of her optimism drained away, leaving her totally deflated.

His businesslike attitude towards her was seriously denting her excitement at living here with him. It was becoming starkly clear that he didn't want to spend any time with her and that he was deadly serious about keeping their relationship emotion-free.

Turning to stare down at the chopping board and the pile of ingredients for the food she didn't really feel like eating any more, she was just about to pick up the knife to start chopping enough onions for one portion, determined not to let him totally disturb her equilibrium, when she realised he was still in the room.

When she turned to look at him she saw he was leaning against the doorjamb, watching her with a thoughtful expression on his face.

'I'm sorry I forgot about our "getting to know each other" dinner last night,' he said when he noticed her questioning eyebrow.

He didn't exactly *sound* sorry though. In fact, from the tone of his voice she got the impression he was actually quite irritated about having to explain himself.

'There's a good chance I won't be around at regular times in the evenings so don't worry about making food for me. I'll eat when I get in,' he went on when she didn't react right away.

So she was going to be eating on her own every evening? How horrible. She hated the thought of sitting in this huge empty house all on her own night after night, not having anyone to talk to. She was so used to being around people all day in the café and then chatting to her mum and sister over their family meals it made her spirits sink to think she'd miss out on all that life while she was here.

For a whole *year*.

Her stomach knotted at the thought of it.

'You know, this house is such a big, lonely place for one person. Perhaps your great-aunt wanted you to get married and raise a family here so you're not on your own all the time,' she muttered, unable to keep her agitated thoughts to herself any longer.

She saw his shoulders stiffen and the air felt suddenly leaden with tension.

'Yes, well, she'll have to be for ever disappointed in me for not having children, I'm afraid,' he said tersely.

'You don't want kids?' She was surprised to hear that.

'No.'

'Why not?'

'Because they're an inconvenience. They mess up your life.'

The bluntness of his tone bothered her.

'You really believe that?'

'Yes.'

But she could have sworn she saw a hint of uncertainty in his eyes. Just for a second.

'That's sad.'

'Sad? Why?' He was scowling at her now as if she was talking utter nonsense.

She shrugged. 'I don't know. I guess I can imagine you being a great dad.'

He looked at her steadily for a couple more beats and

she got the feeling he was trying to decide how to handle this without it turning into a big deal.

'Well, thanks. But I don't think I'm the sort of person who could give a kid the kind of love they need.'

'Because your parents didn't give it to you?' she blurted without thinking, her frustration at his aloofness getting the better of her.

Anger flashed across his face, but he covered it quickly. 'I'd rather not talk about my parents.'

'Okay. Sorry.' But she didn't feel sorry, she felt annoyed with him for being so obstructive. Was he going to treat her like this for the entire year? Perhaps he'd hoped she'd squirrel away in her downstairs bedroom like an animal in a cage, never asking any awkward questions or getting in his way and only showing herself when he summoned her.

He must have seen the irritation on her face because he blinked in surprise. 'Anyway, I have a lot to do this evening,' he said, to her mounting ire. 'I'll leave you to it.'

Before she could utter another word, he strode out of the room, leaving her alone.

Again.

CHAPTER SIX

Articulate—use words cleverly to figure out what your partner is trying to tell you.

THE NEXT FEW DAYS followed a similar pattern, with Soli barely catching Xavier for two minutes over his morning coffee before he left for work and then him coming home at random times in the evening, regularly texting her to let her know he wouldn't be back in time for supper and to eat without him.

As her anxiety grew about how they would fare at the impending party, her concentration levels waned, making it increasingly difficult to concentrate on the marketing she had planned for the café.

So when Friday night came around she crossed her fingers that Xavier would be back at a reasonable hour and finally willing to give her a bit of his precious time so she could finally put her mind at rest.

But when he walked in after nine o'clock he only poked his head into the sitting room, where she'd been trying to distract herself by half watching TV and half checking social media, and said a curt 'hello' before excusing himself to go up to his office.

Having sat on her own, fretting, as she drained a large glass of wine, Soli suddenly found she'd had enough of being ignored.

Springing up off the sofa, she ran into the hallway, where Xavier was already mounting the stairs, his long legs making short work of the winding staircase.

'Xavier!' she shouted, determined to get his attention before he disappeared on her again.

He stopped climbing and turned to look back down on her with a frown of surprise.

'Look,' she said, throwing up her hands in exasperation, 'I appreciate you're busy, but how am I supposed to convincingly pretend I'm your wife—someone that loves you and knows you intimately—if you won't even talk to me?' She held up both hands, palms forward. 'Can you please just give me half an hour of your time? Is that really too much to ask?'

He was looking at her now as if completely stunned by her outburst.

'I'm sorry to snap,' she said quickly, worried that she'd gone too far in her agitation, 'but I've reached my limit of pretending not to mind you treating me like a piece of furniture.' She tried to smile but her mouth refused to play ball. Instead, to her horror, her muscles began to tug downwards at each side and her throat constricted painfully as she fought back tears.

But she wasn't going to cry. No way. She was going to be an adult about this.

'If you really want us to appear like a proper couple

you're going to have to let me in a bit,' she pointed out in a measured tone.

A muscle in his jaw flickered, but after a few seconds of seeming to seriously contemplate what she was saying he gave her a curt nod of agreement.

'Okay, then. And how do you propose I do that?'

She moved to the bottom of the stairs and leant on the newel post, looking up at him, a mixture of excitement and relief surging through her. 'There's this game I've played at a party which helps you get to know the other guests better. First of all you have to look into each other's eyes for three minutes—to begin to feel more comfortable with that person in a physical sense.' She paused, gauging his reaction.

'Go on,' was all he said, walking down one step towards her.

'Then we ask each other a set of questions which are meant to give us some insight into each other's lives— how we see the world, what makes us feel good and bad. Personal self-disclosure, I think it's called.'

'Right.' He seemed less certain about this, but he hadn't said no, so she decided to forge on.

'The shared vulnerability is supposed to make us feel closer and help us trust each other more. I appreciate this is a bit of an ask at this early stage, but I think it'll be a great way to get comfortable with each other pretty quickly, especially since we don't have a lot of time to do that, what with you being so busy at work.'

She tried to keep her scepticism out of her voice about how busy she thought he *really* was, as opposed to how he'd probably been using it as an excuse to avoid her, but from the twitch in his eyebrow she could tell she'd failed.

'Okay, Soli, fine.' He rubbed his hand over his jaw. 'I guess we should do this now since Hugo and Veronica's party is tomorrow.' He walked down the rest of the stairs to where she stood. 'Where do you want to do it?'

'The sitting room would be good. Somewhere we can sit comfortably.'

'Okay. Lead the way,' he said.

She ignored the weariness in his voice, determined not to give him an excuse not to go through with this. Hopefully once they started communicating properly he'd start to relax around her.

In the sitting room she chose the three-seater sofa and sat down on it, patting the cushion next to her to encourage him to sit close by.

He followed her suggestion and turned to face her, laying his arm along the top of the sofa and looking anything but excited about the prospect of doing this.

'Okay, I'm going to set the timer going, then we have to sit looking at each other's faces, particularly the eyes, until the beeper goes.' She shifted in her seat, trying to ignore the wave of heat rising up her neck at the thought of actually doing this now with Xavier.

'Are you ready?' she asked him.

'As I'll ever be,' he drawled.

'Okay, then, I'm starting the timer—now,' she said, tapping on the screen of her phone.

Turning to face him and settling her body into a comfortable position, she fought back a ridiculous urge to giggle, knowing it would spoil the exercise before they'd even started, and took a breath, locking her eyes with his.

He nodded as if resigned to letting this happen and looked back at her with that shrewd, intelligent gaze of his.

Soli swallowed, suddenly acutely aware of every breath she took, every facial muscle she moved. It was intensely intimate, having him looking at her so thoroughly without a break, but she was determined not to look away.

All the hairs on her body stood up and a hot tingle rushed over her skin as the seconds ticked by slowly, but she still didn't look away.

He really was an immensely attractive man, she mused as she gazed at his olive skin with its five o'clock shadow and his long, dark lashes that almost brushed his cheeks every time he blinked.

She became aware of some strange feeling building inside her, something that made her pulse jump in her throat, but before she had a chance to figure out exactly what it meant the timer went off, making them both jump.

'Sorry, I didn't realise I'd set the volume that high,' she said, flustered and grabbing for the phone with fumbling fingers. Finally managing to turn it off, she turned back to him and shot him an apologetic grin.

'Well, that was fun,' she joked.

His mouth actually twitched up at the corner at that, which she considered a personal victory. Of sorts.

'At least we'll be able to describe each other's faces to an outsider in detail now too,' she said, acutely aware of a tell-tale wobble in her voice. 'You know, I hadn't realised your eyes had yellow flecks in them; I thought it was just a lighter shade of green. Oh, and how did you get the small scar by your lip? It's so tiny I hadn't noticed it till now.'

'I fell off my bike here in the garden when I was eight,' he said, lifting his hand to touch the scar she'd mentioned, almost absently. 'Aunt Faith bought it for my birthday and the front brakes were really fierce. I went right over the handlebars.'

'Ouch!' she said, with a grin.

'Precisely,' he agreed, his mouth twitching upwards again.

Yes, progress! It seemed the forced intimacy had opened something up a crack between them. She just needed to press her advantage now and get him talking to her some more.

'Okay, then, now we've done that let's move on to the questions. I'll ask you some first, okay?'

He began to frown, but seemed to change his mind. 'Sure. Fire away.' Shuffling back against the sofa cushions, he crossed his arms in front of him and gave her his full attention.

Soli felt herself flush again under his gaze, but tried not to let it distract her.

'What would be a perfect day for you?' she asked as a starter question.

'Hmm.' He rubbed his hand over his jaw again, but in a thoughtful manner this time.

'Well, I rarely get the chance for a lie-in, so I'd have one of those.'

Soli tried hard not to picture him lying naked and rumpled in bed. And failed.

'Then I'd have a long, lazy breakfast and perhaps a walk across the heath. Maybe have a swim in the lake and a picnic lunch.'

From the faraway look in his eyes now, she got the impression he was actually enjoying thinking this up. The thought of it warmed her.

'In the afternoon I'd go and play tennis then head out for a slap-up meal in town.'

'Wow, that all sounds great,' she said with a grin. 'And when was the last time you spent a day doing things like that?'

This seemed to stump him. 'I don't think I've ever had a day like that. I've always been too busy with work or had other social engagements.'

'Oh. What a shame.'

'Yes, I guess it is,' he said, shrugging his shoulder.

There was a small pause where neither of them said anything.

'When was the last time you sang in front of someone?' Soli asked, to fill the silence.

'Never,' he said with a shake of his head.

'Really? Never?'

'I'm not really into performing,' he said with finality to his tone.

'Oh. Okay, then,' she said, recognising his need to move on.

'How about this: if you could choose one ability that you don't already have, what would it be?'

'To predict the future,' he said with confidence.

Soli thought this was interesting. It clearly pointed to a need for complete control.

'What are you most grateful for?'

He paused infinitesimally before replying, 'My health, wealth and happiness.'

Glib, but okay.

'What would you never joke about?'

'Money.' There was no pause before that answer.

'Is there something you've always dreamt of doing but have never got round to? Tell me about it, then tell me why you haven't done it yet.'

'Hmm.' This gave him pause. 'I think I'm doing what I dreamt of. I wanted to run my own company and live in this house.'

'Okay. Well…well done,' she said with a smile. 'What's your biggest accomplishment?'

'Same answer. My company and finding a way to live in this house.' He looked particularly pleased with himself for that answer.

'Tell me about a happy memory from your school days.'

Suddenly the buoyant atmosphere seemed to drop like a stone.

'I can't think of one right now,' he said tersely, his gaze skimming away from hers now.

There was something heartbreakingly raw about the way he said this, but she didn't press it. From the way his shoulders had stiffened she got the impression he'd happily call an end to the session if she did and that was the last thing she wanted when he was finally starting to open up to her a little.

'What has been your most embarrassing moment?' she asked with a smile, hoping to flip the mood, but was a little taken aback to see his eyes harden at this. 'It can be something really silly,' she added quickly, desperately trying to rescue the lightness they'd had previously.

'Pass. I can't think of anything right now,' he said again, his tone warning her not to push it. Clearly she was treading on dodgy ground.

Okay. She could come back to that another time. She didn't want to ruin the progress they'd made. But something still pushed her to ask the next question anyway.

'What's your relationship with your mother like now you're grown up?'

The light went out of his eyes. She realised with a shiver of disappointment that she'd blown it and that he'd probably clam up completely now, but to her surprise he didn't. Instead, he hooked an arm across the back of the sofa again and looked directly into her eyes as if actively deciding not to dodge her interest in the question any more. Perhaps he was hoping she'd leave him alone if he finally gave her an answer to it.

'I don't really know her, to be honest. We have very little contact these days. She's not exactly the maternal type. I think she fell pregnant with me by accident—at least, that's what I overheard one day when my great-aunt and a friend of hers were chatting. Apparently my father convinced her to keep me, but she and I never really bonded. Not that my relationship with my father was much better. He was always being sent away overseas with work. He was a foreign diplomat. My mother often went with him but they kept me here in England at boarding school. It was for my own good, apparently, so I wouldn't feel unsettled.'

From the expression on his face she gleaned that it had actually had the opposite effect. No wonder he was so attached to this house. It seemed to be the only place he'd ever felt secure. She couldn't imagine how horrible it must have been not to be allowed to live with your family. There were so many good memories from her own childhood, she'd be devastated not to have had the opportunity to experience them. Some of them were only snatched, random moments in her memory, but they still held so much meaning for her. They'd help her grow and form as a person and the knowledge that she'd be able to come home to her family and a safe, loving environment every day after school had kept her going through her most taxing years.

'I suspect it was really because they thought I'd cramp their style if I was living with them,' Xavier went on, his eyes taking on a far-away, troubled look now. 'They were always big socialisers, according to my great-aunt…' He paused, as if weighing up whether he wanted to say the next thing out loud, obviously deciding that he did when he added, 'And not exactly faithful to each other.'

'Oh. I'm sorry to hear that. It must have been really unsettling for you,' she said quietly.

He looked at her again, his expression softer now with what she thought might be appreciation for her understanding.

'It wasn't great, but then no one's life is perfect, right?'

'True,' she said, giving him a supportive smile.

There was another heavy pause as they just looked at each other again and Soli felt a strange sort of pulse beat between them.

'Any more?' Xavier said, breaking the tension.

'Any more what?' she asked, a little shaken by the atmosphere that had formed.

'Questions,' he said pointedly.

'Oh! Yes. Okay.' Pulling herself together, she asked, 'What would you regret not having said to someone if you were to unexpectedly die this evening?'

He raised a wry eyebrow, his eyes twinkling with mirth.

'Don't worry, I'm not thinking about doing you in,' she added with a grin, then muttered, 'yet,' waggling her eyebrows in jest.

He came really close to properly smiling at that and her heart did a little dance of joy in her chest.

'Hmm, I don't know,' he said thoughtfully. 'I guess I wish I'd had a chance to tell my great-aunt how much I appreciated her taking me under her wing like she did. I don't know what would have happened to me if she hadn't.'

Soli became aware of tears pooling in her eyes. 'I'm glad you had her. She sounds like an amazing woman.'

'She was.'

Blinking away her tears and pointing at her eyes, then wafting her hands at either side of them with a strained smile of embarrassment, she asked, 'When did *you* last cry in front of someone?'

He frowned, but didn't meet her eyes. 'I'm not a crier.'

'Really? You never cry?'

'Not in front of other people, no.' He shifted a little in his seat and crossed his arms. 'And it's been years since I cried on my own.'

'Oh. Okay, then.' There was something so heart-wrenching about this it actually caused her physical pain deep in her chest. How awful that he didn't feel he could express his sorrow in front of someone else.

'I cry in front of people all the time,' she said with a self-deprecating grin. 'I find it cathartic. I always feel better afterwards, though sometimes I'm embarrassed by how easily I do it. I cry at anything even remotely sad,' she said, feeling tears pushing at the backs of her eyes again just from thinking about it.

His shoulders had stiffened as if he was really un-comfortable now and he glanced down at his watch, as if wanting to escape from the conversation.

This was confirmed when he said, 'Anyway, Soli, it's been an interesting exercise, but I really do have some work to do this evening, so I'm going to say goodnight.'

'Okay,' she said, watching him get up from the sofa, feeling a swell of satisfaction from getting as far as she had.

It was early days yet, but at least she knew a bit more about him now.

His emotional unavailability made more sense now she knew more about how he'd been ignored by his parents during his childhood. She felt truly sorry for the poor, lonely little boy he must have been growing up, not having a family who loved him or a steady base to come home to during his breaks from school. What must that do to a child? To not feel wanted by the people who were supposed to love you unconditionally?

It was a horrible thought.

Well, she'd make sure she did her very best to support him in the months to come. She'd need to be careful not to get dragged into an emotional quicksand where Xavier was concerned—it wouldn't be sensible to allow herself to actually fall for the guy, she reminded herself with a strange pulse of panic—but she could be a friend to him, as he'd suggested.

Yes, that was exactly what they both really needed at this juncture in their lives.

A good friend.

CHAPTER SEVEN

Would I Lie to You?—keep your cool and think quickly to win this game.

XAVIER SLEPT BADLY that night and woke up later than his usual six a.m. start.

After having that conversation with Soli his dreams had been tangled with memories of his time at boarding school—feeling isolated and humiliated when he'd been the only boy whose parents hadn't turned up to watch an end-of-term performance before they all left for the Christmas break. It had then changed to him standing in the mostly empty register office with Soli. In the dream they were reciting the lines they'd been asked to say, except it wasn't the registrar conducting the service, it was Great-Aunt Faith, who was barking instructions at them as if they were disobedient children.

As he'd turned to apologise to Soli, he'd realised it wasn't her standing next to him after all—it was Harriet.

'Really, Xavier? You had to pay her to marry you? How pathetic,' she'd sneered at him and the ugly look of utter disdain on her face had woken him with a sickening jolt.

It had been so vivid and had drawn such a strong emotional response from him he felt exhausted now, as if he'd not slept a wink all night.

Remembering with relief that it was the weekend, he allowed himself to lie in bed and read the news on an app on his phone, determinedly pushing the unsettling echoes of the dream out of his mind, before finally dragging himself out of bed for a shower then heading down to the kitchen for breakfast.

He'd just got the coffee machine set up and running when the buzzer for the entry phone at the front gate went.

Frowning to himself and wondering who the hell would be so uncouth as to turn up uninvited at this hour on a Saturday morning, he picked up the handset and snapped, 'Yes?'

'Mr McQueen? This is Samuel Pinker. I've been employed by your great-aunt's estate to visit you and your wife at home in accordance with her will.'

Heat rushed across his skin, quickly followed by a wave of cold panic that made his hair stand on end. So they were being checked up on already?

'Okay. Well, you'd better come in,' he said, forcing his tone to sound jovial and upbeat. 'Solitaire is still in bed, I'm afraid. It's a little early for her, so you'll need to give me a few moments to rouse her.'

'No problem,' the voice of Pinker said over the phone. 'I have a quick call to make so I'll park in your driveway and give you a knock in five minutes, if that suits you?'

'That would be fine,' Xavier said steadily.

'Thank you,' the man replied.

Xavier pressed the button to release the gate, then dashed out of the kitchen and down the corridor to Soli's room, where he banged hard on the door.

It was a full minute before he was able to rouse her.

'Xavier? What's the matter?' she asked, hiding a yawn behind her hand and looking a little bewildered to see him standing there.

'There's someone here from my great-aunt's solicitor's office to check up on us. You need to get dressed. Quickly,' he said, determinedly trying not to notice how appealing she looked, all bed-rumpled and sleepy.

Her eyes sprang open at that and she did a little nervous jiggle on the spot. 'Should I get dressed?' she asked, her voice wobbling with panic.

'No,' he said, thinking it would seem more realistic if it looked as though she'd just got out of bed. 'But perhaps put a robe over your pyjamas?'

'I don't have one!' she said, flustered.

'There's one on the back of my bedroom door. Go and put that on. It'll look better if you come from upstairs anyway. As soon as you hear me open the door, come down. Okay?'

She looked slightly terrified now. 'What am I meant to say to him? We haven't worked it out yet!'

'Don't worry. Let me do the talking. Just try and make it look as though you like me and find me attractive,' he said, flipping her a wry smile.

She nodded jerkily. 'Okay. I can do that.'

There was a strange, zingy tension suddenly between

them, but he brushed it off, not having the time to consider what it might mean.

Two minutes after she'd dashed upstairs, the doorbell went and Xavier took a deep, steadying breath before going to answer it.

Their visitor was a portly man, with a shock of russet hair and a cheerful smile.

'Samuel Pinker,' he said, holding out a hand, which Xavier shook firmly.

'Good to meet you. Please come in.'

He guided the man into the hallway, just as Soli made a timely appearance at the top of the stairs.

The two men looked up at her as she descended and Pinker once again held out his hand in greeting as Soli reached the bottom stair.

Soli, to her credit, appeared to be totally relaxed as she shook his hand and introduced herself, giving Pinker a warm smile that lit up her whole face.

Xavier's stomach did an odd swoop as he once again thought how attractive she looked with her wild curls framing her pretty face and her cheeks pink and a little sleep-creased. The robe she'd found in his bedroom was far too big for her, but it only enhanced how feminine and delicate she was.

He had the strangest compulsion to wrap his arms around her, to protect her from Pinker's searching gaze, but he held back, not wanting to spook her and give the two of them away.

To his surprise, Soli appeared to have the same urge to touch him and he gave a small involuntary grunt of surprise as she walked straight up to him and slid her arms around his middle, pulling herself close so they were chest to chest. He looked down to see she was gazing adoringly into his eyes.

His heart did a three-hundred-and-sixty-degree turn.

Remembering the exercise they'd done only the night before, he maintained eye contact with her, immediately recalling that same close connection he'd experienced, so didn't even blink when she stood on tiptoe to plant a light, soft kiss on his mouth.

The sweet, sleep-warmed scent of her invaded his consciousness, making his senses reel and his body instinctively tighten with lust.

Ah, hell. If she pressed herself any closer to him there was a good chance this could turn into a very embarrassing moment indeed.

Luckily, she pulled away before he completely lost control of the situation and turned to smile at Pinker, who was watching them with a focused sort of smile on his face.

'Can I get you a cup of coffee, Mr Pinker?' she asked him. 'We were just about to have one.'

To Xavier's surprise, Pinker shook his head. 'No, thank you, Mrs McQueen. I only popped in so I could tick the "living together" box on the paperwork. It's very clear you both live here, what with me turning up at such an ungodly hour at the weekend and finding you in residence. I do apologise for any inconvenience caused—it's my job, you know?'

'Of course! We totally understand,' Soli said, with warmth in her voice.

'Well, I'll let you good people enjoy the rest of your

morning,' Pinker said, tipping Soli a courteous nod and offering Xavier a smile. 'No doubt I'll see the two of you again at some point. Until then…' He made for the door, giving Xavier a nod of thanks when he opened it for him, and vanished outside.

Xavier waited until he saw Pinker's car pull out of the driveway before shutting the door with a sigh of relief and turning to face Soli.

'Well done,' he said, walking towards where she still stood by the stairs. 'I think we convinced him.'

Soli smiled back, looking a bit sheepish now. 'Sorry for kissing you like that without warning, but I thought it would look more authentic. It's the sort of thing I'd do if we were really married.'

'No problem,' he said, lifting a hand to touch his lips where the ghost of Soli's kiss still lingered. 'It's a good job you insisted on that eye-gazing thing yesterday—it made it a lot easier for me to look at you.'

'Thanks. I think,' Soli said, flashing him a rueful grin.

'I didn't mean…' He shook his head, irritated with himself. 'I meant it made it easier to be immediately intimate with each other.'

'I knew what you meant,' Soli said, widening her grin, evidently enjoying winding him up.

He couldn't help but smile back at her, a surge of relief-filled happiness appearing out of nowhere. Clearly he'd made the right choice in Soli for his pretend wife. Her quick reaction today gave him confidence they'd actually be able to pull this thing off at the party this evening.

'Oh, wow!' Soli said loudly.

'What?' he asked, startled.

'Your smile. It's incredible. You should do that more often.'

'Uh, thanks.' He smiled again in a show of nonchalant acceptance but her words had made a tingle shoot straight up his spine. No one had complimented him on his smile in a very long time. Perhaps because he hadn't had much to smile about.

They stood there, just looking at each other for a couple of beats, and once again Xavier had the weirdest feeling that Soli was someone he could really trust and rely on. Strangely—considering she was still practically a stranger to him—she was one of the few people he'd ever felt that about.

She looked back at him with curiosity in her eyes. And something else. Something that made his skin heat and his body tense with arousal.

He suddenly wanted to kiss her again, just to experience that same thrilling feeling of being connected.

No. No. *Not a good idea.*

Obviously it had been much too long since he'd been physically involved with a woman if he was contemplating messing with this precariously balanced business relationship he'd negotiated so carefully.

'You know, it occurs to me that I didn't ask anything about you when we did that getting to know each other exercise last night,' he said, taking a deliberate step back away from her. 'Want to chat now over coffee?'

The look of surprise on her face made him feel equal parts amused and guilty and a hot sort of discomfort trickled through him. Apparently she'd not expected him to take any interest in her as a person.

'Just in case we're caught out like that again,' he added quickly, not wanting her to read too much into his offer of friendship.

'Er...yes, sure. If you like,' she said, folding her arms around her middle and looking suddenly a little uncomfortable about standing in front of him in her nightwear.

'Feel free to get dressed first,' he said with a reassuring smile, 'but only if you want to. Don't do it for me.'

'Nah, I'm fine,' she said, letting her arms swing down to her sides and pushing back her shoulders. 'Let's do it now.'

He really *liked* her self-confidence.

So they started off by chatting about simple things like their favourite books and films and music, then they moved on to which countries they'd like to visit and why.

'So it sounds like you haven't travelled much yet,' he said as she reeled off the long list of places to visit on her bucket list.

'I've not had much chance,' she said with a sad smile. 'Ever since my dad died I've had to spend all my time working and looking after my mum and sister.'

'Yes, of course,' Xavier said, chastened. He'd almost forgotten how much she'd had to deal with during her relatively short life. 'That must have been pretty tough.'

'Yeah, it was at the beginning,' she said, hunching her shoulders, but maintaining her sunny smile. 'My mum got very depressed after we lost him and started really struggling with her Parkinson's, and Domino was too young to help out. She still needed someone to look after her and I was the only one available. It didn't leave a lot of time for me.'

'No. I bet,' was all he could muster in response. It made him realise how easy he'd had it being an only child with family money behind him. Glancing at his watch, he gave a start of surprise. He'd been enjoying chatting with her so much he'd not noticed how the time had flown. 'Hey, it's nearly lunchtime already.'

'Oh!' she said, looking slightly panicked. 'I'd better get dressed and grab some lunch. I have a hair appointment at two o'clock.'

Once she'd dashed off and changed her clothes they reconvened in the kitchen and ate their fill of the delicious food that Soli had loaded the fridge with—which mostly consisted of Mediterranean-inspired fare like brightly coloured salads, a cold meat platter and a range of healthy grains—before she excused herself to go to her appointment, leaving him on his own.

Experiencing a strange surge of energy once she'd gone, he took himself off for a long, hard session in the gym, followed by a lengthy swim in the pool.

Finally feeling as if he'd got past the odd edgy tension that had kept him moving, he went for a scorching hot shower, coming down from his bedroom to find a wonderful smell wafting from the direction of the kitchen.

Striding in, he found the room empty, though it was clear Soli had been in here recently because there were mixing bowls in the sink and a dusting of flour on the work surfaces. The smell seemed to be coming from the large range oven and he peered through the glass to see a large cake rising inside its tin.

Despite having stuffed himself at lunchtime, he heard his stomach give a growl of hunger. He'd told her he didn't have much of a sweet tooth, but he'd make an exception for something that smelt that good.

'I thought we could take it to the party as a gift for your friends,' came a soft voice behind him and he spun around to see Soli standing in the doorway with a tentative smile on her face.

There was a strange rising sensation in his chest when he noticed how her wild curls had been tamed into sleek blonde waves, making her look a good few years older than she was. Not that he didn't like her usual hairstyle. In fact, he probably preferred her hair au naturel, but he appreciated the effort she'd gone to for the party.

'Your hair looks nice,' he croaked through a suddenly dry throat.

It must be the heat from the oven getting to him.

She gave him a wide, delighted smile. 'Thanks, I'm glad you like it.'

'Are you going to be wearing that later?' he asked jokily to distract himself from the inappropriate way his body seemed to be responding to her now, pointing to the bathrobe he'd loaned her that morning, which she had wrapped tightly around her.

She smiled back. 'I wasn't planning on it, no. I bought a dress especially for the occasion. I hope it's the right sort of thing.' He noticed her jaw twitch and realised she was probably as nervous about going tonight as he was.

'Don't worry, they're a friendly crowd, on the whole.' He took a stabilising breath. 'I probably ought to warn you that there's a good chance my ex, Harriet, might be there, and there could be a bit of tension.' He frowned, wondering how best to explain this without having to go into too much embarrassing detail. 'We didn't part on great terms.'

'Oh. I'm sorry to hear that. So it wasn't a mutual split, then?'

He looked at her steadily for a second, weighing up whether or not to answer that, before shaking his head. 'No. It was her choice. But I'm over it now.'

Soli's eyes narrowed as if suspicious of this bold statement. 'How long were you with her?'

'Four years. We met in our last year of university.'

The usual wave of hurt flooded through him at the thought of Harriet and all that had happened between them, but he was determined not to let seeing her again ruin his night tonight. He needed to concentrate on getting through this thing successfully with Soli and convincing his friends they were a real married couple in order to avoid any more personal humiliation. That had to be his top priority.

'Is there anything specific I need to know? So I don't make a faux pas if we meet her?' Soli asked, her expression open and her voice so kind it reached right inside him and tugged at his heart.

He almost told her everything, right there and then, but decided against it at the last second. She didn't need to know all the sordid details. It wasn't as if everyone would still be gossiping about it now. Surely they'd all moved on.

'No. I think it's probably best if we just avoid her. I don't want to cause a scene, especially not in front of

Hugo and Veronica, who are friends with both of us,' he said stiffly.

'Okay. Well, thanks for the heads up.' She was looking at him now with a concerned expression, as if she suspected there was more to it than he was telling her.

Nothing, it seemed, got past Soli.

There was an awkward beat of silence where they both smiled at each other and he couldn't help but think how pretty she looked. Her pupils seemed to dilate as she continued to maintain eye contact with him and she drew in a soft, breathy gasp, opening her lips a fraction as if she couldn't quite get enough air.

His gaze immediately moved to her mouth and he had to force himself not to start wondering what it would feel like to kiss those soft, inviting lips again.

'I should get the cake out of the oven before it burns,' she said a little over-brightly, jarring him out of his lascivious trance.

'Yes. Okay. You do that,' he said, a little rattled by his body's instinctive response to her. 'I'd better go and get ready for the party. We need to leave in about an hour.'

At the door he turned back to watch her as she busied herself around the kitchen, drawing in a great lungful of the delicious smell of the cake as she opened the oven door and bent down to lift it out.

'There's a good chance that won't make it out of the house,' he joked. 'It's altogether too tempting.'

She turned to give him a startled look, quickly recovering her composure when she realised he was talking about the cake. 'I thought you didn't like sweet things?'

He raised an eyebrow, tamping down on his amusement about the misinterpreted innuendo. It wasn't really appropriate to flirt with her when they were on their own. 'For that,' he nodded to the tin she had in her oven-gloved hands, 'I'll make an exception. It smells incredible.'

Her answering blush brought a smile to his lips and he allowed himself to flip her one last grin before walking away to prepare for the party, hyper-aware of his blood pumping hard in his ears.

CHAPTER EIGHT

Cluedo (UK)/Clue (US)—uncover the culprit with deduction and guile.

IT WAS MORE of a garden party than a posh evening do, as it turned out, which suited Soli just fine. It meant she was less likely to melt into a sweaty, nervous puddle as they mingled with the large throng of elegant, sophisticated guests.

Xavier was received with a mixture of exaggerated bonhomie and friendly curiosity and he seemed, to Soli, to be completely at ease as they moved from group to group, giving a nod here and there and occasionally stopping to introduce her before politely excusing them and moving swiftly on.

The comforting weight and heat of Xavier's arm around her waist kept her grounded as they circulated around the party and after a while she started to relax and chat with the people who asked kind, but slightly bemused questions of her, particularly about how she'd met Xavier. Once she'd given her answer about meeting him through the business she quickly moved the focus of the conversation onto the other person, making sure to ask them lots of questions about themselves.

They'd been there for about twenty minutes without catching sight of the host or hostess, who according to one guest were either down in the wine cellar stocking up on booze or settling a tantrum-throwing child, when there was a shout from behind them. 'Xavier McQueen, where have you been hiding?'

They both turned away from the couple they were chatting with to see a tall, slim woman wearing a flowing cornflower-blue silk cocktail dress striding purposefully towards them. She pushed her long, sleek black hair away from her face as she got nearer and gave them a huge grin, her dark eyes sparkling with delight.

'Veronica. Lovely to see you,' Xavier said, taking a step towards her. Soli could tell from the smile in his voice that he was genuinely pleased to see her. But if that was the case, why had he not seen his friends for so long? He couldn't have been that busy with work, surely.

'I'm so pleased you came! I had a bet on with Hugo that you would. He owes me a fiver, oh, he of little faith!' She raised a playful eyebrow at Soli. 'My darling husband thought the two of you might be a bit too busy "being newlyweds".' She turned to give Xavier a playful wink. 'But I knew you wouldn't be so mean as to deny us your wonderful presence at such an important do. Five years we've been married, can you believe it?'

Without waiting for a response from him she turned to look at Soli with wide, discerning eyes. 'Now, who is this delightful creature? Introduce me to your cute-as-a-button new wife, Xavier.' She held out a manicured hand, which Soli shook, a little surprised by the strength of the woman's grip.

'This is Solitaire—Soli for short,' Xavier said. The sound of her name on his lips gave Soli a strange little shiver of delight. He had such a wonderful deep, gravelly voice—it always did something to her whenever he spoke.

'It's so wonderful to meet you,' Veronica said, pulling her in for an enveloping hug. 'What a gorgeous name!'

Soli believed she really meant it too—she didn't seem at all patronising or false; her smile and touch were too warm for that.

'Lovely to meet you too. Thanks so much for inviting us,' Soli said, returning Veronica's smile. 'What a beautiful garden you have,' she said, gesturing towards what must have been half an acre of land, with its vibrant borders of summer flowers in full bloom and its springy grass that her heels kept sinking into, rooting her to the spot.

'Oh! Thank you! We love being out here in the summer and it's great for the children when they need to burn off some steam. Which is all the time!' She laughed, then glanced at Xavier, her smile faltering as an expression that Soli couldn't quite read flashed across her face. But only for a second. Had she felt as if she'd put her foot in it with him for some reason?

'I probably should mention that we've invited Harriet and her partner here today,' Veronica said, her expression a bit strained now.

'I expected you would,' Xavier said in a neutral tone,

though Soli could have sworn she felt him stiffen beside her.

'I just thought I'd warn you so it wouldn't be a shock if you saw her here. I understand you haven't been in touch since...' She broke off, glancing quickly at Soli before returning her gaze to him. 'I just mean I can understand why you kept a low profile after what happened,' Veronica finished in a sympathetic tone.

Soli stood motionless, listening intently, wondering what the heck she was missing here.

Xavier shrugged. 'I thought it'd be better to let Harriet feel as if she could still see her friends without me being around all the time,' he said gruffly. 'You were *her* friends first, after all.'

Was she imagining it, or was there a hint of pain in his voice? The very idea made her shiver with horror and she experienced the strongest urge to wrap her arms around him, to let him know she was there for him and on his side should he need her. He froze for a second as she gave in to her instinct and slid her arm around his waist, but quickly relaxed again, pulling her closer in to his side.

Veronica smiled at the two of them, seeming to decide that Xavier must be over it. 'Well, I'm delighted that you have this gorgeous creature by your side now.' She gave Soli a warm smile, before moving her gaze back to Xavier.

'You know, there's a real spark between the two of you—something I never saw between you and Harriet. I always thought she was a bit too straight for you. In retrospect I'm sure getting married wasn't the right thing for either of you at the time. It was probably for the best that she called it off.'

Soli's heart gave an extra-hard thump in her chest. So he'd nearly married Harriet, but she'd called it off?

There was an uncomfortable pause before Xavier cleared his throat and said, 'Yes, perhaps so. It would have been nice to have more than an hour's notice that she'd changed her mind though.'

Soli's breath caught in her throat. So Harriet had dumped him at the altar! How humiliating for him. She couldn't imagine anything worse for someone as proud as Xavier. No wonder he'd been so determined not to get married again—and that his great-aunt had felt she'd had to go to such extremes to make him even consider it.

Not that he'd married her for love.

The thought made her stomach do a sickening sort of lurch.

'Oh, darling, I know.' It was Veronica's turn to sound uncomfortable now. 'It was a terrible thing to do to you, but I think she just panicked. She'd been feeling wobbly about it for a while but Hugo and I persuaded her it was just pre-wedding jitters. I'm so sorry we didn't talk to you about it beforehand. Still, it's done now and you're happy with your lovely new wife,' Veronica said brightly, as if sensing the need to move the conversation onto safer ground. 'By the way, where did you two meet? I forgot to ask.'

'Through the business,' Xavier said in a confident tone that even had Soli convinced for a second.

Veronica smiled indulgently. 'You know, Xavier, I

don't think I've ever seen you looking so relaxed. The two of you are obviously good for each other.'

Soli stood stock-still, her heart beating rapidly in her throat, wondering what on earth Xavier would say to that. She hoped with all her heart it would be something nice. It felt incredibly important at that moment that it was.

'Soli is really good for me,' he said, to her surprise. 'The first thing I noticed about her was how vibrant and upbeat she is. I find her positivity really inspiring, to be honest, because, as we know, I'm not always the sunniest of people.' The look of genuine approval on his face when he turned to look at her made Soli's tummy flutter with exhilaration.

Veronica gave a tinkling laugh. 'Don't do yourself down. You're a wonderful person and a great friend—when you deign to accept invitations from us.' She laughed again, but it was plain from her tone that she was genuinely joking around with him.

At that moment a small child ran up to them, shouting, 'Mummy, Mummy!' and did a spectacular trip-dive just before reaching them, splashing her beaker full of blackcurrant juice all over Veronica's shoes.

There were a few seconds of noisy disruption as the child began to wail and Veronica half admonished, half comforted her.

Turning to them with a tearful child pressed up against her, she said, 'I'm so sorry, will you excuse me for a second? I'd better take her inside and get myself cleaned up. Don't run off, now, will you? I want to chat more later. It's been so long! I want to hear all about what you've been up to in the last few years, including all the details about your wedding.'

As soon as she was out of earshot Soli turned to look at Xavier, who was standing stiffly by her side, watching Veronica walk away with a frown on his face. 'So it wasn't just your parents that let you down, it was your fiancée too,' she said quietly.

She waited, looking up at him expectantly, willing him to trust her and tell her the whole story.

His frown deepened, then he gave a curt nod.

So that was all she was getting? Her pulse rate soared as frustration shot through her.

'Why didn't you tell me Harriet stood you up at the altar?' she blurted into the silence, unable to hold on to her patience any longer.

'Why do you think?' he shot back gruffly. 'It's not something I generally like to shout about.'

She sighed. 'Okay, I get that it must have been humiliating and not an easy thing to talk about, but I could have done with knowing about it before coming here and having to find out about it from your friends.'

He took a step away and ran a hand through his hair, looking frustrated with himself. 'Yes, okay. You're right, I should have told you. I'm sorry.'

'It's fine. It's just—it makes it hard for me to react appropriately when I don't have all the information.' She frowned, not wanting to turn this into a fight, but determined to make her feelings very clear. 'I want to get this right, Xavier. For both our sakes.'

Xavier smiled back ruefully, his facial muscles tense.

'I appreciate that. I'll try to be a bit more open and honest with you from now on, I promise.'

'Thank you,' she said, giving him a nod of appreciation.

He looked back at her, his eyes seeming to grow darker as their gazes locked.

'You know, I'm really impressed with how you've handled yourself here today,' he murmured. 'I wasn't sure how it was going to go, but everyone we've spoken to has clearly really liked you.'

'That's probably because I asked them so many questions about themselves and actually listened to their answers,' she joked, a little uncomfortable with his praise.

'No. It's not just that. People really respond to you. You have a real charm about you and you're clearly very intelligent, judging by the way you followed the different conversations you were thrust into.'

She swallowed, feeling a bubble of pride rise through her chest. 'Thanks. That's really nice to hear. I've never thought of myself as intelligent.' She glanced away as heat began to creep up her neck. 'I wasn't great at learning at school—it bored me, to be honest—but I've read a lot since I've been working in the café and I talk to such a wide variety of people in there every day I hear all sorts of interesting things. I guess it's made me good at general-knowledge subjects. In fact, I probably should warn you, I'm killer at Trivial Pursuit.'

He smiled at that and his whole face lit up.

Soli dragged in a breath as her body flooded with heat in response to it. He was such a beautiful man, even more so when he relaxed a little and let himself show his emotions on his face.

She swallowed as he took a step closer to her and reached out to pick a small leaf out of her hair. 'You look lovely today, by the way. I don't think I told you that back at the house. And I really appreciate you making so much effort for the party.'

'You're welcome,' she murmured through lips that were now having trouble forming actual words. He was standing so close to her, all she was aware of was his tantalising scent.

'We should probably slip away home now, before Veronica or Hugo come back out here,' he said, so quietly she was forced to lean in even closer to hear him. Her pulse throbbed hard in her veins as she felt the masculine heat of him radiate towards her. 'Veronica seemed intent on getting all the details about our marriage and I don't think I'm quite in the headspace to make up convincing enough lies right now,' he went on, apparently unaware of how he was turning her to jelly.

'Sure. Whatever you want,' she managed to say, forcing her frozen facial muscles into a smile.

Xavier was facing the house and he glanced towards it, seemingly to check if it was safe to make a sneaky exit, but he must have seen something, or someone, that alarmed him because the smile dropped from his face and his whole body stiffened. He appeared to pale as he continued to stare in shock at whatever had caught his attention.

'What's wrong?' Soli asked, turning to look in the direction he was gazing, a slow, heavy feeling of foreboding sinking through her.

'It's Harriet,' he replied in a tense voice.

'Your ex?' she asked, turning to watch a strikingly beautiful woman walking slowly towards them.

Soli frowned, wondering why she seemed to be moving so awkwardly, then as she looked down she realised the woman was heavily pregnant and the weight of the baby was making her waddle in her heels across the spongy grass.

'Yes,' was all Xavier had time to reply before Harriet was upon them, holding out her arms to Xavier in greeting.

'Xavier! I heard you were here with your new wife, so I thought it'd be all right to come over and say hello. It's wonderful to see you happy.' She offered Soli a friendly smile, the warmth in it only increasing her beauty. 'I'd heard you were becoming something of a confirmed bachelor-stroke-playboy.' She grinned affectionately at Xavier and Soli's stomach gave a sickening twist at how excluded she suddenly felt. These two clearly had some serious history between them.

And Harriet was exactly the sort of woman she'd expect Xavier to be married to. Elegant, intelligent and classically beautiful—the woman seemed to radiate vivacity. By stark contrast, Xavier's face looked stonier than ever.

'Oh, come on, Xave, you know I'm only teasing,' Harriet cooed, giving him a playful slap on the arm. This seemed to wake him up somehow and the corners of his mouth actually turned up for a moment. Not that the smile reached his eyes.

'I'm really happy for you,' he said in a voice that

sounded as though he was having to force the words through his throat. 'You're actually glowing. I thought that was just an expression. I didn't realise pregnancy really did that to a woman.'

'So I've been told,' she said with a kind smile. 'It's all those hormones rushing around my system. I'm sure I won't look like this once the baby's born though. I've never been good with lack of sleep.'

'No. I remember,' Xavier said.

Soli's stomach twisted even harder, making her feel a bit sick. Now she was imagining the two of them in bed together, waking up and smiling at each other in mutual adoration before rolling together and—

No. Not going there right now.

'Well, I'd better get back to Neil—he'll be sending out a search party if I don't show myself soon. He's turned into something of a worrier since I fell pregnant. Calls me umpteen times a day to make sure I haven't gone into labour unexpectedly and forgotten to phone him!'

She shook her head, but from the way she was beaming Soli could tell she didn't mind this show of over-the-top possessiveness one little bit.

She could understand that. It must be wonderful for someone to love and worry about you that much.

'When are you due?' she asked, to cover the slightly awkward atmosphere that throbbed between them all now.

'Three weeks. I can't wait, to be honest—I feel like an elephant lumbering around!'

She really didn't look like one though; she was carry-

ing all at the front, so if you saw her from the back Soli
bet you wouldn't even know she was pregnant.

'Oh, by the way,' she said, turning to Xavier, 'happy
birthday for Wednesday. Are you doing anything special for it?' She glanced between the two of them with
interest.

Soli tensed as an intense desire to protect Xavier from
the hurt this woman had caused him mixed with a sting
of her own hurt that he hadn't even mentioned his birthday to her.

'Yes, of course, but it's a big surprise,' she lied
quickly, giving her a covert wink in the hope she'd believe the bluff. No way was she having this woman
thinking she wasn't as good a partner to Xavier as Harriet had been in the past.

But then, Soli hadn't shredded his heart and humiliated him in front of the people he loved and respected
most in the world, so she was already one up on her.

'Sweetheart, I'm so sorry to drag you away early but
this migraine seems set to stay,' she said to Xavier, linking her fingers through his and feeling him squeeze her
hand in silent thanks. 'It was good to meet you, Harriet.
Good luck with the baby,' she said, giving the woman one
last smile and a nod, then pulling subtly on Xavier's hand.

'Bye, Harriet,' Xavier said, falling into step with her
as they walked back towards the house. They made a
swift exit through the huge throng of people who were
now milling around the large garden and made it back
to the car without encountering any objections to their
leaving.

'Thanks,' was all Xavier said as he pulled the car out of the parking space and set off back to their house.

Soli waited until they were driving down the main road into Hampstead before she asked, 'Are you okay?'

He didn't answer her immediately, just kept staring ahead at the road. 'Yeah, I'm fine,' he said eventually, though he really didn't sound it.

'I take it you didn't know she was pregnant?'

There was a heavy pause in which he stared at the road ahead again. 'No, I didn't.'

'How did it make you feel?' she asked tentatively.

He turned to glance at her and the expression in his eyes made her stomach sink to the floor. 'Not great, to be honest.' He dragged in a sharp breath. 'The main reason she gave for not wanting to marry me was that I wanted to have kids but she didn't. She thought having a family would mean she wouldn't be able to focus on her career—that it'd hold her back.' His jaw clenched tight before he spoke again, as if he was fighting with his emotions. 'But I guess she did want kids after all— just not with me.'

Soli's stomach dropped even lower, making her feel nauseous on his behalf. 'Oh, Xavier, I'm so sorry.'

He shrugged. 'She probably had it right. I'd have been a terrible father and a selfish husband. I've been so focused on work and building my company I probably wouldn't have given my relationships priority—as I'm sure you've noticed,' he added with a grimace. There was a heavy pause before he cleared his throat and said, 'It was for the best that we didn't get married.'

She wanted to reassure him, to tell him that he had

it all wrong, but she couldn't. She didn't know him well enough to be able to say something like that and he knew it.

Her heart went out to him. No wonder he was so unwilling to get close to someone again. Anybody would be wary of allowing themselves to love and trust if they'd been through what he had.

She wanted to help somehow, so much it made her chest physically ache.

But do what?

Taking a breath, she gave him a supportive smile as an idea began to form in her head.

She might not be able to do anything about the past, but she could definitely do something about the future.

Acknowledging a small but insistent voice in her head reminding her not to get too emotionally involved—because she knew, deep down, that if she set out on that path it would be almost impossible to turn back—she assured herself she would only do it to make their time together more enjoyable, and perhaps to say thank you to Xavier for giving her the chance to make a better life for herself and her family.

Yes. She would do it for him because she could.

But, perhaps even more importantly, because she knew that nobody else would.

CHAPTER NINE

Mr & Mrs—discover things about your partner you didn't know.

IT HAD BEEN quite an eye-opener for Xavier, seeing Harriet for the first time in five years. The pregnancy had knocked him off his game to begin with, but once they'd started talking he'd soon regained his equilibrium. Meeting her again had been something he'd been dreading, but now it had happened he realised it hadn't affected him in the way he'd expected.

In fact he'd been surprised, after talking to Soli about it all and reflecting on it later that evening, by the startling realisation that he wasn't angry with Harriet any more, despite the pregnancy she'd sworn she'd never want. Thinking about what he'd had with her just conjured a sense of bittersweet nostalgia now, but that was all it was. It seemed he'd finally moved on from the hurt and bitterness he'd felt about her rejecting him.

It was actually quite liberating. He'd been walking around with this sense of loss and inadequacy for so long, it was a huge relief to finally feel it lifting.

He had a strong suspicion that Soli's steadfast support

and compassion had had a hand in breaking the grief he'd been living with too. Her tackling the subject head-on had made him realise how he'd bottled his feelings up, and how unhealthy that had been. He'd not talked to anyone about what had happened to him before, worried it would make him seem weak, and had cut everyone who knew about it out of his life so that he hadn't had to face it. But he knew now he couldn't hide for ever. It was time to get past his hang-ups.

He had an inkling that Soli wouldn't let him carry on the way he'd been going anyway.

She was a real force of nature.

They'd spent the next day in the house together, with her reading a book in the garden and him moving between his home office and joining her on the terrace to eat, where they'd chatted about inconsequential things. He'd appreciated her allowing him some personal space and leaving the subject of Harriet alone, but also making it clear she was happy to talk if he wanted to.

It seemed he'd made a good move in choosing her to be his stand-in wife. He found he was actually enjoying her company now and could imagine them getting on fine for the next few months. Until it was time to call a halt to it all.

Strangely, the thought of that brought with it a heavy, tense feeling, so he pushed it to the back of his mind. There was no point in dwelling on what would happen when their arrangement came to an end. It was months away yet.

Walking into the kitchen on the morning of his birthday to grab a quick cup of coffee, he stopped in amazement as he saw that the table was set for two and there was a plate loaded with Scotch pancakes covered in maple syrup and two large mugs of coffee sitting on it. Soli was standing at the stove, attending to what looked like poached eggs.

'Happy birthday!' she said brightly when she noticed him standing there, open-mouthed. 'I thought I'd make you breakfast. You like eggs, right?'

'Er…yes. I love them.'

'Great. Take a seat and dig in to the pancakes. I made them fresh. There's more coffee if you need a refill after that one too.'

'You didn't have to do this—' he began to protest, but she waved his words away.

'Of course I did! It's your birthday. Everyone should get special treatment on their birthday.'

Never having had 'special treatment' like this before, Xavier went to object, but snapped his mouth shut at the last second, feeling it would be rude and unkind to contradict her. Just because no one else had done it for him, it didn't mean he couldn't accept it from her. Tingly heat rushed across his skin as he made the conscious decision to accept her indulging him today. It would actually be pretty nice to celebrate his birthday for once.

'Well, I appreciate the thought,' he said, sitting down at the table. 'I'll wait for you before I eat though.'

'Okay,' she said, shooting him a warm smile.

A minute later, she came to join him, laying down plates of buttered wholemeal toast with two poached eggs balanced on top.

'So! What are you going to do with your day?' she

asked, sitting down opposite him and picking up her cutlery.

He frowned at her. 'Go to work.'

She looked aghast. 'Really? Can't you take the day off for once?'

'I wasn't planning to. There's a lot going on at the minute.'

'But you have a large staff working for you.'

'Yes.'

'So let them do the work today. You're the boss, right? Take the day off and hang out with me. Treat yourself.'

He considered this for a moment, feeling a throb of unease about not going in to work at such short notice. Though, if he thought about it, he'd not had a day off in five years, so it was probably overdue. Soli was right too—his staff were more than capable of getting on with what needed doing without him for one day.

'Well, I suppose I could—'

'Great!' She grinned at this and began tucking into her breakfast.

After they'd finished the delicious meal, Soli ordered him to go and sit in the garden and read the papers that she'd nipped out and bought earlier while she cleared up. She wouldn't hear of him helping her, even though he pointed out he should be the one to do it since she'd cooked.

They spent a lovely morning looking out across the garden, reading and chatting about current affairs, which she seemed impressively clued up on—another by-product of working in the café, he supposed.

Just before lunchtime, Soli stood up and brushed

down her skirt. 'Right! It's time for a walk on the heath, then lunch. I've already put together a picnic. You'll need your swimming trunks, your trainers and your tennis racket,' she called over her shoulder, as she walked away into the house.

He stared after her, dumbstruck, his body rushing with endorphins, as it occurred to him what she'd done. She'd planned the 'perfect day' he'd told her about for his birthday.

Heat pooled in his belly and he was horrified to find his eyes had welled with tears.

No. No! He couldn't allow himself to feel sentimental about this. She was just fulfilling some obligation she felt she had as his wife, that was all.

Still, a little voice told him, she hadn't *needed* to do it, and from the glee he'd heard in her voice he suspected she was actually enjoying it.

A couple of hours later they were stretched out on picnic blankets, groaning happily after wolfing down the fabulous lunch she'd put together, which included slices of her amazing—and apparently legendary—chocolate fudge cake.

'I can see why that's so popular in your café', Xavier said, nodding towards the now empty container that had held the cake. 'I don't think I've ever tasted anything like it.'

'An "orgasm in food form", one of my friends calls it,' she said with a grin.

There was a small pause, where they didn't look at each other for a moment and pretended to watch a couple of squirrels running up a tree trunk instead.

Xavier cleared his throat, reminding himself what a bad idea it would be to act on the kinds of thoughts that had just popped into his head following that comment.

'So tell me what *your* perfect day would consist of,' he said, attempting to circumnavigate the strange atmosphere now zinging between them.

Her brow furrowed as she appeared to think about this for a moment.

'Well, if I could choose anything, I'd probably go for spending the day on a Mediterranean island. I'd eat lunch on the beach and go for a swim in the sea. Then I'd spend the evening having someone servicing my every need.'

'That sounds good,' he said, smiling at her and noticing how her cheeks had flushed an adorable shade of pink. 'I think I could probably manage to enjoy a day like that too.'

'Well, maybe we'll do it for your next birthday,' she quipped, her face falling as it obviously occurred to her that they wouldn't be together for his next birthday. Their time, and their marriage, would be over by then.

'When was the last time you had a holiday abroad?' he asked hurriedly, attempting to sweep past the awkwardness.

'Er…' She thought about this for a second, looking relieved to have the conversational diversion.

'I guess it was about four years ago, just before my dad died. We went to Brittany on the ferry. It was a great holiday. We were all really happy.' He saw grief flash across her face and a sudden and acute instinct to make her happy again overwhelmed him.

'You know, it's probably been that long for me too.

I've been so focused on building the business, I've not stopped to take a proper break.' He dragged in a breath, throwing caution to the wind. 'You know, I own a holiday property on Corsica. It's just been renovated and they've completed the fit-out early, so it's just sitting empty at the moment. We could go and stay for a week.' He shrugged, trying to appear nonchalant. 'It would do us both good to get away.' He smiled. 'And there wouldn't be any solicitors there, checking up on us.'

Her eyes had lit with excitement as he'd talked and as soon as he finished speaking she blurted, 'That would be amazing! I've always wanted to go there. It sounds like such a beautiful place.'

'Okay, then,' he said, satisfaction coursing through him at being able to bring back her smile. 'I'll arrange for us to go this Saturday. I'll just need to let my colleagues know.' He paused and smiled to himself. 'They're going to wonder what's happened to me. I never take time off.'

'I guess they'll just assume you're having a honeymoon with your new wife,' she pointed out with a grin.

'Yes, of course.' He blinked, realising it was a detail he'd overlooked and feeling pleased it would still fit their story. That solidified it as a really good practical excuse to go.

Satisfied with his decision, he lay back and stared up at the fluffy clouds floating slowly across the sky above him.

Yes. Getting some sun on their faces, eating good food and relaxing would be a great thing for both of them.

Soli's stomach had jumped with excitement as they'd stepped off the plane that Xavier had chartered into the balmy Corsican air. She'd not been able to believe it when he'd led them to a private lounge at the airport and announced in a really matter-of-fact voice that their pilot would be there to greet them soon and they would be in Corsica within a couple of hours.

Soli's only experience of being on a plane had been on a family holiday to Spain when they'd gone with a budget airline. This trip had been entirely different, what with the separate leather seats, à la carte food and total lack of general public.

And then when he'd led them over to a soft-top classic car and loaded their bags into the boot her insides had done a little dance of excitement. The trip to his hillside house had been a thing of joy.

The cliff-top cottage where they were to stay for the next week was quite a bit smaller than the Hampstead house, but no less impressive. It had been newly decorated in fresh Mediterranean colours and filled with French-style furniture, all of which looked incredibly expensive and dauntingly classy.

'It's a rental aimed at the high-end market,' Xavier said conversationally as they walked inside and Soli gasped in delight at the amazing view of the sea through panoramic bi-folding doors. 'We have our own private cove down there,' he said, walking to the doors and opening them back so the sweet, briny smell of the sea below them rushed inside and tickled her nose.

'It's a bit of a walk down a narrow path in the cliff, but well worth it.'

Soli followed him onto the deck, which housed a couple of comfortable-looking loungers as well as a small dining table with a canopy flapping gently in the warm breeze, and turned to give him a smile that felt as if it might split her face in two. 'I love it!' she said, her voice raspy with delight. 'I can't wait to explore.'

'Let me show you your room first,' he said, strolling back inside.

She followed him through the living area and down a short corridor to where two doors stood opposite each other.

'You're in here,' he said, opening the door on the right. They walked inside and stood by the king-sized bed that was dressed with white linen sheets and an abundance of pillows in a soft blue-grey colour.

'There's an en-suite bathroom over there,' he said, gesturing to a small door on the right.

'Oh, Xavier, it's wonderful!' she said, turning to give him a grateful smile. It was a long time since she'd been this excited about being somewhere and her whole body felt jittery with adrenaline. Or was it that she was nervous about being here with him? The whole place shouted *Romance!*

He smiled back at her with the genuine, wide grin that always made her tummy flutter whenever he decided to trust her with it. 'I'm glad you like it.' He huffed out a breath, frowning down at the floor before looking back into her eyes. 'I wanted to say thank you—for all the support you've given me recently. It was above and beyond the call of duty and I want you to know I really appreciate it.'

She suddenly felt a bit shy. 'It was my pleasure. Anything to help.'

The air between them felt prickly with emotion. Or was she imagining it?

Something in his expression made her breath catch in her throat.

'You know, you're the most genuinely caring person I've ever met,' he murmured, taking a step closer to her.

Soli was suddenly intensely aware of how alone the two of them were, and how close to the enormous, inviting bed.

Heat throbbed through her, making her head swim.

'Thank you,' she breathed through numbed lips. She suddenly wanted to kiss him so badly her whole body ached with it.

The look in his eyes mesmerised her, keeping her suspended in a state of such intense longing she knew she had no hope of escaping from it. It wouldn't take much to be close enough to touch him. Just one more step. She could feel the heat radiating from his body and his enticing scent filled her nose, making her mouth water.

His Adam's apple bobbed in his throat as he swallowed and her gaze flashed down to it for a second.

The break in eye contact seemed to shock him out of whatever state he was in and he gave a rough cough and took a step backwards, sweeping his hand towards the door.

'Okay, well, I'll grab the bags from the car and you can get settled in. We should go out for dinner. There's a lovely tavern in the next town with magnificent views of the harbour. It's quite a sight.'

It was as if he'd brought the shutters down on his emotions.

'That sounds wonderful,' Soli said quietly, her stomach sinking with disappointment at his sudden change in demeanour.

'Good,' he said, giving her a jerky nod and swiftly leaving the room.

She flopped down onto the bed and took a few deep, steadying breaths.

Perhaps this holiday wasn't going to be as relaxing as she'd hoped after all.

The tavern was as magnificent as Xavier had described and Soli had a hard time choosing what to eat from the comprehensive seafood menu.

'I don't usually eat fish. I've never learnt to cook it because Domino has an extreme aversion to the smell,' she said, her mouth watering at the thought of the meal she'd just ordered. She'd been hesitant to ask for the lobster—she'd always wanted to try it—but Xavier seemed to have sensed her worry and told her to order whatever she wanted. So lobster it was, with a large glass of crisp Sancerre, which he'd recommended.

She was in heaven.

'So, I thought tomorrow we could explore some of the coves. Maybe take a picnic lunch with us. I have a small motorboat moored in our cove which we can take along the coast,' Xavier said, putting down his wine glass and fixing her with his tingle-inducing gaze.

'Oh, wow! I'd love that!' she said. This whole set-up was like something from the movies.

The smile he gave her made his eyes twinkle and she

took a hurried gulp of her own wine to calm her suddenly racing pulse.

She needed to remember that this wasn't real. They were just pretending.

At least he was.

She wasn't so sure about herself any more.

They slept in late the next morning on Xavier's insistence and ate a light breakfast before strolling down the winding path to their cove and climbing into the boat.

The turquoise sea glittered in the late morning sunlight and Soli laughed with joy as they sped through the gentle waves to the other side of the island and one of the other secluded, and usually deserted, coves that Xavier knew about.

Once there, he brought the boat in to shore and tied it to a large rock, making sure it wouldn't float away before helping Soli out. Her hand was warm and firm in his and for a moment he contemplated not letting go of her and pulling her towards him instead.

To do what, he wasn't sure.

No. He was. But he couldn't allow himself to think like that. They'd made a pact and he needed to keep to it. For his own sanity.

After exploring the small cove, where Soli scrambled over the rocks and stood on the largest one with her hands on her hips and her curls blowing in the wind— eliciting in him the strangest feeling of lightness he'd ever experienced—they settled down onto the picnic blanket he'd brought and tucked into the food his housekeeper had stocked the fridge with.

Once they'd finished he lay back on the blanket with his hands behind his head and gazed up at the azure-blue sky, letting the heat of the day wash over him. It had been a very long time since he'd felt this relaxed—even though an undercurrent of crackling energy still pulsed through him. Something he couldn't quite identify, though he had his suspicions.

'Phew! It's so hot!' Soli said next to him. 'I think I'll go for a swim. Want to join me?' She looked at him expectantly.

'Not right now,' he said, unwilling to move from his comfortable position. 'You go ahead.'

He tried not to watch as she took off the light summer dress she'd been wearing to uncover a cherry-red bikini.

Tried and failed.

He also tried to keep his gaze off her as she skipped down the golden sand to the water and tentatively dipped her toes in.

That was a lost hope too.

'It's warm,' she called back, sounding delighted with the discovery.

He gave up and turned to rest on his side, watching her splash around, grinning from ear to ear as she went deeper into the water.

Her body was lithe, but curvaceous, imperfect in places—and wonderfully *real* for it.

It had to be the most alluring sight he'd ever seen.

She was magnificent, standing tall and proud in the waves as they gently lapped at her thighs. The very picture of female beauty.

A sense of contentment washed over him, taking him by surprise.

Being here with Soli felt so very *right*.

He was both amazed and pleased by how much he'd found he enjoyed sharing things with her. Being an only child, he wasn't used to sharing, so he was surprised to find how much he actually liked it. Soli took such joy in being introduced to new things too and she seemed to genuinely enjoy them. The women he usually dated were well used to the high life and didn't tend to comment much on the places he took them or the gifts he bought, so it had been wonderful to see Soli's genuine appreciation. It made him feel as though he was making a valuable contribution to her happiness, and her life. Something he'd never experienced before with a partner.

She was so full of wonder and enchantment with the world, despite the trials she'd been through in her life.

He'd never met such a positive person and it thrilled him to his core.

What was he doing, anyway, just lying there alone? He should take her lead and go and enjoy himself in the water.

With her.

Pushing himself up to standing, he walked swiftly across the hot sand, feeling acute pleasure as the cool sea rushed over his feet and lapped against his legs. He waded towards where she was bobbing about in the water and when she turned and saw him coming her face broke into a smile.

Euphoria swelled in the pit of his stomach, then rushed up through his chest, taking his breath away.

'The water feels incredible against your hot skin,' she called, moving forwards to meet him.

All he could think about at that moment was what it would feel like to touch her slick skin and feel her incredible body pressed against him.

Her smile faltered as he got closer and he realised that the longing he was feeling must be showing on his face.

'Are you okay?' she asked, reaching out to him and putting her hand on his shoulder. Before he knew what was happening a particularly strong wave had pushed her towards him and their bodies connected, their mouths only inches apart now. The feeling of her pressed against him tipped him over the edge and without another thought he dropped his mouth to hers, sliding his hands around her waist to steady them both.

Everything else faded away as the sensation of her soft lips under his took over his entire awareness, plunging him into a state of desire so intense it left him breathless. Instinctively he deepened the kiss and felt her respond, opening her mouth so he could slide his tongue inside. She tasted just as sweet as he remembered, but also salty from the seawater, and he let out a groan of pleasure deep in his throat. Her body was slippery and smooth against his and he pulled her closer to him, losing himself in pure physical indulgence.

He'd wanted to do this *for so damn long*.

His body responded as his desire deepened, hardening and pressing into her with obvious intent.

'Oh!' she gasped against his mouth and the sound of her surprise shocked him out of his erotic daze. He pulled away abruptly, suddenly furious with himself for allowing his need to override his common sense. What was he doing? He couldn't kiss her like this and expect everything to stay the same between them.

But did he really want it to?

Yes. They couldn't afford to let their agreement slip; it wasn't sensible.

'Sorry,' he muttered, drawing away from her and noting with a sting of regret how shell-shocked she seemed by his sudden withdrawal. 'I shouldn't have done that.'

'No. Okay,' she rasped, her confusion clear on her face.

'I'm going for a swim, then we should think about getting back to the house,' he said gruffly, diving underneath the cool water before she had a chance to answer him, praying it would bring him back to his senses and extinguish his driving need to swim right back and kiss her again.

'You know, you're very mature for your age. I guess that comes from taking on so much responsibility when you were so young,' he said to her later, back at the house, while they sat on the terrace gazing out over the water, sipping their second large glasses of wine, trying to pretend that the kiss hadn't really happened.

She turned to shoot him a startled smile. 'Do you think so? Most of the time I feel like I have no idea how to be an adult.'

He gave her a wry smile back. 'I think most people feel like that. We're all just making it up as we go along.'

'That's good to hear.'

There was a small pause where they just looked at each other.

'I'm…er…just going to get a glass of water. This wine's going straight to my head,' she said, standing up quickly and stumbling as she caught her foot on the chair leg.

Xavier shot out a hand to steady her, rising from his chair so he could take her weight.

She gazed up into his face, an expression of embarrassment clouding her face. 'Sorry,' she whispered.

'No need to be sorry,' he said roughly, hyper-aware of his pulse throbbing in his throat. She smelt wonderful, like sunshine and fresh air and her own distinctive sweetness, and he drew in a great lungful of her scent, his chest swelling with a longing so powerful his whole body rushed with it.

'Soli…' He wasn't sure what he wanted to say. A thousand thoughts flashed through his head but words wouldn't form in his mouth.

So he kissed her again. Hard.

She let out a small gasp of surprise, but didn't pull away. Instead she wrapped her arms around his back and pulled him closer to her, forcing their bodies together.

And then his hands were in her hair and his body was responding in all sorts of inappropriate ways, but he couldn't stop himself this time. Didn't want to.

From the desperate sounds in her throat, it seemed as though Soli was having the exact same problem.

'Let's go inside,' she murmured when he pulled back a fraction to breathe, her grip tightening on him as if she was afraid he might change his mind again and let her go.

Through his haze of desire, Xavier couldn't remember any of the reasons why they should stop any more, so without another word he slid his hands beneath her thighs and lifted her up against him and carried her into the house, still kissing her as he went, unwilling to break the connection.

In the bedroom they discarded their clothes quickly and he rolled on top of her, luxuriating in the feeling of her soft skin against his.

Through the fug of feeling a terrible thought struck him like a blow. 'I don't have any condoms,' he bit out, suddenly furious with himself for overlooking such a simple thing. His thoughts swirled wildly as he tried to reconcile all the concerns that were now jabbing at the edges of his brain.

'It's okay, I'm on the Pill,' she muttered back, gazing up into his eyes with a look of such genuine honesty he knew deep down that she was telling him the truth. Because she always told him the truth.

'Thank God for that,' he said, letting out a breath and feeling relief radiate from the pit of his stomach. Sliding his hands back into her hair, he took a moment to marvel at the sensation of the silky strands running through his fingers. 'Thank God,' he repeated huskily, before losing himself in the wonderfulness of her again.

CHAPTER TEN

Dominoes—set them up with a steady hand, then see them fall with the slightest knock.

XAVIER SAT ON the terrace cradling a large cup of coffee in his hands and staring out over the sea as the sun rose in the distance.

He'd left Soli sleeping peacefully in his bed, with her wild curls spread out around her head, having to force himself to leave the room and not slide back in next to her and pull her soft, welcoming body against him again.

What the hell did he think he was doing, messing with their no-sex agreement like that? All day yesterday he'd fought the urge to get closer to her, keeping his physical distance and his tone light and friendly. He'd deliberately not flirted in any way, strictly disciplining himself against giving in to the desire that had swelled and throbbed inside him.

And then it had all gone to hell.

It had been the heady mixture of sunshine and lust and then being forced to touch her again when she'd stumbled that had been his final undoing. The expression of open hunger in her eyes when she'd looked up at him had been impossible to resist.

The sex had been great too. Fun and surprising in its intensity. They'd fitted together so well, delighting in exploring each other's bodies for the first time but also seeming to know intuitively what made the other tick.

They had been around each other a lot recently, of course, so maybe that was why it had felt so *comfortable* being with her.

Not that he was going to let it happen again. No. He'd be a fool to indulge his base desires and potentially ruin the good thing they had going. The last thing he needed was for this business relationship to take a wrong turn and for the solicitors to get wind and it put his inheritance in jeopardy.

That house was much more important to him than sating his physical desires for the next few months.

When Soli got up he'd discuss that with her in a straight and honest manner. He didn't want her to think he'd taken advantage of her last night, but he wanted to make it clear that it had been a mistake on his part and that they should move their relationship back to their being friends only.

Surely she'd understand the necessity of that. She might even wake up this morning regretting what had happened last night too.

Just as he thought this there was movement by the terrace doors and Soli emerged into the sunlight wearing one of the robes from the room.

He swallowed hard and gave her a friendly but controlled smile, not wanting to make her feel awkward, but needing to set the right businesslike tone for the conversation that was to come.

'Good morning,' he said as she moved slowly towards him, appearing to stumble a little on the smooth tiled floor. 'Are you okay?' he asked, feeling a sting of concern as she got closer to him.

She really didn't look good. Her skin was a strange grey-green colour and her eyes looked a little unfocused.

'I don't feel too great actually.'

'Here.' He stood up and pulled out a chair for her. 'Sit down.'

She came towards him and put her hand on the back of the chair, as if not entirely convinced it was what she wanted to do.

'I felt a bit light-headed last night but I thought it was because of the…um…wine.'

And the sexual tension, he filled in silently for her.

There was a sudden flash of panic in her eyes and she took a hasty step backwards. 'Sorry. Excuse me for a second—' and with that she dashed back inside, the door to her bedroom slamming loudly behind her.

Panic inched through him. He had no idea what he should do. Should he go into the bedroom to check if she was okay? If she was being sick she might prefer that he leave her alone. Or was she hoping he'd go in there and hold her hair and rub her back? No. He couldn't imagine her wanting that. Especially with their relationship being so…*confused* right now. So he stayed at the table and waited, with his pulse beating hard in his head, until he heard her bedroom door open again.

Striding into the living area, he saw her standing in

the doorway, seemingly holding herself up by propping her hands against the door jambs.

'You should go straight back to bed,' he said, noting how she was trembling now.

'I don't think I drank too much last night, I think I'm ill,' she murmured, looking at him with bloodshot eyes. 'I must have picked up a tummy bug from somewhere, or perhaps it was something I ate—'

'I agree. Straight back to bed for you.' She nodded and turned around, heading back into her room, where she climbed shakily under the fresh cotton sheets of her bed.

Good that we used my bed last night so her sheets are clean, he thought as she snuggled into the pillows and let out a small sigh of relief. At least she'd be able to lie there without being constantly reminded of what happened between them last night. He didn't want her associating it with feeling ill.

Not that *that* should be his priority right now, he reminded himself sternly. 'I'll go and fetch you a glass of water,' he said, heading quickly out of the room and into the kitchen.

He filled a glass for her and searched out a small bowl from the cleaning cupboard, which he then took into her bedroom.

'Here you go, just in case you feel ill again and don't think you can make it to the bathroom. Not that it'll be a problem,' he added quickly, not wanting her to think he'd be angry if she made a mess.

'Thank you,' she whispered, clearly trying to smile at him, but not quite managing it.

'Try and sleep,' he said quietly, backing out of the room. 'If you need me, shout. I'll be right next door.'

He saw her give him a small nod before he turned around and headed back to the living area.

It looked as if the conversation about what had happened last night was going to have to wait.

Soli slept fitfully, weaving in and out of consciousness, sometimes aware of Xavier's presence in the room, other times thinking she must have imagined it.

In the middle of the night she rolled over and stretched out her arm to see whether he'd got into bed with her, but had found the other side cold and empty.

Not that she could blame him. Who'd want to sleep next to someone who had to get up to vomit every half an hour? She hoped to goodness he wasn't sick too—that would really make her feel wretched. He'd been really kind, looking after her, coming in to check on her regularly and refreshing her water. Luckily she'd not needed the bowl he'd brought in. The thought of him having to deal with that had given her the horrors.

She couldn't bring herself to think about what had happened between them the night before though. As wonderful as it had been, it made her stomach tie into knots just thinking about it, so she pushed it to the back of her mind. It would be something she'd mull over once she was feeling better—which would hopefully be soon.

She hated being ill.

Especially when she was meant to be on holiday.

And with Xavier right next door.

She was still sick the following day and only got out of bed to dry heave before crawling back under the covers to sleep, but the next morning she woke up feeling as if the worst of it had lifted and tentatively sat up in bed to check the time.

Ten o'clock.

She'd been in bed for nearly two days.

Poor Xavier—he must have been bored out of his mind.

Slowly, carefully, she swung her legs out of bed and tested how she'd feel standing up, finding she wasn't as dizzy as she'd been the day before, and instead of lurching, her stomach gave a growl of hunger.

Thank goodness for that.

It seemed it was only a forty-eight-hour bug. Still, as she pulled on her robe and made her way to the door she had a moment where she thought she might pass out.

Better take it easy, Soli; no need to rush.

After pressing her hands to the wall and taking a few deep breaths to give her head a chance to catch up with the movement, she walked slowly out of the room and into the living area.

It appeared to be deserted, though there was a smell of coffee in the air and a plate and a mug next to the sink.

'How are you feeling this morning?' came a voice from outside and she turned to see that Xavier was sitting on the terrace, looking at her with concern in his eyes.

'A lot better, thanks,' she said, walking slowly out onto the terrace and over to where he was sitting on one of the loungers with a tablet on his lap.

'You still look a bit pale. Are you sure you're okay to be up?' he asked, his gaze raking her face.

She cursed herself for not even looking in the mirror

and flattening down her hair before leaving her room, but decided just to brazen it out now she was here. He certainly didn't look disgusted by her appearance. If anything his expression was one of friendly concern.

'A bit of fresh air will probably do me the world of good,' she said, sitting down carefully on the lounger next to him and offering him a tentative smile. 'I'm so sorry for ruining your holiday.'

He waved a hand at her. 'Don't be ridiculous. It's not as if you got ill on purpose.' He sat up and swung his legs to the side, putting the tablet onto a coffee table next to him. 'Could you eat?'

'Actually, yes. I think I could.'

He nodded. 'Okay. Stay there. I'll fetch you some breakfast.'

Before she could object, he stood up and strode swiftly and purposefully back into the house, returning a few minutes later with a mug of coffee and a plate of wholemeal toast.

'Here,' he said, handing her the food, then putting the drink onto the table next to his tablet. 'I thought something quite plain would be good to start with.'

'Thank you,' she said, gratefully accepting the plate and sitting up on the lounger to eat.

She felt him watching her as she took her first tentative bite, then when it was obvious she wasn't going to be sick again he went back into the house, returning a couple of minutes later with a mug of coffee for himself.

'I guess you were hungry,' he said, gesturing to the now empty plate she had on her lap.

'I guess I was,' she agreed, giving him a grateful smile.

'Listen. We don't need to rush off anywhere today, if you're worried about that,' he said, his expression sincere. 'I'll be very happy to hang out here until you feel more up to going out. Perhaps you could teach me how to play a board game or something.'

'That would be great,' she said, immediately perking up at the thought. Lazing around and recuperating whilst playing one of her favourite games would be her idea of heaven right now. 'Except I didn't bring one with me.'

'No problem,' Xavier said with a twitch of his eyebrows. 'We have some here in the house. Apparently they're popular with holidaymakers who want to switch off their phones and get back to a screen-free existence for the duration of their stay, or so the interior designer told me the other day. It made me think of you actually.'

She blinked in surprise. 'Well, that's great. I guess the lure of board games isn't dead after all.'

'I guess not,' he agreed, the corner of his mouth turning up. 'I'll go and fetch them and we can have a game now if you feel up to it.'

'Great,' she said, 'but we should move to the table. I take my playing very seriously.'

'I'd expect nothing less,' he said with a smile.

So he went to the fetch the games that he'd had stocked in a cupboard in the living area for guests—as a reaction to her love for them? she wondered hopefully—while she went to get dressed.

They played happily for the next couple of hours, sipping coffee and feeling the warm sea breeze on their faces as they alternated between asking questions and answering them, each taking great pleasure in challenging the other's knowledge of random facts.

'I really appreciate you looking after me. It's kind of you,' Soli said after they'd finally called a halt to the game. She'd been intensely aware of all the things they hadn't said to each other since 'the other night' and wanted to clear the air so she could breathe properly again. Even if it meant dealing with something she didn't want to hear. Which, from Xavier's careful avoidance of touching her or maintaining eye contact for too long, she suspected might be that he believed they'd made a mistake in sleeping together.

Nausea rose from her stomach as she waited for his response, only this time it came about through nerves.

'Well, I did agree to be there for you in sickness and in health, so I guess I'm just fulfilling my promise,' he quipped, though she couldn't help but notice how his whole body had tensed.

She shot him a sheepish smile. 'Still, it's good of you.'

He shrugged, clearly uncomfortable with her praising him. 'You deserve to be looked after too,' he said gruffly.

Letting out a low breath, she leant back in her chair and crossed her arms. 'I guess I'm just not used to it any more. It's been a while.'

'Since your dad died?' he asked, their gazes locking.

The sudden swell of emotion she experienced made her suck in a breath.

'Yeah,' she said, telling herself to pull it together. This was no time to go to pieces.

Xavier seemed to sense her discomfort and gave her

an understanding nod. 'Hey, I forgot to ask—how's your sister doing at Oxford?'

'Great! It sounds like she's really enjoying herself,' she said, grateful for the change in conversation.

'Good for you for making that happen. I'm seriously impressed. I'm not sure many siblings would go to the lengths you did to make sure their sister was set up like that.'

She shrugged, but her face heated at the compliment. 'It would have been a crime not to let her go to university. She's so smart. The world is going to thank me one day.'

'I'm sure it is.' He sat back and studied her for a moment. 'I guess I should thank you too. You saved me from losing my home. And perhaps my sanity.' His smile was wry.

'Well, you've been very generous. You've given me more than I asked for.'

He laughed, perhaps to cover his unease. 'We seem to have turned into the Mutual Admiration Society.'

She smiled. 'Yes, I guess we have.'

'Well, why not? We are pretty amazing people, are we not?'

'We are, I suppose.'

'No! No "suppose" about it. We are.'

Their gazes locked and Soli got lost in a sudden flash of memory as she thought of how he'd looked into her eyes while they were making love.

'Listen. About what happened the other night,' he said in a careful tone that made her spirits plummet.

'Yes?'

'I don't think it's a good idea to let that happen again. Especially since we still have rather a long time to live together. It could make things tricky.' He didn't say *if we end up falling out* but it was implicit in his manner.

'Oh. Er...okay.'

She tried not to sound disappointed, but obviously failed because he said, 'It's for the best, Soli,' in a tone that brooked no argument.

'I'm not looking for you to fall in love with me or anything, you know,' she said without stopping to think too hard about what she was saying. 'We could keep it as a purely physical thing. No strings.'

'I'm not sure those arrangements ever work,' he said, his expression radiating extreme scepticism.

Even though her brain was telling her he might have a point, her libido didn't want to listen. They'd crossed the line now and there was no real way back, it pointed out. In fact, it actually felt to her as if she'd turned a corner in her life after sleeping with Xavier—that she'd finally stepped into adulthood. Now she'd pushed herself over the ledge and found her heart had survived it, she was confident she was mature enough to keep sex and love separate.

'We'd make it work. We both know we're not in this for the long haul. It's just temporary. And it'd make living together much more fun and much less frustrating.' She flashed him a smile, which he returned. 'Especially since we agreed not to see other people during the time we're married,' she added.

There was a short pause while he appeared to consider this.

'No. I don't think it's a good idea,' he said eventually and she could tell from the resolute look in his eyes that he'd made his mind up and was unlikely to change it.

The businessman was back.

Her heart sank.

'Okay, whatever you think,' she said brightly to cover her frustration. Perhaps he was right. It might make things more complicated.

But it didn't stop her from hoping he'd change his mind.

The journey home was just as luxurious and comfortable as the one out there, except for a strange sort of stiffness between them that hadn't been there previously. They'd been really careful around each other ever since they'd had that conversation about not having sex again, as if they were tiptoeing around a bombshell that could trigger the second they relaxed and took a misstep and it was making both of them act in an over-the-top, super-polite way towards each other.

So by the time they walked in through the front door to the Hampstead house, Soli was completely and utterly exhausted from nervous tension.

So much for having a relaxing holiday.

Xavier immediately excused himself and she found herself alone again in the kitchen, fixing herself a meal for one, wondering whether her life would ever be normal again.

She came to the conclusion that it was very unlikely. Especially now she knew how wonderful it could be to be wanted by Xavier McQueen. She'd so enjoyed being able to get close to him. They'd been good together in bed. He was certainly a lot better than the men—well, boys really—that she'd slept with in the past. He'd known exactly what to do to give her the most pleasure and had been incredibly attentive to her needs. She'd never experienced anything like it. And she wanted more. Much more.

The idea of living with him until the year was up, with this sexual tension throbbing between them the whole time, and not being allowed to act on it, made her stomach turn over with restlessness. They'd go insane, surely.

They'd be much better to give in to their physical urges and ride things out till the marriage was up. They'd probably be bored with each other by then anyway.

Refusing to listen to a niggling little voice that told her not to bank on that, she decided to keep herself open to the chance it could happen, but not push for it in any way. Xavier was definitely the kind of man who needed to feel in control of his decisions—and his destiny—so if it was going to happen it would need to come from him.

It would be fine with her either way.

Absolutely fine.

To keep herself occupied, so she wouldn't go crazy thinking about it all day, she went into the café to check everything had run smoothly without her.

After being away for a while she found to her shock and distress that the place seemed shabby and cluttered to her now, and the warm, cosy atmosphere that she'd been hanging on to as the excuse not to change a thing about it was sadly lacking. It had all been in her head. A phantom of the past.

She'd been desperately hanging on to her father's vision for the place, to try and keep a part of him alive, but it was actually holding the business back. Destroying it, in fact.

He never would have wanted that.

She knew now, with absolute clarity, that it was time to let go. She needed to stop being afraid of the future and allow herself to finally move on.

It was time to make some changes.

It took two more days of Xavier making himself scarce in the evenings and acting all stiff and formal with her again before Soli's resolve to be cool and indifferent about how their relationship would go from now on snapped.

'Are we really back to you treating me like a piece of furniture again?' she bit out in frustration the morning of the third day when Xavier swept into the kitchen, poured himself a coffee and gave her a polite nod before starting to retreat outside with it.

He turned back, then carefully put his mug down on the nearest work surface, the coffee slopping over the edge as if his hand had been trembling.

'That's not what I'm doing, Soli,' he said quietly, his expression surprisingly tortured.

Her stomach flipped at the sight of it, but she held her nerve. They really needed to address this and the sooner the better.

'Look, I get that you don't want to have a physical

relationship with me, but I'd really prefer it if you at least acknowledged my presence in the house. We can be friends, surely?'

The muscle in his jaw was working overtime. 'It's not that I don't want a physical relationship with you, Soli,' he ground out, taking a step towards her, his shoulders rigid and his eyes flashing with frustration, 'it's that I do.'

'You do?' she whispered, shocked by the passion in his voice and the intensity in his eyes.

'Yes,' he said, letting out a low, frustrated-sounding breath.

'Oh. Okay. I see.'

'And seeing you every day but not being able to touch you, when I know how good we can be together, is driving me insane.' His chest rose and fell in rapid movements as if he was fighting for control and barely keeping it together.

The idea that she was doing that to him thrilled her to her core. Without thinking, she took a step closer to him, unable to fight the instinct to push him a little bit further to see what he'd do.

They stared into each other's eyes, their breath coming fast and their bodies tense.

Xavier made the first move, closing the gap between them and sliding his hand into her hair, then pulling her towards him so her mouth met his. The kiss was rough and full of the longing they'd clearly both been battling since the last time they'd given in to the need to touch each other.

He let out a low growl in the base of his throat as she

wound her arms around him and pressed herself closer to him, feeling exactly how much he wanted her right then.

She pulled back from the kiss to look him in the eyes again, wanting to make sure they were both thinking the same way before this went any further so they didn't end up in an even more awkward position later.

'I thought you said—'

'I know what I said, but I decided not to listen to myself for once,' he ground out, his brow pinched in a half-relieved, half-frustrated sort of frown. His eyes were alive with pleasure though, which her body responded to by sending a throb of pure desire through her.

She couldn't help but grin at him. 'Good decision. Let's be wild. It's a healthy life choice.'

'I don't know about healthy...' His words tickled her lips.

'Liberating, then. We're grown-ups. We can handle it. Both of us know the score and we're not looking for anything in addition to our agreement.'

'You mean that, right?' His expression was deadly serious now.

'Yes,' she said, matching his seriousness with her own. 'I absolutely do. I promise.'

His hands had been tight on her back, holding her against him, but they relaxed a little as something seemed to occur to him. 'Still, we need to be sensible, so we should use condoms too from now on, just to be extra-safe,' he said.

She nodded. 'Fine by me.'

And it was fine, because the last thing she needed right now was an added complication in her life.

CHAPTER ELEVEN

Battleships—sink your opponent with a blow to the heart.

XAVIER WAS LATE for work, for the first time ever, after taking Soli to bed then having a lot of trouble forcing himself to get out of it again and leave her there, all warm and sexily rumpled.

It had definitely been worth it though. More than worth it. All the pent-up frustration and jagged need that had been stressing him out—to the point where he was having trouble concentrating at work—completely evaporated the moment he let himself give in and do what he'd been desperate to do again ever since that incredible night in Corsica.

Ever since they'd crossed that line it had been inevitable they'd not be able to go back to their platonic existence.

He felt pretty confident it would be okay though. They'd had another talk about sex not changing anything about their deal and had both agreed they were still happy with that. Their physical relationship would only last as long as the marriage; after that they'd both walk away.

A clean break.

Now the thought of having Soli at home, waiting for him every evening, had a very different impact on his mood.

He even started coming home from work earlier, looking forward to spending his evenings with her, eating her wonderful food, or seeing the look of astonished approval when he insisted on cooking for her instead.

Life was pleasingly satisfying and straightforward, with his rapport with Soli on an even keel, both knowing exactly where they stood with each other.

There was no pretence and no underlying conflict of interest.

It was the most simple and rewarding relationship he'd ever had.

She seemed to know just how to pull him out of one of his funks with a few choice words and a smile, and she charmed him with her positivity and humble joy. For those few weeks he felt as if he was finally living the life he'd always wanted.

A few days after they decided to ignore their no-sex agreement Soli moved into his bedroom—which he'd suggested, saying it was ridiculous for her to return to her own room every night.

He loved waking up with her beside him. It had been a long time since he'd shared his bed like this and he was surprised to find how much he'd missed it.

Setting off for the office bright and early one morning, he turned back from opening his car door to see

Soli standing on the doorstep, still wearing the short silky pyjamas she looked so damned alluring in, blinking in the sunshine.

'Where are you off to so early?' she asked, carefully picking her way over the gravel towards him in her bare feet.

He met her halfway and lifted her into his arms so she could wrap her legs around his middle and save the soles of her feet from the sharp stones.

Walking back to the car, he put her down gently onto the bonnet and leant in to kiss her, breathing in the enticing, sleep-warmed scent of her.

'I'm off to the office. I want to get everything that needs doing today finished in good time so I can come home early and take you out for dinner. I've booked that new place on Hampstead High Street that you mentioned the other day.'

'Really?' she said, beaming at him. 'That's so thoughtful of you.'

He smiled back. 'It's mostly a selfish move on my part. I really fancied checking it out too.'

Leaning back in, she kissed him hard and he felt her smile against his lips.

'What are you going to do today?' he asked when they broke apart.

'I'm going in to the café. The marketing I've been doing seems to be paying off and we've seen a real increase in business recently.' She took a breath and he felt her fingers dig into his back as she tightened her grip on him. 'And I've decided it's time to give the place a new fit-out.' Her brow pinched in a frown as if she found this idea troubling. 'I can't keep clinging on to my father's vision for the place. It's looking so shabby now and needs modernising.' Her eyes welled with tears. 'Time to let go of the past and look to the future.'

'I think that's a good decision,' he said, running a finger gently under her eye to brush away a tear. His heart gave an extra-hard beat in his chest as it suddenly occurred to him that she was talking about a future he'd have no part in. His time with her would quickly slip away and at some point soon so would she.

'You know, I think my time with you has really made me grow up and look at life from a new perspective. So thank you for that,' she added with a sad sort of smile.

'I'm glad to have helped,' he said roughly, leaning in again and kissing her hard to try and disguise the troubling emotions that were now raging through him. Emotions he didn't know what to do with.

She let out a small sigh of contentment and pressed herself harder against him.

His mind went mercifully blank. All he wanted to think about right now was the feel of her soft, supple body against his and the luscious, honeyed taste of her in his mouth.

So it was a few seconds before he realised there was someone standing on the driveway with them, clearing his throat to politely get their attention.

Pulling away from Soli, he turned his head to see Samuel Pinker, his great-aunt's spy, looking back at him with a slightly sheepish look on his face.

'Sorry to interrupt you. The front gate was open so I thought it'd be okay to come right in. I have some documents from your great-aunt's solicitor to drop off and as I was in the area…'

They nodded politely, all of them patently aware that it had actually been another ruse to check up on the two of them, as per Aunt Faith's decree.

'That's quite all right, Mr Pinker,' Soli said with a grin in her voice. 'I was just sending my husband off to work in the best possible way I know.'

Mr Pinker cleared his throat again as a red flush appeared to creep up his neck and brighten his cheeks. 'Your husband's a very lucky man, Mrs McQueen,' he replied, 'and could I just say, I think the two of you make a lovely couple?' He turned to look at Xavier. 'Your great-aunt would be very pleased to see you so happy, Mr McQueen.'

And with those incisive words hanging in the air, he handed the envelope he was carrying to Xavier, gave them both a friendly nod of goodbye and strolled away back towards the open gates.

Soli couldn't help giggling. 'I don't think we need to worry about him thinking we're not behaving like a real married couple any more,' she said with a grin.

Something about the way she said this, on top of Pinker's parting shot, made a shiver of discomfort rush across his skin. Were they acting like a married couple? He wouldn't have said so. They were just enjoying each other's company whilst they were forced to live together. In order to be convincingly married there would have to be a palpable emotional connection between them as well as a physical one. Which he didn't think they had.

Did they?

He mentally shook himself. It wasn't important. They both knew the score. At least, he was pretty sure Soli did. Though from what she'd just said he was a little worried now that she was allowing herself to become more emotionally attached to him than was wise.

That wasn't what he wanted at all.

Was it?

No. That wasn't what he'd signed up for.

His chest suddenly felt tight.

He needed to get out of there and off to work before his concern became apparent to Soli and potentially started a conflict he really didn't want to deal with right then.

'Anyway, I'll see you later,' he said, forcing himself to give her an unconcerned smile.

'Looking forward to it,' she replied, not seeming to notice the sudden tension in the air. 'Have a good day, darling!'

Soli strolled back into the house, closed the front door and stopped abruptly in the hallway as a sudden horrifying knowledge that she was going to be sick assaulted her.

Her stomach lurched and churned as she dashed to the nearest bathroom, only just making it there in time.

The bug she'd had in Corsica couldn't have got her again, surely. She'd only had it a couple of weeks ago.

Was that right?

No. Hang on, it couldn't have been that short a time ago.

Life had been such a whirl; she'd barely had time to

notice how the weeks had flown by. It seemed like only yesterday that they'd been in Corsica.

But it wasn't. It was at least six weeks ago.

A cold sensation trickled down her spine as something alarming occurred to her.

She should have had her period by now. She remembered spotting a bit a couple of weeks ago, which wasn't unusual because of the pill she was on, but she'd forgotten to write down when her last proper period was.

Her heart gave a painful thump in her chest and she dragged in a breath as she felt suddenly dizzy.

She couldn't be pregnant though. Could she? They'd used double protection, apart from that time in Corsica when they'd just relied on her pill.

Which she'd not taken for the following two days after they'd had sex because she'd been so ill.

But there was no point panicking. She needed to be sensible and keep a cool head about this.

Pulling herself together, she got dressed then went straight out to the nearest chemist for a pregnancy test, using it as soon as she got home. Just because some things pointed towards her being pregnant, it didn't mean she actually was, she reminded herself as she waited for the results to show. It could be another bug, or stress or—something else that her whirling brain couldn't think of right now.

The lines appeared in the little window.

It wasn't anything else.

She was pregnant.

Sitting slumped on the bathroom floor, staring at the

little white stick in her hand, she felt hot tears press at the backs of her eyes as her stomach dropped to the floor.

This wasn't supposed to happen. This wasn't the plan.

What was Xavier going to say? He'd been so definite about this thing between them being a sex-only arrangement.

But perhaps he'd actually be happy about it, a determined little voice in her head whispered. He'd told her that he'd wanted to have kids before Harriet had left him, after all.

She took some deep breaths and forced herself to calm down.

It could be a wonderful thing for both of them. They were good together. They worked, both in and out of the bedroom. He made her laugh and feel good about herself. She seemed to bring out the best in him. He'd even told her that a couple of times in the last few weeks— perhaps not in those words, but he'd certainly alluded to it. He enjoyed her company, and she his.

But could she really have a child with someone who didn't love her?

Someone who didn't love her as much as she loved him?

Because she knew, in that moment, without a doubt in her mind that there was no point denying it to herself any more.

She was in love with him.

Completely and utterly.

She let out a cynical, broken laugh. So much for being mature enough to deal with a sex-only arrangement. She'd been kidding herself this whole time.

She'd not wanted to admit it to herself before now because she'd been terrified that he didn't feel the same—he was so guarded with his emotions it was difficult to know how he really felt sometimes.

But she knew what she really wanted.

She loved him and wanted them to raise this baby together. For them to stay married after the year was up.

But would he feel the same way?

Could he?

She got up from the floor and brushed herself down with trembling hands.

There was only one way to find out.

Soli was in the sitting room, anxiously biting her thumbnail, when she finally heard Xavier's car pull into the driveway that evening.

Getting up from the sofa, she went to meet him in the hall on trembling legs. Her heart was racing so hard she felt light-headed.

The door opened and, almost in a dream, she watched Xavier stride inside.

Her stomach flipped right over when he flashed her the smile she loved so much.

'Hi,' he said, dumping his laptop case by the hall table. When he straightened up to look at her the smile fell from his face and was replaced with a concerned frown.

'Are you okay? You look a bit pale. You're not ill again, are you?' He walked towards her and put his hand on her forehead. 'You don't feel hot.'

The compassion of this gesture gave her the confidence to blurt out what she needed to tell him.

'I'm not ill, I'm pregnant.'

It seemed to take him a couple of seconds to process what she'd said, then, shockingly, he took a swift step away from her.

'What?' he said, his voice as hard as stone. 'How? We've been using condoms.' The expression in his eyes was wild as he stared at her in angry denial.

Her heart plummeted, provoking a fresh wave of nausea.

That was not the joyful reaction she'd been hoping for.

She swallowed hard, telling herself he was just in shock and to give him a minute to process it. 'I did a test. It came out positive.' She took it out of her back pocket to show him. 'I think it might have been that night in Corsica.' She dragged in a shaky breath. 'Or maybe one of the condoms failed and my pill wasn't working properly again after I'd been ill.'

He shoved his hand roughly through his hair. 'This wasn't part of the deal, Soli,' he bit out, his voice icy cold and the expression in his eyes so hard it made her shiver.

A feeling of pure dread flooded through her body.

'I take it you want to keep the baby?' he asked.

'Of course I do,' she gasped, horrified that he'd even think for one second that she'd consider not doing so. 'But if you don't want to be involved I'll find a way to look after it on my own,' she shot back angrily, wounded by his harsh reaction.

'The hell you will,' he snapped.

'What's that supposed to mean?'

'It means there's no way I'm going to abandon my child. Or its mother.'

'But you've been so sure about not wanting to stay married after the year's up,' she pointed out, unable to keep the hurt out of her voice.

He just shrugged. 'We'll work something out. I can speak to Russell and get him to make some amendments to the contract,' he said, his stiff practicality sending little shocks of dismay through her.

'You want us to continue having a *contract*?' she said, appalled by the thought of it. Had it really come to this? Was he going to keep treating her—and now their child—like a commodity? Just as his parents had done to him?

'Isn't that what every mother wants?' he said coolly. 'To know that she and her child will never have money troubles again?'

His dispassion shocked her. She'd seen him flip into business mode before but this was a step way beyond that.

'No! That's not what I want! I want a partner who loves me. Who wants to be with me for *me*. Not because he feels he has to because we have a child together.' She wrapped her arms around her body, aware that she was shaking now. 'We'll only end up resenting each other. It'll be hell living in the same house and I can't let my child grow up in that sort of toxic environment. I can't spend the rest of my life with you if you don't love me back, Xavier. Because I love you!'

He wasn't looking at her now, but down at the floor instead, with a muscle flicking in his jaw.

'Do you love me?' she whispered brokenly, her heart thumping painfully in her throat.

He didn't answer her right away, but even before he opened his mouth to speak she could tell what he was going to say from the tension in his body language.

'I'm not sure I'm capable of loving anyone any more.'

The expression in his eyes was as hard as marble when he finally looked at her.

Grief squeezed her chest, stealing her breath away.

'If you can't love me, I can't stay here with you any longer,' she said, her voice barely making it past her lips. 'I'll make sure this child has all the love it needs and a happy life, but I'll do it without you and your money.'

She went to sweep past him but he put out a hand to stop her. 'Soli, don't be ridiculous—'

Her whole body was suddenly hot now. Burning with anger. 'Don't call me ridiculous! I'm sick of hearing that from you. I know you think I'm just some naïve idiot with money problems, but know this: I'm capable of being happier than you'll ever be because I let people into my heart and treat them with genuine respect— like an equal. If you can't get past that block you have, if you're not willing to, then there's no hope for you, Xavier McQueen. No matter how many houses you own or how much money you have, you'll never be happy if you can't learn to let go and fall in love again, to trust and share your life with someone else. With *me*!' Her voice broke on the last word but she fought back the tears, determined not to cry.

Letting out a loud, painful-sounding sigh, he sat down on the edge of the hall table and looked up at her with such cold resentment she felt a shiver run down her spine.

'Where do we go from here?' she whispered, panic rising in her chest.

He frowned and shook his head. 'I don't know, Soli. I just don't know. I don't think I can give you what you want.'

She saw his throat move as he swallowed but his gaze remained implacable.

After what felt like a lifetime of silence, where it became plain he wasn't going to tell her what she needed to hear, she realised the only thing she could do now was get out of there, just so she could calm down and think straight again. She needed to figure out what the hell she was going to do without him.

'Okay. Well, it's clear how you really feel about me.' She coughed to ease the painful tension in her throat. 'So I'm going to go home,' she said shakily, willing herself to hold it together, just for a few more minutes.

He didn't say anything as she turned and walked away. He didn't follow her up to the room they'd shared so happily for the last few weeks and he wasn't at the front door when she let herself out with a small bag she'd packed.

In short, he made it crystal-clear that he wasn't going to stop her from leaving.

CHAPTER TWELVE

Game of Life—spin the wheel of fate for a chance at the life you want.

IT WAS VERY QUIET in the house once she'd gone.

Xavier paced the floor for what felt like hours, trying to reconcile his thoughts about what Soli had said to him. And what he'd said to her.

Her out-of-the-blue revelation had blindsided him—his harsh words a reaction to the crushing fear that he'd been wrong to relax around her. He'd been totally unprepared for how to handle her unexpected and shocking news, and something dark and instinctive had reared up from deep inside him, making him lash out at her. To protect himself.

The whole time they'd been sleeping together he'd been afraid of this happening, but he'd pushed it away, not wanting to dwell on it, telling himself he was worrying for no reason. He thought he'd been so careful, so clever, using extra protection and making sure they were both on the same page. But he'd forgotten about Corsica. The one weak spot in the whole game.

A restless sort of dread lay heavily in his stomach

as he paced around, his veins on fire with adrenaline and terror.

He couldn't give himself fully to her, not in the way she wanted. He'd protected himself from loving anyone else ever since Harriet had torn his heart to shreds and he'd seriously believed he wasn't cut out for that sort of relationship with anyone ever again. He was his parents' son, after all.

And he'd managed to keep his feelings under control and his heart protected, until Soli had come along and turned his world upside down.

Letting her in had been such a gradual process, he'd barely noticed it. He thought they were just having fun, but from the way he was feeling now that she'd walked out on him it was clear she'd worked her way firmly into his affections.

He spent a rough night, barely sleeping a wink, Soli's sweet scent on his sheets haunting his dreams when he did sleep.

Getting up groggy and tired the next day, with his head heavy and tight with stress, he made his way down to the kitchen in the hope that a strong cup of coffee would help him think straight.

Just the sight of the empty room where he and Soli had spent so much time enjoying each other's company made him want to punch a wall in frustrated regret.

What was he going to do? How would he handle this? He suddenly desperately wanted her to be there to talk to—to see her kind, reassuring smile again. Supporting him. Caring for him.

Not that she was ever likely to be doing that again after the way he'd treated her.

Did he really believe he couldn't love her?

He didn't know any more—his head felt as if it was stuffed with cotton wool, and his blood was like sludge in his veins.

Dropping his head into his hands, he let out a loud, frustrated sigh and sank back against the work surface, feeling the hard ridge of it digging in to his spine, but he didn't move; instead he revelled in the pain it caused him, glad of the distraction from the more problematic pain in his heart.

The next few days were hell.

Soli kept her word, staying away from the house, and from him.

He'd thought it would be okay, that it would be hard but he'd be able to cope without her there, but he felt sick every time he came downstairs and found she still hadn't returned. The house was so silent and dark without her, as if she'd taken all the life and colour of the place with her when she left.

Most distressingly, the house no longer felt like his home.

There was a constant, tight ache in his chest, which he accepted, when he finally allowed himself to acknowledge it, was because he missed her.

He missed her like crazy.

The following Saturday he woke up early, the sense of doom he'd been carrying around with him since she'd gone weighing on him more heavily than ever.

Once downstairs he found he couldn't settle to anything. It was too quiet, too still in the house, so he grabbed his jacket and walked to Hampstead Village in search of something to distract him.

He was just passing some seating outside a coffee house when he heard someone calling his name. Turning to see who it was, he felt his pulse leap as he saw Harriet sitting in one of the chairs, cradling a tightly swaddled baby.

'Harriet. How are you?' he asked, his voice a little unsteady with a strange kind of yearning that had swelled in him at the sight of the child in her arms.

'I'm really well, thanks. Meet Harry, my son,' she said, beaming down towards the baby.

'Hello, Harry,' Xavier said, bending down to look more closely at the tiny human in her arms, fighting back an intense surge of emotion that was threatening to engulf him.

Would his and Soli's child be a boy? he wondered wildly, his heart thumping hard at the thought.

'Where's Soli?' Harriet asked, as if sensing his turmoil.

'She's at home,' he lied, standing up straight again, pain throbbing hard through his chest at the sound of her name.

'I guess the two of you might be having your own little bundle of joy soon,' Harriet said with a twinkle in her eye. 'I always thought you'd make a fabulous father, despite what I said all those years ago.' She appeared to swallow and blink, as if suddenly uncomfortable. 'Listen, I just wanted to say sorry for the way I treated you back then,' she went on before he could respond. 'It was an incredibly selfish way to behave.' Her smile was full of what looked like genuine regret now. 'I was afraid you didn't really love me for *me*, you just thought I ticked all the boxes for the sort of woman you thought you should be marrying.' She hugged her son a little tighter to her.

'But I guess it all worked out for the best. You and Soli looked so happy together when I saw you at the party.'

'We were,' he said, realising with a shock that he was actually speaking the truth now. He *had* been happy then. 'And I forgive you for what happened with us. You were right; we wouldn't have been good for each other. We probably would have made each other miserable.'

And he really meant that too.

Because he recognised now that Soli *was* right for him. She'd brought him back from the brink of despair and helped him realise that he wasn't like his parents at all; that he *was* capable of loving someone other than himself. Soli made him happy because she truly cared about him, *for him*, just as Great-Aunt Faith had. The warmth that the two most important women in his life had bestowed on him had instinctively made him feel secure. Wanted.

Loved.

Which was what he'd really been trying to hang on to all along. Not the house, but the security he'd thought it had represented.

He turned away from Harriet to stare at the empty space beside him, remember how he'd grown used to turning to find Soli smiling at him and how it had felt like being given a shot of adrenaline straight to his heart.

His life was empty without her.

Dragging in a deep, fortifying breath, he turned to glance in the opposite direction, towards the rental units he owned on the High Street, suddenly so clearly knowing exactly what he wanted.

He wanted Soli back. And he wanted their child too.

He wanted them to be a family—something he'd always longed for, but had previously accepted he'd never have. Until now. Until her.

So what the hell was he doing still standing there?

Blood pulsing hard through his body, he said goodbye to Harriet and started off in the direction of the board game café. He was going to talk this thing out with Soli once and for all. Exactly what he was going to say, he wasn't sure, but he felt confident it would come to him as soon as he set eyes on her.

He knew some sort of grand gesture was in order if he had any chance of winning her back though. He'd done too much damage with his selfish silence to just expect her to listen to his demands.

She was too self-possessed for that.

He needed to find a way to prove to her that he was genuinely sorry and that he meant it when he told her he couldn't live without her. That he wanted them to be a real family, something he'd never had before—had never felt worthy of—but had ached for his whole life.

But what if she turned him down? What if she just laughed in his face?

His pace slowed as the idea rattled through him and he stopped and leant a hand against the window of the nearest shop as a dark kind of fear seized him.

That was probably what he deserved after the way he'd treated her, but could he really put himself through that sort of humiliation again? It had nearly killed him the last time it had happened to him.

On the other hand, was he really prepared to lose everything he'd ever wanted because he was too afraid he might lose it later? That made no sense at all. His damn stupid pride was getting in the way of his happiness, and Soli's too, and he couldn't allow that to happen. She was the only person that had never let him down.

She loved him. That was abundantly clear.

And he knew without a doubt that she'd make an incredible mother to his child and the most loving, caring partner he could ever hope for.

Even if he struggled to get the loving thing right, he knew that Soli would be there the whole way, backing him up and evening him out. They would make a brilliant team.

He wanted her back. The woman who had helped him live again and appreciate everything he had for more than just its monetary worth.

The woman who made him happy.

The woman he loved.

He knew with absolute clarity now that the house meant nothing to him if she wasn't in it. It was just bricks and mortar, full of ghosts and regrets—an empty shell without her.

She, and her love and affection, was what he'd really needed all along.

The house was his past, but she was his future. She and their baby.

With unwavering resolve making his heart thump hard in his chest, he started walking swiftly towards the café again, prepared to do everything in his power to save their marriage.

He was in love with Soli and he was going to do whatever it took to prove it to her.

* * *

Soli was practically dead on her feet.

She'd not slept properly since leaving Xavier's house—the place she'd previously begun to consider her home too until she'd been made to feel supremely unwelcome there—and it was really beginning to show.

Even her mother had noticed her lack of energy and positivity in the last few days.

Xavier's initial, shocked reaction to the pregnancy had been understandable—she recognised that—but to reject her love, then let her leave and not contact her again, was just plain heartless.

To be perfectly honest, it had broken her heart.

But then, she'd not contacted him either, she accepted with a thud of despair. She'd been too afraid to in case she saw that look of cool reproach on his face again.

Sighing loudly, she picked up a mug from a tray of newly washed crockery and rubbed the tea towel over it. It was all very well holing herself up here, but she was going to have to face him again eventually so they could work this thing out between them. She'd signed a contract to stay married to him for the next few months after all and there was no way she was going to welch on their deal. She wasn't a quitter.

She was just finishing this thought when a familiar and stomach-twisting scent hit her senses.

Looking up, she found herself staring into the dark intensity of Xavier's gaze.

'Hi, Soli,' he said quietly.

'What are you doing here?' she blurted, completely

losing any poise she'd coached herself to exude when next confronted with him.

'I came to talk to you.'

'Here?' she said, glancing around her, unable to keep the incredulity out of her voice.

The corner of his mouth twitched up. 'Yes. I figured it's as good a place as any.'

'It's not exactly private,' she said, gesturing round at the tables full of customers and at her sister and mother, who were currently drinking coffee at the other end of the bar, celebrating a successful end to Domino's first term at university. The two women were now watching them, their interest clearly piqued.

'That's my sister and mother over there,' Soli hissed under her breath so they wouldn't hear her.

'Have you told them about us?' he asked.

'No. Not yet.'

He gave a sharp nod, but didn't move away from the counter. 'Well, we could go somewhere a bit quieter if you like.'

Suddenly she didn't want to move away from behind the counter. She wanted to make him pay for his indifference towards her by forcing him to say whatever he had to say in front of all these people. To hell with his manly pride. She didn't need to take his feelings into consideration any more, especially when he obviously had no intention of protecting hers.

'No. Whatever you have to say to me you can do right here. I'm busy doing my job—I don't have time to leave just so you can reject me again.' She folded her arms and stared him down, determined not to let him win this time.

She might love him, much more than she was willing to admit right now, but she was damned if she was going to let him hurt her any more than he already had.

She and the baby would be fine without him and his money. She had enough love in her to count for two parents.

Out of the corner of her eye she noticed her sister was still staring at them both.

'Soli, did this guy break your heart or something? Is that why you've been moping around looking so broken since I got back?' Domino called out.

Obviously they weren't being as discreet as she'd hoped.

She swallowed and was about to answer when Xavier spoke over her.

'Yes, I'm afraid I did. And I came here to apologise and tell your sister how much I love and miss her.'

He turned back to face her and looked directly into her eyes.

She just stood there dumbstruck, with blood rushing in her ears, wondering if she'd misheard him.

'I'm sorry,' he said, with such emotion in his voice she knew immediately that he genuinely meant it. 'I'm so sorry for hurting you.' He put his hands on the counter and leant in closer to her. 'I don't work properly without you. You've changed me, changed the way I think about life and what love really is. I don't deserve you, Soli, I know that, but I want you back. I want us all to be a family.'

'Really?' was all she could think to reply to that, her scrambled brain slow to catch up with everything he was saying.

'Yes. Really. I got spooked when you told me about the baby because I'd promised myself I wouldn't fall for you and it made me realise that I had. That I wanted you more than I should. I've been a complete idiot. You're the best thing that's ever happened to me—you and the baby.'

There was a loud gasp and a squeal from the direction of her mother and sister, but Soli ignored it, her attention focused solely on Xavier now.

'You really want me back?' she asked shakily.

'Yes,' he said with more determination in his voice than she'd ever heard before. He moved round to the opening in the counter and took her hand in his, gently tugging on it to ask her to follow him out to the floor of the café.

When they were both standing in front of the now mostly silent room—since the whole of the clientele appeared to have stopped playing their games to stare at them instead—Xavier dropped to one knee and looked up at her with such intensity in his eyes her heart nearly flew out of her body with excitement. His hand was shaking as he held onto hers tightly, their palms pressed hard together, and she realised with a shock that he was scared. He was afraid she would reject him, but he was still going through with this, in front of all these people.

He wasn't hiding any more.

He swallowed, looking as though he was having trouble starting his sentence, but his voice was loud and clear when he spoke. 'As you're aware, I find it really hard to trust people, but I know—I guess I've always known, deep down—that I can trust you, Soli. I love the idea of you being the mother of my child. You're the most wonderful, caring, compassionate person I've ever met and it would be a huge privilege to spend the rest of my life with you.'

There was a low murmur from the crowd, but he didn't let it distract him.

'I promise you, I will do everything in my power to make you happy. I'll give you everything I have, *everything*, if you'll come back home with me.'

She could barely breathe as the reality of his words began to sink in.

'I love you, Solitaire McQueen. Will you marry me,' he paused and smiled before adding, 'for real this time?'

Soli thought her heart might explode with happiness. Xavier loved her and he wanted them all to be a family. A real family.

'I love you too,' she sobbed, unable to control her emotions any longer. 'And yes,' she took a steadying breath, 'I'll marry you.' She grinned through her tears. 'Again.'

He kissed her hand before standing up and pulling her into his arms, where he held her to him so tightly she could barely breathe, before finally drawing away just far enough to kiss her deeply, with the love and emotion she'd always known he had in him.

'We'll make one hell of a team, Mrs McQueen,' he murmured against her lips, and she knew, right then, that there would be no more games.

She'd won the ultimate prize.

EPILOGUE

Bingo—hold your nerve for the ultimate prize.
Five years later

'FOUND YOU!' CAME the excited voice of four-year-old Faith McQueen as she pulled back the curtain to reveal her mother crouched on the window seat behind it.

'Darn! And I thought I had the perfect hiding place,' Soli said with a grin, ruffling the hair of her eldest daughter and pulling her in for a kiss.

'Mum, let go—I still need to find Dad and Joy,' Faith said, struggling out of her arms, but not before dabbing one last wet kiss on Soli's cheek.

'Okay, go ahead,' Soli said, unfolding herself from her cramped position with a sigh of relief and heading back to the kitchen, where she still had some last-minute preparations to do for Xavier's birthday meal.

She'd made one of her famous chocolate fudge cakes for dessert and she needed to get it out of the oven now so it'd be absolutely perfect.

It wasn't long before Xavier came striding in through the door with two-year-old Joy on his shoulders and

Faith clinging around his waist with her feet on top of his, doing the penguin walk.

'You seem to have a new hat and pair of trousers,' she joked. 'Did you get them for your birthday?'

She laughed as Xavier shot her a rueful look while he tried, and failed, to prise his children off him.

He was amazing with them, as Soli had always suspected he would be, and they'd both become real Daddy's girls to prove her right. He clearly adored them and had even hinted he'd be very happy to have more kids if she thought she might too.

'Where's everyone else?' Faith asked, her eyes round with excitement when she saw the kitchen table laden with the special birthday meal.

She was talking, in part, about Soli's mother, who had moved in with them and taken the downstairs bedroom when her Parkinson's had worsened and it had become impossible for her to manage stairs. It was a great arrangement because it meant the girls could spend lots of time with their grandmother, and she absolutely adored having them around her. She often said to Soli that they kept her young.

After acing her degree at Oxford, Domino had gone on to do a pure maths MSc, and was starting a PhD at King's College in London, so had moved in with them too last year, latterly bringing with her her boyfriend, who was another PhD in her department and deeply devoted to Soli's brilliant sister. If the two of them had kids, Soli suspected they'd be so smart they'd go on to solve all six of the remaining mathematical Millennium prize projects or something.

The house was no longer the silent show home it had

been when she'd first moved in. It was now always full of life and laughter, which Xavier happily asserted would have delighted his great-aunt Faith, and openly admitted that he loved too.

Soli had sold the business on to another board game enthusiast when she fell pregnant for the second time and had decided she wanted to be able to spend more time at home with both the children and her mother. She didn't regret it for a second. It had always been her father's dream really, and it had been high time she'd chased her own.

To that end, she'd enrolled in college to study fashion design, something she'd really enjoyed at school, and was now in the process of setting up her own clothing line, which she'd decided to call Solitaire.

It was all up for grabs, which was exactly the way she'd come to like it.

'Speaking of birthday presents—' she said to Xavier once he'd finally freed himself from his daughters' vice-like grip.

'You know I didn't want you to get me anything.' He gave her a mock-stern frown, then pulled her hard against his body, wrapping his arms around her. 'Just this,' he said, dropping his mouth to hers for a long, sweet kiss.

'Well, I'm afraid I ignored your instructions,' she teased, when they finally broke apart, flashing him a smile.

He let out a long, fake sigh. 'Why am I not surprised?'

'I thought you might like this though,' she said, pulling out a long, flat package.

He frowned, taking it from her and pulling off the wrapping paper to reveal a pregnancy testing kit.

'You're pregnant again?' he asked, his eyes lighting up with excitement.

'I am,' she said, grinning as he pulled her back against him and planted little kisses all over her face.

'Well, that's the best birthday present I've ever had,' he said gruffly, grinning from ear to ear.

'You realise there are going to be even more years of hide-and-seek to get through now,' she joked, laughing as he began to kiss down her throat.

'That works for me,' he said, his voice muffled against her skin. 'I know all the best hiding places in this house now.'

She smiled, thinking how much he'd changed since she'd first met him. He was so full of love and happiness with his place in the world now she barely recognised the withdrawn, emotionally scarred man he'd been then.

Contentment swelled in her chest as she looked at her family gathered around her.

Right at that moment she couldn't have been happier. She had everyone she loved right there with her and an exciting future stretching ahead with Xavier by her side.

A future she was no longer afraid to face.

She was proud of the brave, strong and confident person she'd become, thanks to Xavier's belief in her.

In fact, they'd made a pact that there would be no more hiding from life—for either of them—ever again.

He'd been absolutely right: they made the perfect team.

* * * * *

HER MAN ON
THREE RIVERS
RANCH

STELLA BAGWELL

To all my wonderful readers,
with much love and many thanks.

Chapter One

Blake Hollister was fuming when he walked out the front entrance of Yavapai Bank and Trust. So much so that he didn't see the woman on the sidewalk until he'd barreled directly into her, the force of the collision causing her to stagger backward.

With lightning-quick reflexes, he grabbed a steadying hold on her upper arm to prevent her from falling to the ground.

"Oh, pardon me, ma'am. I—"

"Blake? Blake Hollister, is that you?"

His hand continuing to grip her upper arm, he stepped back to survey the young woman he'd very nearly knocked off her feet. Shiny black hair, ocean-gray eyes and a soft wide mouth tilted in a tentative smile. Did he know this beautiful lady? She definitely seemed to recognize him.

"I'm sorry," he said, his face growing warm with

embarrassment. It wasn't like he was acquainted with a long list of women. Particularly one with a tall, curvy figure and a face like a sweet dream. If he'd met this one before, he damn well should've remembered the occasion. "Should I know you?"

The smile on her pink lips deepened. "It's probably been too long for you to recall," she told him. "I used to visit Three Rivers Ranch with my mom. She did sewing projects for your mother, Maureen."

As he continued to take in her lovely image, recognition struck him. Could this be the raggedy little teenage girl who used to sit on the floor of the front porch and play with the dogs while their mothers discussed items to be sewn or mended?

"Don't tell me you're little Katherine Anderson! I can't believe it!"

Her gray eyes sparkled, making her smile even warmer. "That was many years ago. And I wasn't sure you even knew my name back then. My name is O'Dell now."

Katherine Anderson had been several years younger than Blake and traveled in a totally different social circle than he and his family. And although he'd not paid any extra attention to her, he had noticed her from time to time. Mostly because she'd always looked unusually somber for someone so young.

"I remember," he told her. "And your mother is Paulette, right?"

Appreciation flashed in her gray eyes. "That's right."

Recognizing his hand was still clamped around her arm, Blake dropped his hold and forced himself to put a respectable step between the two of them. "Sorry for not recognizing you right off," he said with a rueful smile. "But you look…all grown-up."

She laughed softly. "Believe me, you not recognizing me is a compliment. I'd hate to think I still look like my teenage years."

He smiled at her. "I, uh, I apologize for plowing into you like that. The bank had a little mix-up on some of my accounts and the steam coming out of my ears must have blinded me."

"No problem. It was nice running into you again. Even if it was literally," she added impishly.

"Nice, yes."

"Well, I'll let you be on your way." She extended her hand to him. "Perhaps we'll run into each other again in another twelve years."

Blake took her offered hand and was instantly surprised at the trusting way her fingers molded around his. Her grip was strong and warm, a reflection of the woman she'd become.

"Uh, are you busy right now?" The question blurted past his mouth before he'd realized the words were anywhere near his tongue. "If you'd like, we could walk down the street to Conchita's and have a cup of coffee."

Her eyebrows arched and then she glanced over both shoulders as though to make sure he was actually inviting her, rather than someone who may have been standing behind her.

"I'm running a few errands this morning," she explained. "But a few minutes for coffee shouldn't hurt."

A ridiculous little thrill rushed through him. "Great, I have a few minutes, too."

Liar, liar. You don't have a minute to spare. Not with all kinds of work waiting on you back at Three Rivers. What the hell has come over you, Blake? She said her name was O'Dell now. That means she's married. Or doesn't that matter to you?

It didn't matter if she was married, Blake mentally argued. Buying an old acquaintance a cup of coffee was hardly an indecent gesture.

He reached for her arm. "Let's walk on this side of the street until we reach the end of the block."

She nodded in agreement. "I was about to suggest the same thing. It's only the first week of April, but it feels like July. And this side of the street offers a bit of shade from the blistering sun."

As they walked along the quiet street of Wickenburg, Arizona, Blake was acutely aware of the soft, sweet scent of her perfume, the way the sun put fiery sparks in her shoulder-length black hair and the graceful sway of her hips.

"So are you here in town for long?" he asked as they paused at the street corner to check for traffic.

"I live here now," she told him. "I moved back almost three years ago."

Blake hoped the red he could feel on his face wasn't that noticeable. "Oh. Mom mentioned something about you moving away. That was several years ago. I wasn't aware you'd returned. I…don't get away from the ranch all that much. There's always so much to do."

"I can understand that," she replied. "I remember Three Rivers always being a very busy place."

Busy? That was a mild way to describe his family business, Blake thought. As the general manager of Three Rivers Ranch, he barely had time to draw a good breath. If not for the mix-up at the bank requiring his personal attention this morning, he wouldn't have been in town at all, much less taking time to have coffee with a woman. But that wasn't the sort of information he needed to share with Katherine O'Dell.

They crossed the street, then traveled another half

block until they reached Conchita's coffee shop. The small pink stucco building was shaded by two large mesquite trees and offered customers outdoor seating. As they walked over a group of stepping stones that served as a sidewalk, Blake gestured to one of the tiny round tables situated on the stone patio.

"Go ahead and take a seat, I'll get the coffee. What would you like?"

"Thank you, Blake. Make mine plain coffee with one sugar."

He seated her at one of the wrought-iron tables and entered the coffee shop through a wooden screen door. As usual, Emily-Ann Smith was behind the counter. In one corner of the small room, a radio was playing an old standard, while a table fan stirred the scents of fresh-baked pastries displayed in neat rows inside a large glass case.

The instant Emily-Ann spotted Blake, a wide smile came over her face. "Well, Blake Hollister! Should I be worried the roof is going to crash in? It's been ages since you've been in for coffee."

The quirky young woman with long auburn hair was a childhood friend of Blake's youngest sister, Camille. "Hello, Emily-Ann. How are things going for you?"

She shrugged one shoulder. "Boring without Camille around. Is she ever going to come back home?"

"Hard to say. I think she likes living down on Red Bluff."

"Living. Hmm. You might call it that. Hiding is the way I'd put it," she muttered, then shook her head. "Sorry, Blake. I shouldn't have said that. What would you like this morning? I've sold at least fifty lattes since I opened at six. Want to try one?"

"No, thanks. Just two plain coffees." He placed the

correct amount of bills on the counter plus a tidy tip. "One with cream. The other with one sugar."

"Two coffees? You must be needing extra caffeine today," she said as she turned to make his order. "Guess running a ranch like Three Rivers takes a lot of energy."

Energy? No, it took working every waking moment, along with his very heart and soul, to make sure the one-hundred-and-seventy-year-old ranch not only remained solvent, but also kept improving. It was a task that had consumed his life for the past five years and the main reason he was still single at the age of thirty-eight.

"I have a guest with me," he explained. "She's waiting out at one of the tables."

Emily-Ann peered past his shoulder to the small square of window overlooking the coffee shop's patio.

"Oh! That's Katherine!" She quickly made a shooing gesture toward the door. "You go on outside and I'll bring the coffees to your table. Anything else? The brownies are still warm."

Blake pulled more bills from his wallet. "Okay, Emily-Ann. You're a good saleslady. Two brownies. If Katherine doesn't want it, I'll take it home to my niece."

"Coming right up," she cheerfully replied.

He left the building and joined Katherine at the tiny table. "The coffee is coming right out," he informed her. "Along with a couple of brownies. So I hope you're hungry."

A wide smile spread her lips and Blake was struck all over again by the warmth of her expression.

"Does anyone have to be hungry to eat a brownie?" she asked, then glanced toward the small building. "I wasn't aware that Emily-Ann served customers outside. She must consider you very special."

He let out a short laugh. "Not really. I've known her

since she was just a little kid. She and my youngest sister, Camille, went through twelve grades of school together. They're still good friends."

"I see. I remember Camille. She was a year or so younger than me, I think. And you had another sister, too. Vivian, right?"

She apparently remembered far more about his family than he did about hers. But that wasn't unusual. The Hollisters had lived in Yavapai County for over a century and a half. The folks who didn't know them personally were at least familiar with the name.

"That's right."

"So how are your sisters? And the rest of your family?" she asked.

She was wearing a white skirt that hugged her hips and legs, with a pale blue sleeveless blouse. Every now and then the desert breeze caused the thin fabric to flutter against the thrust of her breasts, giving him a vague glimpse of some sort of lacy garment beneath. Blake couldn't remember the last time he'd noticed a woman's clothing or the way she smelled. He couldn't even remember the last time he'd wanted to take a few minutes out of his day to talk to one. Yet being here with Katherine was causing everything inside him to buzz with excitement.

"They're fine. All the family is fine," he said, then, forcing himself, added, "Except for Dad. He died five years ago."

A somber expression stole over her face. "Yes, my father mentioned to me that Joel Hollister had died. Something about a horse accident, is that right?"

Blake nodded stiffly. "Yes. There was a horse involved, but we're not sure how it happened."

At that moment Emily-Ann emerged from the coffee

shop carrying their orders. She smiled coyly at Katherine as she placed the coffees and brownies on the table.

"Hi, Katherine. You're keeping some bad company this morning, aren't you?" she teased, her gaze rolling to Blake.

"Blake was kind enough to invite me for coffee," she told Emily-Ann. "We've not seen each other in years."

Emily-Ann chuckled. "That's not surprising. Blake treats us townsfolk like we have the plague. He only comes around in a blue moon. You two enjoy your coffee."

With a swirl of her long skirt, Emily-Ann turned and walked back into the building. Across the table, Katherine cast him an awkward smile. "She likes to tease."

"It wouldn't be Emily-Ann if she wasn't joking about something," he said. "Which is easier than talking about herself, I suppose. She's not had an easy life."

Tilting her head, she gently stirred her coffee. "Most of us haven't."

The wistful note in her voice caused question after question to swirl through Blake's thoughts. The most important one being whether she was married or attached to a special man.

He took a cautious sip from his coffee. "So what brought you back to Wickenburg?" he asked, trying to sound as casual as possible.

"My father. He suffered a stroke and wasn't mobile enough to care for himself. My brother, Aaron, wouldn't offer to help and Mom didn't really care what happened to Dad. You see, she divorced him when I was eighteen—right after I'd graduated high school. That's when she moved me and Aaron to San Diego. She's still living there near her sister."

So Katherine had been positioned between bitter parents, he thought ruefully. Although Blake and his siblings had lost their father, they'd been spared that kind of misery. "So you decided to shoulder the responsibility of helping your father," he mused aloud. "How is he doing now?"

She shook her head and Blake was certain he saw a mist of tears in her gray eyes.

"He passed away a year ago, last spring." She let out a heavy breath. "After I'd dealt with his funeral, I kept thinking there was nothing here in Wickenburg for me and then I decided I was wrong. My son likes it here. He's made lots of friends in school and I've made new friends, too. Along with getting reacquainted with old ones. Plus, I have a job I like. So I decided not to uproot again."

She had a son! Blake's gaze instantly slipped to her left hand, but there was no sign of a wedding ring. Yet he wasn't ready to make the deduction that she was single. She could've simply left the piece of jewelry off today.

"I'm sorry about your father," he said. "I hadn't heard."

She shrugged. "At least he's not suffering now."

He took a bite of the brownie as more questions darted through his mind. "Tell me about your son."

Her smile held the same sort of pride he saw on his mother's face when she spoke of her children.

"Nick is my only child. He's ten years old and at the moment he can't decide whether he wants to be an air force pilot or a point guard for the Phoenix Suns. Next week, he might want to be a neurosurgeon. At least he loves school. So that's one worry I don't have."

Envy slashed through Blake. At one point in his life, he'd hoped and planned to have a wife and several children of his own. But the closest he'd ever gotten was a broken engagement. Now, after three years of trying to forget the humiliation of being dumped before the wedding, Blake had pretty much convinced himself that marriage and a family weren't meant for him.

"What about your husband? What does he do for a living?"

Her gaze turned out toward the street. "Cliff died seven years ago in a single-car accident. After that, it's just been me and Nick on our own."

Blake was stunned. This warm, beautiful woman had been a widow for seven long years? Raising a son on her own? It didn't seem possible.

"I don't know what to say, Katherine. Except that I wish things had gone better for you."

She shrugged and Blake's gaze was once again drawn to the shiny black waves brushing the top of her shoulders. He figured if he was ever close enough to bury his face in her hair, it would smell like flowers and sunshine. And her skin would feel just as smooth as it looked.

"I wish so, too," she murmured, then cast him a lop-sided smile. "But that's enough about me. What about you? I imagine you've been married for ages and have at least three kids."

His gaze fell to the brown liquid swirling in his cup. "You imagined wrong. I had a fiancée once but never had a wife. No kids, either. I guess you could say I'm married to Three Rivers Ranch."

At least that was what Lenore had told Blake when she'd slipped off her engagement ring and handed it back to him. Even though the memory of that humiliating scene was still as fresh as the day it had happened three years ago, he wasn't about to share it with this woman. Katherine hardly needed to know he'd been unable to hold on to his intended bride.

Blake Hollister was single! Katherine was dumbfounded. He'd seemed like the type of guy who would mature into a family man like his father, Joel. Or perhaps that was just the way Katherine had wanted to see him.

When she'd been a senior in high school, Blake had been twenty-six. Katherine had thought he was the best-looking man on earth. Tall and muscular with thick sable-brown hair and handsomely carved features. Just getting a glimpse of him had set her eighteen-year-old heart aflutter. And if by chance he did happen to pass close enough to say hello to her, she'd felt like she'd been transported to heaven.

All those years ago, she'd had a major crush on the eldest Hollister son. Yet even at that tender age, Katherine had realized dreaming about Blake in a romantic way had been as futile as wishing for snow in the middle of July. It wasn't going to happen in this part of Arizona. Not then. And not now.

"I'm surprised, Blake," she admitted. "Of all of your brothers, I thought you'd be the first one with a bunch of kids and a sweet wife at your side."

His rich brown eyes focused on something beyond her left shoulder and Katherine could see her comment had left him uncomfortable. Which only made her want to ask him all kinds of personal questions. Ones that she had no business asking.

"I thought the same thing. But it hasn't worked out that way. Actually, my brother Joe is the only one of us Hollister boys who's taken the matrimonial plunge.

He and his wife, Tessa, are expecting their first child in a few months."

"Congratulations to them. I hope everything works out well." She pinched off a morsel of the brownie and popped it into her mouth.

"I do, too," he said. "They're madly in love and Mom is excited about becoming a grandmother again."

"Again?"

Nodding, his gaze returned to her. "Vivian has an eleven-year-old daughter, Hannah."

"Oh, do Vivian and her family live around here? I've not seen her around town."

"Viv's been divorced for several years now. She and Hannah live on the ranch with us. Actually, she never moved away. I think her ex thought living on Three Rivers would be easier than making a home elsewhere. Guess it just wasn't easy enough for him."

"I'm sorry to hear things didn't work out for your sister." She sipped her coffee and tried to ignore the way Blake's eyes were roaming her face, as though he was trying to decide if there was still a part of that poor Anderson girl in her, or if she'd changed completely since she'd been away.

When he'd invited her to have coffee, she'd accepted, thinking it would be nice to catch up with news about him and his family. But now that she was sitting across this tiny table from him, she realized she'd made a huge mistake. He was making her feel things she shouldn't be feeling, remember things she'd tried so hard to forget.

"Vivian didn't need a man like him in her life," he said bluntly.

Like she hadn't needed a man like Cliff in her life, Katherine thought dolefully. At least, not the man he'd turned into during the latter half of their marriage.

Shoving that dark thought away, she said, "Actually, I'm surprised Vivian hasn't married again. I remember her being so warm and beautiful."

"She's gun-shy, I think."

Katherine knew the feeling. "Since I moved back to Wickenburg, I've not run into any of your family around town. But I do hear snippets of gossip from time to time."

His grunt was full of humor. "Mostly about Holt, I imagine. He still likes to break wild horses and party afterward."

She broke off another piece of the brownie and popped it into her mouth. Not because she was hungry, but because it tasted good and something about Blake was making her so restless she needed to do something with her hands. She only wished she could make her eyes find a different object to stare at. Just looking at his rugged face reminded her that she was a woman. One who hadn't been touched by a man in a long, long time.

"I think most of the single ladies in town think of him as a man on the prowl. I mostly remember him playing football in high school. And your brother Chandler played baseball. They were both good athletes."

"I'm sure you've seen Chandler's animal hospital on the edge of town. He's pretty much tied to his practice and seeing after the animal health on Three Rivers. As for Holt, he manages the horse division. Even though I joke about him being a rounder, he has more knowledge in his little finger about horseflesh than I'll ever know in a lifetime." He paused, a slow grin spreading across his face. "I've said enough about my family. What about your brother, Aaron? What is he doing now?"

"He went into law enforcement. He works as a deputy for Inyo County in California."

"The Death Valley area. He must be tough. Is he married?"

Katherine tried not to grimace. "No. He doesn't think he's cut out to be a family man. And frankly, I think he's right. He has a cynical attitude about…well, love and family. I don't think any woman could put up with him for long."

"Ouch. Sounds like the two of you aren't exactly close."

"Oh, we talk occasionally. And we care about each other. At least, I care about him. But we have different ideas about things, that's all. I tried to get him to come to Wickenburg before Dad died, but he never would. That hurt. A lot."

He studied her closely. "And your mother? She doesn't want to come back?"

Katherine shook her head. "She likes the Southern California climate and being close to her sister. And she says there are too many bad memories for her here."

Before she realized Blake's intention, he suddenly reached across the table and covered her hand with his. The physical contact practically took her breath away, but the jolt of his touch couldn't compare to his next words.

"I'm glad you don't feel that way, Katherine. It's nice to have you back home."

Home. Was she really home? Since Cliff's death, and more recently her father's, Katherine had begun to wonder if she would ever know the true feeling of home again.

A hard lump suddenly lodged in her throat and she tried to swallow it away before she spoke. "Thank you, Blake. When I came back—to help Dad—I wasn't sure I was doing the right thing. To say the least, our relationship had been strained. But now...well, long before he died, we made peace with each other. And that's the most important thing. Don't you think?"

"Absolutely."

Lifting her gaze to his, she gave him a grateful smile. "Coming from you, Blake, that means a lot."

He didn't say anything. Instead, he continued to study her face as his thumb slowly stroked the back of her hand. The touch ignited a spark somewhere deep inside her and shot a wave of uncomfortable heat straight to her cheeks. Inside her head, a voice was commanding her to ease her hand away from his and run down the street as fast as her high heels would carry her. Yet she couldn't seem to make herself move, or even speak.

"Katherine, I—"

The sound of his low voice snapped her paralysis and she managed to ease her hand from his hold and reach for her purse.

Before he could stop her, she rose to her feet. "Thank you for the coffee, Blake, but I really must be running. I have to be back at work by ten."

He glanced at his watch, then got to his feet. "When we get back to my truck, I'll drive you."

"No need for that. My car is parked in the parking lot at Yavapai Bank and Trust. I was about to go in to do some banking business when we crashed into each other," she explained.

"Okay," he told her. "I'll clear the table and then we'll walk back."

After tossing their coffee cups and scraps of uneaten brownies into a nearby trash bin, he reached for her arm and guided her back onto the quiet sidewalk.

"So where do you work, Katherine?"

Although the touch of his hand on her arm was

featherlight, it was enough to send electrical shocks up and down her arm. No matter what man was at her side, the odd reaction would have been troubling. But this was Blake Hollister. The eldest son of the prominent ranching dynasty. The man who made sure Three Rivers Ranch remained a cattle kingdom in Southern Arizona. The only thing he could ever be to Katherine was a friendly acquaintance.

"I'm a secretary to the superintendent at St. Francis Academy. A private school over on South Saguaro."

"You said earlier that you liked your job. Have you been there long?"

Had he always been this tall and dark? This strong and broad-shouldered? Everything about him seemed magnified ten times over since she'd last seen him. But then a man could change greatly in a matter of a few years, she thought. Her late husband was proof of that.

She answered, "Almost three years. I went to work there shortly after I returned to Wickenburg. Juggling my job and caring for my dad wasn't easy, but I managed."

"School will be out soon," he remarked. "Will you have to work during the summer?"

"Only for half of each workday. I'm looking forward to having the extra time to do things with Nick. He wants to go camping."

"Most little boys do. My brothers and I used to put up a tent out behind the cattle barn and pretend we were miles away on some lonesome mesa. That way we had to worry and watch for coyotes and mountain lions. Sometimes that was hard to do, though, when a pen of weanling calves was bawling right next to us."

Katherine chuckled. "No doubt it was still an adventure for you. I'm not sure Nick is ready to sleep out in the backyard on his own, though."

His smile knowing, he glanced at her. "I have an idea it's more like his mother isn't ready for Nick to sleep outdoors."

She sighed. "I confess. I have sheltered him somewhat," she admitted. "It would be different if he had siblings. But that never happened."

Katherine had no idea why she'd added that last bit of information. Blake wasn't interested in her past family life. He was simply carrying on a polite conversation. He didn't care that all of her hopes and dreams for a big family had vanished as Cliff had turned away from her and buried himself in his job.

"Well, at least you have one child," he said. "That's more than I have."

She started to ask him if he still hoped to have a family someday, but a quick glance ahead told her they'd reached the bank building. Which was probably a good thing. She didn't need to know about Blake's wants or wishes. It was none of her business whether he had a special woman in his life now, or even if he was looking to find one. Money in the bank and a closet full of fine clothes didn't change the fact that her maiden name was Anderson.

"Here we are," she said in an overly bright voice. "Thanks again for the coffee, Blake. And please tell your family hello for me. Especially your gracious mother."

He released his hold on her arm, but instead of stepping away, he reached for her hand and lifted it to the middle of his chest. "I'd really like it, Katherine, if you'd come out and have dinner with me at Three Rivers."

Was he serious? Her gaze roamed his face as she tried to figure out the motive behind his invitation. Was he simply being polite? She couldn't think of any other reason.

"Oh, I wouldn't want to impose on your family."

He frowned. "Don't be silly. They'd all be glad to see you. But if you'd rather, we could go somewhere else for dinner."

Totally bemused now, she looked around her, then back at him. "Are you asking *me* for a date, Blake?"

Her question caused his square jaw to turn a shade darker. "That's exactly what I'm doing. Why? Is there anything wrong in that?"

Only that she was the daughter of one of the town's worst drunks. It didn't matter that Avery Anderson was dead and gone now. That didn't change the fact of Katherine's upbringing.

Stuttering, she tried to give him a reasonable answer. "Uh, well, it's just that I— Dating is something I don't do. I mean, not very often."

"Then you need to let me change that."

Her heart was suddenly tripping over itself. Blake Hollister wanted to take her on a date! If such a thing had happened twelve years ago, she would've fallen over in a dead faint. And she was darned close to it now.

"I don't—"

"I know," he interrupted. "You've already said you don't date very often. Well, I don't, either. So that puts us on equal footing."

If possible, her heart leaped into an even faster gait. "I suppose I could think about it," she hedged. "And you could give me a call."

"Great!" He dropped her hand and pulled a smartphone from his pocket. "Give me your number. Or are you in the book?"

"No landline." She gave him the number. "That's my cell. And I can't answer during working hours."

"Don't worry," he said with a grin. "I'll call at a respectable time. And soon."

Completely flustered now, she tugged the strap of her handbag higher onto her shoulder. "I really have to run, Blake. Goodbye."

Stepping around him, she practically ran into the bank building. But as soon as she reached the lobby, she paused and looked through the darkened plateglass wall overlooking the street.

Blake's tall, commanding figure was sauntering toward a black pickup truck covered with gray dust. As she watched him climb into the vehicle, then back it into the street, she decided she didn't have anything to worry about. Blake would never call her. In fact, before the day was over, she'd bet he would delete her number from his phone and forget all about her.

And that was the way she wanted it, she thought as she continued through the lobby and straight to the nearest teller. She wasn't about to let Blake Hollister, or any man, start filling her head or her heart with romantic dreams.

No. She had more important things to do. Like raising her son. And trying to forget that she was responsible for her husband's death.

Chapter Two

"What are we doing here, Joe?" Blake asked cynically as he and his younger brother trudged through a narrow gulch filled with rocks and sage. "I mean, we come out here every couple of weeks and poke around like a pair of old prospectors looking for gold. And we have about as much chance of finding anything as those dream chasers did a hundred and fifty years ago."

"We're not looking for gold, Blake," Joseph bluntly reminded him. "We're looking for some sort of clue to solve our father's death."

"Just because Holt found our dad's spur rowel here in this same gulch back in February, doesn't mean we'll find anything else," Blake reasoned. "Besides, I've been thinking. Dad could have already been hanging from the stirrup when Major Bob galloped through this gulch and the rowel was raked off by a rock or bush. Whatever caused him to lose his seat in the saddle could've happened a long way from here."

"That's true," Joseph replied. "But I don't think so. I think he met someone here in the gulch or at the well pump. It's only about twenty yards from here."

Joseph had worked as a deputy sheriff for Yavapai County for more than ten years and his mind operated in a different way than Blake's.

Straightening away from the gravel bed where he'd been searching, Blake tugged his straw cowboy hat lower over his forehead. Midafternoon in Arizona was usually hot at this time of year and today was no exception. Even with his eyes shaded by a pair of dark aviator glasses and the brim of his cowboy hat, the brightness of the sun caused him to squint as he looked across the rocky slope to where his brother stood.

"It's been five years, Joe. Maybe it's time we gave up."

Joseph stared at him for a long, awkward moment, then walked over to him. "I can't believe you're saying that. What the hell is wrong with you? Everybody knows Major Bob didn't spook or buck. You could set off a firecracker under that horse and he'd just stand there with a sleepy look on his face. You and I both know someone killed Dad and tried to make it look like an accident."

"Yeah," Blake mumbled. "But after all these years, Joe, how can we ever find enough evidence for the law to make an arrest?"

"We found the rowel. We know Dad was here on this part of the ranch even though he'd told the ranch hands that day he'd be riding a good five miles west of the ranch house. If we can find the reason why he wound up here instead, we'll figure things out." Joseph reached

for Blake's shoulder and gave it an encouraging shake.
"Come on, brother. You've always stuck with me on
this. Don't start losing faith now."

Blake tried to smile—something he admittedly didn't
do very often. It wasn't that he was a grouch or a negative person. It was just that smiling and laughing felt
awkward to him. His family often called him the judge.
They didn't understand that ever since Joel had died, the
heavy weight of running this seven-hundred-thousand-
acre ranch had landed squarely on his shoulders. Not
only did the family's financial security depend on Three
Rivers's solvency, but there was also the family legacy
to continue. Hollisters of past generations had first built
Three Rivers back in 1847. It was Blake's job to see the
ranch remained sound well into the next generation. With
that kind of responsibility, he didn't have much urge to
laugh or smile.

"I'm not losing faith, Joe. I only wish some sort of
definite clue would turn up. And I—" He paused, his
gaze scanning the rocky terrain dotted with thorny
chaparral, chollas and the occasional mesquite tree.
"When I look around this place, I start imagining Dad
and what he must have gone through that day. I wonder
if he was fighting for his life. Or did someone ambush
him from behind and he never knew what hit him? The
questions stab me right in the heart."

"I feel the same way, Blake. Everyone in the family
wonders about those things. Especially Mom."

Blake released a heavy breath. "She rarely mentions
Dad's death. She only talks about the good memories."

"That's because those times are the most important
thing to her. The wonderful years Dad was alive and
with us," Joseph replied. "Not the way he died."

Amazed at Joseph's calm, perceptive attitude, Blake

turned his gaze back to his brother. For years Joseph had been driven to find the answers to their father's death. As a deputy, he'd used every spare hour he could find to pore over the case that the late Sheriff Maddox had ruled an accident. But now that Joseph had fallen in love with Tessa and made her his wife, his priorities, even his attitude, had definitely changed. Instead of being driven, he took things in stride. Instead of going around with a scowl on his face, his expression was one of composed strength.

It was hard for Blake to believe that love and a coming baby had made such a change in his brother, but the evidence was standing right in front of him. And the reality left Blake more than envious.

"Yeah. The most important," Blake muttered.

Joseph gently slapped a hand against the middle of Blake's back. "Come on. Let's head back. It's my day off and I promised to meet Tessa in town. She's still buying things for the nursery. I don't know how much more stuff she's going to squeeze into that room. Our little one isn't going to need clothing for at least two years. She's already bought our child a pair of cowboy boots."

Blake's lips twisted into a semblance of a smile. "Guess she's planning on the kid being a rancher. God help the little tyke."

The two men began to climb up the steep bank of the gorge.

"Why do you say it like that?" Joseph asked. "You, of all people."

Blake didn't bother to answer until he and his brother were both out of the gorge and walking toward a work truck parked a few feet away.

"Ranching is not an easy profession," he reasoned. "Some people think we just buy a herd of cows, then they eat grass and have babies and that's all there is to it. Easy, right?"

Joseph glanced over at him. "Some people think all you have to do to be a deputy is pin a badge on your chest. But we both know that nothing worthwhile is easy."

"Does that include being a husband?" Blake asked.

"Sure," Joseph joked. "I'll say it's as hard as hell and you'll run and tell Tessa."

The two men climbed into the cab of a white ton truck with the 3R brand displayed on both doors. As Blake settled himself behind the wheel and started the engine, he said, "I wouldn't repeat such a thing to my sweet sister-in-law. I was just curious. In case you haven't noticed, I've never been a husband before."

Blake put the truck in motion, and as he steered it in the direction of the ranch house, he could feel Joseph's keen gaze boring into the side of his face.

"You really are curious, aren't you?" Joseph asked.

"Why not?"

"Why not? You never bother to look at a woman, much less date one. Not after Lenore."

Scowling, Blake jerked the wheel to avoid a boulder. "Hell, Joe, did you have to bring her up? Besides, it's not like I'm over-the-hill and washed-up. I'm only thirty-eight. I still have time to hook up with a woman."

"How's that going to happen? You rarely step off Three Rivers."

"You might be surprised, little brother," Blake said coyly. "I might've already met one."

As the truck bounced over the rough terrain, Blake glanced over to see Joseph gaping at him.

"Floorboard this damn truck," Joseph told him, his

voice taking on a note of excitement. "We need to get back to the ranch and knock a board off the barn!"

Rolling his eyes, Blake said, "Let's not take the celebrating to that extent. But I did have coffee with a woman a couple of days ago. A mighty pretty one, too."

Joseph squared around in the seat. "Did you dip into Mom's peach wine before we headed out here?"

"What kind of question is that? Don't you think I might know a girl? A pretty one?"

"Well, yes. I just never figured— Who is she?"

Right now she was little more than a nice, sweet memory. One that Blake couldn't get out of his head. "Do you remember Paulette Anderson? Years ago, she used to sewing and mending for Mom."

"Sure. I remember. Nice lady. In spite of being married to that good-for-nothing Avery. I had to arrest him once. Drunk as a skunk. Driving all over the road. It's a miracle he hadn't killed himself or someone else. I'm pretty sure he lost his driver's license after that."

My brother, Aaron, wouldn't offer to help. When I came back—to help Dad—I wasn't sure I was doing the right thing.

Katherine's remarks about her father suddenly traveled through Blake's thoughts. Without knowing much about her family life, he'd not fully understood what she'd meant. He'd figured her parents' divorce had caused a rift with her father, but she'd decided to put it all behind her.

Frowning thoughtfully, he said, "So you're telling me that Avery Anderson was an alcoholic. I didn't know."

"I thought everybody around here knew that." Joseph shook his head. "What do the Andersons have to do with you having coffee with a woman, anyway?"

"She's their daughter. Katherine. Her name is O'Dell now. Did you know she'd returned to Wickenburg?"

"No. Guess she came back to bury the old man and settle his estate. Which couldn't have been much."

Blake inwardly winced at his brother's remark. He understood Joseph wasn't being snobbish. He was simply speaking the truth. The Andersons had lived in a very modest house on the outskirts of town. They'd never had much in the way of material things. But until this moment, Blake hadn't been aware that Katherine's father had cared more about a bottle of booze than he had his family. How had she found it in her heart to care for him during his failing health? Blake doubted he could ever be that forgiving or compassionate.

Blake pulled his thoughts back to the present. "Katherine lives here now. She's a widow. With a son."

Long moments passed in silence and Blake wondered if his brother was trying to come up with a nice way of telling him to steer clear of Katherine O'Dell.

Eventually, Joseph asked, "You say she's pretty?"

For once, Blake didn't have any trouble putting a smile on his face. "Very."

"Then you'd better ask her out."

"I already have," Blake said flatly. "She hedged on giving me an answer."

Joseph looked at him. "You're not going to let that stop you, are you?"

"I'm not going to let anything stop me."

Later that evening in a small fenced yard behind Katherine's house, she tossed a baseball with a gentle underhanded pitch to her son, then smacked the worn glove on her left hand.

"Okay. Let it rip. I'm ready," she called to Nick.

Nick groaned with frustration. "Aww, Mom, that's not the way to throw a pitch. You gotta go like this. And put some steam behind it!"

He went through the exaggerated windup of a major-league pitcher and then threw a hard bull's-eye that nearly knocked the glove off Katherine's hand.

Somehow she managed to make the catch, but her fingers stung from the force of the ball. "Nick! I am not about to throw the ball that hard. I might accidently hurt you. It's underhanded or not at all," she warned. "Take your pick."

Nick groaned. "Oh, Mom, I'm not a baby. I can catch a fastball."

"Maybe you can, but I'm not going to throw you one. You have to play by my rules."

"Okay," he mumbled with disappointment. "I'll follow your rules. Let's play."

Katherine tossed the ball back to him while thinking how much better things would be for her son if he had a father. Not just a guy in the background, like Cliff, who'd worked too many hours to ever notice he had a son, much less spend time teaching him about sports. Nick deserved to have a father who would give him special love and attention. But finding a man who'd give that much to a stepchild seemed next to impossible.

By the time dusk began to fall and the backyard darkened with shadows, Nick had grown tired of the simple game of pitch and announced he was hungry.

Katherine pulled off the glove and handed it, along with the stained baseball, to her son. "Put your things away and wash up. I already have something fixed, so we'll eat in a few minutes."

"Okay, Mom. And thanks for playing catch with me."

At ten years old, he was tall for his age, with long

lanky limbs and feet that were growing just as quickly as his height. His thick hair was nearly as dark as hers and his eyes close to the same gray. People often remarked that Nick favored his mother, and Katherine had to admit that when she looked at her son, she saw nothing of Cliff O'Dell. And considering the way that things had worked out for her and her late husband, she supposed it was a blessing that Nick didn't resemble his father.

Slinging her arm affectionately around Nick's shoulders, she guided him toward the back door of the house. "You're very welcome."

"Mom, do you think I might go to baseball camp this summer? Jimmy Bainter's dad is going to be the instructor. You know, he played in the minor leagues once. Back before he got so old."

"Old? I've seen Jimmy's dad before. He doesn't look old." Katherine opened the door and ushered her son inside a small mudroom.

"Oh, shoot, Mom, that guy is probably forty!"

Trying not to laugh, Katherine nudged her son on toward the kitchen. "Go on and wash up."

"But what about the baseball camp? Can I go? Jimmy and Shawn have already signed up. And it's going to be over at the park. Every day for two whole weeks!"

"May you go," she said, correcting him. "And maybe. I'll check into it."

"Thanks, Mom." Grinning as though he was already certain she'd conceded, he hugged her waist, then rushed from the room.

Katherine washed her hands at a deep double sink, before entering the kitchen to get the evening meal ready. As she walked toward the refrigerator to pull out a casserole dish filled with lasagna, she decided to detour to the cabinet counter to check her phone. Normally, she didn't get many calls, but she did receive a few texts from coworkers.

Seeing a notification that she'd missed a call, she punched a button to see the caller identity and immediately let out a small gasp.

Blake! Blake Hollister had called her!

Yes, she'd given him her phone number the morning they'd had coffee, but she'd never expected him to use it. In fact, once she'd walked away from him in front of the bank, she'd pretty much decided she'd never hear from the man again.

What was she going to do now? She'd missed his call and he'd not left a voice mail.

The smart thing to do, Katherine, would be to put down the phone and forget the man. So what if he did call you? So what if he did take you out on a date? That's as far as things would ever get with a man like him. You'd only be wasting your time.

Disgusted with the cynical voice going off in her head, she placed the phone on the far end of the cabinet and went about getting the lasagna heated for their supper.

By the time she and Nick had eaten the meal and finished it off with chocolate ice cream for dessert, she'd decided to forget about Blake's call. If he'd wanted to talk to her that badly, he would have left a message. Besides, she had plenty of other things to think about. Like vacuuming the living floor and putting a load of towels in the washer.

"Mom, can I watch one of your Tarzan movies?" Nick asked as he helped her carry the dirty dishes to the sink. "I want to see the one with the elephant stampede. You know, the one where the bad guys are trying to get ivory from the sacred elephant graveyard."

Katherine smiled to herself. She'd always loved the Tarzan movies made back in the 1930s and 1940s, yet the first time Nick had watched one with her, he'd promptly described the whole thing as dorky.

"I thought my Tarzan movies were too cheesy for you," Katherine said as she began to scrape food scraps into the garbage disposal.

"I guess I got to liking them. The animals are neat and so is Boy."

Smiling, she glanced at him. "You think it would be fun to live in a tree house?"

"Yeah. But only for a few days. There wouldn't be any TV."

Since she made sure to limit her son's time in front of the TV, he appreciated the chance to enjoy his favorite programs. "Oh, well, that would be awful. You'd have to get a stick and draw pictures in the dirt for entertainment."

A bewildered look came over her son's face. "Mom, are you feeling sick or something?"

Katherine chuckled. "No. Just feeling my age. And you have my permission to watch the movie. Just make sure you put the DVD back into its case when you're finished."

"Thanks, Mom!"

Nick hurried out of the kitchen and Katherine finished washing and drying the last of the dishes. She was hanging the dishtowel on a rack when her phone rang. The sound caused her to jump as though a firecracker had exploded beneath the table.

Could Blake be calling again? The number illuminated on the face of the phone wasn't familiar, but the prefix was local.

Bracing herself, Katherine snatched up the phone and accepted the call with a simple hello.

"Katherine, this is Blake. Do you have a moment to talk?"

His low, masculine voice caused goose bumps to erupt along the backs of her arms and suddenly her heart was pounding so hard and fast, she felt dizzy. "Uh, yes, I can talk. How are you, Blake?"

"Fine, thanks. You sound surprised to hear from me."

Her legs shaking, she walked over to the kitchen table and eased into one of the wooden chairs. "To be honest, I wasn't expecting you to call."

After a pause, he said, "I was giving you time to think about our date."

She gulped and glanced over her shoulder. Thank goodness Nick was occupied with the movie. Having her son within earshot of her conversation would have made it even more difficult.

"Our date?" She repeated the words in the form of a question. "We don't have a date."

"We will. As soon as you say yes."

Katherine looked around her simple kitchen and wondered if she was dreaming. "I'm not sure that would be the right thing to do, Blake," she said as politely as she could manage.

"Why?" he asked. "You don't like me?"

She practically spluttered into the phone. Like him? What would he think if he knew she'd spent most of her teenage years mooning after him? Probably laugh himself silly, she thought. "Of course I like you. Very much. It's just that I'm... Well, since Cliff died, I haven't exactly put myself back in the dating scene. I'd probably be very boring company."

Another long pause and then he said, "The dates I've had in the past couple of years can be counted on one hand. So you see, I'm just as rusty about this as you are. As for being boring, my family's nickname for me is Judge."

Katherine could hardly imagine a man of Blake's status going without dates. Besides being handsome and wealthy, he was warm and personable and a far cry from boring. He could have any woman he set eyes on. Had he stayed away from the dating scene because his engagement hadn't worked out? She wondered. If so, he must have been crazy in love with his ex-fiancée. The thought was more than off-putting.

"I have my son to consider," she hedged. "He'd have to go to a sitter."

"My mother or sister would be happy to take on that chore."

She absently rubbed her fingertips across her forehead. "Thank you, but I have a neighbor who watches Nick whenever I have to be out at night."

"Then I don't see a problem. What about Friday evening? Say about six? We'll have a nice dinner in Prescott."

The mere idea of sitting at a candlelit dinner table with Blake was enough to make her tremble all over. "I'd rather keep it casual...if you don't mind," she added, then realized she'd just given in without really meaning to.

"I don't mind at all. We can make it as casual as you want," he assured her. "So where do you live? Your father's place?"

When she'd returned to Wickenburg to care for her

father, she'd not been surprised by the dilapidated condition of the home where she and her brother had grown up. The roof had leaked in several places and in most of the rooms the linoleum had worn down to the subflooring. The air-conditioning had gone kaput, and with no window screens, it was impossible to open the house for any kind of relief from the heat. Her father had refused to move anywhere, so she'd been forced to make enough repairs to make the house livable for her and Nick.

Blake had thought she was still living there and yet that hadn't stopped him from asking her for a date. The whole notion amazed her.

"Uh, no. After Dad died, I sold the property. I've moved to the west side of town in a white brick house with green shutters." She gave him the address. "My little car is red and you'll see it parked beneath a carport on the right side of the house. It's easy to find."

"No problem. I'll find it."

A few awkward moments of silence passed and then she asked, "Are you really sure you want to do this, Blake? If you're having second thoughts, don't worry about it. I'll understand."

"Would you understand? Because I wouldn't," he said bluntly. "Listen, Katherine, I've asked you out on a date because I want to spend time with you. Why is that so hard for you to believe?"

Her spine stiffened to a straight line. There was no point in skirting around the issue, she thought. "Surely you can't be that blind. You're a Hollister. You have no business going out with someone like me."

"Someone like you? Since when is it wrong for a Hollister man to want to spend time with a lovely, intelligent young woman?"

Did he honestly see her in that way? "We hardly travel in the same social circle, Blake."

"I don't travel in any social circle. And from what you tell me, you don't, either."

He was making sense. Or did she simply want to believe the two of them could meet on common ground.

"I apologize, Blake. I'm insulting both of us, aren't I?"

"Yes. You are."

She bit down on her lower lip. "I'm sorry. I really do want to see you again."

"Good. That's all I needed to hear. So I'll see you Friday evening."

She could hear a smile in his voice and the sound warmed her far more than it should have. "Friday. Yes. See you then."

He ended the call with a quick goodbye, and with a shaky hand, Katherine placed her phone on the table.

Right or wrong, she was going on a date with Blake Hollister.

Chapter Three

Friday afternoon Blake called Katherine to confirm their date, and before their brief conversation ended, she asked if he'd mind dropping off Nick at the sitter's on their way out of town. Blake had readily agreed and had even felt a bit flattered that she wanted him to meet her son.

But now as Blake walked to the front door of Katherine's brick house, he wondered how Nick was going to react to his mother going on an outing with a strange man. Blake loved children, but that didn't mean Katherine's son would like him. It would make for an awkward start with Katherine if the boy took an instant dislike to him.

Trying not to dwell on that possibility, Blake punched the doorbell and after a moment he could hear footsteps racing through the house. When the door partially opened, he found himself staring at a tall, thin boy with dark hair and clear gray eyes. There was no doubt he was Katherine's child. Her features were stamped all over his face.

"Hello," he said as he warily eyed Blake. "Are you Mr. Hollister?"

"Hello," Blake said, returning the greeting. "And I am Mr. Hollister."

Continuing to study Blake with open curiosity, he opened the door wide and thrust out his hand.

"I'm Nick," he said, introducing himself. "Nice to meet you, sir."

Blake gave the boy's hand a firm shake. "It's nice to meet you, Nick. And it's fine with me if you call me Blake."

"Mom says I have to be respectful of my elders. But you don't look all that old to me," he said. "You want to come in, Blake?"

Blake smiled to himself. At least the boy wasn't sulking. "That would be nice."

Nick stepped to one side and Blake entered a short foyer.

"Mom is still getting dressed," Nick announced as he closed the front door behind them. "She's always slow."

"That's okay. I don't mind waiting."

The boy motioned for Blake to follow him out of the foyer. "Come into the living room. I'll go tell Mom you're here."

With Nick leading the way, Blake entered a cozy room furnished with a dark red couch and matching stuffed armchair. A glass coffee table was covered with books and DVDs, while a television spanned a far corner of the room. Beyond a picture window framed with cream-colored drapes, a view of the desert almost made him forget the house was situated on the edge of a residential area.

"You can sit anywhere you want," Nick instructed before he disappeared through an open doorway.

After taking a seat in the armchair, Blake settled back and allowed his gaze to wander around the room. Almost immediately his attention was caught by several framed photos resting on a wall table off to his left. With only a span of a few feet between him and the photos, Blake could see the majority of the images were of Nick captured at different stages of his young life. There was also an enlarged snapshot of Paulette Anderson with another woman, most likely her sister. He also recognized one small photo of Katherine's brother, Aaron. The fact that there were no images of her late father or husband stood out like a weed in a rose garden.

Considering what Joseph had told him about Avery Anderson, Blake could understand why she might not want to be reminded of her father. But what about her husband? Was losing him still so painful she didn't want to look at his image?

The sound of footsteps had him glancing around to see Nick entering the room.

"Mom says she'll be ready in five minutes," he announced. "But if I was you, I'd be ready to wait another ten. She's just now doing something to her hair."

The boy walked over to the couch and plopped onto the end cushion. Blake noticed he was wearing a black T-shirt with his school's name printed across the front, along with blue jeans and high-top basketball shoes made of black canvas. In a few short years, he was going to be a very good-looking teenager, Blake decided. No doubt Katherine would have her hands full trying to keep him on the right path. Unless she married in the near future and then Nick would have a stepfather to help guide him into manhood.

Shoving away that uncomfortable thought, he asked, "What grade are you in, Nick? The fifth?"

He nodded. "I'm ten. I'll be eleven in three months, though."

"Hmm. I liked being eleven," Blake commented. "It's a fun age."

"I wouldn't know about that. I'm not eleven yet."

Before he could stop it, Blake was laughing and the sound must have eased something in Nick, because he suddenly laughed along with him.

"Are you really a cowboy? Mom says you run a big ranch that has lots of cows and horses."

"That's right. It's called Three Rivers Ranch."

His interest piqued, Nick squared around on the cushion so that he was directly facing Blake. "I guess you know how to ride a horse and all that kind of stuff. Can you rope a bull?"

"I can. But it's not something I do very often. It's pretty dangerous. Especially when they have long horns."

Nick thought about that for a moment. "Yeah, guess it would be. Those long horns are pretty scary. When Gold Rush Days was going on, Mom took me to the rodeo. It was exciting. I liked the bucking horses best."

"Then you'd like my brother Holt. He rides bucking horses practically every day."

Nick was clearly impressed. "Really? Wow, he must be a tough guy."

"As tough as they come," Blake agreed.

"You have brothers and sisters?" he asked.

"Three brothers and two sisters."

"Gosh, that must be great. I don't have a brother. Or a sister. I wish I had some. But I don't think I ever will."

Blake had expected Katherine's boy to utter a few stilted words, then disappear into another part of the house. The fact that Nick seemed to want to talk, especially about such personal things, touched a soft spot in him.

Doing his best to sound casual, Blake asked, "Why do you think that?"

Exasperation twisted Nick's young features. "Because Mom don't like men much. She don't even like to talk about my dad."

Blake wasn't sure what Nick meant by that statement and he was hardly going to pump the boy about Katherine's private life.

"Well, she must like some men," Blake reasoned. "She agreed to go on a date with me."

Nick scooted up on the edge of his seat and leaned closer to Blake. "Yeah. And that's got me stumped. I've been thinking she's gotten sick or something. When Mom walks in here, you take a real close look and see if anything looks funny to you."

Struggling to keep a straight face, Blake said, "Don't worry. I'll study her close."

Nick started to make some sort of reply when his mother suddenly appeared in the open doorway to the living room.

As Blake slowly rose to his feet, he realized his promise to Nick was going to be mighty easy to keep. Dressed casually in a red-and-white-flowered sundress with skinny straps and her long hair pinned behind one ear, she looked like an exotic flower in the middle of a jungle.

"Good evening, Blake. Sorry for keeping you waiting."

"No problem," he assured her. "Nick and I have been using the time to get acquainted."

Her skeptical gaze traveled back and forth between him and her son. "Really? Nick isn't much of a talker around strangers."

"We're not strangers now, though, are we, Nick?" Blake looked over at the boy and winked.

Grinning, Nick immediately jumped to his feet. "Gosh, no!" He turned his attention to his mother. "Blake's been telling me about his ranch. And he has lots of brothers and sisters. Did you know that, Mom? And one of his brothers rides bucking broncos! Isn't that something?"

Katherine's brows inched upward as she darted a look of surprise toward Blake. "It's something, all right," she told him, then gestured over her shoulder. "Go get your backpack. And be sure you have your toothbrush and pajamas."

After Nick disappeared from the room, Blake said, "I hope you're not making Nick stay overnight at the sitter's on my account. We can be back early if you need to pick him up before bedtime."

Katherine shook her head. "Don't worry. It's no problem. Nick is staying with his best friend, Shawn. His dad, Lash, loves for Nick to stay overnight. And Shawn stays with us quite often. Lash is a single parent like me, so it helps both of us to switch off with the babysitting duties. The Ralstons live just down the street, so it's not out of the way."

A single dad with a son the age of Nick? Blake wondered if he should be jealous of Katherine's neighbor, then promptly scolded himself for being such an idiot.

Just because she'd agreed to have one date with him, didn't mean he had exclusive tabs on the woman. She had the right to go out with whomever she pleased.

Shoving away that disturbing thought, Blake said, "It's good you have someone so trustworthy to watch Nick. And by the way, your son is quite a boy. You must be incredibly proud of him."

A faint smile touched her face. "He's everything to me. Without him...well, these past years would've been even harder to get through."

Blake expected her to make a comment about Nick taking after his father in certain ways, or how she hoped he'd grow up to be like the man she'd married, but she didn't. And suddenly Blake was wondering if Nick had been right about his mother not wanting to talk about her late husband.

Before Blake could think of a suitable reply to her remark, Nick bounced into the room with a backpack hooked around both shoulders.

"I got everything, Mom. And don't worry. Lash will make sure we brush our teeth. He doesn't let us get by with anything."

Chuckling, Katherine picked up a clutch bag from a nearby end table. "That's why he's the best babysitter you've ever had."

Blake picked up his cowboy hat from where he'd left it by the armchair and levered it onto his head. "Are we ready to go?" he asked.

"Ready," Katherine answered, then with a gentle scruff to the top of Nick's head, she urged her son toward the door.

Blake followed them onto the front porch, and while she dealt with locking the door, he wondered what might have happened if he'd dated Katherine twelve years ago before she'd left Wickenburg. Perhaps she and Nick would be living on Three Rivers now as his family. But at eighteen, she might've been too immature for a serious relationship between them. Especially one that would last. Either way, he couldn't change the past, he realized. But starting tonight, he was definitely going to try to change the course of his future.

"Since you said you wanted to keep things casual, I didn't make dinner reservations," Blake said as he braked for a stop sign. "Have you thought about where you'd like to eat? Or what you'd like to do?"

Katherine glanced over at him. For Blake, dressing casually meant a pale blue Western shirt that had most likely cost more than her monthly grocery bill, dark blue jeans and a pair of brown, square-toed alligator boots. With his black cowboy hat lying on the console between them, she had a full view of the dark tousled waves of hair edging over the tops of his ears and onto the collar of his shirt. He looked like a man who knew exactly what he wanted and, once he got it, wouldn't hesitate to fight to keep it. To say the man was attractive would be like calling a hurricane a gentle breeze.

She clasped her hands together on her lap as though she needed to prevent herself from reaching across the seat and touching him. "This is probably going to sound silly to you, but I'd like to take a drive through the mountains toward Prescott and eat at some little spot on the side of the road. Is that okay with you?"

He looked over at her and she noticed one corner of his lips was curved faintly upward. The expression was hardly a smile, she decided, yet it was as sexy as heck.

He said, "That sounds absolutely okay with me."

Relieved, she felt compelled to explain her choice.

"I'm not much for fancy, Blake. That's probably hard for a man like you to understand."

His grunt was a mocking sound. "A man like me? I'm hardly black-tie-and-tails, Katherine."

A blush stung her cheeks. "No. But, well, you know what I'm getting at. I wasn't raised like you."

With his gaze fixed firmly on the highway, he said, "Look, Katherine, I thought we'd hashed out all of that. Sure, I remember your parents' little house, where you were raised as a kid. Nobody had to tell me that your family didn't own much. But that has nothing to do with you as a person. Besides, you've grown above all of that. Seems to me, you've been doing very well for yourself and your son."

She smoothed a hand over the hem of her dress. "Yes, things are much better now. Financially speaking, that is. But with Dad gone, my mother too bitter to really enjoy life and my brother keeping his distance, I can't help but wish things had been different. For them and for me and Nick."

"I'm sure you wish things had been different for your late husband, too."

A chill settled over her. Clearly, he'd noticed she'd left Nick's father off her list. "Talking about Cliff isn't something I want to do tonight," she said stiffly.

"Hmm. Nick says you never want to talk about his father."

She stared at his profile. "Nick told you that?"

He glanced in her direction. "Sorry. I shouldn't have mentioned it. But I'm curious as to why you want to avoid the subject of your late husband. Is it because you loved him so much that remembering hurts?"

Katherine groaned. This was supposed to be a date, not a question-and-answer session, she thought crossly.

"It's not that. And I'm not trying to keep Nick from learning about his father. Well, maybe I am in some ways," she glumly admitted. "You see, I'd rather Nick only know about the good parts of his father. It would only hurt my son to learn how his father changed from a loving husband into a man driven by an obsessive need for money."

She paused and waited for him to make some sort of reply. When he remained silent, it was obvious he was expecting her to explain further.

"I had hoped that having a child would help," she went on in a strained voice, "but my getting pregnant actually made things worse. By the time Nick was born, Cliff hardly noticed he had a child. It's no wonder Nick says he can't remember his father. Cliff never spent enough time with his son to make any memories. He was too busy making money."

Blake steered the truck onto Highway 93, and as they headed north, Katherine couldn't help but wonder what he must be thinking about her and her marriage. No doubt he was probably telling himself this was the first and last date he'd have with Katherine O'Dell.

She was about to apologize for sounding so sharp, when he suddenly spoke.

"If my math is correct, Nick must have only been about three when his father died. That's too young for a child to remember much of anything."

Sighing, she looked at him. "Maybe that's a good thing. I don't know anymore. I expect when Nick gets a little older, he's going to start asking more questions about his father. I dread that time, because I can't lie to him. It wouldn't be right."

"No. Lying wouldn't be good. But maybe by the time Nick does start asking those questions, he'll already have another father," Blake suggested. "And the truth won't hurt so much."

Katherine stared at her clasped hands. "I honestly doubt that's going to happen. I can't see myself marrying again."

Another stretch of silence passed and then he said, "Nick wants brothers and sisters."

Her gaze slid over his chiseled features. "I can't believe he was telling you that sort of thing. He doesn't talk about private matters to anyone but me—and sometimes his buddy Shawn."

He shrugged one shoulder. "I guess Nick decided I was someone he could confide in. So what are you going to do about it?"

She frowned at him. "Do about what?"

"About giving him some siblings."

His nerve astounded her. She'd been acquainted with the Hollister family for as long as she could remember. And yes, throughout her teenage years, she'd had a crush on Blake. But she didn't know him in a personal way. Not even well enough to call herself a close friend. So what made him think he could talk to her about such things?

"Do you really think that's any of your business?"

His grin was a bit suggestive and even more endearing.

He said, "Probably not. But I hope to make it my business before the evening is over."

If Katherine had any sense at all, she'd tell him to turn the truck around and take her home. She didn't need some man digging into the deepest part of her. She didn't want him prying at the locked-away spot where she harbored her hopes and dreams. And she especially didn't need a man like Blake, who'd been born into a loving family and a home where he'd never lacked for anything, telling her what she or her son needed in their lives. And yet, she didn't want to go home. She didn't want this evening with Blake to end. Even though he was making her think about uncomfortable things, he was also making her feel more alive than she'd felt in years.

"I suppose you have a right to hope," she murmured.

He didn't make any sort of reply and his silence made the cab of the truck feel even more crowded with his presence. In spite of the air-conditioner vents blowing in her direction, she could practically feel the heat emanating from his body and hear the soft in and out of his breathing.

Swallowing hard, she purposely stared out the passenger window and tried to concentrate on the open landscape. With each passing mile, the terrain appeared to be growing a bit greener. Here and there, huge rock formations towered into the sky, while on the lower slopes of the gentle hills, sage bloomed purple.

After a few moments, the rugged beauty of the land began to soothe her jumpy nerves and before long she was gasping with delight. "Look, Blake, at the water hole! There's a big herd of antelope. Aww—and all those babies! They're beautiful!"

He glanced at the wildlife. "Looks like this area has been blessed with a bit of rain. Grass has greened the slopes and given the antelope and deer plenty to eat."

She stared at the herd of animals until they were completely out of view, then looked over at him. "I have to admit that living in San Diego was nice. But I missed Arizona," she said wistfully. "The desert and the saguaros. The rock bluffs and pine-covered mountains. And all the deer and antelope."

"You forgot to add the blistering heat and months without rain. Along with the rattlesnakes, horned lizards and javelina," he added jokingly.

She smiled. "Strange, isn't it? That a person can get attached to such a rugged place."

"Hmm. It's all I've ever known. So it doesn't seem strange to me. I'd feel stifled if I had to live in a city." He cast a curious glance in her direction. "Is that one of the reasons you decided to stay in Wickenburg after your father died? Because you missed this area?"

She took a moment to think about his question. "I'll be honest, Blake, twelve years ago when I left with Mom and my brother, I never expected to see the place again. I thought I'd never want to return to Arizona. You see, when we left Wickenburg, I had high hopes that my life would change. I desperately wanted to better myself. But my life made turns I never expected. And along the way I think I forgot that better doesn't always equal happiness."

"No. Not always," he quietly agreed.

Emotions filled her throat and she tried to clear away the lump before she spoke. "This is probably going to sound terrible to you, but I dreaded coming back to Wickenburg. I dreaded seeing the place and seeing Dad. There were plenty of things I didn't want to be reminded of. But when I walked into our old house and my father reached for my hand… I can't explain it, but for the first time in years I felt truly at home."

"Maybe that's because you felt needed."

Needed? She stared out at the desert hills, yet instead of seeing the rocky slopes covered with creosote brush and cholla cactus, she was seeing her father as she'd seen him as a child. Staggering home from an evening spent at the local bar. He'd always been knocking things over and spilling food in the kitchen, then yelling at her mother to clean up the mess. And Paulette had always dutifully obeyed his orders. She'd never complained or asked her husband to change his foul ways. She'd simply bided her time until her children had finished high school and then she'd slapped him with a divorce. Oddly enough, the dismantlement of his family had devastated Avery Anderson.

Shoving at the sad memories, she finally said, "My father did need me in a physical sense. To do the things he couldn't do for himself. But I never once thought of him needing me in an emotional way. Maybe because… when I was growing up, he hid himself behind a bottle. Thankfully, these last few years he remained completely sober. But I think it was hard for him to let me or anyone see the real Avery."

When he didn't make an immediate reply, Katherine wondered if she'd shocked him by bringing up the subject of her father's drinking. Although she couldn't imagine why it would have surprised him. Everyone in town had known about Avery Anderson's problem with alcohol.

Another mile passed before Blake asked, "What did Nick think of his grandfather?"

"They got along great. The only thing Nick didn't like was that his grandfather wasn't well enough to do outside things with him. Like fishing or camping. But they played checkers and other games together. Now that Dad is gone, I'm glad that my son had two years with his grandfather."

"What about Nick's other grandparents? Does he visit them often?"

Katherine shook her head. "Cliff never knew his

parents. He went into the foster-home program when he was about two years old."

"I see."

Did he really? Katherine doubted it. Blake Hollister's life had always been stable. Surrounded by a big family with a home that had been anchored in the same spot for more than a hundred years, he'd never had to doubt whether he was loved or had a roof over his head from one week to the next.

Biting back a sigh, she said, "I shouldn't have spoken so bitterly about Cliff a few minutes ago. Down deep, I think he never got over being passed from one family to the next. Of never having much of his own. He worked like a demon for financial security."

"He probably believed that would fill his emotional void, too," Blake said thoughtfully.

Surprised that he'd put his finger on Cliff's problem, she darted a look at him. "You're right, Blake. But that's over and in the past. Now I just want to raise my son to be a happy, well-rounded person."

To her surprise, he reached over and folded his hand around hers. "You needn't worry, Katherine. You've already got him off to a great start." He squeezed her fingers ever so slightly. "And I apologize. I had no right to press you to talk about your private life. It's just that I like you, Katherine, and I want to know all about you."

How could she be cross with him when just the touch of his hand was filling her with a swirl of emotions that warmed her and lifted her spirits?

"There's no need for you to apologize, Blake."

He smiled at her. "Well, just the same. What do you say we start all over? Let's talk about the weather."

His suggestion pulled a laugh from her. "I think I can safely say it's hot and dry."

He made a show of studying the cloudless sky stretched in front of them. "Looks hot and dry to me, too. So we have that topic covered. What else would you like to talk about?"

"I'd love to hear about Three Rivers and all that goes on there. But if you'd rather not talk about your job, I'll pick a different subject."

Blake couldn't believe what he was hearing. Since his broken engagement, the few women he'd dated hadn't been the least bit interested in his family's ranch, other than the profit it made. All of them had preferred talking about Phoenix and the excitement the city had to offer, like shopping, music concerts and big sporting events. And once those subjects had been thoroughly hashed to death, he'd listened to recounts of European vacations or days lounging on a tropical island.

Frowning doubtfully, he glanced at her. "Are you sure you want to hear about cowboy stuff? Most of it isn't pretty. You might be bored."

Smiling softly, she squeezed his fingers. "I would love to hear about you and Three Rivers."

Chapter Four

Less than a half hour later, Blake and Katherine stopped at a little roadside café in Congress. As they sat in a worn, wooden booth, eating jalapeño-spiced burgers on sourdough buns, Katherine continued to listen intently as he described a typical workday schedule at the ranch.

"I don't know how you keep up with everything." She reached for her iced tea. "Your mother must really depend on you."

"Mom depends on all of us," he told her. "Not just me."

As Blake watched her sip from the straw in her glass, he decided her lips looked even sexier now that the food had erased her lipstick.

"I'm sure she does—depend on all of you. But you've stepped into your father's position. Being manager of a ranch the size of Three Rivers would carry a heavy weight."

So she understood that much, he thought with a sense of relief. "To be honest, Katherine, after Dad died, I didn't want the job."

Frowning with confusion, she lowered a forked french fry back to her plate. "Didn't want it? But a few minutes ago you told me you went to college to get a degree in ranch management. Obviously you were training for the job—I mean eventually."

"That's right. I did get my degree. But I thought... Well, none of us were expecting Dad to be taken from us so soon. I thought I had years and years before I'd have to take over the management job. When Dad died, I was too young and inexperienced to step into his boots." Shaking his head, he let out a self-deprecating groan. "Hell. That was a stupid thing for me to say. If I lived to be a hundred years old, I could never fill my dad's boots."

The faint smile on her lips was full of empathy. "You're wrong to sell yourself short, Blake. You've kept the ranch solvent and growing. I'm sure your father would be very proud."

"Proud. I can only hope," he said ruefully while wondering what Katherine would think if he told her that he and his brothers suspected their father had been murdered. She'd probably think the whole family was crazy or paranoid. And maybe she'd be right, he thought. After five long years, there was still no concrete evidence to prove their theory right.

She suddenly reached across the tabletop and touched the tip of her fingers to his. "You know," she said softly, "I wasn't prepared to be a widow or a single mother, either. And sometimes I really doubt the job I'm doing with Nick. But in the end, all you and I can do is try our best. And hope we've made a positive mark on our families."

Something about the touch of her warm fingers, and the soft encouragement of her words, touched him in a deep and powerful way. And before he realized what he was doing, he captured her hand in his and drew it toward him.

"Thank you, Katherine. I needed to remember I'm not the only one who's lost a loved one."

She looked away from him, and for one brief second, Blake thought he saw a look of guilt in her eyes. What was that about? he wondered. Her father or her late husband?

Drawing her hand from his, she reached for her handbag. "Um, if you're finished eating, we should probably be going…before we run out of daylight."

Recognizing the moment between them was over, he said, "I'll take care of the check and we'll be on our way."

They left the quiet little café and headed north toward Yarnell. Behind them, the sun had slipped below the desert floor, sending long shadows over the hills.

"Looks like we should've started earlier," Blake commented. "By the time we reach the mountains near Prescott, it's going to be dark."

"No matter," she assured him. "I'll see them another time."

Another time. Yes, he definitely wanted more time with Katherine. But would she be willing to give it to him? From the moment they'd dropped off Nick at the Ralstons', Blake had felt Katherine put up an emotional guard of sorts. Whether that was because she didn't trust him or herself, he could only wonder.

"Well, we still have a bit of daylight left. Maybe we can make Yarnell Hill Lookout before it gets dark. I'm sure you've seen it before, but it's always worth the look," he said as he helped her into the cab of the truck.

As she settled herself in the seat, she said, "You're probably not going to believe this, but I've only heard about the lookout. I've never actually been there."

About to shut the door, he paused and looked at her with surprise. "You've really never visited the lookout?"

She shook her head. "My parents never took us sightseeing. And the few dates I had as a teenager, I wasn't allowed to leave Wickenburg. Since I've returned, I've not had any real reason to drive up this way."

"Well, you're in for a treat," he promised.

For the next ten miles, Blake pushed the speed limit until they reached the summit of Yarnell Hill and the lookout located on the downhill side.

To his delight, the round parking area surrounded by a low rock railing was presently empty. He pulled the truck to a stop a few feet away from the barrier and killed the motor, while across from him, Katherine leaned forward in her seat to get a better view of the panoramic scene of the canyon below.

"Oh, Blake! This is gorgeous!" she exclaimed. "Especially like this—with twilight falling."

The look of wonder on her face caused his chest to swell with unexpected emotions. Just knowing he'd pleased her in such a small way made him feel like he could jump a mountain.

"Would you like to get out and walk around?" he suggested.

She flashed him a wide smile. "Oh, yes, let's do."

By the time he'd exited the truck and opened the door

to help her down, she'd already flung off her seat belt and was eagerly reaching for his hand.

"Careful. Don't get your high heel hung in the running board," he urged as he assisted her to the ground. "Sorry. No one in my family drives a car or I would've brought it tonight. The rough road in and out of the ranch puts too much wear and tear on a vehicle."

Laughing lightly, she said, "Blake, you make it sound like I'm a princess who needs a gilded coach. Your truck is very nice. It's far more luxurious than my little economy car."

"Some women think they're just work vehicles."

Her expression suddenly serious, she looked up at him. "I'm not *some women*."

A hot southwest wind was playing with her dark hair. When a strand settled on her lips, his fingers itched to reach up and tuck it back in place. But he didn't want to make any sort of move that would cause her to shy away. Having her this close had to be enough. At least, for tonight, he thought.

"No. I'm beginning to see you're definitely not that kind," he murmured. He released a long breath, settled a hand against her back and urged her forward. "Let's go over to the wall."

As they walked slowly, side by side, he could hardly concentrate on the view of the landscape. Instead, the warmth of her back was radiating through his hand and up his arm, while the sweet, flowery scent of her competed with the faint odor of sage carried by the wind.

"So do you come over this way very often?" she asked.

"No. I can't remember the last time. I'm afraid when Emily-Ann told you I don't go to town much, she was speaking the truth. I don't go much of anywhere. Sometimes I go with Holt to a special cattle or horse auction. But for the most part, the ranch takes most of my attention."

Now she was probably thinking he was like her late husband, Blake thought ruefully. So driven to make money, he had no time for anything else. Lenore had definitely thought so, but his ex-fiancée hadn't understood that his devotion to the ranch was all about family, rather than money. He could only hope that Katherine was different.

She asked, "You like staying home? Or do you just not like getting out and socializing?"

"A little of both, I guess," he admitted.

A dimple appeared in her left cheek and Blake was shocked about how much he wanted to press his lips to the soft little dent.

"If that's the case, then I feel very special that you left the ranch just to have a night out with me."

His arm slid around the back of her waist. "I'm glad. Uh, that I've made you feel special," he murmured, then added in an even lower voice, "And that I'm with you tonight."

She looked up at him, and from the wary look in her eyes, Blake could tell she was feeling the same magnetic pull that was drawing him closer.

"Blake, I like you very much," she said in a soft, almost wistful voice. "But I'm not sure that I—"

Her words ended abruptly as she quickly turned her head away. Blake caught her chin with his thumb and forefinger and pulled her face back around to his.

"That you what?" he prompted. "Should be here with me? Like this?"

Even in the twilight, he could see a stain of red darken her cheeks.

"Something...like that," she murmured brokenly.

"Then maybe I should convince you that us being together is...very right."

He saw her eyebrows shoot upward, but that was the only reaction he noticed before he lowered his head and settled his lips over hers.

The intimate contact seemed to momentarily stun her and she went stock-still. And then suddenly the rigidness in her shoulders eased beneath his hands and her soft lips yielded to his.

The tiny signal of surrender was all it took for Blake to wrap his arms around her and let his kiss do all the talking.

Before Blake had arrived for their date this evening, Katherine had wondered if he might kiss her and then she'd promptly told herself she was letting her imagination get way out of hand. She and Blake were just now getting to know each other, she'd mentally argued, and it was far too soon for physical intimacy. Yet as soon as they'd left Nick at the Ralstons' and started out of town, something had changed. Each word they'd spoken, every glance they'd exchanged, had seemed to be ripe with sexual tension.

Now the hungry probe of his lips was causing her senses to spin like a tumbleweed racing across the desert floor. She couldn't think beyond the heady taste of his mouth, the feel of his hard arms wrapped around her and the warmth of his body seeping into hers.

This was too good. This was everything she'd ever wanted. Everything she'd never had or expected to find. But like a lovely dream, it would end. And she'd be left with little more than a memory.

The desperate thoughts racing through her mind gave

her the strength to break the contact of their lips and move a step away from him. Yet ending the embrace did little to ease her chaotic senses.

As she stared out at the darkening canyon, her heart was beating fast, chanting a plea for her to turn back to him and reach for any kind of affection he was willing to give her.

"Katherine, I—"

Not wanting to hear an awkward apology for something that had felt so special, she quickly intervened. "You don't need to say anything, Blake. The kiss was very nice. But I wasn't expecting anything like this to happen."

"Why not?" he asked gently. "You're an attractive woman. And though my family calls me a stuffed shirt at times, I'm not a cold fish."

Cold? The idea was laughable. His kiss had been as hot as the Arizona sun.

"That's not what I meant." She forced herself to look at him and then wished she hadn't as she felt something inside her begin to melt. "I, uh, thought this was going to be just a friendly outing."

"It is." Turning toward her, he rested his hands on her shoulders. "We are…friends. And more…hopefully."

She didn't think it was possible for her heart to beat any faster, but somehow it managed to kick into an even higher gear. "I don't know what you mean by more, Blake, but I don't think I'm ready for anything other than…friends."

Dusk was spreading dark shadows all around them, but there was just enough light remaining to see his gaze was studying her face. The intensity of it sent a shiver rippling down her spine.

"You've been alone for a long time, Katherine. I'd think you were past ready to have a man in your life."

She began to tremble. Yes, she was past ready for a man's love. But Blake wasn't the right man. He'd gone for thirty-eight years without a wife or children. That proved he wasn't in any romance for the long haul.

"And you're expecting me to believe you're that man?" she asked, her voice little more than a hoarse whisper.

"Why not? My limbs all work and so do my senses. At least, most of them. I also have a home and a steady income. What more could you ask for? Other than maybe a sense of humor. And I'm trying to work on that."

Her urge to both laugh and cry caused a garbled groan to slip past her lips. "Oh, Blake, you're a wonderful man. It's me. For the past seven years I've been on my own. I get lonely at times, but no one has broken my heart. And that's the way I want things to stay."

"I don't plan on breaking your heart, Katherine."

She sounded like an idiot. But she couldn't explain that he was too good for her. Not because of his social standing. No, he was simply too good a man to get tangled up with a woman like her. A woman with so many emotional scars she wasn't sure she'd ever be able to give a man like Blake the love he deserved.

"No. Not intentionally. But that's not really important. We need to get off this subject and move on to something else."

Moving from under the grasp of his hands on her shoulders, she walked across the overlook and stared out at the night sky. But instead of taking in the beauty of the twinkling stars, she was reliving his heated kiss and the incredible pleasure that had flooded through her.

If she was a brave, confident woman, she would've slipped her arms around his neck and showed him just how much she wanted him. But she wasn't brave. She was still running from the past, and she knew if she stumbled the least bit, it would catch up to her.

Her dark thoughts were suddenly interrupted as his warm fingers wrapped around her upper arm and tugged her toward him.

"You think we should discuss the weather again?" he asked. "Well, I don't. In fact, I don't think we ought to talk about anything."

"Blake, I—"

Before she could utter a protest, his hands were cupping the sides of her face and the tip of his nose was brushing against hers.

"I think you want to kiss me," he murmured. "Just as much as I want to kiss you."

She couldn't deny the truth of his words and knew it would be futile to try. Especially when a reckless hand seemed to be pushing against her back, urging her to step into his arms.

A split second was all it took for her common sense to lose the battle, and with a groan of surrender, she slid her arms around his neck and tilted her hungry mouth up to his.

"I do want to kiss you, Blake. Very…much."

She'd barely had time to speak the last word before his lips swooped over hers and the passionate connection blotted out everything except the incredible pleasure pouring through every particle of her being.

His kiss was rough, ravaging her lips with a ferocity that left her legs weak and her senses dazed. Each time his mouth lifted for air, she thought it was all going to end. Instead, the longer the kiss went on, the more steam he seemed to be gathering. Over and over, his lips explored hers, filling her with a heat so intense she was on the verge of melting right there in his arms. When his tongue slipped past her teeth and began to mate with hers, she groaned deep in her throat, while her hands clenched a tight hold on the back of his neck.

The taste of his mouth filled up her senses and beckoned her body to arch into the hard warmth of his. At the same time, she felt his hands slipping down her back, cupping the cheeks of her bottom and drawing her hips tight against his.

Through the haze of her desire, she could feel his arousal and was shocked to think the effect she was having on him was as strong as the fire that had ignited inside her.

This couldn't stop now, she thought. It was all too good, too perfect to end.

But suddenly she felt his hands easing away from her hips, his mouth lifting from hers. When she finally found the strength to open her eyes, she saw his face hovering above hers and wondered why the mere space between their lips felt like a giant chasm.

"I, uh, think we'd better stop," he suggested as he drew in a ragged breath. "Before things get out of hand."

As far as Katherine was concerned, the kiss had gotten out of hand several minutes ago. But rather than use a bit of wisdom and step away from him, she'd chosen to throw caution to the wind. Now he was probably thinking she was some sort of sex-starved widow begging for any sort of physical attention he'd give her.

Her cheeks flaming with heat, she backed away from him until the space between them made it impossible for her to touch him.

"I don't know what happened, Blake. I'm...morti-fied."

A frown creased his features. "Mortified? It didn't feel like you were embarrassed to kiss me."

Groaning, she turned her back to him, "I wasn't! That's the problem. Another minute or two and we would've been tearing at each other's clothes, unable to stop."

His features softening, he moved a step toward her, and though she screamed at herself to keep a safe distance between them, she couldn't force her legs to move. Crazy or not, her body was aching for him, longing to feel his hard warmth wrapped around her.

"It felt damn good to me, Katherine."

Good? She'd felt euphoric. But then, he probably already figured that out from the way she'd wrapped herself around him.

He reached out and trailed his fingertips gently up and down her bare arm. "But you agreed to go on a date with me. Not get seduced. And I want us to get started off right."

"Started?" She practically screeched the word. "Right now I'm thinking the last thing we need to do is see each other again!"

He moved close enough to wrap his hands over her shoulders. The warm strength of his fingers pressing into her flesh caused her to close her eyes and wish for the strength to resist him.

"You're afraid of the flash fire between us, aren't you?" he asked gently. "You're terrified that we'll wind up in bed together and then everything will end in a heap of ashes. Right?"

Shocked that he'd read her thoughts so perfectly, her eyes flew open. "Why should we do that to each other?

Wouldn't it be better if we just smiled and waved at each other from across the street?"

Faint humor cocked one corner of his lips. "Waves and smiles are pleasant. But that's not enough to satisfy me."

She clenched her hands tightly together in an attempt to stop their trembling. "And what do you think it would take to…satisfy you?"

"Not what you're thinking," he mumbled, then with a hand against her back, he urged her in the direction of the truck. "Come on. I think we've seen enough of Yarnell Valley."

"Would someone please pass me the tortillas before my eggs get cold?"

The question came from Holt as a portion of the Hollister family began to eat a routine five o'clock breakfast in the Three Rivers dining room.

Vivian, the eldest sister of Blake's siblings, placed the container of warm tortillas within Holt's reach.

"Save some for the rest of us, would you?" she teased while sharing a conspiring wink with Blake, who was sitting next to her. "Reeva says this is the last batch of homemade tortillas she's making. From now on, you're getting store-bought."

Across from Vivian, Chandler, the second oldest of the siblings and the veterinarian of the family, let out a loud grunt. "That does it for me. From now on, I'll eat breakfast after I get to town. Copper Canyon has homemade tortillas. None of those rubber discs."

Near the head of the table, Maureen spoke up. "Oh, for heaven's sake, Viv. Quit pulling your brothers' legs. Reeva would never put anything store-bought on this table. The day she does will be the day she heads to the nursing home."

Blake and his brothers looked down the table at their mother. A tall, slender woman in her early sixties, her tanned complexion was a bit weathered from working outdoors in the Arizona sun. Her dark brown hair, threaded with a few streaks of silver, was shoulder-length but usually twisted up in a messy knot or pulled into a ponytail. She was still an attractive woman and very much a part of the day-to-day work on the ranch. She was also the glue that kept the family tightly adhered to one another.

"Hell, Mom, you're brutal," Holt told her.

She shot him a look that was meant to be stern but was anything but. "I'm going to be brutal if you curse at the table again."

Holt shook his head as he piled a mound of chorizo and eggs onto one of the tortillas and folded it over. "Poor Reeva. That's what she gets for years of service as the family cook. Her last golden years stuck away in an old folks' home. That's real appreciation, Mom."

"Who's going to be stuck in an old folks' home?"

Everyone at the table, including Blake, looked around as Reeva stepped into the dining room carrying a dish of cottage fries.

As she placed them at a spot on the table near Holt's plate, he said, "According to Mom, you are. For serving store-bought tortillas."

The bone-thin woman with a single steel-gray braid hanging down the center of her back let out an unladylike snort. "Don't you worry about it, Little Buck. I'll still be going when you're sitting in a chair with a blanket over your lap watching reruns of *Stoney Burke*."

Reeva marched out of the dining room and Holt

looked over to Blake, as though he needed his older brother to defend him.

"Why does she have to call me that? Nobody has called me by that wretched nickname since I was twelve years old. And who the hell is Stoney Burke?"

Maureen leveled another stern look of warning at her younger son, then ruined the whole effect with a soft chuckle. "You have to remember Reeva is nearly seventy-two. *Stoney Burke* was a television series back in the 1960s about a saddle bronc rider. Sort of fits you, Holt, I'd say."

Holt threw out his chest. "Must have been a good-looking guy."

"He was."

Vivian groaned and rolled her eyes. "Always the Romeo," she muttered.

Picking up her coffee cup, Maureen leaned back in her chair. "Speaking of Romeo, how was your date last night, Blake?"

Blake nearly spewed the mouthful of food he was chewing right back onto his plate. "Mom! I hadn't told anyone about that—except you!"

Unaffected by his reaction, she sipped her coffee, then smiled. "Well, it's sure nothing to keep secret."

Chandler stared at Blake, while Holt appeared to be momentarily stunned.

"My big brother on a date?" Holt finally asked. "Who's the girl?"

Blake cleared his throat. "Katherine O'Dell. Her name used to be Anderson. She's a widow now."

"Katherine? Oh, yes, I remember her," Vivian recalled. "She was a quiet, shy girl back in high school. I thought she'd left Wickenburg a long time ago."

"She returned to Wickenburg to care for her father,"

Blake said, feeling more uncomfortable by the minute. It wasn't that he was embarrassed to have his siblings learn he'd gone on a date. He just wasn't ready for a bunch of awkward questions. Not when he'd been sitting here mentally reliving every moment he'd had Katherine wrapped in his arms.

The explosive passion between them had shocked Blake. To say the experience had left him rattled would be putting it mildly. Never had he wanted to make love to any woman the way he'd wanted Katherine. He was still wondering where he'd found the willpower to put an end to their embrace. And wondering, too, what might have happened if he'd allowed it to go on.

"I remember hearing the old man died," Chandler commented. "The bottle finally got him, I suppose."

A pang of regret passed through Blake. Compared to most, Avery Anderson might not have been an admirable person. But he'd been Katherine's father and losing him had hurt her.

"The man suffered a stroke," Blake said bluntly.

Chandler cast him a rueful glance. "Sorry. I shouldn't have said anything."

"You haven't answered Mom's question," Holt interjected. "How was this hot date of yours?"

His time with Katherine hadn't been hot, Blake thought. It had been more like sizzling. A fact that had him wondering if he'd already burned his chances to build any sort of relationship with her.

Looking down at his plate, he said, "Nice. And that's all you're going to hear out of me."

Holt let out a loud guffaw, which was a typical reaction from his younger brother. From the time he was a little scamp, Holt had been cocky, confident and all cowboy. He loved horses and women, in that order.

And never took the latter seriously. Sometimes Blake wished he could be more like Holt. Then it wouldn't matter if he ever had a wife or children. But his hopes and dreams were far different than Holt's. Blake wanted a family of his own.

With a glance of warning at Holt, his mother said, "Frankly, I'd love to see Katherine again. I hope you'll invite her out soon, Blake."

"I'll invite her," Blake said. "But I won't promise she'll come."

How could he? He wasn't even sure Katherine would agree to go out with him again, much less show up for a family dinner.

Chapter Five

The following Monday morning at work, Katherine was attempting to juggle her attention between the ringing phone on her desk and the ledger sheet on her monitor screen. Through a row of windows to her right, the sun was already bright in a cloudless sky. The varsity baseball team was on the field practicing, while nearby a maintenance man was mowing grass around a stand of bleachers. So far it was a routine school day at St. Francis Academy, yet Katherine was struggling to get back in the work groove.

For the past forty-eight hours she'd tried to shove thoughts of Blake Hollister out of her mind, but so far everything about the man seemed to be stuck in her brain. Kissing him had been wildly delicious and she'd not wanted those passionate moments in his arms to end. However, now that a bit of time had passed since Friday night, she'd come to realize it was more than

Blake's kiss that had mesmerized her. His dark hair and rugged profile, the husky note in his voice, his reserved smiles and even the way he wore his clothes had all fascinated her. A woman couldn't think straight with that kind of stuff going round in her head.

She was staring blankly out the window when Prudence Keyes, the superintendent of the private high school, stepped through the open doorway between their offices.

"What's wrong?" she asked. "A headache?"

Katherine jerked her attention around to the other woman. "Oh. No. I was just…thinking."

"About a sandy beach and a tall margarita?"

Katherine swiveled her chair until she was facing Prudence. "No. But it does sound nice."

"To you and me both," Prudence said wryly, then placed a slip of paper on the corner of Katherine's desk. "Here's all the info on the math books. I want you to go ahead and place the order today. I realize this school year is about to end, but sometimes these things are put on back order and then we'd have to scramble around to find another distributor. Since we already have the money appropriated, I don't see any need to wait."

Nodding, Katherine said, "I'll get it done this morning."

"Has Coach Lyons handed in any information on the basketball jerseys yet? We need to get those ordered also."

"No. He hasn't. And from what I understand, he'll be at a coaches conference in Phoenix today and tomorrow."

Prudence heaved out an exasperated breath. "Jocks! All they think about is winning. Everything else is chicken feed."

Katherine stared at her boss. At thirty-five, Prudence

had been divorced for a few years. With a petite figure and caramel-brown hair curling over her shoulders, she was a lovely woman. Her delicate features were soft and an aura of pure femininity surrounded her. Only Katherine and a few others were aware of her iron-fisted approach to running St. Francis Academy. As far as her divorce went, Prudence never discussed the reason for her broken marriage and Katherine never asked.

"That is what a coach is supposed to do, Prudence," Katherine reminded her. "Focus on having a winning season."

"A man should have more than one responsibility. But God knows some of them can't even handle one, much less two or three."

Katherine didn't often hear this much cynical sting in Prudence's voice. Before she could ask the other woman what had started her Monday off so badly, Prudence eased a hip onto the corner of her desk.

"Speaking of men," she said, "you've not mentioned how your date with Mr. Hollister went. Did you have a nice time?"

Try as she might, Katherine couldn't stop a wave of heat from coloring her face.

"The evening was...very nice."

Folding her arms against her breasts, Prudence regarded her thoughtfully. "Nice. Hmm. Nice enough to see him again?"

Other than Prudence and her babysitter, Lash, Katherine hadn't told anyone about her date. And she'd only confided in Prudence because she was the closest female friend she had in town. Now she almost wished she hadn't. She didn't want to discuss Blake Hollister. Not when the mere thought of him turned her into a helpless romantic fool.

"I'm not sure about that," Katherine hedged.

"You mean, not sure he'll ask you again? Or not sure you'll agree to go?"

Sighing, Katherine leaned back in the big leather desk chair and crossed her legs. "Oh, he's asked me already," she admitted. "I got a call from him last night. He's invited me to dinner at his family's ranch."

"Dinner at Three Rivers. Mmm. After one date? You must've made quite an impression on the man."

Impression? She probably had, Katherine thought ruefully. That she was ripe and ready for a lover. But that simply wasn't the case. For the past few years, sex had pretty much dropped off her radar. The only thing she'd been focused on was caring for her ailing father and seeing that Nick had the kind of home a child needed. Now Blake had come along and stirred up some sort of monster inside her. All she could think about was the way he'd kissed her and the way she'd kissed him back.

"Not really," she said. "Blake is a homebody. He's probably invited me to Three Rivers for dinner so he won't have to leave the ranch."

Prudence grimaced. "If that's the reason, I'd be telling him to go take a flying leap off the south rim of the Grand Canyon."

Katherine refrained from rolling her eyes, but just barely. "Why the south rim? Is it better for leaping?" she asked drolly.

"It's the nearest to us," Prudence quipped, then straightened away from the desk. "In all seriousness, Katherine, I'm glad you're seeing Mr. Hollister. You're the kind of woman who needs a man in her life. And from what I gather, no one can say a bad thing about him."

"That doesn't mean he'd be right for me," Katherine replied. "Why would you have the idea that I need a man, anyway? I've managed on my own for years now."

Prudence gave her a wan smile. "There are other things a man can give you besides financial security."

Not according to her late husband. Cliff had believed financial security was the cure-all. He'd never stopped to notice that she and their baby had needed love and attention. He'd never realized that she would have gladly traded their comfortable suburban home for a three-room shack in order to get back the man she'd first married.

Shoving at those dark thoughts, she said, "I don't know why you're telling me this, Prudence. You're not married and you're happy."

The smile on her face took on a mocking twist. "Am I?"

Katherine was still trying to come up with an answer to that loaded question when the other woman suddenly turned all business and started toward the door.

"I'm headed to the cafeteria. The cooks are complaining about one of the ovens and a walk-in freezer is trying to quit. While I check out the kitchen problem, see if you can find Coach Lyons's cell number. I'm going to give him a reminder about those jerseys."

"I'll get right on it."

At the door, Prudence paused and looked over her shoulder. "Kat, we women don't often get a chance to have a real man—a good man in our lives. Don't let this chance for you slip away."

Katherine had been given one chance with Cliff and she'd not been woman enough to hold his interest. With Blake she'd have to compete with Three Rivers for his attention. She'd be a fool to think she'd come out the winner.

"I'll think about your advice, Prudence."

Smiling, the superintendent turned and left the office.

"Mom, you've been driving forever," Nick grumbled. "If you keep going, we're gonna be in California."

Katherine glanced over at her son, who was leaning forward in the seat, staring out the passenger window. Since Nick had been a town boy all his life, it wasn't often he got to see the rugged countryside. But after several miles, he was restless to be out of the car.

"You must be sleeping through geography class. California is to the west. We're traveling east."

He groaned. "Aww, Mom, you know what I mean. How much longer till we get to Three Rivers Ranch?"

"It isn't too much farther."

As best as she could remember, the ranch's entrance was only a mile or so away. But more than twelve years had passed since she'd visited Three Rivers Ranch with her mother. She'd not remembered the dirt road being this rough. It felt like her car was being rattled to pieces. She wished now that she'd taken Blake up on his offer to come into town and take them to the ranch. But she'd wanted to save him the bother. Plus, she'd wanted to have her own vehicle with her, just in case she decided to make a quick exit.

"There's a sign!" Nick eagerly pointed to an entrance up ahead on the right of the road. "Bar X Ranch," he said. "Darn, that's not it."

"No. Blake's brother Joseph lives there with his wife. He's a deputy sheriff."

Clearly impressed by this news, Nick looked at her. "Wow! That would be neat to have a brother who's a deputy sheriff. And another brother who rides broncs. Blake's lucky, huh?"

Nick wants brothers and sisters. What are you going to do about it?

Try as she might, she'd not been able to forget Blake's words. His observation was something Katherine lived with every day. Nick truly wanted siblings. He brought up the subject often, and each time she listened to his wishes, the guilt inside Katherine grew darker and heavier. But what could she do about it? She couldn't marry the first man available just to give Nick a brother or sister. Ending up in another bad marriage would be far worse than Nick not having siblings.

You should feel guilty, Katherine. You haven't tried to change the direction of your life. You haven't allowed yourself to look at any man in a romantic way. No, these past years you've worked very hard to steer clear of love and marriage. Because you want to keep your life safe and uncomplicated. But what is that doing to your son?

Glancing at Nick, she did her best to smile. "Yes, Blake is very lucky. He has a third brother who's a veterinarian, too."

"Wow, that would be neat to get to doctor animals. Are we going to meet all of Blake's brothers and sisters when we get to Three Rivers?"

"I'm not sure. But whomever we meet, I want you to remember to be polite."

His expression said he was clearly offended. "Aww, Mom. I won't mess up. I'll remember to keep my elbows off the table and use my salad fork first. And I won't ask personal questions. Like money and marriage, and stuff. That's boring, anyway."

Thank goodness he was still young enough to consider such things boring, Katherine thought. In a few more years he'd be all grown and dealing with the responsibilities that came with being an adult. For now she wanted to make sure his childhood was stable and happy.

She glanced at him and smiled. "Are you glad we're visiting Three Rivers this evening?"

"Sure. I want to see Blake again. He seems like a neat guy."

"I'm glad you think so."

From the corner of her eye, she could see a wide grin on his face. "Yeah. Guess it would be kinda bad if I didn't like your boyfriend."

Boyfriend. She'd had one date with the man and already Nick considered Blake as someone important in his mother's life. She wasn't sure whether Nick's view of the situation was a child's naivety, or if she was the one who refused to see what was developing with her and Blake.

"Is that what you think he is? My boyfriend?"

Nick's boyish chuckle was smug. "Well, he's not your husband yet."

Katherine came close to stomping the brake and stopping the car in the middle of the road. For Nick to call Blake her boyfriend was one thing, but her son's imagination seemed to be making a giant leap. She needed to make it very plain to him that she had no plans to marry anyone. Especially a cattle baron whose family owned a fair portion of Yavapai County.

But Three Rivers Ranch was only a few minutes away and now wasn't the time for such a lecture. She didn't want to ruin Nick's evening before it ever got started. For now she'd ignore her son's provocative remark. Tomorrow would be soon enough to set him straight on the matter.

With that decision made, she pressed on the gas and braced herself for the moment she'd see Blake again.

On Three Rivers Ranch, Blake and his eleven-year-old niece, Hannah, were sitting on the front porch of the ranch house when the girl spotted Katherine's dark red car coming up the long, tree-lined drive to the house.

"Here they come, Uncle Blake." Wearing jeans and boots and a T-shirt with the image of a running horse on the front, the blond-haired girl jumped from the lawn chair. "Let's go down to the driveway and wait for them."

"Wouldn't that look a bit overeager?" Blake asked, even though he was already rising from his chair.

She looked at him and rolled her eyes, as though she had little patience with grown-up games. "Uncle Blake, you are excited to see her, aren't you? Why not show it?"

Why not, indeed? Blake thought. All week long, he'd been counting the hours until this Friday evening arrived. It would be silly to hide his feelings now.

"You're right. Let's go."

The two of them left the porch and stood at the edge of the circle drive. By the time Katherine stopped the car in a graveled parking area beneath one of the cottonwoods, Blake was there to open the door for her. On the opposite side of the car Hannah was already waiting for Nick to climb out.

"Looks like you made the trip all in one piece," he said as he gave her a helping hand onto the ground. "Did you have any trouble remembering the way out here?"

She smiled at him and Blake was amazed at the feelings rushing through him. He wasn't a happy-smiley-type guy, so why was Katherine's grin making him feel goofy with pleasure?

"No trouble. I was surprised to see very little has changed between here and Wickenburg." Her gaze swung to the three-storied white house, with its shaded wraparound porch. "Oh my, this all looks just like the last time I was here and that was twelve years ago. Except the wicker chairs had green cushions instead of red. And the tree at the north end of the porch wasn't nearly that tall."

That she remembered his home so vividly touched a soft spot in him. "That's right. Mom changes the cushions when they start to wear thin." He reached for her arm. "Everyone is out on the back patio. We'll go through the house."

Blake glanced over to see Hannah already had Nick by the hand and was leading him away from the car. His niece didn't possess one shy bone in her body and thankfully Katherine's son appeared to be thoroughly enjoying the female attention.

"Hannah, you and Nick come here," Blake called to his niece. "I want to introduce you to his mother."

The two kids skirted the front of the car and stood hand in hand in front of Blake and Katherine.

"Hello again, Nick," Blake told the boy. "Welcome to Three Rivers Ranch."

"Hello, sir," Nick politely replied, then cast a shy grin at Hannah.

Hannah giggled and smiled back at him.

Oh, to have the innocent trust of a child, Blake thought. He glanced at Katherine to see she was also taking note of the sudden bond forming between the two youngsters.

"Hannah, I want you to meet Nick's mother, Mrs. O'Dell," Blake said. "And, Katherine, this is Vivian's daughter, Hannah."

Hannah thrust out her free hand to Katherine. "Nice to meet you, ma'am."

Smiling gently, Katherine shook the girl's hand. "It's my pleasure, Hannah. And you look very much like I remember your mother."

"Thanks! Everyone tells me that, so I guess it must be true." She turned an imploring look on Blake. "May I take Nick down to the barn and show him my horse?"

Nick turned wide eyes on Hannah. "Oh, wow! You have a horse? Do you ride it?"

Hannah nodded. "Sure. All the time. But we can't ride him this evening. It's too close to dinner. But you can pet him and give him treats."

Blake looked at Katherine. "Hannah knows her way around the barn and the horses. It's fine with me, if it's okay with you."

Katherine studied the two children for a long moment, before finally conceding. "All right. As long as you stay right with Hannah," she told Nick.

Both children were so exuberant they were practically dancing on their toes.

"Don't worry, Mrs. O'Dell, I'll take good care of him." Hannah tugged on Nick's hand. "C'mon. Let's run!"

They raced off toward the barn with shrieks of laughter and Blake noticed a tiny frown suddenly creasing the middle of Katherine's forehead.

"Don't worry. Hannah is an old hand around the animals. She's eleven going on eighteen. She'll take good care of Nick. And a few of the ranch hands are always around the barn. They'll keep an eye on them."

She turned slightly toward him and Blake was struck all over again at the fresh beauty of her face. All those years ago, she'd been a pretty teenage girl with simple

clothes and a sad, somber air about her. He'd sometimes paused to speak to her, but little more than that.
If anyone had told him she'd return to the ranch one day
as such a lovely woman, or that he'd be looking at her
with such longing, he would've laughed away the idea.

"I'm not worried," she told him. "I'm just amazed
at Nick. He buddied up with Hannah almost instantly.
He never does that with anyone. Especially with a girl."

Blake chuckled. "Well, Hannah does have a way
about her. And she is cute, even if she is my niece.
Maybe Nick is starting to get the idea that girls are
fun, too."

Katherine let out a good-natured groan. "Oh, please.
Not yet. I'm just now getting used to him being in the
fifth grade and playing Little League baseball."

"I wouldn't start worrying about him getting a broken heart just yet," he told her. "It's grown-ups like us
who manage to make a mess of our feelings."

"Yes. Unfortunately," she said wryly.

Oh, Lord, why had he said something like that? Now
she was going to think he had some sort of phobia about
love and marriage and everything in between.

*No use hiding the truth, Blake. You do have a fear
about trusting your heart to a woman. So if you ever
plan to get anywhere with Katherine, you better get rid
of it, and quick.*

Determined not to dwell on those negative thoughts,
he placed a hand at the back of her waist and urged her
toward the house. "Let's go in. The family is waiting
for us."

Chapter Six

The moment Blake ushered Katherine into the living room of the big ranch house, she realized very little had changed. Although the leather furniture had been updated to a lighter shade of brown, it replicated the comfortable style that had graced the large room twelve years ago. The same cowhide rugs were scattered on the parquet floor, while huge pictures and paintings of Three Rivers's ranching scenes still adorned the sand-colored tongue-and-groove walls.

Pausing, Katherine allowed her gaze to soak up the entire room. "Everything is just as beautiful," she murmured.

"I'll tell Mom you said so. That will please her. She doesn't consider herself much of a homemaker. Not when it comes to decorating. But give her a horse and a branding iron and she has plenty of confidence."

"I remember her being a remarkable woman. I'm sure

that hasn't changed, either," Katherine murmured while wishing she could say the same for her own mother. Paulette had never had the self-confidence to stand up for herself. Instead, she'd wanted someone else to rescue her from a miserable marriage.

They moved on to a wide hallway, where a long staircase led up to the second and third floors. Katherine pointed to the bottom step. "There's one of my old sitting spots. Sometimes I'd wait there while Mom and Mrs. Hollister went upstairs to go over all the items to be altered or mended. Mostly I sat out on the porch so I could pet the dogs."

"I remember."

She glanced up at him, and as her gaze roamed his handsome face, she realized just looking at him had the same startling effect it had on her all those years ago. Her heart was pounding and her thoughts were swimming with all sorts of romantic notions. What was wrong with her, anyway? Weren't teenage crushes supposed to die with time?

"Really? I'm surprised," she said. "You barely even paused to say hello."

"Sorry. I never was good at talking to girls back then. I'm not much better at it now."

"You hardly seem to be having a problem at the moment," she said drily.

"That's because you're different."

She shot him a skeptical look and he quickly added, "I meant different in a very nice way."

He was certainly different from any man she'd ever met, she thought as her heart continued to helplessly pitter-patter against her ribs. Even though he was dressed very casually in faded jeans and a green plaid shirt, he wore the clothes like a tailor-made suit.

"Then I'll take that as a compliment." They continued on through the house before she suddenly remembered the handbag hanging on her shoulder. Pausing, she said, "I'd rather leave my handbag here in the house. Can you put it in a safe place for me?"

"Sure. I'll put it in Mom's desk."

"Uh, give me a second. I have something inside for your mother." She slipped the bag off her shoulder and dug into the contents until she pulled out a tiny box. "Just a little token."

His eyes took on an odd look as she handed him the bag.

"I'll be right back" was all he said.

So what was he thinking now? Katherine wondered as she watched him disappear down the hallway. That she was trying to get her foot in the door with a gift to his mother?

Stop it, Katherine! Quit trying to read every little expression on the man's face. You're only here for dinner. What he thinks about your motives doesn't make a whipstitch of difference to your future. Because your future certainly isn't destined to be intertwined with this man on Three Rivers Ranch.

The chiding voice going off in her head was suddenly interrupted with Blake's return, and once he took her by the arm and guided her onto the back patio, she was too busy meeting his family to worry about tomorrow.

"Katherine, you look amazing! It's so good to see you again!" Vivian reached for her hands and gave them a tight squeeze. "We only just learned from Blake that you'd returned to Wickenburg. You should've let us know!"

Holt nudged his sister out of the way and reached for

Katherine's hand. "Hello, Katherine. Remember me?" he asked with a charming grin.

"Of course I remember you, Holt." She glanced down at his black cowboy boots. "You were always wearing spurs, though. And the brim of your hat was usually bent cockeyed."

He laughed and so did Vivian.

"That's because Holt spends more time with his face in the dirt than he does in the saddle," Vivian said with a teasing wink.

Holt pulled a face at his sister. "Keep it up, sis, and I'm going to start telling tales on you."

"Let me through, you two. I want to get my hands on this young lady."

A female figure plowed her way between Vivian and Holt until she was standing directly in front of Katherine. After one long look, Maureen Hollister grabbed her and enveloped her in a tight hug.

"Little Kat. It's so wonderful to see you again." She put Katherine at arm's length and, through misty eyes, took another survey. "And what a beauty you've turned into! It's no wonder Blake is so smitten."

Directly behind her right shoulder, Katherine could hear Blake awkwardly clear his throat.

Holt turned a baited grin on his brother. "Smitten, eh?"

"Knock it off, Holt," Vivian ordered, then grabbed her brother by the arm. "Come with me. Mom and Katherine can't talk with you around."

Vivian jerked Holt away from the group, and with a rueful smile, Maureen said, "Sorry, Kat. Holt gets a kick out of provoking his siblings. Don't pay any attention to him."

"I'm not offended by Holt's teasing," Katherine assured her. "And I must say you don't look a day older, Mrs. Hollister."

Her laugh was full of skepticism. "Oh, honey, the wrinkles and sunspots and gray hair are quickly catching up to me, but I try not to notice. I have too much work to do to worry about those little things." Her gaze made a search of the patio. "Did your son come with you this evening?"

Before Katherine could answer, Blake said, "Hannah has already captured Nick and taken him down to the horse barn."

Maureen chuckled. "My granddaughter is horse crazy. Dog and cat crazy, too. I think she's going to end up being a veterinarian like her uncle Chandler."

"Speaking of Chandler, will he be coming to dinner tonight?" Katherine asked. "It's been so long since I've seen him I'm not sure I'd recognize him."

Maureen shook her head. "Unfortunately, he had an emergency call out on the T Bar O. He won't be able to make it."

"What about Tessa and Joe?" Blake asked his mother. "I thought they'd be here by now."

"I just got a call from Tessa a few minutes ago. Joe's shift ran overtime and they're running a bit late. But they're coming, and Sam, too." She turned her attention back to Katherine. "So how is your mother, Kat? I used to get a card or short note from her in the mail, but I've not heard from her in a long time."

"She's doing okay. She lives just a few houses down from her sister."

"Is Paulette still sewing?" Maureen asked.

"No. She gave that up once she moved away from Wickenburg. She works as a checker in a grocery store."

Katherine handed Maureen the small box. "This is for you."

A look of pleased surprise crossed Maureen's face as she accepted the box and lifted the lid. "Oh, this has to be your mother's thimble."

"It is. When I returned home to Wickenburg, I discovered Dad had collected all the sewing equipment Mom had left behind and stored everything away in a chest. I thought you might want the thimble for a keepsake."

"Oh, I do. Your mother was a wonderful seamstress. I could always count on her to fix whatever I needed. Or to make me something new. You'll never know how much I missed her once you all moved away." She put the thimble back into the velvet-lined box, then leaned forward and kissed Katherine's cheek. "Thank you, Kat. I'll go put this away in the house. Blake, you take Katherine over and fix her something nice to drink."

Maureen moved away and Blake snared an arm around the back of Katherine's waist. "That was very thoughtful of you, Katherine. Mom will cherish the thimble."

"Your mother was always extra nice to me, Blake. I've never forgotten that. I also think there were times she had Mom mending things that normally she would have thrown in a charity box. Just because she knew we needed the extra income."

He cleared his throat and his gaze softened on her face. "Mom has always liked to help others. I noticed she called you Kat. Is that your nickname?"

"Yes. My dad called me Kat at times."

"Hmm. It suits you. Even though I've never seen you stick out your claws." Grinning impishly, he nudged her forward. "Let's go over to the bar. Jazelle, the housekeeper, has stocked it with anything and everything. Including chocolate milk for the kids. But I doubt we'll see the youngsters until it's time to eat. I'll probably have to call the barn and have one of the ranch hands shoo them back to the house."

"That's okay. I want Nick to enjoy himself."

His warm brown eyes settled on her face and Katherine wondered if the man had put some sort of magic spell on her. Just feeling his gaze slipping over her skin was causing her heart to melt.

"And what about you?" he asked gently. "Are you enjoying yourself so far?"

Knowing that Blake wanted to spend time with her when he could have most any woman he wanted for a dinner guest made her feel desirable. Something she'd not felt in a long time. And that alone was a joy.

"You're probably not going to believe this, Blake, but there were times these past twelve years that I thought of you and this ranch. I'm glad I'm here tonight."

Holt and Vivian were sitting nearby, but that didn't deter him from bending his head and brushing a kiss on her cheek.

"You've made me feel very special, Katherine."

Her face stinging with color, she forced her gaze up to his. "Um, I think you'd better get that drink you promised me."

She desperately needed something to stop her dreams from heading in the same foolish direction as her son's, Katherine thought.

Blake wasn't her husband. Nor would he ever be. The more she could embed that hard fact in her brain, the safer her heart would be.

After a meal of grilled T-bone steaks, charro beans, twice-baked potatoes and strawberry shortcake for dessert, everyone gathered in the living room for coffee. Except for Hannah and Nick. As soon as the kids had gulped down dessert, Katherine had given her son permission to go to the den with Hannah and watch a G-rated family movie.

Since then, Blake had been listening to stories being swapped between his brothers and Sam, the foreman at Joseph and Tessa's Bar X Ranch. Across the room, the women had gathered in a tight circle, no doubt discussing the things they deemed important.

By the time Blake had swallowed the last of his coffee, he was silently groaning with frustration. As much as he loved his family, he wanted nothing more than to be alone with Katherine.

Apparently his wishes were so strong she must have picked up on them, because she suddenly excused herself from the group and joined Blake where he stood on the cold stone hearth of the fireplace.

Smiling, he rested a hand at the side of her waist. "I've been standing here wondering if you'd like to stretch your legs a bit," he told her. "We could walk down to the barn and I'll show you my office."

She looked at him with interest. "I assumed you did your office work here in the house."

He shook his head. "Dad used to keep his office here in the house. But I decided it would be better for me to be in the middle of the action. So I had a room built onto one end of the cattle barns and furnished it with everything I needed."

She wrapped an arm through his and Blake thought how natural it felt to have her touching him. How perfect it felt to have her and Nick here with his family.

"I'd love to see your office," she assured him. "But maybe I should tell Nick where I'll be."

Blake shook his head. "No need to interrupt the kids' movie. We'll go out through the kitchen and I'll tell Jazelle to check in on them."

A few minutes later, after the two of them had excused themselves from the rest of the family, Blake and Katherine strolled slowly through the moonlight toward the barns and feedlots that made up the working ranch yard.

"The breeze feels lovely tonight." She sighed with pleasure. "And it's so quiet and peaceful out here."

He chuckled softly. "A pen of weanling calves are bawling up a storm and a pair of stallions are exchanging trash talk. You call this quiet?"

A wan smile tilted her lips. "This is different than human noise. I can see why you don't like to leave this place."

As they walked along, Blake could feel her hip occasionally brush against his and the sweet scent of her hair and skin drifted up to his nostrils. The hand she had resting on his forearm felt small and warm and it was far too easy for him to imagine her fingers moving over him, lighting a fire wherever they touched.

Clearing his throat, he said, "It's not that I'm against getting out and seeing other places and people. It's just that the ranch is my life. And the work to keep it running smoothly doesn't allow me much free time."

"I know."

Her short reply caused him to stop and turn to her. "Does that bother you, Katherine?"

Her gaze suddenly dropped to the ground between their feet. "Why, no. Why should it?"

"Well, because of your late husband. You told me he was obsessed with his job and making money."

"I'd rather not talk about him, Blake. This evening has been too nice to ruin it now."

She brought her gaze back to his and Blake could see she was trying to force a smile on her face.

"I don't want you to talk about him. I'm trying to ask how you feel about my job."

She tugged on his arm and the two of them continued walking in the direction of the barn.

"Oh, Blake, there's no point in asking such a question. Like you said, managing Three Rivers is your life. I'd never expect you to change that for my sake. Or any woman's, for that matter."

She might not ask him to change his management role with the ranch, but could she accept it? Or would she be like Lenore and feel ignored and neglected? One thing was certain: he'd be damned before he set himself up for another broken engagement.

He glanced at her profile etched against the silver moonlight. She'd already endured more hardships and loss in her young life than any one person should have to bear. He wanted to wipe away all that sorrow. He wanted to give her everything she needed and wanted. But it was clear to Blake that she wasn't ready to accept anything from him. Especially not love.

Chapter Seven

At a big white cattle barn with a roof of corrugated iron, Blake guided Katherine to a door on the north end. When they stepped inside the large room, a small desk lamp was already on, shedding a dim pool of light across the hardwood floor.

"I'll turn on another light so you can see things better."

He crossed the room to a floor lamp positioned near a wall table. The second light flooded the office with a warm glow and Katherine studied her surroundings with interest.

Near the back wall, a large mahogany desk, equipped with a computer and other technical necessities, faced the door. To the right, near a row of windows shaded with partially opened blinds, a long, oxblood leather couch was flanked by two matching chairs. In front of the furniture a large cowhide rug, similar to those in the ranch house, spread over a portion of the floor. Behind the desk, along one wall, were rows of file cabinets. Next to those, a table was equipped with a sleek coffeemaker and a stack of glass cups and saucers.

No cheap foam cups or plastic chairs in here, she thought as she moved across a wide expanse of beautifully designed ceramic tile. Blake was accustomed to the best.

As she meandered around the room, she paused to examine a set of large framed photographs hanging along one wall. Most of them depicted images of cowboys hard at work with smoking branding irons and boiling dust. "So this is where you take care of the business end of things. It's very nice. Do you have a secretary to help you?"

He moved over to the desk and rested a hip on a corner. "No. Holt and Chandler keep harping at me to hire one. Especially Holt, because he hates paperwork. He scratches down the necessities, then throws it all at me and expects me to deal with keeping his transactions straight. That's a headache I don't need. But the pain isn't bad enough for me to hire a secretary."

She joined him at the desk. "Why? Having one would help ease some of your workload."

He shrugged one shoulder. "It would. But I'm, uh, I'll put it like this—I like things done my way. I'd probably butt heads with a secretary. Anyway, Dad never had one. If he could handle the job on his own, then so can I."

She wanted to point out that he didn't need to follow in the exact footsteps of his father just to prove his worth as a man. But that would be getting personal and she was already becoming far too entwined with him and his family. If she intended to walk away from this man with her heart intact, she needed to keep things as casual as possible. Yet nothing felt casual about the way she felt every time she looked at him.

"A secretary would free part of your time for other things," she suggested.

He eased off the corner of the desk. "Could be," he said wryly.

Now that he was standing, his arm was very nearly touching hers, while an earthy-smelling cologne emanated from his shirt and swirled around her senses. The urge to wrap her arms around his waist and feel the hard warmth of his body next to hers was so strong she had to fight to keep her hands at her sides.

"Do you ever go out with the ranch hands and do cowboy things? Like roping and branding?"

"I do. Especially when I want to get a close-up look at the herds. And when we have roundups, I want to be there to help and oversee things."

"You have a foreman for that, don't you?"

"Matthew Waggoner. Great guy and I'd trust him with my life. But he can't be everywhere at once. When you're dealing with several thousand head of cattle, you need all the help you can get."

"Matthew Waggoner," she repeated thoughtfully. "I don't recall his name. He must have come here after we moved to California."

Blake nodded. "He's been with us about nine years. He was married when Dad first hired him as a wrangler on the horse division. But after living in Phoenix for most of her life, his wife wasn't very content with ranch life. After about two years, she got a divorce and lit out."

His brown eyes were fixed on hers and she got the impression he was waiting to see her reaction.

"That's unfortunate."

He moved a step closer, and as his hands settled over her shoulders, Katherine realized she was already in trouble. Her heart was pounding and all she could think about was having his lips on hers, his arms crushing her against his hard body.

"Not very many women are cut out for this sort of life."

Even though his words were spoken in a soft voice, they still held a cutting edge. Katherine wondered why any of it should matter to her. She wasn't interested in living here on Three Rivers with this man. At least, that was what she'd been telling herself. Yet right now, with his warm hands on her shoulders and his face only inches away, she wanted him with a longing that took her breath away.

"Is that why you've stayed single all these years?" she asked. "Because you think you'd end up like Matthew Waggoner?"

"Matt's failed marriage isn't the reason I'm still single. Neither is my sister's divorce. I've just not found the right woman. Yet. But I think I'm…getting awfully close to finding her."

His face dipped toward hers, until all she could see was his hard lips and the faint dent in the middle of his chin.

"Blake. This is—"

"Delicious."

She barely had time to suck in a deep breath before his lips settled over hers. The slow, searching kiss warmed her blood and spun her senses into a swirl of sweet oblivion. Drawn to the magic he was creating, she stood on her tiptoes and circled her arms around his neck.

In response, his arms wrapped around her and then

suddenly the front of her body was crushed against his. Groaning, she shifted in an effort to fit herself more perfectly to the contours of his body. At the same time, his tongue delved deep into her mouth and demanded more than just the mating of their lips.

And like the reckless moments they'd shared at the Yarnell lookout, he was soon kissing her over and over until every ounce of breath was gone from her lungs and the strength in her knees threatened to give way.

Just as she felt herself wilting against him, he lifted his head just enough to slide his lips over her cheek in a slow, sweet circle. Goose bumps erupted on her arms and marched down her spine. She dug her fingers into the back of his neck and willed herself not to wilt in a helpless puddle at his feet.

"Wait here," he whispered.

He walked over to the floor lamp and switched it off, causing the room to fill with soft shadows. By the time he returned to her side, her heart was pounding madly and a voice in the back of her mind was screaming at her to turn and run from the office as fast as she could. But the words of warning couldn't begin to compete with the need to have this man touching her, loving her.

All too willing, she allowed him to take her by the hand and lead her over to the couch. Together, they sank onto the middle cushion, where he promptly gathered her into the tight circle of his arms.

"I've thought about this all week long, Kat. I think I've counted each minute—until I could hold you, taste your lips." To underscore his words, he fastened his lips over hers in another long, dizzying kiss.

Letting her mind go blank, Katherine clung to him, until finally he eased back his head and cupped her cheeks with the palms of his hands. The tender touch caused a lump in her throat and turned her voice to a husky whisper.

"Something happens to me, Blake, whenever I'm near you. I think I go a little…crazy." She smoothed her hands over the slopes of his shoulders, then pushed her fingers up the back of his neck until they were meshed in his dark hair. "You asked me to have dinner with you and your family tonight. Not to have a necking session. But I…"

Her words trailed away on a shaky sigh as his lips began to track a hot, wet trail down the side of her neck.

"You want me as much as I want you," he murmured.

The movement of his lips as he spoke against her skin was as erotic as a kiss. Pleasure shot through her and she wondered how he could make her feel this much. Want this much.

Sighing, she whispered, "Yes. I do."

With a triumphant groan, he tilted her head back and nuzzled the tender spot beneath her chin. "That's all that matters. That we want each other. The rest will come—I know it will."

The rest? What was he talking about? She started to ask, but he chose that moment to dip his head to where the neckline of her blouse parted near the shallow indention between her breasts.

To have his mouth touching her in such an intimate spot shot liquid fire through her veins. The sensation erased her resistance and turned her into a willing puppet. She hardly noticed as he eased the both of them down on the leather cushions and began to unbutton her blouse. When he finally pushed the pieces of fabric aside and his hands cupped around both breasts, she was suddenly flooded with a need so intense she could scarcely breathe, much less think.

It wasn't until he lowered his head and fastened his mouth over one lace-covered nipple that a cool burst of sanity managed to pierce her thoughts.

What was she doing? She couldn't make love to Blake! Not here. Not now. Maybe never.

With a whimper of frustration, she anchored her hands alongside his face and lifted his head away from her.

Dazed by the sudden interruption, he frowned down at her. "Kat—what's wrong? Did I hurt you?"

"No. I... Oh, please, Blake, let me up."

He instantly moved away from her and Katherine snatched the pieces of her blouse back over her breasts and scrambled to a sitting position. Unable to look at him, she gulped in deep breaths of air.

"I'm confused," he said, his voice gruff with desire. "You just told me how much you wanted me. Was that just a lie? A way to tease me?"

Feeling miserable and stupid at the same time, she forced herself to meet his gaze, then immediately felt worse. There was a wounded look in his brown eyes and she could tell the pain had nothing to do with manly ego. No, her rejection had clearly hurt something deep and the notion shook her. He wasn't supposed to care that much. Or want her that much.

"I'm sorry, Blake. I do want you. And I wasn't trying to lead you on. But I can't— I have to think sensibly about this. We can't just make love as though we have a right to!"

His expression incredulous, he stared at her. "Why can't we? We're both grown, unattached adults."

He made it sound so simple. As though giving in to their physical desire would be as natural and right as breathing. And maybe for most people it was those things, Katherine thought. But not for her. All she could think about was the misery she'd gone through with Cliff. The guilt and senseless loss she'd felt when he'd crashed his car. She couldn't give all of herself to another man without knowing his feelings for her were deep enough to last a lifetime.

She swallowed and fought to compose herself. "Because I have more than myself to think about. I have a responsibility to Nick."

The frown on his face deepened. "What does making love to me have to do with your son? You'll always be his mother and a damn good one as far as I can tell. But you're more than a mother, Kat. You're a woman. Why don't you want to let yourself be one?"

He was making too much sense to suit her and she quickly jumped to her feet and walked over to the windows. With her back to him, she gazed through the partially opened blinds while her fingers fumbled with the buttons on her blouse.

"After Cliff died, I told myself if I ever got involved with another man I was going to do things differently. I was going to be smarter and take each step slowly and wisely." She looked over her shoulder at him. "So far there's been nothing slow happening between us. And that's just as much my fault as it is yours. But it's…too much, too soon."

She didn't realize he'd left the couch until he was standing directly behind her and his hands gently curled around her upper arms. "Okay, so we got a little carried away a minute ago. But you're making far too much of it. I'm not asking or expecting you to have sex with me here in this office…tonight! If, or when, that ever happens, it will be somewhere more private than this. And it won't happen unless you're ready."

No doubt he was thinking she was behaving like an inexperienced teenager, rather than a mature woman. The idea caused tears to sting her eyes and she bit down on her lower lip in an effort to stem them.

"Oh, Blake. I'm sorry. I think—" Drawing in a steadying breath, she turned and rested her palms against his broad chest. "You should forget about me. I'm only going to make you miserable. And that's not what I want. You deserve to be with a woman who's not afraid to give you what you want. One who will make you happy."

A lopsided grin twisted his lips. "I deserve to be with the woman *I* want. That's what will make me happy."

Her head swung back and forth. "Can't you see, Blake? I'm not the person you think I am. I'm flawed. I'm—"

"Shh. Don't say that." He gently cradled her face between his strong hands. "You're beautiful and kind and strong. You're the woman I want. Just give me a chance to prove it. That's all I'm asking."

"But you don't know about my marriage and everything that—"

He softly touched a forefinger against her lips. "You've told me enough. And that's in the past. Besides, do you think my life has been perfect up until now? Not hardly. But I'd like to think the two of us can start again—together."

Start again. So many times these past years, she'd wished that she could start her life over. She'd dreamed about finding love and giving Nick the siblings and father he often asked for. But so far she'd been too afraid to let herself take that step. Blake was giving her a chance to reach for all that she ever wanted. It would be worse than cowardly not to give him, or herself, a chance at happiness.

With a tiny groan of surrender, she slipped her arms around his waist and pressed her cheek against the solid warmth of his chest. "I'd like to try, Blake."

A long week later, Blake looked away from the spreadsheet on the monitor to the stack of papers Holt had just tossed onto the corner of his desk.

"What are those?"

Holt grinned. "Registration papers. I need you to fix them all up for me. You know, send them to the quarter-horse association. Pay the fees and that sort of thing. There should be ten or eleven there. Our mares have been busy."

Biting back a weary sigh, Blake reached for the papers and quickly scanned over the first sheet. "You haven't finished filling in the information. And I don't see any name suggestions. I can't send these in like this. The association can't register a name unless they have choices to pick from."

The grin on Holt's face turned even more persuasive. "Well, damn, brother. You think I don't know that after all these years? I thought I'd give you the honor of doing that task. You've always been good with names. Let's see, eleven times three. That's only thirty-three choices you'll have to come up with. That'll be a snap for you."

Blake wanted to curse a blue streak at his brother. Instead, he fought to control the urge and leaned back in the black executive chair. "Like I have time for that? What's wrong with you doing it? You manage the horse division. You're familiar with these particular wean-lings. Not me."

Holt plopped into one of the armchairs and crossed

his boots out in front of him. Blake didn't miss the fact that the rowels on his brother's spurs were a fraction away from gouging holes in the flooring.

"I am familiar with each and every one of them. And they all have different personalities," Holt said, "but I'm not good with paperwork. Like you."

Blake huffed out a heavy breath. "Look, Holt, I'm up to my eyeballs in paperwork already. And Matt wants me to ride out with him to look at Gila Valley. Grass is getting sparse on that range and we damn well don't want to start haying at this time of the year. He thinks that herd might need to be moved, so I've got to figure out where there's enough forage to put seven hundred head."

"Well, why are you getting all huffy with me? I got my own problems to worry about."

Blake pointed to the stack of registration papers. "Including those. You finish filling them out and I'll do the rest. Not before."

Holt's jaw dropped. "You're going to force me to take them to Mom for her help."

"You're not taking anything to Mom. She's already working twelve-hour days. You want to keep her up until midnight?"

Holt shot straight up in the chair and glared at him. "Mom stays busy because that's the way she wants it. Not because I'm putting a burden on her! And what the hell has come over you, anyway?"

Blake left his chair and walked over to the coffee-maker. Jazelle had made the coffee for him long before daylight. After sitting several hours on the warmer, the java had now turned into black soup, but he poured himself a cup anyway and stirred in a heaping spoon-ful of sugar.

"Nothing has come over me. Except that I'm getting damn tired of doing your job. I have a life, too, you know," he muttered.

Every day this week, Blake had been trying to find enough time to drive into Wickenburg and meet Katherine for lunch, but so far he'd managed to have only a short phone conversation with her. Tomorrow was Saturday and he'd promised to take her and Nick and Hannah to Lake Pleasant for a picnic outing. But even that would have to be postponed if he didn't catch up with the most pressing issues on his desk.

Holt shoved back the brim of his hat and stared at him. "Well, excuse me. Maybe you'd like to change jobs with me for a few days. It might be good for you to eat a little dust and get kicked in the ribs. Now that I think about it, saddling twenty or thirty colts a day would be good for those puny arms of yours."

Blake strode back to his desk. "Keep it up, Holt, and I'll be more than glad to show you what I can do with these puny arms. And as far as changing jobs, you'd do well to last one day cooped up in this office."

Holt's stare turned into a glare. Then with a resigned shake of his head, he began to chuckle. "Sorry, Blake. You're right, as usual."

Blake wearily thrust a hand through his hair. "I don't want to be right. I want to be happy."

Frowning again, Holt rose from the chair and walked over to Blake. With his hands resting flat on the desktop, he leaned intently toward his brother. "Blake, are you all right this morning? You're the judge. Hell, you've never cared about being happy before. What's this talk about, anyway?"

Oddly enough, Holt was right. Ever since their father had died, Blake hadn't allowed himself to think about whether he was a contented man. He'd been too busy putting the ranch, his mother and siblings all before himself. Even when he'd gotten engaged to Lenore, he'd not really went around in a blissful state of mind. He'd simply considered getting married as one more step toward meeting all the goals he'd set for himself. He'd never stopped to consider whether fulfilling those steps in life was the same as being happy.

"I've never... Well, that was before, uh, things changed," he finally said.

"Oh. You mean now that you're seeing Katherine O'Dell." Holt straightened away from the desk and folded his arms against his chest. "When she was here last week for dinner, I could tell you really liked her."

Liked? This thing he was feeling for Katherine was far more than *like*. He feared he was falling for the woman and the chance of him holding on to his heart was about like a snowflake surviving on a hot sidewalk.

"Yes. I do—really like her. But I'm not entirely sure that's a wise thing."

He looked up to see Holt was studying him closely. As though he considered a man with more than an overnight interest in a woman a rare sight.

"Why? She seems like a lovely, intelligent woman. Far too nice for my taste, though."

Blake grimaced. "Yeah, you like yours on the wild side."

Holt's chuckle was smug. "That's the best kind. Like a paper plate after a nice meal. Easy to clean up. Just toss it away and get another one."

Blake shook his head before taking a long sip of the syrupy coffee. "I'm going to try to forget I heard that."

"What? No lectures about breaking hearts and taking a woman seriously?"

"No. I'd be wasting my breath. Besides, one of these days you're going to pay for your rowdy behavior."

Holt chuckled again, although this time the sound didn't carry as much arrogance. "Okay, one day I'll get a lance through my heart. But that's me. What about you and Katherine? Are you getting serious about her? If you ask me, that's kind of quick."

From the moment Blake had run into Katherine on the sidewalk, he'd been serious. He realized that sounded like love at first sight. But he couldn't confess such a thing to Holt. That would only produce more laughter from his Romeo brother.

"I'll put it this way. She's, uh, becoming important to me. But I'm not sure things between us will ever go anywhere. She's had a rough time of it—losing her husband and all. And I'm not exactly the kind of man she thinks she needs."

"Well, why the hell not? You're so good it's sickening."

"Thanks," Blake said drolly.

Holt made a dismissive gesture by batting a hand through the air. "You know I meant that as a compliment."

Blake let out a rueful sigh. "Katherine wants a man who can devote plenty of time to his family. I haven't forgotten what happened with Lenore. Neither have you."

"Listen, Blake, if a man tries to spread himself too thin, he'll end up with a bunch of holes in him. If Katherine can't be happy with what you can give her, then I'd be moving on to a woman who's not so demanding." He picked up the stack of registration papers and headed for the door. "I'll go get Lonesome saddled for you."

Surprised at the offer, Blake said, "Thanks, Holt.

And as for the horse papers, I'm sure Hannah will be glad to help you with them. She loves to name animals."

Holt's face lit up. "Hey, you're right. I should have thought of that."

Giving his brother a backhanded wave, Holt departed the office, leaving Blake to turn his focus to the spreadsheet. The list of vet supplies the ranch had used the prior month was huge and the cost even more worrisome. He was going to have to do his homework to find better suppliers with more competitive prices—a tedious task that would eat up his time.

A secretary would free part of your time for other things.

Katherine's suggestion gnawed at his thoughts until, finally, he leaned back in the chair and scrubbed his face with both hands.

Hiring a secretary would be like admitting he couldn't keep up with his job as ranch manager. That his shoulders simply weren't broad enough to carry the load his father had always handled with ease. No, Blake thought, he was the eldest of the family. He was the one holding the reins of the ranch. He didn't want anyone thinking the job had become too much for him. Especially Katherine.

He was surprised Holt hadn't brought up the subject of a secretary. Normally, his brother was hounding him about hiring extra help here in the office. Instead, he'd suggested Blake find a woman who wouldn't be so demanding. This from a man who considered the opposite sex little more than a paper plate?

Hell, he wasn't about to take Holt's advice. The two of them were polar opposites. As for Katherine, the only thing she was demanding from Blake was that they put their relationship on the slow burner.

Slow. Fast. Whatever the speed, he had to convince Katherine they were perfect for each other.

Blake's thoughts were suddenly interrupted as the phone on the corner of his desk began to ring. Seeing the call was coming directly from the horse barn, he punched a button and lifted the receiver to his ear.

Holt said, "Lonesome is ready and Matt's waiting on you."

"I'll be right there."

Blake switched off the computer and reached for his hat. Outside, the sun was a white ball of fire and had already heated the morning to a fierce temperature. Gila Valley was an hour ride, or more, from the ranch yard. By the time he and Matt got there, both men and their horses would be covered with dust and sweat.

But he wouldn't want it any other way, he realized as his long strides carried him across the sunbaked ground to the horse barn. Like his father and the generations of Hollisters before him, Blake was a cowboy at heart. And nothing could change that fact. Not even Katherine.

Chapter Eight

"Mom, do I need to put my swim trunks in my bag?"

Standing at the closet door, Katherine glanced around to see Nick standing in the open doorway of her bedroom. In spite of it being only eight thirty in the morning and the fact that Blake wouldn't be picking them up for another hour, he'd already shouldered his backpack.

"I'm not sure, Nick. Blake didn't say anything about getting in the water. But let's take our swimwear just to be safe."

"Hooray! We haven't been swimming in a long time. Not since Grandpa died."

Caught off guard by Nick's comment, she tossed the jeans she'd been holding onto the bed and walked over to him. "Has it really been that long since we've gone to the lake?"

He nodded. "You're always working or doing something, Mom."

Always working. She'd flung those two words at Cliff more than she cared to remember. Now it looked as though she was guilty of doing the same thing. "Yes, I guess I am. But that's going to change. I promise."

He tilted his head to one side as he considered her last remark. "Why? Because of Blake?"

Warm color washed over her face. "No. Not exactly. I'm just going to make an extra effort to make sure we do more things together."

"Gee, Mom, we do lots of things together. Shawn doesn't get to do anything with his mother. He never even sees her! So I'm lucky!"

Katherine didn't know what had caused the divorce between Lash and his ex-wife. But she was aware that the woman had totally turned her back on her son. Which was unfathomable to Katherine.

Rubbing a hand over the top of Nick's dark head, she said, "I'm glad you think so. Are you excited about the picnic today? With Blake and Hannah?"

His eyes lit up. "Sure! Hannah's really fun—even though she is a girl. And Blake is fun, too. He talks to me about important things. And I like that."

The night they'd had dinner at Three Rivers, Blake had made a special effort to give Nick some personal attention. Katherine had deliberately stayed out of the way so her son could have one-on-one time with Blake and apparently the interaction had left an impression on her son.

"Important things, huh. Like what?"

"Oh, like grown-up stuff. Like what I want to do when I get to be a man and things like that. He showed me some trophies and ribbons that his brothers had won when they were a kid, like me. Playing sports and doing horse shows. That was pretty neat. And you know what, Mom? Blake doesn't brag about anything. He just talks about doing your best and being honest. Billy Johnson's dad brags all the time. And Billy gets embarrassed. When I get a dad, I hope he doesn't talk that way."

When I get a dad. Nick's words struck her hard. So did the longing on his face.

Taking him by the hand, she led him over to the end of the bed. "Sit down for a minute, Nick. I want to talk to you."

"Aww, Mom. We don't have time for that. Blake's gonna be here in a few minutes and I want to be ready!"

With a hand on his shoulder, she nudged him into the chair, then took a seat on the end of the bed. "I promise I won't keep you here long. You just said you liked to talk about important things. Well, this is something important."

His eyes widened and then he said glumly, "Oh. What have I done this time? I made A's on all my test grades this week. And I didn't get into trouble even once at school."

She gave him a reassuring smile. "You're not in trouble, Nick. I just want to…talk to you a little about Blake. And me. I can tell you really like him."

His wide grin spoke volumes. "Oh, yeah!" he exclaimed, then just as quickly his grin was replaced with a sober expression. "Before I met him, I didn't think I'd like him. But he's not like I thought he'd be. He's pretty super. You know what I mean, Mom?"

She knew exactly what her son meant. Blake was super. And that made her have even more doubts about her ability to hang on to a man like him for any extended length of time.

Smiling gently, she said, "Yes, Blake is a nice man. And I'm glad you like him. I just don't want you to... well, get too many ideas about him."

A confused frown puckered his forehead. "What kind of ideas?"

Talking to her son about something that affected both of their lives shouldn't be this hard, she thought. But since Cliff died, she'd not had a man in her life. This was something new for the both of them.

"Like Blake might eventually be your father some-day. I don't want you to wish for something that will probably never happen."

He stared at her for long moments and then the corners of his mouth began to tremble ever so slightly. *Please, God, don't let him cry*, she prayed. Otherwise, she'd be crying with him.

"What would be wrong in wishing for that? You just said he was a nice guy. And if you don't want to marry him, then why are you going out with him?"

The reproachful tone in his voice had Katherine groaning inwardly. "Listen, Nick, just because two people go on dates, it doesn't mean they plan to get married. It just means they like each other's company. And they want to spend time together."

"Maybe you and Blake will want to be together for a long time. Then you'd want to get married, wouldn't you?"

"Well, maybe. I just don't want you to get your hopes up and then have them squashed. Understand?"

He kicked the toe of his athletic shoe against the carpet. "Yeah. I understand," he mumbled. "But I think—"

"You think what?"

"Oh, nothing." He suddenly jumped to his feet. "May I go finish getting ready now?"

"Yes, you may."

Nick made a quick escape and Katherine returned to the closet to search for something appropriate to wear for a picnic at the lake. But instead of seeing a row of garments hanging on the rack, all she could see was the quiver of disappointment on Nick's lips.

What was she doing? Setting herself and her son up for a major heartbreak?

Shaking the dismal questions away, she tossed a skinny blue tank top onto the bed and promised herself she wasn't going to let another dark thought enter her head today.

Since Blake had started dating Katherine, he'd not seen her in a pair of jeans. He'd thought she looked incredibly sexy in a dress, but throughout the forty-five-minute drive to Lake Pleasant, he struggled to keep his gaze focused on the highway instead of her.

The tight denim outlined the provocative curves of her hips and long shapely legs, while the skimpy blue top she was wearing exposed the creamy skin of her chest and shoulders. With her hair pulled up in a ponytail, she looked more like a teenager than a widowed mother.

"Uncle Blake, let's go to that place with the big rocks," Hannah suggested as they began to cross the long New Waddell Dam that created the lake. "We can swim there. And Nick and I can hike up the mountain."

Blake glanced at the two children in the back seat of the truck. From the moment they'd left Katherine's house in Wickenburg, Hannah and Nick had chattered nonstop. At the moment, they were exchanging grins and high fives as though they were already certain Blake would agree to their choice of picnic spots.

"Sounds okay with me," Blake said. "As long as somebody isn't already camping there."

The children responded with shouts of approval, while across the console Katherine smiled at him.

"I believe you have a pair of happy campers back there."

"Well, so far," he agreed. "The place Hannah is talking about is a private little cove near some rock bluffs. Not many people know of it."

"So how did you find the place?"

"Have you forgotten?" he asked coyly. "My sister is a ranger here at the state park. It pays to have an inside track."

She chuckled. "The other night after dinner, Vivian told me she'd been working as a ranger ever since her divorce. I could tell she loves her job. I'm glad. She didn't deserve the heartache she's gone through."

He glanced at her. "Neither did you."

"No one does. It just happens," she said curtly, then abruptly changed the subject by gesturing at the scenic sight of the lake. "I'd forgotten how pretty this place is. I'm very glad you had the idea for a picnic today. Nick reminded me this morning that we've not been here since his grandfather died."

Blake wasn't about to admit that it had been years since he'd gone on a recreational outing like this. She'd think he was doing all this just to impress her. And maybe in a way, he was. But yesterday, after Holt's visit to his office, Blake had done plenty of thinking about his job and Katherine. And he'd come to the conclusion that if he truly wanted to be a family man, he was going to have to make changes in his life. He just didn't know how or where he could make those changes.

"I'm glad you're looking forward to this. Instead of

worrying about the ants and horned lizards and rattle-snakes."

She chuckled under her breath. "Now, why should I worry? I have you to keep me safe."

Such simple words, yet they made Blake feel ten feet tall.

He reached over and squeezed her hand. "I'll do my best."

Once they entered the park, Blake turned onto a graveled dirt road that appeared to be taking them away from the lake rather than toward it. But soon the road began to curve eastward, through low desert hills sparsely dotted with chaparral and an occasional saguaro.

When they finally reached the secluded cove and everyone departed the truck, Katherine gazed at the rock ledge that formed a natural roof over the ground. Less than fifteen feet away, clear blue water lapped at the shoreline. Two desert willows covered with pinkish purple blooms fluttered in the brisk breeze.

Clapping her hands with delight, Katherine exclaimed, "Oh, this is a little paradise!"

Her display of pleasure put a broad smile on Hannah's face. "This place doesn't really have a name like some of the other camping spots. But Mom and I call it Apache Cove."

"Apache Cove!" Nick exclaimed. "Why do you call it that? Did Apaches use to live here?"

"They must have," Hannah told him, as though she was quite certain of her state history. "Uncle Joe and I have found arrowheads here before. We might even find some today."

Nick turned wide eyes on his mother. "Did you hear

that, Mom? We might find arrowheads! Wouldn't that be neat?"

She patted the top of the red ball cap he was wearing. "Very neat. I hope you do find some."

"Hey, you three. Am I going to get some help over here?"

Katherine glanced over her shoulder to see Blake lifting a large ice chest from the back of the truck. As her eyes took in his tall lean body dressed in jeans and a white T-shirt, she realized the splendid beauty of the cove was merely a backdrop for Blake's handsome image. The thought had her wondering if she was simply lucky to have caught his eye, or cursed for dating someone so out of her reach.

No. Don't go there, Katherine. Remember? Today is nothing but good, happy thoughts.

For once, she followed the uplifting voice in her head and her laughter came free and easy as she slung an arm around both children. "Come on, you two. We'd better help get our picnic."

In a matter of minutes, the four of them had toted everything from the truck over to a weather-worn wooden picnic table situated near the rock ledge. Blake dug a checked tablecloth from a tote bag and spread it over the tabletop.

"There. Fit for a king's banquet," he said as he carefully smoothed out the wrinkles.

"What's in the basket to eat?" Nick asked as Katherine placed paper plates and plastic utensils onto the table.

"All sorts of good things," Hannah told him. "I asked for fried chicken and Uncle Blake wanted sandwiches, so Reeva made both. And she put homemade chocolate-chip cookies in, too. They're yummy."

"Anything with sugar is yummy to Hannah," Blake teased, then looked to Nick. "What about you, Nick? Does your mother give you plenty of desserts?"

The boy wrinkled his nose. "Only if I eat all my meat and vegetables. I like the meat, but not the vegetables. Yuck!"

"Well, don't worry. We don't have a bunch of vegetables for our picnic today, but maybe your mother will allow you to eat cookies anyway," Blake told the boy, then gave Katherine a conspiring wink.

So far the amount of time Nick had spent with Blake wasn't all that much, yet Katherine could already see a bond developing between the two. Having a father figure was exactly what Nick needed at this time in his life. And the fact that Blake cared enough to give her son undivided attention endeared her even more to the man.

"I think we can forget about the vegetable rule for today," Katherine said.

Nick gave a triumphant fist pump, while Katherine and Blake shared amused glances.

"But that doesn't mean the both of you are only going to eat cookies," Blake warned the two kids.

"Oh, Uncle Blake," Hannah said with a groan. "You're such a stuffed shirt."

"Stuffed shirt, eh? Just wait until we go swimming. I'm going to throw you and Nick up so high out of the water you'll have birds flying around your heads."

Nick's and Hannah's mouths flew open and then they both began to giggle.

"Oh, wow! This is gonna be fun!" Nick exclaimed.

Hannah danced on her toes. "Let's hurry and eat, Nick, so we can jump in."

Blake held up both hands. "Whoa! There isn't going to be any jumping in the lake right after we eat. I don't want a bunch of tummy aches around here. You two can hunt arrowheads or go for a hike before we do the swimming. Okay?"

To Katherine's amazement, both children agreed without too much complaining. After Hannah and Nick meandered off together toward the shade of the ledge, she looked at Blake and smiled. "Are you sure you've never been a dad before? You handled that like a pro."

"I haven't forgotten how Dad dealt with us kids. If we got rowdy, he could get mighty firm. But we always knew he was a lovable teddy bear underneath."

The wan smile on his face held a touch of sadness that she understood all too well. "I can tell you still really miss him," she said gently.

His gaze moved past her and out toward the wide stretch of blue water. "I'll never stop missing him."

"I miss my father, too," she admitted with a long sigh. "Knowing what he was, that probably doesn't make much sense to you. But there was parts of his life when he, uh, wasn't always a bad or neglectful father. Now I find myself hanging on to the good memories of him much more than the bad."

His gaze returned to her face and then he surprised her by reaching for her hand. The comforting warmth of his strong fingers wrapping around hers made something in the middle of her chest melt like a marshmallow over a burning log.

"It makes all kind of sense to me, Katherine. But today is for fun. Not for us to get melancholy."

He squeezed her hand, and as she watched an engaging smile spread across his handsome face, she decided the man had put some kind of spell on her. Just the touch of his hand and the smile on his face made her world seem bright and beautiful. It was an exhilarating thought, but also a very scary one.

Flashing a smile back at him, she said, "You're right. Let's put the food on the table before the kids start howling that they're starving."

Blake couldn't remember the last time he'd been on a picnic. Probably not since he'd been in high school, when he and a bunch of friends had gathered here at the lake for a Fourth of July party. Years had passed since those carefree days. Now as the four of them sat around the table enjoying the lunch Reeva had packed for them, he realized he'd almost forgotten how it felt to eat outdoors with the lake water lapping close by, the sun shining in a bright blue sky and a pretty girl sitting next to him.

No, she was more than pretty, Blake thought. With her face practically bare of makeup and her black hair teased by the wind, she was sexy and womanly. She was also making him wish the two of them were alone. At least long enough to kiss her senseless.

Forcing himself to ignore the erotic images in his head, he glanced at Nick. The dark-haired boy was busy chomping on a fried chicken leg. So far he seemed to be taking in everything about the day with great enthusiasm. Blake was relieved. If Nick wasn't happy, Katherine would hardly be enjoying herself.

He turned his gaze on Katherine. "How long has it been since you two have gone on a picnic?"

She gave his question a moment's thought before answering. "A few months ago we went to the park in town."

Nick groaned a loud protest. "Aww, Mom, that wasn't

much of a picnic. We just ate sandwiches, then got up and went home. This is a real picnic."

"My mom doesn't have much time to take me on picnics," Hannah said. "But she makes up for it in other ways, I guess. Uncle Joe takes me riding a lot. And that's super fun."

"Uncle Joe takes you riding more often now that he's married to Tessa and they have a ranch to care for," Blake pointed out.

"That's right. Tessa is fun. She likes to do all sorts of things. And Uncle Joe is a lot more fun now that's he's married." As soon as she spoke the last word, Hannah's expression lit up as though she'd just made the obvious connection. "Gosh, I hadn't thought about that idea before. Maybe Mom needs a husband to make her happier."

"Your mother doesn't need fixing. She's happy as she is," Blake told his niece.

"Yeah, but there's nothing wrong with being happier." The girl turned a crafty glance on Blake and Katherine. "Maybe that's what you need, too, Uncle Blake. A wife!"

A wife. Ever since Lenore had broken their engagement, Blake had been asking himself if he was actually meant to have a wife and children. Sometimes at night, when he fell into bed, exhausted from trying to do too many jobs in one day, he told himself his only lot in life was to manage Three Rivers. And most of the time, he was content to accept that lonely idea. But now that he'd met Katherine again, he wanted more. Much more.

Glancing down the table, he noticed Nick was staring at the three of them, clearly hanging on to every word. Blake awkwardly cleared his throat and tried to think up a neutral reply to Hannah's suggestion.

"And maybe you need to eat the rest of your lunch and leave the matchmaking to the adults," he told her.

Hannah looked at Nick and rolled her eyes, then both children giggled.

"Okay. I won't talk about that kind of stuff." She pulled a handful of potato chips from an open bag. "I want to talk about riding horses. I've been thinking Nick needs to learn how to ride. And quick. That way he can go on spring roundup with us."

"Roundup!" Nick squealed with excitement. "You mean like herdin' cattle and all that kinda stuff? Do you get to go?"

Nodding, Hannah answered, "Sure do. Some of the other ranch hands let their kids go, too. All we get to do is ride drag. So we won't get in the way. But it's fun. And we get to eat off the chuck wagon and at night we sleep in bedrolls. Uncle Holt sings around the campfire, too. Sometimes he sounds sorta like a wounded coyote, but most of the time it sounds nice. I wouldn't tell him that, though."

The excitement on Nick's face turned to doubt. "I don't know about ridin' drag."

Hannah batted a dismissive hand through the air. "Oh, it's easy. You mostly just eat a bunch of dust. But we tie kerchiefs over our faces when it gets too bad. But you need to learn how to ride first. Good enough so that you can trot and canter without falling off. I can teach you." Hannah looked hopefully at Katherine. "Will you give him permission, Katherine?"

Blake could see tense lines forming around Katherine's mouth and across her forehead. Clearly, she was concerned about Nick's safety. But she might also be worried about the boy becoming emotionally invested in the Hollister family. If so, Blake wanted to erase her fears. He wanted her to see that he and his family would be a constant anchor in their lives. If only she would give Blake a chance to prove it.

"I'd have to think on it, Hannah," Katherine said cautiously. "Being around livestock can be very dangerous. And Nick isn't like you. He's a city boy."

"I can learn, Mom! And I'm not afraid of any ol' horse or cow! I'm not even afraid of a bull—with long horns," Nick added for good measure.

Katherine turned a worried frown on Blake. "What do you think about all this?"

He glanced at Nick and the eager, hopeful look on the boy's face tugged at his heart. From what Katherine had told him, even when he'd been alive, Nick's father had been absent in his baby son's life. With only one debilitated grandfather, Nick had never had a chance to experience the outdoors with a father figure at his side. Blake desperately wished he had the right to take Nick under his wing and guide him into manhood.

"I think it would be a great experience for Nick. He'd learn a lot about ranching," Blake told her. "And Hannah makes a great riding instructor. She's taught a few other kids before. Besides, climbing into a vehicle and going down the highway can be dangerous."

Her face suddenly blanched white and Blake wished he could kick himself. Reminding her of her late husband's death was the last thing he'd intended to do. "I'm sorry, Katherine. I wasn't thinking how insensitive that sounded."

"Forget it. I know you were only talking in general terms." She smoothed back a few tendrils of hair that the wind had whipped loose from her ponytail. "Will you be going on spring roundup?"

"I always do. I like to get a firsthand look at the herds

and make sure everything is going smoothly. But it will be a few more weeks before the roundup takes place. Nick has enough time to learn how to ride."

Nick must have felt the momentum of the issue was gravitating to his side. He was practically bouncing in his seat. "Can I, Mom? Can I?"

Katherine turned a gentle smile on her son. "I'm not promising anything yet, Nick. But I'll think about it."

Seeing that as a positive response, the two excited children began exchanging high fives.

Blake looked over at Katherine and smiled. "I've heard the scariest part of being a parent is letting go."

Her lips twisted to a wry slant. "Just wait until you have your own. You'll find out just how scary."

His own kids? At one time Blake had dreamed of having a whole brood of children. But then his father had died and his responsibilities on the ranch had taken a drastic change. During his brief engagement to Lenore, he'd let himself believe that children and a woman to love him was finally coming true. After that dream had died an abrupt death, Blake had refused to think of himself as being a husband and father someday. Until now.

Meeting Katherine again had injected him with newfound hope. And though a part of him was yelling that he needed to put a foot on his burgeoning emotions, the other part refused to do anything to dampen the first real joy he'd felt in years. There was a good chance she might never fall in love with him. But being with her made him feel like a wanted man again. And for now, that had to be enough.

Chapter Nine

More than an hour later, after the meal was finished and the leftovers packed away, the four of them hiked up a nearby trail until they reached the summit of a tall hill covered with saguaro cacti, thick chaparral and blooming wildflowers. Blake and Katherine found a comfortable rock seat, shaded by a lone mesquite. Since the rock wasn't all that wide, there was hardly an inch of space between them. The closeness made Katherine acutely aware of his thigh pressed against hers and the masculine scent of his skin swirling up to her nostrils. Touching him, even in an innocent way, filled her with the memory of his kisses and made her long for more.

Several yards away, but still within view of the adults, Nick and Hannah were content to search for arrowheads along a bare rocky shelf along the side of the hill.

"This is a gorgeous spot." Katherine's gaze studied the rugged landscape before landing back on Blake's face. "Thank you for bringing us, Blake. This is a day Nick will never forget."

He glanced over at the kids before turning his warm brown gaze on Katherine. "I don't think I'll forget it, either." He reached out and smoothed a tendril of loose hair off her forehead. "As much as I'm enjoying Hannah and Nick, I wish the two of us could be alone. For a few minutes, at least."

His suggestion put a hot blush on her cheeks. "It's probably a good thing we have two chaperones."

His head leaned closer to hers and longing fluttered in the pit of Katherine's stomach.

"We won't always have chaperones with us," he reminded.

"No. We won't."

"Does that worry you?"

She leveled a knowing look at him. "Everything about us worries me. But—"

"You want to be with me," he interrupted. "More than you want to run and hide."

She let out a long breath. "Something like that."

He reached over and folded his fingers around hers. "I want to be with you, too, Kat. More than you can imagine. And today has set me to thinking."

When he didn't continue, she asked, "About what?"

"Oh, about me and the ranch. About you and Nick. And all the things I'd like to share with you two."

The serious look in his eyes scared her. This was Blake Hollister, not just some regular Joe who drove a delivery truck or worked on a highway crew. His family name was known far and wide. Three Rivers had a reputation as being one of the largest, most productive ranches in the state. Money was not an issue with him. He and his family had more than enough. As for women, he had the looks and charm to have most any-one he set his eyes on. So what made him think she was special? Katherine wasn't special. She'd been born an Anderson. Pretty clothes and a decent house didn't change that fact. And sooner, rather than later, he would realize she wasn't suitable wife material for a man like himself.

Her heart fluttering, she purposely turned her gaze on Hannah and Nick. "You're thinking too much, too fast, Blake."

His thumb gently caressed the back of her hand and Katherine desperately wanted to rest her head upon his shoulder. To let herself believe the three of them could be a real family.

"I'm thirty-eight years old. I don't want to waste any more time." His thumb and forefinger wrapped around her chin and guided her face around to his. "It's been seven years since your husband died, Kat. You shouldn't want to waste any more time, either."

A lump of emotions stuck in her throat. Seven years. She'd hung on to the memory of her tragic marriage much too long. And through it all she'd believed a chance to love again would never come to her. Now Blake was at her side, offering her all sorts of dreams and passion. Even if their time together was short-lived, she'd be a fool to push it all aside.

"I don't intend to," she murmured.

Surprise flickered across his features and then his hand was gently cradling the side of her face. "Do you really mean that?"

Her heart racing, it was all she could do to keep from

throwing herself in his arms and begging him to never let her go. "I really mean it."

His eyes full of promises, he started to say something. But shouts from Hannah and Nick suddenly interrupted the moment.

"Mom! Mom! We've found an arrowhead! Come look!"

With a wry smile on his face, Blake stood and pulled Katherine to her feet. "I think we'd better go share in the excitement."

Her heart suddenly full, she squeezed his hand. "I think you're right."

Monday morning, shortly before her lunch break, Katherine carried a handful of papers into Prudence's office and placed them on the superintendent's desk.

"Those are all ready for you to sign. The set of papers on top is the work order for the gym floor repair. The contractor won't appear until he has everything in writing," Katherine informed her. "The secretary for the construction company made that clear to me over the phone this past Friday."

Prudence reached for the papers and began to scratch her signature on the appropriate lines.

"Send these off as soon as you get back to your office," she told Katherine. "The coaches have a basketball camp already scheduled for the last week in June. The new flooring needs to be in place before camp begins."

"Right. I'll try to get a fixed date as to when the work might start."

Prudence pushed the signed papers back toward Katherine, then looked up and smiled. "So how did your weekend go? Did Mr. Hollister come through with the picnic?"

Katherine wondered if the smile on her face looked as dreamy as it felt. "He did. And he brought his young niece, Hannah, along so that Nick would have company. We all had a—" Not wanting to sound like she was gushing, she stopped short of saying glorious. "We had a great time."

"It must have been more than great," Prudence replied as she carefully scanned Katherine's face. "Your eyes are lit up like a Christmas tree."

Katherine unwittingly touched a hand to her warm cheek. "I guess I do feel happy this morning," she admitted, then let out a short laugh. "It's been so long since… Well, I'd forgotten what it's like to be courted by a man."

Prudence pointed to the chair in front of her desk. "Sit. Tell me about it."

The phone on the superintendent's desk began to ring, and thinking the woman would answer, Katherine hesitated about taking a seat. Instead, Prudence ignored the phone and motioned impatiently to the chair.

"I'll get back to the call later," she insisted. "Right now I want to hear about your day at the lake."

Katherine crossed her legs and tried to look casual. "Well, there's not that much to tell. Blake took us to a private little cove that hardly anyone knows about. It was a beautiful spot and we had it all to ourselves. Our lunch was delicious and afterward we hiked around the nearby hills. The kids explored and searched for arrowheads. Then we swam and played in the water for hours."

"Sounds like you made a long day of it."

Katherine nodded. "It was well after dark by the time

we got home. Nick was so tired from all the play he fell asleep on the couch."

Prudence's expression turned clever. "And what did Nick think about the outing?"

"Oh, gosh, I don't think I've ever seen him so animated and happy. He was still talking about it this morning at breakfast."

The other woman leaned back in her chair as though she had all day to discuss Katherine's date. "Does he like Mr. Hollister?"

Katherine's smile slowly vanished. "That's the thing that worries me the most about all this, Pru. Nick adores Blake. He sees him as some sort of hero cowboy and father figure all rolled into one."

"That's something to worry about? You should be thanking your lucky stars that he isn't jealous and resentful of the man."

Katherine groaned. "I am grateful that the two get along so well. Already Blake and Hannah have plans to teach Nick how to ride a horse and take him on spring roundup. Nick's so over the moon with it all there's no way I can refuse to let him."

Prudence thoughtfully tapped her ink pen against a notepad. "I'd probably fire you if you did. Your son needs to learn and do. And the family connection he'll get with Blake and his niece will be great for him."

Katherine nodded. "I agree. Nick does need all that. But he's already dropping little remarks that tells me he believes Blake will soon be his father. I've tried to caution him about getting his hopes up, but he's only ten years old. He doesn't understand that love and marriage are complex matters. Tell me, Pru, what happens when all of this ends? Nick is going to be devastated. He'll lose all trust in his mother!"

Frowning, Prudence leaned earnestly forward. "Why are you already talking about everything ending? My Lord, Katherine, do you think everything good in your life is always going to end?"

She let out a long sigh. "It's hard not to think in those terms," she admitted. "Dad is gone and the rest of my family is a disjointed mess. My marriage turned out to be a failure and then my husband loses his life because of me. Aren't those enough reasons to expect the worst?"

Without saying a word, Prudence left her chair and crossed the room. After closing the door firmly behind her, she marched over to Katherine. "Listen to me, Katherine. I don't ever want to hear you say such a thing again. Your late husband didn't die because of you or anything you did. He died because he was stupid enough to drink himself into a foggy stupor and get behind the wheel of a car! Once and for all, you need to put him and everything that happened behind you."

"That's easier said than done," Katherine retorted. "I told Cliff I was divorcing him. That's why he drank himself into a stupor. If not for me—"

"You didn't put a bottle of liquor in his hand. You didn't force him to drive. The man was emotionally weak. He had issues that you couldn't begin to fix."

Katherine grimaced. "Thanks for reminding me I was married to a psychologically disturbed man."

Shaking her head, Prudence walked over and placed a comforting hand on Katherine's shoulder. "Look, Katherine, there's hardly a woman alive that hasn't made some sort of mistake over a man. Yours was Cliff. Now with Blake you have a wonderful chance to change your life. A chance for you and Nick to be happy. Don't blow it by clinging to a ghost."

"I don't want to blow anything." But when Katherine tried to look into the future, she couldn't see herself with Blake. Still, on the day of the picnic she'd indicated to him that she was ready to take their relationship to a deeper level. And no matter how many doubts she had concerning the two of them, she wasn't going to run from that promise now. "I'm just not sure that I'm the woman Blake wants to spend the rest of his life with."

Smiling cleverly, Prudence shrugged one shoulder. "If you two decide you're not right for each other, then at least you can say you had a hell of a ride trying to find out."

Katherine rolled her eyes, then in spite of herself, she began to chuckle. "Pru, you're crazy."

"True. But maybe no one else but you will find out about my condition. Otherwise, we'll both lose our jobs," she teased.

The phone on the desk began to ring again. As Prudence went to answer it, she gave Katherine a backward wave. "Don't worry. Be happy."

By Wednesday, Blake had worked nonstop to catch up on the tasks he'd left undone in order to take a day off for the picnic. But today, he decided he couldn't wait any longer to see Katherine. Earlier this morning, he'd called to see if she could possibly get away from work long enough to have lunch with him. To his delight, she'd agreed.

Now, after making the trip from Three Rivers into Wickenburg in record time, Blake wheeled his truck into the school parking lot. At the same time, Katherine was emerging from the back entrance of the building.

Not bothering to cut the motor, he climbed from the cab and hurried over to greet her.

"Hello," he said, then bent and pressed a swift kiss on her cheek.

A soft smile curved the corners of her lips. "Mmm. That was a nice hello."

The welcoming light in her gray eyes made Blake feel warm and wanted. "I hope I'm not late. I was detained at the last minute by a cattle buyer wanting to purchase a pair of bulls. Thankfully, Matt took over the job of showing him the animals."

"Oh, I hope you don't lose a sale because of me."

Loving the feel of her walking at his side, he slipped an arm around the back of her waist. "Don't worry. Matt would tell you he's a much better salesman than me and he'd be right. I don't have the patience for it."

At the truck, he helped her into the cab, then quickly took his place behind the wheel. As he began to back the vehicle from the parking spot, he glanced over to see she was snapping the seat belt across her lap.

"Wow. You look gorgeous today. That dress is something else." Buttoned from the tight-fitting bodice all the way down to the flared skirt at her knees, the garment showed off her tiny waist and fluttered around her bare, slender legs.

Smiling modestly, she looked over at him. "Do you like it? I wasn't so sure about the bright green and yellow flowers, but it makes me feel good whenever I wear it."

The dress made Blake feel more than good. It was making him ache to hold her in his arms and run his hands over her womanly curves. "Well, I'm glad you wore it today. So where would you like to eat? Or maybe I should be asking how long your lunch break is? We might not have time for much more than fast food."

After checking for traffic, he steered the truck onto the street, toward the business section of town.

"I normally have an hour for lunch. But today my boss knew you were coming, so she gave me an extra fifteen minutes."

"That was very nice of her."

"Where I'm concerned, Pru is a hopeless romantic. As for herself, I've never known her to date anyone."

"What is she? One of those old-maid schoolmarms?"

Katherine laughed. "Not hardly. She's in her thirties and very attractive. She's also divorced. I've never asked why her marriage ended and she keeps that part of her life private."

Blake figured most everyone in Yavapai County had heard about his broken engagement to Lenore. But whether anyone knew the reason for it, he couldn't say. How could he? He hardly knew the answer to that himself. Lenore had blamed her change of heart on the long hours he'd devoted to the ranch, rather than her. But after thinking about it for three long years, he wondered if that had only been a partial excuse for not wanting to marry him. Hardly six weeks after the woman had handed him back his ring, she'd hooked up with a wealthy car dealer up in Prescott.

"Hmm. Maybe this pretty superintendent could make my brother Holt walk the straight path."

"From what you've told me about your rowdy brother, Pru wouldn't put up with him for five minutes."

"Neither will any other woman," he said drily, then gestured toward a fast-food joint in the distance. "There's a burger place. Is that all right with you?"

When she didn't answer immediately, he glanced over to see she was staring out the passenger window, while her fingers fidgeted with the hem of her dress resting across her knee.

"What's wrong?" he asked. "You want to eat something different?"

She looked at him and the raw longing on her face was unlike anything he'd seen on her before. Like a lightning bolt, it struck him hard, leaving his whole body sizzling in its wake.

"I thought—if it's all the same to you—we could go to my place. It's only three blocks from here. And I have plenty of leftovers from last night's meal."

She was doing more than inviting him to her home for lunch. She was finally telling him she wanted to be close to him. Really close. Like a kid just handed a prize gift, he wanted to shout with joy. Instead, he tried to act like a mature man and hold his elation down to a grin.

"With the kids around all day at the lake, I didn't have a chance to even kiss you. How did you know I've been aching to be alone with you?"

Reaching across the console, she rested her hand on his forearm. The simple touch had the power to send sparks flying all the way to his shoulder.

"Probably because I've been aching, too," she murmured.

If Blake could have safely broken the speed limit, he would have. But only seconds earlier a car had pulled onto the street in front of them and was forcing him to drive at a snail's pace. The five minutes it took to get to Katherine's house seemed more like twenty.

By the time they'd stepped through the door and Katherine had locked it safely behind them, Blake was reaching for her.

"This is what I've been hungry for." His voice gruff with desire, he gathered her in the tight circle of his arms.

She let out a breathless laugh as her hands latched on to the slope of his shoulders. "You don't want to eat lunch?"

"I can eat anytime," he answered. "But I can't do this."

He fastened his lips over hers, and though he was promising himself to keep the kiss gentle, Katherine had other ideas. Nipping, searching, tasting. Her soft lips were making a ravenous feast upon his. At the same time, he felt her arms slip around his neck, then tighten as though she never wanted to let him go.

Her eager reaction pushed any plan for gentleness out of his mind. He opened his mouth and coaxed her to come inside. She gladly accepted his invitation, and when her tongue began to glide over the rough edges of his teeth, Blake lost all sense of thought.

The kiss turned into a fierce dance, with each of them fighting to get closer, to quench the fires they were building with each taste, each delicious sup. In a matter of moments, Blake was lost in a fog of heat with only one thing on his mind: the burning urge to make love to the warm, giving woman in his arms.

When the need for air finally forced him to lift his head, Katherine grabbed him by the hand. "Let's get away from the door," she whispered.

She led him out of the short entryway and into the living room. There, Blake eased her onto the couch, then stretched out next to her on the long length of cushions. Her arms promptly came around him, and as he shifted his body to a more comfortable position, he realized his arousal was perfectly aligned with the juncture of her thighs. Which only made the ache to thrust himself inside her even worse.

"I didn't know this was going to happen," he said

against her lips. "I mean…happen today. I only knew I wanted to see you. Now I…I'm about to lose it, Kat. I don't want to hurry, but—"

She moved her head just enough to plant a row of tempting little kisses down the side of his neck and the hot throb in his lower body grew unbearable.

"You don't have to wait," she whispered. "I'm ready. So ready."

Blind with a desire that had been working on him for days, he reached up under her dress until his fingers came in contact with her panties. Curling his fingers over the waistband, he yanked the silky garment down her legs, pausing only long enough to remove her high heels.

With the shoes and undergarment out of the way, he shoved the bottom half of her dress up to her waist, then hurriedly released himself through the fly of his jeans.

"You don't need protection," she said in a whispered rush. "I'm on the Pill. Uh—not for this reason. But to keep my cycles regular."

"Damn good thing. Because I don't have any protection with me."

Even as he said the words, he was straddling her and bracing his weight on his knees. She looked up and their gazes locked. The tender invitation in her gray eyes caused an odd sort of stinging to prick the center of his chest. The unexpected feeling rattled him, but she didn't give him a chance to wonder what sort of upheaval was going on inside him. Not when a cat-like purr was suddenly vibrating in her throat and her hands were linking at the back of his neck, drawing his mouth down to hers.

"Come here," she whispered.

The sweet, mysterious taste of her lips wiped away

the last tenuous hold on his self-control, and with a helpless groan, he thrust himself deep into the damp warmth of her body.

Her soft, needy moans managed to penetrate the roaring in his ears and he lifted his mouth just long enough to glance down at her. The passion etched upon her face was more than he deserved. More than he'd ever dreamed this woman could feel for him.

"Kat! My Kat! This—you—are all I want. All I need!"

"Love me, Blake. Don't stop!"

She wrapped her legs around his and lifted her hips so that she could take him in fully, completely. At that moment, Blake's senses exploded and the next thing he knew he was driving into her, his thrusting fast and deep.

All at once a shower of hot arrows pricked his skin and sent sensations up and down his body. His scalp was surely lifting from his head, while a lungful of breath hung in his throat. Beneath him, he felt her shifting and straining to match the rhythmic thrusts of his hips. At the same time, he was aware of her hands racing over him, touching every spot within her reach.

The need to feel her fingers against his bare skin had a part of him longing to stop long enough to tear off his clothes. But not even the thought of that pleasure was enough to make him draw away from her. Even if the roof was tumbling in on his head, he couldn't stop this frantic journey to paradise.

Over and over their bodies crashed together, until the fierce movements caused them to slip off the edge of the couch and onto the floor. Still connected, Katherine's back ended up lying flat on the braided rug, while

Blake's head was only inches away from the corner of the coffee table.

Easing his mouth from hers, he panted, "Let me lift you back onto the couch."

"No! Don't move! Don't stop!" she gasped.

She wrapped her legs tightly around his and arched her hips desperately upward.

She was like a bright flame, consuming him with a wet heat that took his breath away and controlled his every thought. He couldn't get enough of her. He'd never get enough of her.

Delving his hands into her black hair, he lowered his lips back to hers and thrust his tongue deep into the honeyed pool of her mouth. Her groans came one after the other as her fingers dug into his back and her hips ground against his.

Like the tattered edge of a tow sack, Blake's self-control began to unravel. He fought to hang on, but it was a hopeless battle against the fiery wind that was spinning him into a vortex he couldn't escape.

The storm lifted him up and carried him to a cloud so bright and golden that it blinded him with pleasure. From a place far away, he heard her cries of delight, felt the spasms of her body tighten around him.

Forever. Forever. Like a sweet promise, the words tumbled through his thoughts. This was the way it was meant to be. Her loving him. Him loving her.

Shuddering with his release, he crushed her tightly in the folds of his arms and whispered her name.

When Blake's awareness fully returned, he realized the two of them were still on the floor, wedged between the coffee table and the couch. Katherine's face was pressed between his shoulder and the braided rug, but he could see her eyes were tightly shut, her forehead covered with beads of sweat.

Tendrils of damp hair curled at her temples and he pressed his lips to the tender spot before he pushed his weight off her and climbed to his feet.

By the time he'd fixed his clothing, he turned to see she was standing directly behind him, shoving a cloud of tangled hair away from her face.

Swallowing at the emotions suddenly burgeoning in his throat, he reached for her. With her head tucked beneath his chin, he held her tightly against him. "Oh, Kat. I didn't mean for that to happen—not that way. I wanted it to be sweet and slow and special. Now you're thinking I'm some sort of animal."

Her shoulders began to shake and after a few seconds he realized she was chuckling. Surprised by the reaction, he eased her head back far enough to see her face.

"Why are you laughing? Was I that awful a lover?"

The amusement on her face was suddenly replaced with a tenderness that struck him smack in the middle of his heart.

"Oh, Blake. How could you ask that? You were incredible." Slipping her arms around his waist, she snuggled the front of her body next to his. "In fact, I was wondering if we have enough time left for a…repeat. Or would you rather I dig the leftovers out of the refrigerator?"

He arched his eyebrows in surprise and then it was his turn to chuckle. "You little brazen hussy," he softly accused.

Smiling wantonly, she tilted her lips up toward his. "Now that you've discovered the real me, what are you going to do about it?"

Bending, he slipped an arm beneath the back of her knees and lifted her into his arms.

"I'm going to carry you to the bedroom," he told her. "And make the most of the time we have left."

Chapter Ten

Two days later, on Friday evening, Katherine sang along to the radio as she prepared a simple evening meal of macaroni and cheese with grilled smoked sausage. Behind her at the small kitchen table, Nick placed silverware and napkins next to two plates.

Less than an hour ago, Blake had called to invite her and Nick to Three Rivers tomorrow. Other than a few brief text messages, it was the first time since the day they'd made love on her lunch break that she'd actually talked to him. Hearing his voice had filled her with sweet joy and the excitement of seeing him soon was humming through her like the music on the radio.

"Mom, I haven't heard you sing in a long time." His task finished, he walked over to where his mother was standing at the gas range and peered impatiently at the cooking food. "You must be happy that we're going to Three Rivers tomorrow and we'll see Blake again."

Katherine could feel a broad smile stretching across her face. Making love to Blake had made her feel like a reborn woman. The heated kisses they'd shared on their first date had given her a hint of the explosive chemistry between them. Still, she'd not expected their lovemaking to be so scorching hot that just thinking about it put a blush on her cheeks.

"I guess I am pretty happy." She gave the top of his head a playful scruff. "And what about you, son? Are you looking forward to your first riding lesson?"

"Boy, am I! I can hardly wait! When I talked to Hannah on the phone, she told me she already had a horse picked out for me. His name is Moondust. 'Cause he has a moon-shaped spot on his forehead and little white dots on his hips. Hannah says he's the best horse for learning to ride, and she promises that if I fall off, Moondust won't step on me. He'll stand real still and wait until I get up and get back on."

Katherine managed to stifle a groan and keep her motherly fears to herself. Nick was ten years old going on eleven. Hannah had been riding since she was four. To treat Nick like a baby, especially in front of Hannah, wouldn't just humiliate him, it would crush his self-confidence. And it was important to Katherine that her son grow up believing he could accomplish anything he put his mind to.

"It's good to hear that Moondust is so trustworthy. But I have a feeling you won't fall off. Blake says Hannah is a great teacher. If you do everything she tells you, you'll be a wrangler in no time."

"You really think so, Mom?"

"Sure I do."

"You know, Mom, before I met Hannah, I thought spending time with a girl would be yucky."

She glanced down to see Nick's face scrunched up like he'd just tasted something sour. "Why did you think that?"

"'Cause the girls at school are all silly. They only talk about things like clothes and cheerleading and boy bands. Boring stuff. I thought Hannah would be like those girls. But she's really cool. She knows how to do fun things that boys like. And she doesn't act like a smarty-pants just 'cause I don't know about ranching. She says not to worry, she'll teach me all about it!"

Katherine smiled while thinking about how much this past month with Blake and his little niece had changed Nick. He'd always been a fairly happy child. But now he seemed enthused about everything. He'd even quit complaining about cleaning his room, when before she'd had to plead and threaten to get him to pick up his dirty clothes and carry them to the hamper.

"You really like Hannah, don't you?"

"Yeah! I like her a whole lot! You know what, Mom? We decided to call each other *cousin*."

His remark grabbed Katherine's attention. "You did?" she asked, careful to keep her voice casual. "What made you two decide that you're cousins?"

Nick's expression turned a bit sheepish. "Well, we think you and Blake are gonna get married soon. So that will make me and her cousins."

Married. Katherine wasn't surprised her son had been thinking such things. Hardly a day went by that he wasn't hinting at the possibility of Blake becoming his father. She'd tried to temper the boy's hopeful dreams by explaining how marriage was a serious issue and that she and Blake might not ever want to be man and wife. But so far all her warnings had fallen on deaf ears.

Tonight she wasn't going to warn her son that his

dreams might never come true. Instead, she simply asked, "What makes you two think Blake and I are going to get married?"

"We can just tell. Hannah says she's never seen her uncle Blake smile or laugh like he does with you. And you never liked any man until Blake came along."

A dark cloud of guilt settled onto Katherine's shoulders. Nick had been too young to remember anything about his parents' relationship and he'd never questioned her about her feelings for his father. Nick simply assumed that his parents had been a loving married couple and she'd never had the heart to tell him otherwise. In spite of their four-year marriage and a child together, she hadn't felt the same strong bond with Cliff as she did with Blake. Never during the years of their marriage had she felt the hot, reckless passion she'd felt with Blake in the one short hour of time they'd been together. If that made her a bad person, she couldn't help it.

"Mom? You're not saying anything."

She turned off the blaze beneath the macaroni and cheese, then turned to Nick. With a hand on his shoulder, she guided him over to the table and eased him into one of the chairs.

When she took a seat across from him, he leaned forward, his whole face a look of eager anticipation. "Listen to me carefully, Nick. I understand that you and Hannah want to be cousins. And I've known for a long time that you want a father, but—"

Before she could say another word, Nick blurted, "I don't want just any ol' guy to be my dad. I want Blake to be my father! And he wants me to be his son! I know he does!"

Katherine studied Nick's stubborn face and realized she was wasting her breath with cautions and warnings.

The boy wasn't going to allow his mother to pour water on his dreams. Besides, it was far too late to be worrying about the future. She'd trusted Blake enough to invite him into her bed. Now she had to go a step further and trust him with her heart. And Nick's happiness.

Smiling faintly, she ran a hand over his dark hair. "You love Blake, don't you?"

His head bobbed up and down. "He's good to me. But not too good."

She arched an eyebrow at him. "What does that mean?"

He tilted his head to one side as he contemplated his mother's question. "You know what I mean, Mom. Blake gives me attention, but he isn't going overboard to make me like him. He's letting me decide about that. He mainly wants me to grow up strong and tough. And to be smart, too. That's the way Lash is with Shawn. And that's the way I want Blake to always be with me. That means he cares."

Her heart filled with pride, along with a pang of sad regret. If not for her, Nick's dad might still be alive today. But whether he would've changed and turned into a real, caring father, she could only guess.

"Yes. Blake does care about you. I think he always will."

A happy light was suddenly twinkling in Nick's gray eyes. "Gosh, Mom, it's gonna be great having a dad. Maybe he can come watch me play baseball. He might even teach me how to throw a curveball!"

Seeing that nothing she could say was going to dampen Nick's hopes, she decided to simply go along. After all, a boy did need dreams. And so did a woman.

"I'm not sure Blake played baseball in high school

or college. He might not know anything about curveballs and that sort of thing."

"Blake played baseball," Nick promptly insisted. "He told me so. He said he wasn't as good as his brother—the one who's a vet—but he made the team. Gee, Mom, I know more about him than you do."

Smiling at that, Katherine left the chair to attend to the cooking food. "Give me time," she said. "I'm learning."

She had switched off the burner beneath the sausage and was forking the meat onto a serving platter when Nick rushed up behind her and hugged his arms tightly around her waist. Displaying his affection was something he'd done quite often when he was much younger. Now that he was beginning to consider himself close to being a teenager, episodes such as this were becoming few and far between.

"Oh my, what's this all about?" Turning slightly, she tucked an arm around his shoulders and gathered him in a tight hug.

"I just feel good. That's all." He leaned his head back and peered up at her. "Can I tell you something else?"

She pressed her finger to the tip of his nose. "You can tell me anything."

"Well, I got a confession to make," he said sheepishly.

"Uh-oh. Sounds like you got in trouble at school. Where's the note?"

Nick's head swung back and forth. "No way. I made a hundred on my geography test today! And Ms. Canfield let me clean all the blackboards for her."

"Oh, you must have been the star pupil, then." She gave him a playful smile. "So what is this confession all about?"

"It's about you and Blake," he said. "When you first told me you were going to go on a date with him, I was thinking he was going to be a jerk. I decided that when I met him, I'd be polite because I promised you I would be. But I sure wasn't going to like him. How could I be so wrong, Mom? Now I feel bad for thinking such things."

She gave him another tight hug. "Oh, Nick. You're the best son any mom could ever have."

Still unsure, he looked doubtfully up at her. "You're not mad at me for being a dope?"

Laughing, Katherine playfully scrubbed the top of his head. "No. I'm not mad. Ready to eat supper?"

Nick hurried over to the table and took a seat at his usual chair. "Yeah! I'm starved. And I want to go to bed early tonight. That way when I wake up, it'll be time to head to the ranch."

Yes, Katherine thought as she carried the food to the table. She was more than ready to see her man on Three Rivers Ranch again.

By the time Blake entered the ranch house later that night, it was past midnight. His shirt was covered with dirt and sweat and his boots were dragging as he made his way to the gas range and opened the warming drawer.

Damn! It was empty and he'd not eaten since five o'clock this morning. Where the hell had Reeva put the leftovers?

After washing his hands at the double sink, he opened the refrigerator and stared wearily at the crowded shelves, when a footfall alerted him that someone else in the house was still awake.

"Blake! Where the hell have you been? And you're

still wearing your chaps. I thought you and Joe had gone out for a short ride. That was hours ago! Holt has gone to town and Chandler is on an emergency call. I was about to send the boys at the bunkhouse out to search for you two!"

He turned to see his mother striding toward him. In spite of the late hour, she wasn't dressed for bed. Instead, she was still wearing her jeans and a white shirt with the sleeves rolled up past her elbows. The stressed look on her face told him she'd been deeply worried.

"Sorry, Mom. After I put up my horse, I didn't take time to take off my chaps. I'll put them in the mudroom before I go upstairs."

"You think I'm worried about those damn chaps?" She took him by the arm and led him over to the kitchen table. "You sit. While I make you a sandwich, you can tell me why you've been out so late."

While she carried an armful of things from the refrigerator over to the cabinet, Blake swiped a weary hand through his hair.

"We were about to head home several hours ago," he told her. "But then Joe thought he spotted a trail of smoke in the direction of the number-nine well pump. I thought it looked like smoke, too, so we decided we'd better check it out. If that part of the range caught fire… well, I don't have to tell you it would scorch everything for miles."

Slathering a slice of bread with mayonnaise, she paused and directed a sharp look at him. "Dear God, was something burning?"

"We searched all around and couldn't find anything burning or where any fire might have been. It was spooky."

"So you've been all these hours looking for a fire that

wasn't there?" She turned back to her sandwich making. "You should've come on home. But I know how Joe's mind works, and yours, too. You were both thinking that area is close to where you believe your father was killed. You still think you might find some other kind of clue over there. Don't you?"

"We weren't really thinking about clues, Mom! The fence that crosses the gorge had been cut. The cattle were out on the old road that goes up to the Fisher property."

Maureen slapped the sandwich onto a paper plate and carried it over to him. "Cut? Are you sure about that? If I remember right, the motley bull, the one Chandler calls Tiger, is over in that section. He's been known to break a fence before."

"This wasn't broken, Mom," he said bluntly. "We could both see where wire cutters had been used."

Shaking her head, she went back to the refrigerator and pulled out a long-necked bottle of beer. After she placed it in front of Blake, she eased down in the chair next to his.

"I don't understand this, Blake. Why would anybody do something so malicious?"

He shrugged while hoping he could smooth his mother's fears instead of sounding an alarm. She already had more than enough on her mind. She didn't need to be worrying that Three Rivers might possibly have an enemy out there.

"Joe and I figure it was probably hunters."

Maureen was more than doubtful. "Blake, hunting season doesn't start for months."

"I should've said poachers. It's not enough that they hunt during illegal months, they want to trespass to do it."

She scowled. "Maybe we ought to send a couple of men over there on a regular basis to ride fence line. Say, three times a week. At least, for a while."

"I agree. I'll talk to Matthew about it and see who he can spare."

"What about the cattle?" she asked. "Did you get them rounded up?"

"There's hardly ever any cell signal over there. Tonight it was nil. My phone was useless and so was Joe's. So we couldn't call the hands for help." Shutting his eyes, he used his thumb and forefinger to rub at the stinging grit. "For a few hours, we had hell. But we finally managed to get the cows and the bull back onto Three Rivers land. After that, we patched up the fence well enough to hold them until some of the guys can get over there in the morning to make permanent repairs."

His mother studied him for a long moment, then shook her head and slumped back in the chair. "I'm sorry I yelled at you, Blake. Of all my sons, you're the last one to deserve a scolding. I've just been so worried. I kept trying your phone and Joe's. Then about two hours ago, Tessa finally called me, wondering why Joe hadn't made it home. I tried to calm her by telling her I thought you two might have gone to look at a horse for sale up at Yarnell."

"Lord, I didn't know you could make up such whoppers, Mom. Why didn't you just tell her the truth? That you didn't know what we were doing."

"Blake, in case you've forgotten, your sister-in-law is five months pregnant! The last thing she needs is to be working herself into a worried frenzy."

"Looks like you've worked yourself up into a worried frenzy, too." He took three bites of the sandwich, then washed it down with a third of the beer.

From the corner of his eye Blake could see his mother reaching up and massaging both temples. In that moment, he forgot his own weariness and frustration. It wasn't often that Maureen Hollister ever showed a crack in her strong armor. Seeing her a bit rattled reminded Blake that she was more than a worried mother. She was a woman who'd lost her husband, a man she'd loved with all her heart. Only God knew the real depth of her grief.

"Don't tell your brothers," she said. "They'll think I'm losing it."

Blake gave her a lopsided grin before turning his focus back on the sandwich. After he'd eaten a few more bites, he looked over to see the tense lines on her face had eased somewhat.

"Mom, may I ask you something personal?"

"I'm your mother. You may ask me anything. That doesn't mean I'll always answer, though."

His smile weary, he said, "I've been wondering. Do you think you could ever love a man the way you loved Dad?"

A look of faint surprise crossed her face and then she shook her head. The negative response left him feeling even more exhausted.

"I could never love any man the way I loved Joel. He's the father of my babies. We were partners in everything. But—" She paused and gave him a pointed smile. "If the right man happened to come along, I could love him. It would just be a different kind of love in a different kind of way."

"I see. I guess that answers my question."

Maureen grimaced. "After the night you've just put in rounding up cattle and fixing fence, why would you be asking me such a thing?"

Leave it to his mother to make him blush, Blake thought wryly. "Well, because Katherine is a widow, too. She doesn't much like to talk about her late husband or the accident that took his life. I don't know whether that's because it's still too painful for her, or if it's just her way of putting him and their marriage behind her. But sometimes I wonder if—"

Unsure of how to go on without making himself sound like a silly sap, he reached for the beer and downed several swallows.

Next to him, Maureen said softly, "You wonder if she could ever love you. Right?"

He nodded, then let out a cynical grunt. "It's stupid of me to be wondering about such a thing now."

"Meaning?"

"Meaning I think I've already fallen in love with her. And if she doesn't love me back, then I'm—" he settled a hopeless look on his mother "—in the same fix I was with Lenore."

She frowned. "You're making a big mistake, son, in comparing Kat to that woman. Lenore could only love one person and that was Lenore. You could've given her your devoted attention for twenty hours a day and she still wouldn't have been satisfied."

Groaning, he scrubbed his face with both hands. "Why didn't I see that about her before I ever asked her to marry me? It's a scary thought to think I was that blinded. Now I catch myself stepping back and wondering if I... Well, that maybe I'm reading too much into Katherine's feelings for me."

Maureen left the chair and crossed the room to where a baker's rack was loaded with sweets Reeva had baked earlier in the day. As she cut a wedge of two-crust pie and scooped it onto a small plate, she said, "Hannah tells me that Kat and Nick are coming here to the ranch tomorrow. I'm glad. Do you have something special planned?"

"Nick wants to learn how to ride. That's the main thing we're going to do."

She carried the pie and a fork to the table and placed it in front of Blake. "I'm surprised at how close Hannah seems to be getting to the boy. She's always been picky about who she gets close to, but she seemed to take up with little Nick right away."

"That's because the two of them have something in common. Neither has a father."

Frowning, Maureen said, "Hannah's dad isn't dead."

"As far as she's concerned, he is."

He picked up the fork and sliced into the pie. "What is this I'm eating? Looks like yellow grapes."

Maureen chuckled. "That's gooseberry pie. And the berries don't come cheap, so enjoy it."

He scarfed up another bite as his mother lingered near his shoulder.

"Hannah used to talk about wanting her mother to get married again. But she hardly ever brings up the subject now."

"Good thing. Vivian likes her life the way it is."

"And what about you, Blake? Would you like to become Nick's father?"

He'd not expected his mother to ask such an outright question and long moments passed as he gave careful thought to his next words.

"Nick is a fine boy," Blake told her. "Any man would be proud to call him his son."

"That's a standard answer if I ever heard one. I'd prefer a simple yes or no."

He twisted his head around just enough to allow him

to see her face. "It's not that easy, Mom. But yes, I'd like for the boy to be my son. I'm just not certain that Katherine feels the same way—that she wants me to be Nick's father and her husband."

Her hand came to rest on his shoulder. "I understand, Blake. You're wondering if she has room enough in her heart to love you the way you want to be loved. Well, most women aren't equipped with a one-size-fits-all heart. I think Kat's happens to be a whole lot bigger."

Bending, she pressed a kiss on his cheek. "Good night, son."

She'd already headed out of the kitchen when Blake called to her and she paused long enough to look back at him.

"Yes?"

"I'm sorry Joe and I worried you so."

"Forget it. That's what mothers are for."

The next morning, inside one of the ranch's many huge horse barns, Katherine stood next to Blake and watched her son stride back and forth over the hard-packed ground to test the cowboy boots Hannah had given him a few minutes ago.

"How do they fit, Nick?" Hannah asked as she walked along beside him. "Since they're old, they ought to feel good and soft. Old is always better. I keep 'em till the soles get holes. Then Mom makes me throw them away."

Pausing, Nick rocked back on his heels and gazed in wonder at the snub-toed boots. The upper leather was creased and scarred, but from the look on Nick's face they were the grandest footwear he'd ever owned.

"They feel good," he said. "Do they look like girls' boots?"

She waved a dismissive hand through the air. "No. They just look like regular boots. I wear boy boots lots of times. You can't tell the difference."

"Really?"

"Really." She stuck out her foot to show off the chocolate-colored pair she was wearing. "See. These came from the boys department. Bet you couldn't tell."

Nick shook his head. "No. So now what? Do I get to put on a pair of spurs?"

Hannah's mouth popped open. "No way! They're for giving commands and going fast. If you don't do it right, the horse might buck! You have to learn how to ride really good before you wear spurs."

"Oh," he said. "Well, I might get good enough to wear spurs someday."

Grinning, Hannah wrapped her arm around his shoulders. "Sure you will. In no time at all. So come on and I'll show you how to put a halter on Moondust. Then we'll tie our horses to the hitchin' post and get them ready to be saddled."

"Okay!"

The two kids took off in a run toward the back of the barn. Behind them, Katherine looked at Blake and smiled.

"Hannah really is going to take care of him. And those boots. He's in heaven."

Blake chuckled. "Before you know it, we're going to have Nick turned into a little cowboy. I hope you don't mind."

"Are you kidding? It's wonderful to see him so happy."

He slipped an arm around the back of her waist and urged her in the same direction the children had taken.

"It's pretty wonderful to see a smile on your face, too. I'm so glad you're here."

"I'm glad, too. Ever since you, uh, came for lunch, I've been thinking about you and—"

She paused abruptly as a tall ranch hand with rusty brown hair and a long handlebar mustache approached Blake.

"Sorry to interrupt, Blake," he said with a polite nod in Katherine's direction. "I thought you should know that Red Feather is limping on her right front this morning. I can't see anything wrong, but her ankle does feel a bit warm."

"Damn! I rode her last night in the pitch-dark. But she seemed to be fine when I turned her out in the paddock. She must've stepped in a hole. Has Chandler taken a look at her yet?"

The cowboy grimaced. "No. Chandler was called out this morning to the Johnson Ranch over in Maricopa County. Poor folks have an outbreak of shipping fever running through their remuda."

"If that's the case, Chandler will be busy for hours." He paused to consider his options, then said, "Put her out in the back patch behind the mares' paddock. I'll send Holt out there to take a look at her as soon as he gets a chance."

"Right," the other man said, then hurriedly strode away.

Concerned by the two men's conversation, she looked at him. "Blake, if you need to attend to your mare, please do. Don't worry about me. I'll stay with the kids."

"No. It's not that serious. And trust me, Holt will know how to fix her far better than me."

"Well, if you're sure. I don't want to be an interference with your work."

He urged her on down the alleyway of the barn. "You could never be an interference, Kat. And this is a special day. Nick is going to get on a horse for the first time in his life. I wouldn't miss this time with him for anything."

I want Blake to be my father! And he wants me to be his son!

Could it be that her son had already picked up signals from Blake? Signs of commitment that she'd been too afraid to see? She didn't have the answers. But one thing she knew for sure—at this moment her heart was overflowing for this man.

"Thank you, Blake. For doing all of this for Nick. You can't know how happy it makes me."

He smiled at her and for a brief second she glimpsed something in his eyes that spoke of love and lifelong promises. The idea filled her with warm joy, even while the cautious part of her mind, the part that remembered all the pain and sorrow of her broken marriage, tried to push the gladness away.

"Look closer, Kat, and you'll see it makes me just as happy."

Chapter Eleven

Blake and Katherine walked to another section of the barn, where the horses were to be saddled. Moondust and Hannah's horse, a sorrel she called Bandana, were already tied to a long hitching post. Hannah had placed a brush in Nick's hand and was patiently showing him how to groom the most important parts of his mount.

For the next few minutes, Katherine was content to stand to one side and watch as Hannah saddled her own horse and Blake handled the chore for Nick. During the process, he painstakingly showed Nick how the blankets and saddle should fit on the animal's back and the importance of keeping the girth tight.

Normally, Nick wasn't keen on taking instructions. More often than not, he allowed them to fly right over his head, but this morning Katherine could see her son was soaking up every word Blake was telling him.

"Okay, kids, looks like we're ready to go to the

arena," Blake announced. "But before we leave the barn, I have something else for Nick."

He disappeared inside the tack room and emerged a moment later carrying a dark brown cowboy hat. The brim was bent and the crown sweat-stained. A brown feather was stuck into the Native American beaded headband.

Wide-eyed, Nick asked, "Is that really for me?"

Blake placed the felt hat on Nick's head and levered the brim up and down to test the fit. "Sure is. A cowboy can't get on his horse without a hat. Feel like it will stay on?"

"I think so." Nick bobbed his head, then seemingly satisfied with the fit, he pulled off the headgear to examine it more closely.

Katherine met Blake's indulgent grin and her heart suddenly filled with warm emotions. What Blake had just given her child was much more than a hat, she thought. It was a show of love.

"Gosh, this is cool! Really cool!" Nick exclaimed. "It looks like the real deal."

Blake laughed. "That's because it is. If you work spring roundup on Three Rivers, you have to wear real cowboy gear."

Grinning from ear to ear, Nick plopped the hat back onto his head and pulled the brim nearly to his eyebrows. "How do I look, Mom?"

"You look like a regular cowhand," she said, smiling at the sight of him. "So don't you think you should thank Blake and Hannah for the riding gear?"

Without further prompting from his mother, Nick stepped forward and flung his arms around Blake's waist. "Thanks, Blake! The hat is super!"

A soft look came over Blake's features as he patted Nick's back. "You're welcome, son. I'm glad you like it."

After moving away from Blake, Nick looked awkwardly at Hannah. "Thanks, Hannah. The boots are great, too."

She pulled a playful smirk at him. "Well, you can hug me, too, Nick. The girl part won't rub off."

He tilted his head to one side as he tried to decide about her invitation. "Okay," he said finally. "But don't tell anybody. Promise?"

Hannah rolled her eyes. "Oh, all right, I promise. And anyway, cousins hug each other. Didn't you know that?"

A dumbfounded look came over his face. "No. 'Cause I don't have any cousins. Except for you," he added.

As Hannah considered his reply, her jaw slowly dropped. "Gosh, now that I think about it, I don't have any cousins, either."

Blake looked at Katherine and winked. "But you will after Tessa has her baby," Blake told the girl.

Hannah clapped her hands together. "Yay! That's right! When Uncle Joe's baby gets here, we'll both have two cousins, Nick!"

Not waiting for Nick to make the next move, Hannah grabbed Nick up in a hug so tight that once she turned him loose he staggered backward.

Blake exchanged an amused glance with Katherine, then said to the kids, "Come on, you two. Unhitch your horses. We're burning daylight."

Two hours later, after plenty of instructions and coaxing, Nick was riding Moondust in a slow circle inside the arena. Hannah rode safely alongside him to offer help and guidance in case he had trouble making the horse go.

Outside the wooden fence surrounding the arena, Katherine sat on a partially shaded stack of hay bales, watching her son grow more confident with each passing minute. If only Prudence could see him now, Katherine thought. Her friend would be smiling with approval.

Too bad Katherine's mother wouldn't have the same sentiment, she thought sadly. Ever since Katherine had made the decision to return to Wickenburg and care for her dying father, Paulette had considered her a traitor. Her calls to Katherine and Nick were few and far between. However, last night, just as Katherine was about to climb into bed, her mother had called.

Katherine wasn't sure why she'd ended up telling her mother about Blake, or their plans here at Three Rivers today. She supposed Nick's excitement had bubbled over onto her and she'd wanted to share it with someone.

Katherine, when are you ever going to quit dreaming? The Hollisters are quality folks and you're an Anderson. You'll only end up hurting yourself and Nick.

Katherine's lips pressed into a tight line as her mother's bitter warning played through her head. Yes, she was an Anderson. But that didn't mean she had to forget her dreams and settle for less.

"Hey, is that a hungry look I see on your face?"

She glanced to her left to see Blake standing next to the haystack. The brim of his gray Stetson partially shaded his face, but she wasn't having any trouble spotting the sexy grin on his lips. The sight of him instantly chased away her brooding thoughts.

After a quick glance around to make sure there

wasn't anyone within earshot, she asked coyly, "For food? Or you?"

His husky chuckle sent a provocative shiver down her spine.

"Uh, unfortunately for food. Mom just sent me a text. Lunch is ready." He reached a hand up to her. "Come on and we'll see if we can pry the kids off their horses."

Katherine laughed. "Right. That might take some doing. I think they're having fun."

"Just a little."

He helped her down to the ground, and as she stood close to his side, she had an overwhelming urge to rest her cheek against his chest, to tell him exactly how special he was becoming to her. But was that something he wanted to hear from her now? Would he ever want to hear it? Or was this family-type gathering just his way of keeping her content until he decided adding a woman and child to his life was more than he could handle?

The questions rolling around in her head must have reflected on her face. He suddenly stroked his fingertips over her cheek.

"What are you thinking, Kat? A few seconds ago you were laughing and now I see shadows in your eyes."

Smiling wanly, she shook her head. "I was just thinking how special this day is for Nick and how much his grandmother is missing by not taking much interest in his life."

Frowning, he said, "Maybe if you gave your mother a call and told her all about the things Nick has been doing and how fast he's growing up, she might get interested."

Katherine shook her head. "She actually called me last night and for a minute—when I first heard her voice—I held hope that she might be softening. I was wrong. She was terribly negative through the whole conversation."

Blake whistled under his breath. "Sorry, Katherine. She sounds awfully bitter."

Katherine shrugged. "She has reason to be bitter over Dad. But ignoring her grandson is taking it too far."

With a hand on her shoulder, he guided her away from the haystack and toward a gate that entered the arena.

As they walked, he asked, "Does Nick realize how his grandmother feels?"

"He does. But thankfully, it doesn't appear to bother him that much. He says his grandmother isn't fun to be around anyway."

"Hmm. So basically, where family is concerned, you and Nick are pretty much alone," he mused aloud.

"That's right. Unfortunately."

"Well, I hope Nick knows he can be a part of my family for as long as he wants."

What would Blake think, Katherine wondered, if she told him that Nick was already planning on him becoming his father? Would he run as far and as fast as he could?

Trying not to think about it, she murmured, "Thank you, Blake."

It took a few minutes for Bandana and Moondust to be unsaddled and put out to pasture. After the horses and tack were both tended to, the four of them walked back to the ranch house. Along the way, they were intercepted by Matthew Waggoner, the ranch's foreman. Without breaking stride, Blake explained what was needed to repair the broken fence near the number-nine well pump. He also added the order for two men to ride the ten-mile fence to the end to make sure it was all still intact.

By the time they reached the ranch house, Blake had explained what had happened the night before when he and Joe had been out riding. He'd blamed the downed fence on poachers. But after hearing the suspicions he held over his father's death, Katherine could only wonder if someone other than a poacher had trespassed onto Three Rivers land. Still, she kept the notion to herself.

When the four of them walked beneath the shade of the patio, Maureen was there waiting for them.

"Finally! Someone has shown up to help me eat all this lunch!" she exclaimed. "You guys go wash up. Everything is ready."

After a trip inside the house to freshen up, they returned to the patio to see Maureen had made a small charcoal fire in the barbecue pit so that hot dogs and marshmallows could be roasted. There was also an assortment of condiments, chips of all kinds and sodas to wash it all down.

"Oh, boy—thanks, Grandma, for fixing us a cookout," Hannah said. "Nick and I are starving, too. We've been riding all morning."

The woman gathered a child beneath each arm and guided them over to the fire. "I want to hear all about it," she told the kids. "Now, be honest, Nick—was Hannah a good teacher? Or was she bossy?"

"No. She was mostly nice. The only time she was bossy was when I was doing something wrong," Nick answered.

Hannah jammed a hand on one hip. "That was because I didn't want Nick to get hurt. And anyway, he was a good pupil."

"And you were a good teacher," Maureen said with

a grin for both children. "Sounds like the riding lesson went well. Your mother will be glad to hear it."

"Where is Vivian, by the way?" Katherine asked. "I was hoping I'd get to see her today."

"Mom had to fill in for another ranger today," Hannah explained, then sighed and added, "Of all days. I wanted her to see me and Nick ride together."

"There will be other rides," Blake assured his niece.

Maureen began to help the kids with their franks and roasting sticks, while Blake and Katherine fared for themselves.

"I didn't know you were planning on all this, Mom," Blake said a few minutes later as everyone sat around a long wicker-and-glass table, munching on the simple food. "I was going to talk Reeva into making sandwiches for us."

"Reeva needed to do some things in town, so I told her to go on," Maureen explained. "Besides, I'm taking the day off. Not even one hour in the saddle for me today."

Katherine looked at Blake's mother. "Do you ride very much, Maureen?"

"Much? Haven't you noticed her bowed legs?" Blake teased.

Laughing, Maureen shook her finger at him, then said to Katherine, "Every day. The boys tell me they can do without my help around the ranch. But I don't believe a word of it. And even if they could handle things without me, I'd go crazy cooped up in the house all the time. Especially since…well, since Joel is gone."

Katherine nodded while hoping she didn't look as uncomfortable as she felt. "I understand completely."

Maureen's smile was perceptive. "I'm sure that you do."

Clearing her throat, Katherine purposely changed the

subject. "This is awfully nice of you to fix our lunch. But you should have waited and let me help you."

"Nonsense. How much effort does it take to carry out a bag of franks and buns?" Her thoughtful gaze traveled back and forth between Blake and Katherine. "You and Nick are going to stay for dinner tonight, aren't you? That's one of the reasons I sent Reeva to town. I wanted her to pick up something special from the grocery store."

"Oh." Katherine looked questioningly at Blake. "I don't know about dinner. Blake didn't mention it and—"

"Blake just assumes things, Katherine. After a while, you'll learn that about him."

"Mom, don't worry," Blake told her. "I wasn't about to let Katherine and Nick leave before dinner. In fact, I was thinking I might drive her out to the old house and show her around. With any luck, the falls might have a little trickle of water."

Across the table, Nick hurriedly swallowed a chunk of hot dog. "Can Hannah and I go, too?"

Blake glanced over at Katherine and she realized his little plan was to gain them some alone time.

"Well," he began, "if that's what you two want to do. Then you're invited, too."

Before Nick could make a reply, Hannah cupped her hand to his ear and whispered behind it. After a moment, his face lit up and then he looked at Hannah and nodded vigorously.

"We don't want to go, Uncle Blake," Hannah informed him. "You and Katherine can go. We can show Nick the cabin some other time."

Katherine was wondering what Hannah had said to cause Nick's sudden change of heart, when Blake spoke up.

"Okay. But what are you and Nick going to do to keep yourselves occupied? The ranch is shorthanded today. I don't want you and Nick roaming around the barns unless someone is around."

"We won't go to the barns," Hannah promised. "We're going to watch the horse races on television. I'm going to teach Nick how to handicap."

"I don't care how much horse racing you watch," Blake told her. "But you're not going to teach Nick how to gamble. So forget it!"

Keeping up with the whole exchange between her son and granddaughter, Maureen suddenly wagged a finger at him. "Blake, don't be such a stuffed shirt. Handicapping isn't gambling. It's calculating which horse will win first, second or third. The kids will be exercising their math skills and learning how to spot good horseflesh at the same time." She turned to give Katherine a confident look. "Don't you agree, Kat?"

In spite of Blake's disapproving scowl, Katherine chuckled. In her opinion he was making much ado about nothing. "Well, it's not like Nick or Hannah will be laying money down at the ticket counter," she reasoned. "I'm perfectly fine with it. Actually, I've always wanted to go to Turf Paradise and watch the horses run. But I never had anyone offer to go with me."

Maureen groaned with dismay while darting a censuring look at her son. "Oh, Kat, all you need to do is call me or Vivian. We love to go to the track whenever we have the chance. So does Hannah."

As if on cue, the girl tossed down the last bite of hot dog and leaped to her feet. "Riders up!" she yelled, then pretending she was holding a bugle, she loudly hummed out the call to post parade.

Clearly impressed, Nick grinned at her. "Hey, that's pretty good, Hannah. You ought to take band in school."

"Thanks," she told him, then glanced hopefully at the adults. "When can we all go to the track? Soon? Please!"

"As soon as your uncle Blake realizes he needs to see more than the back end of a cow," Maureen told her.

Katherine glanced over to see Blake wasn't looking at her or his mother. He was staring moodily off into space.

"Somebody around here has to look at the cows, Mom," he said with a heavy dose of sarcasm. "Or Three Rivers won't last another hundred and seventy years."

Maureen cast a rueful glance at Katherine, then took a moment to scrutinize her son's sullen face.

"One of these days, Blake," Maureen said bluntly, "you're going to see there's more to life than Three Rivers."

Katherine watched Blake's jaw drop. Clearly, his mother's remark was not something he'd ever heard from her. Or if he had, it wasn't often.

She was wondering if Blake was going to make some sort of retort, when Maureen suddenly rose to her feet and began gathering plates and utensils.

"Come on," Maureen said to Hannah and Nick. "Help me carry these things back to the kitchen and I'll dig out the ice cream. We have two flavors today. Strawberry and rocky road."

Both children eagerly jumped to their feet and began helping Maureen clear the table. Katherine pitched in to help and in a few short minutes the lunch remnants were cleared away and she and Blake were alone on the patio.

So far he'd not made a move to leave his chair or say a word, and Katherine decided if he had some sort of issue with her, she needed to hear about it now rather than later.

"I hate to ruin the rest of Nick's afternoon, but I think we should go on home," she told him. "You obviously need a breather."

Her announcement seemed to jolt him as if she'd sloshed a bucket of cold water in his face. He instantly jumped to his feet. "What are you talking about?"

Awkwardly, she turned and walked over to the edge of the patio. From where she was standing, a portion of the arena was visible. Dust was flying high in the air as Holt cantered a black horse through a series of figure eights. Obviously the Hollisters continued to work right through the weekend, she thought. And even more obvious, the time Blake was spending with her and Nick was out of character for him. She wasn't sure if she should feel flattered that he considered them important enough to interrupt his work. Or fearful that she was a temporary thing.

"I…think you've had a bit too much of the family thing today. We're getting on your nerves."

Quickly, he moved up behind her and rested his hands on the tops of her shoulders. "You're wrong," he said gently. "And if I seemed cross a few minutes ago, I'm sorry. I wasn't really."

"You sounded like it."

His hands began to knead her tense shoulders. "Mom's remark did irk me, but I wasn't angry at you, or her, or anybody, except myself."

She turned to look at him. "Why would you be angry with yourself?"

Anguish twisted his features. "Because I finally realized my family has it right when they call me the judge."

"I'm sure they do it with affection, Blake."

"That doesn't make it any less true," he said ruefully. "Judge, stuffed shirt, workaholic. Ever since Dad died, I've had all those monikers thrown at me. And I've always let them roll off my back. But now—with you and Nick here—it's different. I don't want you to start thinking of me in those terms."

"Oh, Blake, if that talk about going to the track upset you, that's not important. I understand—"

She paused as he cupped a hand tenderly to the side of her face.

"No," he said gently. "It is important. And Mom is right. I do need to ease up. I need to let myself enjoy time away from the ranch. I just don't know how to balance it all, Kat. Not the way my brothers do."

She could feel his frustration and she desperately wanted to take it away. "You shouldn't be beating yourself up about this," she said softly. "A man can just stretch himself so far without breaking. You've been giving me and Nick lots of attention. I wouldn't ask you for more."

"No. You wouldn't ask now. But if we were married, you'd feel differently. You'd expect your husband to put you first."

She stared at him in wonder. Was he actually thinking about marriage? No. He was simply using the term to make a point. One that she didn't want to think about. Not today.

"But we're not married," she said, softening her words with a smile. "So let's enjoy our time together today. You said something about showing me an old house. I'd love to see it. That is…if you're still in the mood."

A slow grin eased the tension on his face and it suddenly dawned on Katherine that her happiness was completely intertwined with his. So what if Blake became unhappy with her the same way Cliff had? What if he decided she wasn't worth the effort of wasting his precious time? Oh, God, this was getting too serious, she thought. She was caring too much. Wanting him too much. Yet she was beyond shutting down her feelings. Now she could only move forward and hope she hadn't made the same mistake she'd made with Cliff.

"I'm definitely in the mood." Grabbing her hand, he led her off the patio. "There's a work truck parked out by the back gate. We'll take it."

Fifteen minutes later, after traveling several miles north of the ranch yard, Katherine asked, "How far away is this old house?"

Too far, Blake thought. For hours he'd been aching to get his hands on Katherine, and now that he was finally going to get his chance, he was getting impatient. Although, after that episode on the patio with his mother, he should probably count himself lucky that Katherine was sitting here beside him at all, he thought grimly.

He wasn't sure what had come over him. But all of a sudden every doubt he'd ever had about his future with Katherine was suddenly crowding into the dreams and hopes he was trying so desperately to hold on to. And when his mother had made the remark about him being unable, or more aptly, unwilling to pull himself away from the responsibility of running the ranch, he'd basically wanted to blow his stack. Something that Blake Hollister just didn't do.

"Ten more minutes or so," he said as he maneuvered the truck between two rock abutments. "Sorry about the rough ride. Getting tired?"

"Not at all. I'm loving every minute of it. The mountains in the distance are so beautiful." She glanced at him. "Are you sure we're still on Three Rivers? It seems like we've been gone forever."

He laughed. "I'm sure. On the east side, Three Rivers goes all the way past Constellation to the edge of the Tonto National Forest. To the north it reaches Kirkland Junction. The house is located somewhere in between."

"And is this house something that was built recently?" she asked.

Smiling, he said, "We call it 'the house,' but compared to nowadays standards it's a three-room cabin. My great-great-great-grandfather built it in the summer of 1845. Actually, it's the original ranch house on Three Rivers. He and his bride of sixteen lived there together until 1847, when he built the big house where we live now. By then she'd given birth to a son, Joseph. He turned out to be our great-great-grandfather. My brother Joe is named after him."

He glanced over to see she was staring at him with a look of disbelief.

"What's wrong?" he asked. "You don't believe me?"

"I believe you. I'm amazed, that's all. And wondering how it must feel for you to have so much family history."

"Everyone has family history, Katherine."

"Yes, but not the sort that a person is proud to share with outsiders."

He grunted. "Trust me. Down through the years there've been several rascals in the Hollister family. Vivian swears Holt should be added to the list."

"The night Nick and I came to dinner, I noticed Vivian and Holt seemed very close. Have they always been that way?"

Blake nodded. "Holt is two years younger than Vivian. Mom says when he was born, Viv wanted the baby to be hers. By the time Holt started walking, Viv had become a little mother hen. They have their separate lives now, but they're still very tight."

Katherine sighed. "For years Aaron and I were like that. Whenever things were bad at home, we leaned on each other. But after Aaron reached high school, he started drawing away from me. It was like he needed to prove he was a tough guy and didn't want a sister close by to back him up."

"And now?"

"I think I told you before how Aaron refused to help after Dad had the stroke. Well, he, uh, holds all of that against me. He called me a traitor for moving back to Wickenburg and caring for Dad."

Her father was dead, her mother distant and her brother had turned his back on her. Her family situation was hard for Blake to fathom. He'd always been surrounded by loving, supporting relatives. He couldn't imagine how alone Katherine must feel.

"Sounds like he's just as bitter as your mother."

She sighed again and the sad sound made Blake want to stop the truck and gather her into his arms. He wanted to assure her that she'd never be alone again. Not as long as he was alive. But making that sort of long-term promise would be like saying "I love you—I want to marry you." He wasn't yet comfortable that Katherine was ready to hear such a vow from him.

But she's going to have to get ready. Time is spinning by and you're not so young anymore, Blake. You want a wife to love you and warm your bed. You want children and lots of them.

Katherine finally spoke, breaking into the nagging voice going on in Blake's head.

"Yes, Aaron is extremely bitter," she agreed. "And it's going to take more than his sister to change him."

Blake reached for her hand, and as he gave her fingers a comforting squeeze, he wondered what it was going to take to make Katherine and Nick his family. Or was that a wish that might never come true?

Chapter Twelve

A few minutes later, Katherine stood in front of the original Three Rivers Ranch house and tried to imagine how the sixteen-year-old bride of Edmond Hollister coped with living in such rugged wilderness. And bearing a baby, at that.

Long years of weather had eaten the bark from the chinked logs to leave the small structure a smooth gray color. A heavy planked door sat directly in the center, and to one side of it, a tiny window was covered with board shutters. There was no porch and only a flat rock to serve as a step.

In spite of its crudeness, there was a rustic charm to the little house that tugged at Katherine.

"Oh my, Blake. It's so lovely here. I wasn't expecting the house to sit beneath a mountain bluff or there to be so many trees around. From the size of those cottonwoods, they'd have to be very old."

Standing next to her, he slipped his arm around the back of her waist. "I'd guess the trees are nearing the century mark. Which means someone must have planted them after the big house was built."

"Or could be the trees came up by chance," she suggested. "From a seed carried by the wind."

"Do you believe in chance?" he asked.

She looked up to meet his gaze and not for the first time today she saw doubts and questions swimming in his eyes. Was he beginning to think their relationship wasn't going to work? No. She couldn't allow herself to start worrying. They were together. And alone. That was all she needed to think about now.

She smiled faintly. "You mean like the two of us running into each other on the sidewalk in front of Yavapai Bank and Trust?"

"That wasn't chance," he murmured, his brown eyes softening. "That was luck—on my part."

Her smile turned impish. "You still think so?"

"I'll always think so," he said gently.

Always. She was trying to decide whether to take that one word to heart, when he reached for her hand.

"Come on," he urged. "Let's go around to the back. We'll see if the falls are running."

"We're not going in the house first?" she asked as he led her around the side of the small, chinked-log structure.

A twinkle flashed in his eyes. "No. I'm saving that tour for last."

The area behind the cabin was densely shaded with more cottonwoods and several tall pines. A faint breeze carried the tangy scent of evergreen and Katherine turned her face up to the cool, fresh air.

"I wonder what made your ancestors decide to build

here first?" she asked as they continued walking toward the hundred-foot bluff rising in front of them.

"The availability of water from the falls. And the bluff provided shelter from the north wind and whatever predators, animal or human, that were around in those days."

Katherine looked around her and tried to imagine the area before there were highways and towns and lawmen to keep the peace. "Did Edmond Hollister first come here as a prospector or a rancher?" she asked.

"That's a question that's been tossed around the family many times down through the years," he said. "Dad always thought Edmond was a rancher through and through. Personally, I think when he arrived at this part of the state, he was mostly searching for gold and silver. And when he happened to find a bit of both, he put the money into cattle. And the rest, as they say, is history."

"Hmm. One thing's for sure," Katherine mused, "he must have been a true adventurer."

They pushed their way through a thick stand of brush and pine boughs until they reached an opening. The tiny meadow was lush with green grass, making it evident that water had to be nearby.

Pulling her to a stop next to a twisted juniper trunk, Blake pointed to their left. "Over there. Can you hear the falls?"

She listened more closely and caught the faint sound of splashing water. "Yes! I do."

"It's not often the spring goes dry. But it does happen when a drought is going on. Thankfully, this year we've had a bit of rain."

Bending, Katherine peered through the limbs of a desert willow and spotted a tiny waterfall trickling over slabs of rock. "Oh, there it is! Can we get closer?"

"I think so. Walk behind me—just in case a rattler has decided to find a nice cool spot in the shade."

"Lead the way," she told him. "I'll keep a watchful eye out for reptiles."

A dim trail curved through a stand of trees until they were standing next to a small pool of water surrounded by large boulders.

Katherine immediately kneeled and dipped her hands in the cool water. Except for the chirping and chattering of birds and a breeze sifting through the pines, the woods around them was quiet and still. "This is beautiful. And the water is almost cold."

"Compared to the water hole on Joe and Tessa's ranch, this one is like a teacup next to a bathtub. The falls on the Bar X are really tall and have a pool of water large enough to swim in. One of these days I'll take you over there and show it to you. Do you know how to ride a horse?"

"Uh, no. But don't tell Nick. He thinks his mother knows how to do everything."

He chuckled. "Then you need to be taking riding lessons, too."

She straightened to her full height. "Me on a horse? I'm not sure I'm brave enough for that."

"You're more than brave enough. You've raised a son for the past several years without any help. That takes real courage, Kat."

He'd given her compliments before, but this one touched her deep inside, and before she knew it, she was stepping forward and resting her cheek against his chest. "Coming from you, that means so much to me."

His hands were moving up and down her back, drawing her closer. "You mean, coming from a stuffed shirt like me?"

Even though there was a teasing note in his voice, she sensed a serious undercurrent in his words.

Slipping her hands to the middle of his chest, her fingers teased one of the pearl snaps on his shirt. "The day you came to my house for lunch, I discovered your shirt was stuffed with a very hot-blooded man. In fact, I, uh, eventually took off your shirt," she said huskily. "Would you like for me to get this one out of the way?"

He smiled down at her and the glint she spotted in his brown eyes had her heart beating a rapid dance against her ribs.

"I think it's time we went inside the house."

With his hand on hers, he led her over the tangled trail until they reached the back of the little log house. A wide porch sheltered this end of the structure and Katherine stood to one side of the planked floor while he opened a heavy wooden door. The hinges creaked as he pushed it wide.

"Wait out here," he instructed. "There's no electricity and it's pitch-dark inside. I'll have to light a lamp and open the windows."

He disappeared into the house and after a few short moments Katherine could see a faint light appear beyond the open doorway.

She ventured up to the threshold and peered inside. "Is it safe to come in now?"

He emerged from the shadowy room and reached for her hand. "Please come into the old Hollister homestead, my lady. It's a bit dusty, but mostly clean. Right now you're standing in the kitchen."

Katherine glanced around the small area to see a small set of crude cabinets, a cast-iron wood-burning cookstove and a table with a white granite pitcher and matching wash pan.

"I'd probably burn everything to a crisp on that stove," she said.

"It's hard to imagine living this crudely," he said. "All the water used in the house had to be carried from the falls."

Blake guided her through a doorway and into the next room. The space was illuminated by the open window and the faint glow of a hurricane lamp sitting on a round wooden table.

Katherine looked around with interest. "Are the walls and floors original? I'm surprised how sturdy they are."

"We've not done anything to the place, except patch the roof from time to time." He gestured around the room. "It's anybody's guess how Edmond and Helena used this space. We call it the living room. Mom had the hands bring that sofa and chair up here a couple of years ago. Before those were brought in, there was only a rocker and some cane-bottomed chairs." He urged her to the right, where a calico curtain covered another doorway. "And this is the bedroom."

Katherine stepped past the curtain to find a tiny room with one open window. Fresh air was blowing through the small square, filling the space with the scent of evergreens and sage. A small iron bed covered with a patchwork quilt and two pillows was situated in one corner. At the footboard was a long cedar chest, the edges worn smooth by years of use.

Touched by the simplicity, Katherine stared at the bed as thoughts of Helena Hollister drifted through her mind. The woman had conceived a son in this room and Katherine didn't have to wonder how she'd feel if she conceived Blake's child. She would love his baby fiercely, just as she loved Nick.

Her throat thick with emotions, she turned and

reached for him. He gathered her into his arms and then he was kissing her with a hunger that swept all thoughts from her head.

"I wanted to be alone with you," she whispered as he lifted her onto the bed. "I just didn't realize we were going to be *this* alone. We're miles away from the ranch house—from everything. And it feels...wonderful."

He sat on the side of the bed and began to tug off his boots. After he'd tossed them aside, he went to work removing hers. "There is no cell signal here. No one can call and say I'm urgently needed back at the ranch house. This afternoon belongs to us, Kat. And we're going to enjoy every moment of it."

Her boots joined his on the floor and then he was stretching out beside her, drawing her into the circle of his arms.

His kisses ravaged her lips and kindled a desire in her that knew no bounds. In a matter of moments their clothing joined the pile of boots on the floor and then he was inside her, moving slowly, teasingly, until she was writhing beneath him, crying out for more.

With her arms tight around his back, her legs tangled with his, she closed her eyes and let the pleasure of his body carry her away. Eventually she found herself in a velvety place where there was no sound, only bursting lights, rocketing her senses to the top of a mountain. The descent came much slower, and as she drifted back to awareness, everything inside her turned so soft and vulnerable that tears burned her throat and stung her eyes. A strange swelling filled her chest and it wasn't until she opened her eyes and saw his handsome face hovering over hers that she recognized the feeling was her heart overflowing with love.

* * *

The following week was filled with ups and downs for Blake. Twice he'd made plans to drive into Wickenburg to spend time with Katherine and Nick and both times he'd been forced to cancel at the last minute.

Katherine had seemed to take the canceled dates all in stride. At least, she'd said all the right words about understanding the nature of his job. But Blake wasn't tone-deaf. He'd heard the disappointment in her voice. And tonight he meant to make it up to her in a monumental way. Tonight he hoped to change his life and hers for the better.

"Hey, Blake! You going out tonight?"

About to climb into his pickup truck, Blake paused to see Matthew hurrying toward him.

"I am. Don't tell me something else is going on. Let's see, this week there's been sick bulls, three lame horses, two missing saddles and a well pump on the blink. Not to mention the shipment of feed being four days late. Oh, yeah, I forgot the broken hydraulic lift on the tractor. A few feet closer and the damn bucket would have fallen on Rowdy's head! Am I missing something?"

"Hell, Blake, what's eating you? That's a normal week for Three Rivers."

Hating himself for sounding like such a jerk, he shook his head. "Sorry, Matt. You didn't deserve that."

"Forget it," the foreman said. "The week has been hectic and you've had to carry the biggest load."

"That's what I'm supposed to do. It's just that—"

"You'd like a little time for Katherine," Matthew said, finishing Blake's thought with a knowing grin.

Blake let out a long breath. "Is it that obvious?"

"No. It's just that I sort of know how your mind works. And I can see she's become important to you.

That's good, Blake. It's time you had a woman in your life."

Yes. But was he going to be able to keep her in his life? The afternoon they'd spent together at the old Hollister house had been magical. It would've been the perfect time to tell Katherine exactly how he felt about her.

He loved her more than anything and she needed to know the depth of his feelings. But try as he might, he'd not found the courage to speak the words. Each time he'd even come close to saying the word *love*, he'd choked up. Since then, he'd been kicking himself over and over for not finding the courage to tell her how he really felt.

Blake let out a wry grunt. "I wouldn't have expected to hear that from you."

Matt's chuckle was a cynical sound. "Well, as long as it's you and not me, I'm tickled for you."

Blake glanced at his watch. "I'd better get going. Was there something you needed to tell me?"

"Only that I saw Farley Wilkins in town today. I don't know what he was doing in Wickenburg. Trying to cheat somebody out of something, I suppose. Anyway, he said he wanted to buy two hundred head of Three Rivers's heifers. I told him no and to get lost and stay lost."

Blake gave Matt's arm a playful swat. "Good man. He's lucky you didn't give him a pair of black eyes."

Matt grimaced. "I won't forget how he carried off two of our saddles, then tried to lie his way out of it. And one of these days I'm going to get the three thousand dollars that he owes us, or I'm going to beat it out of him."

"Don't fret about it. What goes around comes around. Farley will eventually pay for his bad deeds." Blake opened the truck door and climbed in. "Just do me a favor tonight, Matt. If some catastrophe happens, don't call me. Just pretend you manage this ranch."

"Don't worry. I got you covered. Big night planned, huh?"

The biggest night of his life, Blake thought. To Matt, he said, "I'm hoping so. See you later."

"Blake, where are we going? To Prescott?" Twenty minutes ago, after he'd picked her up, he'd driven straight to the main highway and turned north. Now the evening sun was waning, sending pink-gold fingers across the desert floor and shrouding the distant mountains with purple shadows.

"If you'd like. But first I want to stop at a very special place."

They were on the same route he'd taken her on their first date, oh, so many weeks ago, and Katherine couldn't imagine what he had planned. So far he'd not given her any hint. Only that they'd eat at some point before the night was over.

"A special place? Where?"

He grinned at her and Katherine decided she'd never seen him looking more handsome. A crisp white shirt was tucked neatly into a pair of dark blue jeans, and a bolo tie fashioned with a piece of hammered silver set with turquoise was pushed tight against his collar. When he'd first arrived at her house, his dark hair had been slicked back away from his face, but now a few dark tendrils had plopped onto his forehead. He looked dashing and rakish at the same time and just looking at him stole her breath.

"We'll be there in a few more minutes," he assured

her, then he asked, "Was Nick disappointed that he wasn't invited?"

"Not at all. It's been a while since he's spent the night with Shawn, so he was looking forward to tonight. And I think I should tell you there's a conspiracy going on with him and Hannah."

"Really? What kind of conspiracy? They're trying to think up some way to get me to take them to Turf Paradise?"

Katherine laughed. "No. Although, I don't have to tell you that he had a blast watching the races on television with Hannah. Somehow he managed to pick a winner and now he's hooked. As for the conspiracy, Nick confessed that he and Hannah wanted to stay behind at the ranch so that you and I could have time alone together at the old house. As if we needed to be thrown closer together," she added sexily. "Thank goodness, the kids don't know exactly how close we already are."

"Are we close?"

The pointed question had her studying the serious expression on his face. "There've been times a thread couldn't be wedged between us. I'd say that's pretty darn close."

"I'm not referring to closeness in physical terms, Kat."

Her heart began to beat hard and fast. So far he'd not pushed her to talk about her feelings concerning him and their relationship. But he seemed to be pushing tonight and she didn't know where it was all leading. Was he about to tell her that he thought they were getting too serious? That he wasn't in the market for anything long-term?

Uncertainty swirled in her voice as she replied, "Oh. Well, yes. I like to think I mean something to you. And you certainly mean something to me. Does that answer your question?"

"Sort of."

She reached across the console and felt a measure of relief as he closed his fingers tightly around hers.

Ten minutes later Blake parked the truck on the Yarnell Hill Lookout, while Katherine appeared surprised with the destination.

"Is this what you're calling the special place?" she asked. "This is where we came on our first date."

"I'm so glad you remembered." He released his seat belt and opened the door. "Let's get out and walk over to the railing."

He helped her down from the truck cab, and though he wanted to pull her into his arms, he didn't. If he started kissing her now, he probably wouldn't be able to stop. And then his plans for the evening would be sidetracked.

Resting a hand against her back, he guided her over to the low stone fence surrounding the parking area. Except for a few pink streaks of dying sunlight, the valley below was dark. As Blake gazed out at the undulating hills, he kept remembering when he and Katherine had visited this spot. The first kiss they'd shared had knocked him sideways. And from that moment on, something deep inside him decided she was the woman he wanted in his life. Not just for a few days or weeks, but forever.

Katherine sighed. "It looks almost the same as it did the other time we came here. So beautiful."

His heart thudding hard in his chest, he slowly turned her to face him. "Not nearly as beautiful as you, Kat. And that night we were here—it's burned into my memory."

"Mine, too. I was very afraid of you that night. I wanted to run as fast as I could."

"Afraid? Of me? Oh, Kat, I would never hurt a hair on your head."

The corners of her lush mouth turned upward. "Silly, I wasn't that kind of afraid. It was the way you were making me feel—so wild and wanton. I knew if I didn't run from you, we'd end up making love. And we did."

"Yes. We did. And since then, I've decided I want to make love to you and only you for the rest of my life."

The smile on her face turned to a look of confusion. "The rest of your life," she repeated. "What are you saying?"

He spoke the words he'd been holding inside of him for the past few weeks. "I'm saying that I love you, Kat. I want you to marry me. To be my wife and the mother of my children. It's that simple."

"Children. Wife." She whispered the words in stunned fascination. "Blake, are you proposing marriage to me?"

"That's exactly what I'm doing." His hands trembling, he dug a black satin pouch from the front pocket of his jeans and removed an engagement ring from its folds. "I drove to Phoenix this morning for a ring. I think it's perfect for you. I hope you think so, too."

Before she could gather herself to speak, he lifted her left hand and pushed the ring onto the proper finger. The huge square-cut diamond was flanked by smaller blue sapphires of the same shape. Even in the rapidly falling twilight, the gems glittered brightly. Like his love for her, he thought.

"Oh. Blake. This is— It's incredible." Clearly astonished, she held up her hand and gazed at the ring. "I've never owned such a piece of jewelry like this in my life!"

"You do now."

Her face a picture of conflicting emotions, she traced a fingertip over the diamond and then the sapphires.

Blake said, "I realize it's not the traditional type of engagement ring. But I wanted it to be different and special. The way you are. And the sapphires match your eyes."

"It's lovely, Blake. Really, it is. But—"

"What? It doesn't fit? Don't worry, I'll get it sized." He reached for her hand and lifted the back of it to his lips. "You're going to make a beautiful Hollister bride, my darling. Now all we need to do is choose a date and a place to have the wedding. And I'll leave all that up to you. As long as you make the date soon. Very soon."

He started to pull her into his arms, then paused as he spotted a pair of glittery tears slipping down her cheeks.

"Aww, Kat. I'm sorry. I'm just a cowboy—I don't know much about romance or how to go about it. I probably haven't done anything right about this proposal. But if you'll look into my heart, you'll see my love for you and Nick is as true as the sky is blue."

She began to cry in earnest and Blake suddenly felt chilled to the bone. Clearly all the happy excitement he'd been feeling was totally one-sided.

Choking back her tears, she said, "I don't doubt your feelings for me, Blake. It's because you do love me that I have to say no."

She might as well have walloped him with a two-by-four. "Explain that to me, Kat. Because nothing about it makes sense. Especially the *no* part. I thought—" Cupping her face with his hands, he tilted her head back so that he could look into her misty eyes. "All this time, you talked about us being so close. When you touched me, made love to me, I believed it. I believed you. Has this all just been a game to you, Kat?"

Her head moved negligibly back and forth. "No game, Blake. This time with you has been like heaven for me. But I wasn't expecting marriage from you!"

Unable to believe what he was hearing, he stared at her. "What were you thinking? That we were just going to go on like we have been for the rest of our lives? Seeing each other once or twice a week? Is that what you want? Because I sure as hell don't! I believe I deserve more and so does Nick."

She pulled away and promptly turned her back to him. "Don't bring Nick into this," she muttered.

"Why not? This involves him just as much as it does you and me. I want him to be my son. I want to be the father he needs. Doesn't that mean anything to you?"

Her head bent forward as though his questions had stabbed her. "Don't you think I understand that Nick needs a father? It's something I live with every day. Especially since I— Since his real father died. But that doesn't mean I'm going to marry the wrong man just to give Nick what he needs."

Anger poured through Blake and he cursed under his breath. "The wrong man! Is that what you think I am? The wrong man?"

"No! Yes, I—" Groaning helplessly, she whirled back to him. "Blake, you don't understand. You and I—dating is good with us. But living together as man and wife wouldn't work. A marriage takes more than just saying 'I love you.'"

"You would know that, wouldn't you?"

Even through his anger he could see his sarcasm had hurt her. But he was beyond caring. After Lenore had jilted him, he'd decided it wasn't in the cards for him to have a family. He'd stopped looking at women, period. Then Katherine had walked into his life and he'd allowed himself to start dreaming and hoping again. What a gullible chump he'd been!

"Probably better than anybody," she said flatly. "It takes commitment. And the way I see things, you already have too many of those to include me and Nick."

She stalked off in the direction of the truck and Blake hurried after her.

"So that's the problem." He flung the accusation at her. "You're angry because I had to cancel our dates this week. You think just like Lenore—that I won't devote enough of my time to you!"

She paused in her tracks and Blake could see her tears had dried. Now her eyes were shooting daggers straight at him. "No. That is not what I'm thinking. I want to spare you another heartache."

Blake barked out a short, cynical laugh. "Spare me? What do you think you've just done?"

"The only thing I could do."

She rushed on to the vehicle and climbed in before he could offer her a helping hand.

His blood boiling, Blake slid behind the wheel, but before he fastened his seat belt, he reached to the floor behind the seat and plucked up the bouquet of flowers he'd hidden beneath a jean jacket.

"Here. Those go with the ring," he said, tossing them into her lap. "The blooms are all yellow. Like sunshine. Because that's how I always thought of you. My sunshine. Yellow flowers and sapphires to match the blue flecks in your gray eyes. What a damn sap, I am. But never again!"

He started the motor and rammed the truck into gear.

Across from him, Katherine's face was etched in stone as she stared straight ahead.

"I hardly feel like dinner after this," she said in a clipped voice. "Please take me home."

"It'll be my pleasure. And as far as I'm concerned, I'm not about to waste my time seeing you again!"

"I wouldn't have expected anything else from you."

The drive back to Wickenburg was made in stone silence. When Blake finally pulled into the drive in front of Katherine's house, she slipped the ring from her finger and held it out toward him.

"I'm sorry I couldn't accept the ring," she said in a raw, husky voice. "It's very beautiful. Too beautiful for me."

He didn't understand her last comment. No more than he understood her refusal to marry him. None of her reasons had made sense.

Face it, Blake. It's very simple. Katherine doesn't love you. She enjoys spending time with you. She enjoys the sex you have together. But that's where it ends. Didn't Lenore teach you anything? You should've seen this coming.

Swallowing at the bitter gall in his throat, he said, "Keep the ring. It's yours now. I don't want it back." To make sure she got the message, he gathered up the original box it came in, along with the satin pouch, and tossed them on top of the flowers she clutched in her lap. "Whenever you need a good laugh, you can open the box and look at the engagement ring that never was."

Her silence spoke volumes as she returned the ring to its box and stuffed the whole thing in her purse.

"There's no need for you to see me to the door," she said as she released the seat belt. "I can make it on my own."

"You may think I'm not worthy of being your husband, Katherine, but I do have manners."

He left the truck and went around to help her down. Once she was standing beside him, he was instantly overwhelmed with her sweet, feminine scent, and the tempting warmth of her body. He'd thought he'd be spending this night making love to her. He'd planned for the two of them to be celebrating their engagement. Instead, everything was dead. Over.

The silence between them was palpable as they walked to the small porch, where a dim light illuminated the entryway. Blake stood to one side while she unlocked the door.

With her back to him, she paused at the threshold. "Goodbye, Blake."

"Goodbye." *And tell Nick I love him.*

The words were aching in his throat as he stepped off the porch and walked away from her.

Chapter Thirteen

By the middle of the following week, Katherine was close to collapsing. Eating was something she had to force herself to do and sleep came in fitful snatches. Her heart was breaking more each day, while her mind was haunted with thoughts of Blake.

She could understand his anger. No doubt he believed she'd been leading him on, allowing him to invest his feelings in her and Nick, all the while knowing she wouldn't marry him. The mere idea that he believed that about her was enough to crush her entire being.

But that's exactly how it looks, Katherine. You made love to the man over and over. You gave yourself to him in a way that said "I love you. I need you. Forever." What were you thinking then? And why did you have to be a complete fool and turn him down? Other than Nick, he's the most wonderful thing to ever happen in your life. Now you've lost him.

The recriminating voice in her head was enough to bring tears to her eyes. She desperately tried to blink them away as she sank onto the edge of her bed and pulled open the top drawer of the nightstand. Next to a hairbrush and a jar of night cream, the box with the engagement ring sat like an ominous reminder of everything she'd lost. What was she going to do with it? With this awful sadness weighing her down?

Lifting the lid, she gazed at the ring he'd slipped onto her finger. Even to her untrained eye, she could see the piece of jewelry was worth a small fortune. The square diamond alone was huge and the sapphires equally impressive.

Yellow flowers because you're my sunshine. Sapphires to match the blue flecks in your eyes.

Each time she remembered Blake's words, she had to fight off a rush of tears. Oh, why had she ever allowed herself to fall in love with him? And how long would it be before this crushing pain inside her went away? Or would it ever go away?

"Mom, are you about to go to bed?"

Closing the lid on the ring box, she looked up to see Nick standing in the open doorway of her bedroom. More than thirty minutes ago, she'd told him to change into his pajamas, but he was still dressed in jeans and a grubby T-shirt.

"In a few minutes," she answered, then followed with a question of her own. "It's getting late. Why aren't you ready for bed?"

Glum-faced, he walked into the room and stood in front of her. "I've been on the phone."

"I heard you talking with Shawn. That was more than an hour ago."

Nick let out a hefty sigh and it was plain to Katherine

that something was troubling him. As of yet, she'd not mentioned anything to him about her split with Blake. Mainly because she didn't have a clue as how to gently break the news, or shield him from being hurt.

"He's getting ready for baseball camp," Nick explained. "It starts in a few days."

"Oh. I almost forgot about camp. You still want to go, too, don't you?"

He shook his head. "I did. But not now. I'd rather go out to Three Rivers and ride with Hannah. She's the one I was on the phone with just now."

Three Rivers. Blake's home. It was never meant for her to live in a place like that, she thought. With a family like his. But God help her, she'd dreamed about it. And now those dreams were dead.

"I see. Did you call her?"

"No. She called me. So we could talk about the roundup. She says it always happens in the middle of May and that's next week. She wants me to come out for another riding lesson before then. Can we go, Mom?"

Oh, please, God, give me strength, she prayed. "I doubt it, son."

She expected him to burst out with a protest. Instead, he stared at her in glum silence. "Hannah said she figured you would say that. She says Blake is acting really strange and he hardly ever comes to the house anymore. We think something bad has happened with you and him."

Before Katherine could come up with an explanation that would make sense to a ten-year-old boy, he suddenly noticed the box in her hand.

"What's that? It looks like a gift."

Deciding there was no easy way around this, she opened the box and showed him the ring.

"Wow! That's a real sparkler! Where did that come from?"

She patted the spot next to her. "Sit down, Nick. I want to talk with you."

His gray eyes wide with uncertainty, he eased onto the edge of the mattress. "About the roundup?"

"Sort of. Mostly about me and Blake and you." She drew in a bracing breath. "You see, Blake asked me to marry him. That's what this ring is about. It was meant to be my engagement ring."

Before she could stop him, Nick leaped to his feet and let out a joyous yell. "Yippee! Blake is gonna be my daddy! My real daddy!"

Shaking her head, Katherine reached out and grabbed a hold on his arm. "Wait a minute, son. You need to hear the rest. I told Blake no. Understand? I'm not going to marry him. In fact, Blake and I won't be seeing each other anymore."

Nick went stone-still, while the joy on his face suddenly turned to total shock.

"I'm not sure what this change is going to mean for you and Hannah," Katherine went on. "I truly want you to get to spend time with her. So I'm planning to have a talk with Vivian and work something out with her about you two."

The color drained from Nick's face to leave it the sickly shade of bread dough.

"Mom, you're kiddin', aren't ya? You wouldn't tell Blake no. He's the best! And I know you like him a lot. The kind of like with hearts and flowers and all that mushy stuff."

She closed the lid on the ring box and put it away in the nightstand. Yes, her love for Blake was full of all that mushy stuff, she thought miserably.

Turning back to him, she said gently, "I'm sorry that I've disappointed you, Nick. Believe me, I never planned for this to happen."

A look of horror came over his face. "Yes, you did!" he yelled. "Blake is the only dad I ever wanted! And Hannah is my cousin and my best friend, too! Now I can't see them! You've gone and ruined everything!"

He turned and raced out the door as though demons were on his heels.

Katherine's first instinct was to call to him and order him straight back to her side. But she didn't. Not when she could already hear heartrending sobs coming from his room across the hallway.

Anyway, what could she say to him? She'd squashed her son's most fervent wish to have a father. She'd made Blake angry and embittered. And she'd ruined any chance she might have for future happiness. Was she crazy? Or would all three of them eventually come to realize she'd done the right thing?

The next morning, Blake took a long swig of syrupy coffee and wearily wiped a hand over his face. It wasn't yet ten and he'd already been at his desk for six hours. And that was after getting only two hours of sleep.

Tossing aside his pen, he left the desk and walked over to the window overlooking a portion of the ranch yard. Twenty tons of alfalfa from northern New Mexico had arrived on semitrucks minutes earlier and now several of the hands were stacking the large bales in a barn next to the horse stalls. On the opposite side of the work yard, a cloud of dust was flying above the cattle pens, where a new shipment of heifers was being roped and dragged to the branding fire.

The busy sight told Blake it was a typical morning

at Three Rivers. At least, it was for everyone else on the ranch. Just not for him. Nothing would ever be normal for Blake again. Katherine's refusal to marry him had turned everything dark and somber. And he didn't know how to fix the pain in his heart or change his life into what he wanted or needed it to be.

A light knock on the door interrupted his miserable thoughts and he glanced over his shoulder to see his mother walking into the office.

She was wearing tall high heels and a beige dress with a pink scarf draped around her neck. She looked prettier than he'd seen her in a long time, yet he couldn't find the energy or the spirit to smile at her.

"So here you are," she said. "I missed you at breakfast."

"I didn't have any."

"I should've known," she said with a disapproving smirk. "Have any coffee left?"

"It's burned black. You'll have to put a bunch of sugar in it."

"I'm tough. I can handle it."

Yes, his mother was tough, Blake thought. She had more fight and fortitude in her little finger than he did in his whole body.

"So where are you off to?" he asked as she drained the last of the coffee into a thick mug.

"I'm going to Phoenix today," she told him as she stirred sugar into the mug. "To look at a pair of horses for Holt and possibly purchase them for the ranch. We'll see. After that, your uncle Gil has offered to take me to lunch. He's in the city this week attending some sort of special training for county lawmen."

Gil Hollister was Joel's older brother by two years. As a very young man he'd lived and worked on Three Rivers, but eventually he'd decided being a rancher wasn't his calling. By the time he'd reached his midtwenties, he'd moved away to Tucson and become a law officer. Blake and the rest of his siblings considered Gil their favorite uncle, in spite of having three more uncles on their mother's side of the family.

"Hmm. Is Joseph down there? I've not heard from him. Not since we found the cut fence."

"He didn't go," Maureen said. "Seems he took the training last year."

"That's good. He doesn't need to get too far away from Tessa right now." Raking a hand through his hair, he walked back to his desk and sank into the chair. "Uh, did you stop by this morning for a reason? Other than to make sure I'm still as good-looking as I was yesterday?"

Moving across the room, she stood in front of his desk and carefully studied his haggard face. "Good-looking? Maybe you'd better go find a mirror. You look like pure hell. And to be honest, I'm not one bit happy about it. That's what I stopped by to tell you. From what Reeva tells me, you're not eating and I can plainly see you've not been sleeping, either."

"Reeva needs to stick to her cooking and quit worrying about my eating habits. And I'm getting enough sleep."

"Sure. Like the cow can jump over the moon. I'm sorry, Blake, but you can't go on like this. You've got to snap out of this and put Katherine completely behind you. Or make up with her."

Leave it to his mother to lay everything out in simple terms. With her, there was no being wishy-washy. Either you did or you didn't. She wouldn't tolerate anyone straddling the fence.

"Make up! Like hell!" he sputtered forcefully. "I'll

never trust another woman as long as I live. I'll never touch another woman as long as I live. And that includes Katherine!"

She cast him a withering look. "I'm very disappointed in you, Blake. And troubled. Why are you sitting around, letting your best chance at happiness slip away?"

He tossed up his hands in a helpless gesture. "Slip away? Mom, in case you didn't know, I asked Katherine to marry me and she turned me down flat. There's no point in begging or pursuing. She doesn't love me. Or if she does, it's not enough. She and I are over. Done."

Her expression softened. "You're letting your ego blind you."

"Am I supposed to grovel? Is that what it takes to get a wife? If so, then I don't want one. A man has his pride, you know. And if he doesn't have that…well, he's pretty damn worthless."

"Looks to me like you're feeling pretty damn worthless right now," she retorted. "And groveling isn't what you need to be doing. Instead, you should be finding out why she turned you down and go about fixing the problem."

"I just told you. She doesn't love me."

"Baloney. You can't convince me of that. Kat is crazy about you. There's something else going on with her and I think I might know what it is."

Blake stared moodily at his mother while silently yelling at himself that he didn't want to know what Katherine's problem might be. She'd kicked him and stabbed him and cracked his heart right down the middle. The farther away he could stay from her, the better off he'd be.

Except that he was still crazy in love with her, Blake

thought. He still ached to hold her in his arms. To make love to her until there was no breath left in his body.

Maureen thoughtfully sipped her coffee, then asked, "Do you want to hear my theory? Or is hanging on to your precious pride more important?"

Frustration pushed a groan past his throat. "Mom, don't you think I've been asking myself over and over where I failed?" He shook his head. "At first I thought it was the same as Lenore. That she was afraid my job as ranch manager would take time away from her and Nick. But now...I'm not sure. I was so angry and hurt I couldn't see straight. Much less figure out what was going on in her head."

She placed the coffee mug on the corner of his desk. "You're still so hurt and angry you're not seeing straight," she told him. "Otherwise, you would've already figured out that Katherine is afraid."

His jaw dropped. "Afraid? Of me? That makes no sense at all."

Pushing the coffee mug aside, Maureen eased her hip onto the corner of the desk. "I don't know how much she's talked to you about her father, but I know for a fact that he was an abusive man whenever he was drunk. Which was quite often. That's why Paulette moved Katherine and Aaron to California. To get away from him."

A sick feeling swam in Blake's stomach. "Katherine has talked a little about her father's drinking. I figured at the most he was a neglectful father and husband, but abusive—no. Kat never said that about Avery. She came back to care for him before he died."

"Because her heart is as big as her head. Because she's a forgiving, compassionate woman. I'm not sure I could've ever done what she did for her father."

And she'd paid dearly for it, Blake thought grimly. Her mother and her brother regarded her as a traitor and had basically pushed Katherine out of their lives. Thoughtful now, he said, "Even if you're right, Katherine can't be thinking I'd ever be like Avery Anderson."

"Or her late husband?"

His head snapped back. "What does Kat's late husband have to do with anything?"

Maureen sighed. "When a woman gets to be my age, son, she can sense things. Especially about another woman. I'm a widow and so is she. But we're not the same sort of widows."

"You'll have to explain that one, Mom."

"Okay. It's damn obvious to me that Kat's marriage was not good," she said bluntly.

The cogs in his mind were suddenly turning faster and faster. "I think you're right about that. From what little she's told me about her marriage, it wasn't all that grand. I think he neglected her and Nick."

Maureen nodded. "Get my point now? She grew up in a troubled family and then her marriage ends up being troubled, too. The woman can't imagine herself in a happy home. She doesn't believe it's meant for her to be a part of a real family. It's going to be up to you to convince her that she's worthy of your love."

"I've been trying for weeks to show her what she means to me. How am I supposed to convince her?"

Smiling smugly, Maureen slipped off the desk and started toward the door. "You're a smart man, Blake. You'll figure it out."

A short while later in town, Katherine and Prudence sat at one of the little round tables outside Conchita's and sipped at the fresh brewed coffee Emily-Ann had prepared for them.

"Eat your apple fritter," Prudence ordered. "You need it. You look like you've lost ten pounds or more."

Katherine rolled her eyes. "I don't know what we're doing here. It's only an hour or so to lunch. Eating a fritter now will ruin my appetite."

Prudence's short yelp was closer to a snort than a laugh. "Oh, please, who are you kidding? You don't have an appetite to ruin."

Reluctantly, Katherine pinched off a corner of the pastry and placed it in her mouth. Normally, she would have savored every succulent bite of the sweet concoction. Now the taste very nearly sickened her.

"Okay, so I don't want to eat. The problem will pass."

"Problem? Are you talking about your lack of appetite? Or Blake Hollister?"

Everything inside Katherine wilted. "Please don't mention his name. And if you dragged me over here to Conchita's just to get me out of the office to talk about... *him*, then we need to end this coffee break right now and go back to school."

Prudence glared at her. "Look, I have a stack of work on my desk that I need to be attending to right this minute. But I care about you and I thought getting you out for a talk might help."

Bending her head in shame, Katherine pressed a hand to her aching forehead. "I'm sorry, Pru. You're my friend and I'm grateful that you care—that you want to help. But there's nothing you can do. And being here at Conchita's is... Well, this is where Blake and I came that first day we ran into each other."

"Oh. You should've told me," she said contritely, then quickly followed that up with a shake of her head. "No.

Maybe it's good that you're being reminded of all you're throwing away."

"Throwing away? Pru, I've tried to explain. I turned down Blake's proposal because I thought it was the best thing for him—and everybody involved."

Prudence was not only unconvinced, but she was also downright angry. "Really? Best for you? For little Nick? You've squashed every bit of hope that boy had—simply because you're a coward!"

Katherine gasped. "Pru! How can you be so heartless?"

"You think telling the truth is heartless? I think sitting around and allowing a friend to ruin her life would be far crueler."

Feeling totally defeated, Katherine slumped back in her chair. Coward. Scared. Worthless. When Blake had asked her to marry him, she'd felt all those things and more. Now, after thinking about it for several days, she'd come to the conclusion that she was a failure as a woman.

"You're right," she mumbled. "I am a coward. To think about making a man like Blake happy, not for just a few weeks or months, but for a lifetime—it's scary, Pru. When it comes to the men in my life, it's not been good. My father, I couldn't pick. But Cliff was different. I did pick him and ended up making him miserable. And now my brother hardly speaks to me."

"Cliff made himself miserable. And your brother is the one losing out. Not you," Prudence argued.

"No matter. It's obvious my relationships with men, relatives or otherwise, always end up lacking. And I don't want Blake to be another casualty of my failures. I love him too much for that."

"Maybe that's something you ought to tell him," Prudence suggested.

Katherine closed her eyes as a chunk of pain settled in the middle of her chest. "Yes, maybe I should. I'll talk to him…soon."

"No. You'll talk to him now. Like, right now."

Katherine opened her eyes to see Prudence staring out toward the tiny parking area in front of the coffee shop.

Her heart beating wildly, Katherine turned in her chair to see a cowboy in a black hat and dressed all in denim striding toward them.

Blake! The sight of him was like a ray of sun after a violent storm.

"Oh."

The one word rushed out of her at the same time Prudence was jumping to her feet.

"I'll see you back at school. Later," Prudence said under her breath. "Much later!"

The other woman hurried away, acknowledging Blake with a nod as she passed him on the walkway.

Even though her heart was yelling at her to run straight into his arms, Katherine remained glued to her seat and waited for him to reach the table.

"Hello, Katherine. Mind if I sit down?"

A zillion questions raced through her mind as she gestured toward the chair Prudence had just vacated. What was he doing here? To ask her to return his ring? To talk about Nick?

"Just push Pru's things out of the way," she told him. "She, uh, had to rush back to work."

A half grin touched his lips. "The minute she spotted me, I noticed."

Katherine's cheeks were suddenly stinging with

color, and though she tried to smile back at him, her face felt frozen. "Did you come to town on business or just needed some of Emily-Ann's coffee?"

"Not the kind of business you think," he said. "I went by St. Francis to speak with you, but someone at the front entrance told me you'd left a few minutes ago with the superintendent. I just happened to be driving by Conchita's and spotted the two of you sitting out here."

He'd driven into Wickenburg to see her specifically? Oh, Lord, what did it mean?

Her heart was beating so fast she was finding it difficult to breathe. "Pru thought we both needed a little break."

The grin on his face deepened and Katherine desperately wanted to reach across the table and press her fingertip against the dimple in his cheek. Touching him had been a precious privilege. These past few days without him had taught her exactly how precious.

"Ironic, isn't it? That I'd find you here," he said. "Where we first had coffee together."

As her gaze hungrily roamed over his dear, familiar face, a lump of painful tears collected in her throat. She tried to clear it away with a little cough.

"That seems like a very long time ago, Blake. So much has happened since that day we met. Again."

Regret was etched upon his rugged features. "Yes. Everything in my life seems different now."

Summoning all the courage she could find, she asked, "Why did you want to see me? To ask for your ring back? It's at home. In a safe place. I realize it's worth an enormous amount of money. And—"

All of a sudden he reached across the table and snatched up her hand. As his fingers squeezed around hers, she met his gaze and the beseeching look in his brown eyes turned her heart to pure liquid.

"I'm here to ask you to put the ring back on your finger, Kat. I'm asking you again to marry me."

Even as she tried to tamp it down, hope surged through her. "Apparently these past few days haven't given you enough time to think," she said in an anguished voice. "I'm an Anderson, Blake. I'm not supposed to marry a Hollister or live in a home like Three Rivers. I'm not even sure that it's meant for me to be... loved."

"Oh, Kat, you're so wrong. You are loved. By me. Always. I know you're afraid. I understand the men in your life haven't always been the kind you deserved. But—"

"No, wait, Blake. Before you go any further, I have to tell you about Cliff. He—"

"It doesn't matter about Cliff. Nothing about that time in your life matters now. All I want to know is if you love me."

By now tears were streaming down her face. "How could you ever doubt it? Of course I love you, Blake. With all my heart and soul. That's why... I desperately want you to be happy. And you need to know that what happened with Cliff was all my fault. He died because of me. Because I told him I was going to divorce him."

Unfazed by her admission, he said, "You didn't make him go crash his car. He did that on his own. And I just thank God that you and Nick weren't in the vehicle with him."

She groaned with misgivings. "Yes, but I was the reason he got raving drunk and climbed behind the wheel. I must have been the reason he was miserable in the first place—the reason he found work more important than me or his baby."

His eyes glowing with tender love, he touched her cheek. "Oh, Kat, a man's happiness begins on the inside. He has to feel good about himself first, or no amount of love or adoration from a woman will make him feel good or right. Your late husband clearly had more problems than you could fix. That's no reason you should blame yourself or suffer for the rest of your life."

More tears oozed from her eyes, but this time they were tears of joy and relief.

"Oh, Blake, I've been such a coward. Such a fool. Are you sure you really want to marry me?"

Smiling, he picked up a napkin from the table and dabbed away the tears on her cheeks.

"Let's go get your engagement ring. I want to slip it back on your finger. Where it belongs."

Her heart bursting with joy, she smiled back at him. "And what are people going to say when they see that poor little Anderson girl wearing such a ring? That I latched on to you for your money?"

Rising from the chair, he pulled her to her feet and into his arms. "No, they're all going to wonder how such a stuffed shirt managed to snare a beauty like you."

She laughed. "Oh, Blake, we are going to be happy together. You and me and Nick and all the babies you want."

"Damn right," he murmured, then leaned over and fastened his lips over hers in a kiss to seal the deal.

Even though they were partially shielded from the street by the limbs of a mesquite tree and there was no one around but the two of them, they were still standing outside in the open for anyone to see. But that hardly seemed to matter to Blake.

He was still kissing her when a quiet little cough sounded from somewhere behind them. They pulled apart to see Emily-Ann standing a few feet away, and from the clever smile on her face, it was clear she'd already seen plenty.

"Excuse me," she said. "I came out to ask if Blake wanted coffee. But I see he already has what he wants."

Blake looked down at Katherine and the love she spotted in the depths of his brown eyes chased away all the hurt and loneliness of the past.

"Yes," he murmured. "Everything I want is right here in my arms."

Epilogue

Six months later, on a beautiful November day, Katherine was in the Three Rivers kitchen, helping Reeva, Maureen and Vivian prepare a massive Thanksgiving meal for the family. As she stuffed pieces of celery with pimento cheese, the back door suddenly opened, bringing with it a gust of cool wind.

From her spot at the cabinet counter, Katherine watched Blake enter the room with Hannah under one arm and Nick under the other. The broad smiles on the faces of her husband and son never failed to make Katherine's heart swell with joy.

She and Blake had gotten married the last weekend in June at an outdoor ceremony here on Three Rivers. A huge reception had followed with tons of food and champagne, live music and dancing that had gone on long into the night. Their wedding had been like a fairy tale, and since then, Katherine sometimes had to pinch herself to make sure she wasn't living a dream.

Three months ago, Blake had hired a secretary to help with the endless paperwork associated with the ranch. At first, he'd not been sure if he was going to get along with the staunch older woman. But as time had passed, he'd started to wonder how he'd ever gotten along without Florence's help. Now, Flo, as Blake called her, was getting to be more like family than anything else.

Katherine was continuing to work as Prudence's secretary, but she'd promised Blake that when she became pregnant, she'd cut her work hours down to part-time. Something that Prudence had already agreed to let Katherine do.

As for Nick, she'd expected him to be pleased to be living here on the ranch, but she'd never imagined he'd take to the cowboy life with such gusto. In spite of his young years, he was eager to learn about the livestock and the land, and Blake was always keen to teach him. Each day, she could see him growing closer and closer to Blake and, in return, her husband never failed to let a day go by without giving Nick a block of undivided attention.

"So where have you three been? Riding the range?" Katherine asked.

"I can tell by the smell where they've been," Vivian teased. "In the feedlot. The scent of manure will go great with turkey and dressing."

"We've been looking at the cows that Dad is going to ship down to Red Bluff," Nick said. "There's a bunch of them, too!"

"How many?"

This came from Maureen, who was busy pouring whipping cream into a mixing bowl.

"About a thousand head," Blake answered his mother. "We'll send the rest up to the Prescott range."

"Sounds good," Maureen replied. "Camille will be happy to hear the cattle are coming. She won't feel so alone then."

"Camille wants to be alone, Mom. That's why she's at Red Bluff," Vivian said, then pointed at her daughter's dirty boots. "You stink. Get out of here."

"Okay, we're going, Mom," Hannah told her mother, then snatched a hold on Nick's hand. "Come on, Nick. Let's go change our boots and see if Little Joe is awake."

As the two children raced out of the room, Maureen yelled after them, "You two leave that baby alone! He's been jostled around enough today already!"

"Yes, and who's been doing most of the jostling?" Blake asked his mother as he walked over and slipped an arm around Katherine's shoulders. "Little Joe is only two months old and you're already trying to decide what horse he's going to ride in the next Gold Rush Days rodeo parade."

Maureen laughed. "I'm not that bad. But Joe is. You'd think he was the first man on earth to have a son. And I can only imagine how bad you're going to be once you and Katherine have a baby."

"Well, if I have anything to do with that," Blake replied, "you're not going to have to wait long."

Vivian turned an excited look on the two of them. "Oh, are you pregnant, Katherine?"

"Not yet. But we're trying."

"That's the best part," Blake said, directing a promising wink at Katherine.

Laughing under her breath, she offered him a celery stick. "Get out of here and go talk to your brothers. This kitchen is getting too steamy."

A few hours later, after everyone was stuffed with rich food and the dishes and leftovers all cleaned away, Katherine joined her husband and his brothers Holt and Joseph on the front porch of the ranch house.

Walking to the edge of the wood-planked floor, Katherine gazed at the distant mountains bathed in a red-gold sunset.

"All finished with the dinner mess?" Blake asked as he came to stand at her side.

"Everything is in its place. So I thought I'd get some fresh air. Have you and your brothers been having a nice visit?"

"Very nice. It's not often that we get to spend leisure time together." His eyebrows pulled together in a thoughtful frown. "And Joe was just telling me something very interesting."

"Oh, what's that? He and Tessa are going to have another baby?"

"Not this soon. No, he was telling me that Mom found an old personal notebook of Dad's. Seems it's been missing for years. Ever since he died, in fact."

Curious as to what this might mean, Katherine asked, "Does this notebook hold some significant information?"

He shrugged. "We're not sure. Dad had scheduled a name and date he'd planned to meet with a cattle buyer down in Phoenix. But he never got to meet with the man. Dad died the day before."

"And you're thinking this cattle buyer might know something about Joel's death?"

"Well, Mom doesn't recall the man and Joe has already run the man's name through the database at the sheriff's department. No person by that name showed up. So he's going to try some different search angles. It's a very long shot, but if this man can be found, he might have a helpful clue. We just don't know."

She said, "For you and your whole family's sake, I wish you could figure out what actually happened to Joel. I wish even more that your father could've been here with us all today."

Wrapping an arm around her, he pulled her close to his side. "With all my heart, I wish Dad was here, too. And that your mother and brother had been gracious enough to call and wish you a happy Thanksgiving."

Neither her mother nor her brother had attended Katherine and Blake's wedding. But she'd not allowed their absence to ruin her very special day. She had too much happiness in her life to dwell on their negative attitude.

"Don't let it bother you, Blake. I'm not. Thanks to you, I have a huge family now. And hopefully, one of these days, Mom and Aaron will realize that they'll never get over the past unless they start forgiving."

His eyes glowed with love as they traveled over her face. "Have I told you how very special you are?" he asked.

She smiled impishly up at him. "Only about a hundred…no, make that two hundred times."

"Well, you've heard it two hundred and one times now."

Resting her cheek against his arm, she said, "I have a confession to make."

"With my stomach so full, now's a good time to tell me."

She gave his arm a playful pinch. "Years ago, when I

had such a teenage crush on you, I would often imagine you proposing to me. In my girlish dreams, you'd put a ring on my finger and dance me away from all the poverty and pain waiting for me back at home." She shifted her head so that she could look up at him. "I never imagined any of those dreams would someday come true and I'd actually be married to my cowboy prince."

Bending, he pressed a kiss to the tip of her nose. "Just goes to show you, my darling wife, that fairy tales can come true."

* * * * *